Means to Deceive

Alex Craigie

This is a work of fiction. Names, characters, events and incidents are the products of the author's imagination. Any resemblance to actual persons, living or dead, or actual events is purely coincidental.

ISBN-13: 978-0-9956966-2-4
Ashford Carbonel Publishing

Dedication

Dedicated to David and to Laddie, his border collie who died unexpectedly just before the completion of this book. Atticus, with his grey-flecked legs and lovable nature, was modelled on Laddie but didn't inherit his remarkable intelligence. Known and loved by the community, Laddie befriended people on his walks, displayed a commendable grasp of the Highway Code and understood an impressive vocabulary. He is much missed by us all.

Chapter 1

I can feel the scream build in the pit of my stomach as my hands grab at the slowly spinning ball drifting beyond my reach.

'Mummy! Daddy! Get it back! Quick!'

I hear my mother, happy and reassuring. 'It'll come back in a minute. Build a sandcastle while you're waiting.'

'No! It's going away!'

'Don't be silly, pumpkin. If it doesn't come back, I'll buy you a new one.'

'It's my Kermit ball. ***Please****, Mummy,* ***please****!'*

I promise you can choose any ball you want if this one doesn't come back

'No! I want **this** *ball. I don't want any of the others.' I hear my childish voice plead and whine.*

The terror wrenches me back to the present and I pull myself up, hunched over my clutched knees as I struggle to control the breaths shuddering raggedly through me.

It's been a while. Sometimes my dream comes out of nowhere, but usually I can trace the trigger. I know the trigger for this one:

I remember Ian Weston taking hold of my hand across the pub table; confusion leaving me witless until I'd abruptly snatched it back, hot colour sweeping my face.

'I don't understand, Ian.' Embarrassment had made my voice squeak and I'd pulled it down to a harsh whisper. 'I thought we were going to discuss the Vulnerable Kids Project.'

His eyes had narrowed a little.

'And we will, Gwen, we will, but I thought we should get to know each other a bit better, first.'

His hand had reached for mine again and I'd stumbled to my feet, trapped by my heavy wooden chair.

‘I’m sorry, Ian, but you’re labouring under a misapprehension.’ I’d sounded like an affronted heroine from a Regency novel. ‘I think I’d better leave.’

The chair scraped backwards as I’d snatched my bag off the floor and fled towards the exit.

I’d been standing in the car park, wondering how I was going to get home, when my arm had been grabbed roughly from behind. Ian was tugging me towards a straggly shrub.

‘Now listen here, missy. You’ve been stringing me along for weeks now and I know when someone is interested in me. Don’t make me beg for what we both want.’

As his face loomed into mine, I’d squirmed and twisted, releasing one hand to deliver a slap that cracked loudly in the air. Then I was free and standing several feet away, watching him. Wary.

My breath had come in broken, noisy gasps as I’d faced him, poised to strike out again–or run.

There was a dull red imprint of my palm on the side of his face and his eyes were hooded now. The genial smile had been replaced by a thin-lipped sneer.

‘So that’s the way you’re going to play it, eh? You’re going to regret this, Gwen.’ He’d stared coldly at me. ‘I’m going to make very, *very* sure of it.’

I take another shuddering breath, and turn towards my little clock radio. 5.45 a.m. Experience tells me there’s no point trying to recapture sleep and the bright light piercing the room through gaps in the curtains promises a continuation of hot, sunny weather. Just one more day of school and then it’s the summer holidays. Good. I need this job. I can go in a bit earlier today, greet Ian cheerfully, and there will be plenty of time before next term for any animosity between us to dissipate. All will be well. The churning sensation inside me eases.

My feet are cool against the wooden floor as I pad my way quietly through to the kitchen. Sunlight is striking the burnished copper pig that sits on the counter. I run my fingers over its pleasing curves. It was a gift to Granny from Grandad Meredith and I love its rounded shape and the solid weight of it. Grandad had an eye for antiques and there are several still on display around the house. Sometimes Granny will ask for one to hold. Her expression as she handles them betrays a love and loss that always moves me.

Whilst the kettle clicks and murmurs on the counter, I watch Bramble stroll across the slabbed patio before turning and stalking towards the rectangular pond behind it that contains some lazy goldfish. Everything is neat. Impeccable. This is the way Granny likes it. Past the yew hedge perimeter is rolling Pembrokeshire countryside, and beyond the fields and meadows the ground dips away to a distant glimmer of sea. My dream swoops painfully to the surface and I look away, busying myself with the comforting ritual of tea-making to push it back below the surface.

I'm raising the cup to my mouth when I hear her. The sun still picks out kitchen details in bright pools of light, but something has dimmed a little inside of me and I brace myself as I head for Granny's room.

'Gwen! Come here.' It's not a request. That's not Granny's way. Granny commands. 'Gwen! Where are you?'

'I'm here, Granny. It's all right.'

Her heavy brocade curtains keep out all but an intense sliver of light where they meet in the middle. I cross the gloom and switch on the lamp by the bed. She squints up at me, her face drooping with displeasure.

'What time is it?'

'Quarter past six. I've just boiled the kettle. Would you like a cup of tea?' I make my voice cheerful and perky.

'Quarter past six? In the morning?'

I nod.

'Why are you dressed so early?' she purses her lips, the deeply etched lines crinkling in irritation.

'It's a beautiful day. Shall I open your curtains now?'

She peers at my face, her eyes narrowed suspiciously.

'You've had that nightmare again.'

She doesn't say anything more, but her eyes crinkle in a familiar way – an intent gaze that squeezes my chest and makes me want to weep or lash out. I do neither, of course. I cross to the window and drag the heavy drapes apart.

Granny's room overlooks the view to the side of the bungalow and it's a continuation of lawn, flowerbeds and hedge, beyond which is the equally impressive home of Vera and her partner Rachel. There are a few modest houses in Dernant, but most of the properties in the village are large, detached and very expensive. It's not a quaint village of thatched cottages around a sleepy duck pond but a modern take on it with gleaming, glass-fronted buildings set back in smoothly manicured gardens. You have to be seriously wealthy to live here.

Over a year ago, I gave up my life in Manchester to come back to this impressive bungalow. I miss my shabby little flat dreadfully.

'Would you like to get up now or would you prefer a cup of tea first?' My voice is still resolutely cheery.

'Tea.'

'Shall I prop you up a bit?'

'No.'

The tone bodes ill for the rest of the day.

At 7.45 the scraping of a key in the lock heralds the arrival of Becky Hughes. She's my favourite of the carers. Some of the others do what's needed quickly and efficiently, some prattle on patronisingly until Granny snaps at them, but many are like Becky – professional, respectful and friendly. When met with a stony refusal to take medication or have a shower, Becky knows when to cajole or convince her reluctant patient to do what's necessary. She never rides roughshod over Granny's wishes but neither does she accept a refusal as an excuse to give up and leave early.

'Morning, Gwen. It's a beautiful day out there.'

'Hi, Becky. Going to be another scorcher, I think.'

She puts down her bag by the kitchen door and removes a pair of latex gloves from her tunic pocket.

'Is your grandmother awake?'

'She's sitting up in bed with Sunday's colour supplement and a cup of tea.'

'No problems?'

'Nothing medical, but you might need to call on all your reserves of tact and diplomacy to get her onside this morning.'

'Not the happiest of bunnies then.'

We're sharing a chuckle at the ridiculous notion of my grandmother as a happy bunny, when there's a sudden commotion from the kitchen. We both rush through in time to witness Bramble burst through the cat flap and turn, all arched back and bristles, to glare at the head of a border collie that struggles to follow her. A spindly white leg, flecked with grey, squeezes past the bobbing head and then no further movement is possible – in or out.

I scoop up a stiff and spiky Bramble, and drop her through the sitting room door, closing it securely behind me.

'What do we do now?' Becky is as flummoxed as I am. 'Whose is it?'

'I've no idea,' I mutter, studying the trapped, squirming creature.

We turn as one when we hear footsteps on the gravel drive and a male voice calling, 'Atticus! Atticus! Here boy!'

Atticus makes little mewling noises as he attempts to obey and I'm galvanised into action, running through to the front door and pulling it open. A man is standing there with a dog leash in his hands.

'Sorry to trouble you. My dog escaped and I think I saw him come this way.'

He's very tall and his broad shoulders blot out the sun.

'It's all right. He's here.' I grin. 'And, don't worry, he's not going anywhere else for the time being.'

His face materialises as he bends down to look more closely at me.

'Not going anywhere? Why?'

His eyes are brown and troubled and I can understand the worry he's transmitting.

'Don't worry. He's fine.' I'm normally very cautious with strangers, but his concern has broken through my social barriers and I pull the door wide open and beckon him through.

'Your Atticus has taken a shine to our Bramble and is now hopelessly gripped in his pursuit of her.'

I turn back, and I can see him better now. There's a deep groove furrowing his forehead as he tries to make sense of what I'm saying. I spin away, open the connecting door between the sitting room and hallway and point to a dark shape crouched on top of one of the bookcases.

'That's Bramble.'

'Bramble's a cat?'

'Correct.'

I seal Bramble inside again, lead him further along the hall and usher him into the kitchen, closing the door firmly behind us. I'm not worried about Bramble; if they were to find themselves in an enclosed space it's far more likely that Atticus would come off worse. Bramble is aptly named, with needle-sharp teeth and claws to match.

Atticus now adds excited little yelps to his repertoire and his master's face is creased into a broad grin of understanding and amusement.

'Oh, Atticus. What have you got yourself into this time, boy?' He crouches down to soothe the bobbing head and looks back over his shoulder at me. 'I called him Atticus because I fondly pictured him as a calm, patient and wise companion.' The bobbing head stills and a long, pink tongue gently laps the hand that supports his jaw. 'Right now, he simply looks like a failed contortionist.'

Becky and I exchange amused glances as he runs his hand over the protruding leg. 'What are we going to do with you?'

There's no room for manoeuvre but Atticus has faith in his master and waits quietly now. Becky heads off in the direction of my grandmother's room and I stand, with one hand on the nape of my neck, trying to think of a way to help.

'Perhaps it would be easier if we opened the door?' I suggest at last. 'It's worth a try.'

I carefully pull the door inwards and Atticus scrabbles with his three good legs until both ends of him are in the kitchen.

Ten minutes later and Atticus is still no nearer freedom. I go through to the utility room and return with a set of screwdrivers and spanners.

'Time for these, perhaps.'

'What are you suggesting?'

'We take off the cat flap and see if there's enough flex in it to release him.'

'But your door —'

'Will be fine. We can replace the flap afterwards. It's that, coat him in grease or starve him for a few days. I know which option *I'd* go for.'

He smiles again. 'If you're sure about this?'

'I am.'

I kneel down beside him and select a screwdriver. Before I can slot it in place, Atticus, terror in his eyes, squirms and bucks until he reappears as one solid object on the outside of the cat flap.

We flop back on our heels and laugh as the liberated collie bounces with delight around the kitchen and makes repeated forays towards his master, almost knocking him over.

'I can't thank you enough. It's not a great first impression to make on my new neighbours, is it?'

The penny drops.

'You've just moved into The Willows over the road?'

He stands and holds out his hand. 'Ben Pascoe.'

'Gwen Meredith,' I reply as we shake hands. There's a lull of perhaps a second before either of us breaks free and when we do I look away, self-conscious.

'I'd offer you a cup of tea and a biscuit as a token thank you,' he says, attaching the leash to the now panting dog, 'but everything's in crates and boxes. Perhaps we could meet up for some lunch later instead?'

'Oh no!' It comes out as a squawk. 'Sorry. I'd completely lost track of the time and I'm late for work.' I grab my bag and keys off the counter and head for the door. 'Let yourself out, Ben. Becky will lock up later.'

I don't even have time to look back at him for a response. I wanted to be early today so that I could smooth things over with Ian before everyone else started to arrive. On the plus side, it's nice to have met our new neighbour and maybe I can take this is an omen that things are going to go well.

Chapter 2

It's not a long drive to the school and, ignoring the insistent ringing of the phone in my bag on the floor, I rehearse in my head what I'm going to say. There's a parking place near the entrance and I hurry up the steps, sneaking a look at my phone as I go. Six missed calls from Catrin and five messages. She'll have to wait until I've cleared the air with Ian.

I'm intercepted by Delyth Parry, the head's self-important secretary. She's heavily made-up today and has squeezed herself into a rather low-cut dress.

'Gwen, a word with you, please.' She's wearing higher heels than usual, too, and there are large diamante earring studs in place of her more sensible dainty ones. I'm not overly fond of Delyth, and her overbearing, meddlesome nature alienates the rest of the staff too.

'Can it wait, Delyth? I need to have a quick word with the head.' I'm moving towards his door when Delyth dramatically flings herself between it and me.

'Mr Weston is not to be disturbed.'

'It'll only take a moment.' I take a step to the side, which she instantly mirrors.

'*Not* to be disturbed, I said.' She draws herself up, accentuating the discrepancies between our heights. I wish I were taller.

'I'll be less than two minutes.' I'm torn between exasperation and the need to get round the indomitable form in front of me. 'Please, Delyth. Just two minutes.'

She folds her arms.

'Mr Weston made it perfectly clear that he is not to be disturbed by anyone – and that includes you. He says I'm to tell you to wait here until he sends for you.'

Is that a tiny smirk I detect? Something's going on and I feel anxiety build. He wants to see *me* specifically. This must be to do with last night. He can't fire me, surely? I'm good at my job and there have been no complaints about me.

Most of the school will be going to the pool soon for the end of term swimming gala, leaving me here with the problematic kids who are too naughty, timid or frail to take part. The vast majority of these children will probably be kept home today, anyway. I have a sudden image of him cornering me in a cupboard but I know that I'm safe here. Mrs Lawson, the lovely additional learning needs teacher is staying and so is Angie, another of the learning support assistants.

'Mrs Parry!' I jump as Ian's voice bellows from the other side of the door. Delyth spins round, wobbling slightly on her unaccustomed heels. She raps on the door as she enters and closes it decisively behind her.

Moments later she's back.

'Mr Weston will see you now,' she declares haughtily as she stands to the side to admit me. The door closes and it's just him and me. He's standing by the window and his features are hidden by the sun's glare.

'Ian, look, I'm sorry –'

'*Mr Weston.*' He turns. He's calm, controlled and, from the expression on his face, very angry. I'm taken aback by the rebuke and flustered. There's a cut on his cheekbone that's been masked by some ill-matching concealer.

'Mr Weston, of course. Well, I just wanted to-'

'Enough!'

This is a side of him I've never seen before and I'm shocked into silence. He sits down behind his desk and says off-handedly, 'There have been some changes made to today's schedule.' He holds out a piece of paper that I take and scan.

'There must be some mistake.' I look at him, bewildered.

'There's no mistake.'

'But you've put me down at the poolside. I always stay here with Mrs Lawson.'

'Not today. Today you go with the others to the gala.'

'But I can't. You know I can't.' I'm aware of the desperation in my voice and the shocked tears perilously close to the surface. I drag them back down. I know what he's doing and I don't want to give him the satisfaction of seeing me grovel.

'I make the decisions here and I expect you to follow them. Is that quite clear?'

'You and the governors know the issues surrounding this. Please.' I despise my pleading tone. 'I'll happily stay here, as usual, with the remaining children.'

‘If I say ‘go’, you go. *I’m* in charge here.’

‘Ian.’ Distaste flickers across his face. ‘Mr Weston.’ I aim for calm reason. ‘The other staff have always supported me on this.’

‘Here we go again,’ he affects a bored drawl, but his eyes are alert. ‘It’s been nearly twenty years. You can’t expect to hide behind that old sob story forever.’ He leans forward across the desk and whispers, ‘I’ve not done with you yet.’ Abruptly, he pushes himself back. ‘Off you go now. We both have more important things to be getting on with.’

Delyth is by the door as I leave, eavesdropping no doubt. She goes in front of me to the other side of the office where she stoops to mutter in my ear, ‘This is what happens when you get above yourself, Gwen. You’re not in his league and you never will be.’

She turns back and normally I’d have pointed out the big sales tag dangling from the expensive dress but I’m feeling angry, scared and mean. Let her look ridiculous

As I make my way along the corridor, I see two of the other assistants with their hands by their mouths and I’m sure that they’re talking about me. They barely suppress their giggles as they pass and I feel uneasy. Ewan Jenkins, the young Class 2 teacher, holds open the door for me and gives me a stage wink as he does so, saying, ‘It’s always the quiet ones, eh?’

I stop.

‘What do you mean by that, Ewan?’ It comes out a little more sharply than I intended, but he simply grins and says, ‘Dark horses, Gwen.’ He heads off quickly towards his class and I don’t have the time to pursue it further.

~~~

Fifteen minutes later and I’m at the back of a long crocodile of animated children waiting to be walked to the Leisure Centre. A whistle sounds at the front and the queue is starting to shuffle forwards when I hear a vehicle pull up behind me. I turn in time to see little Kaylee Johnson jumping out of her father’s van followed by her older brother, Justin, who pushes past his sister and elbows his way through to join his friends. I
~~~

find Justin a difficult child, full of aggression and at the centre of much of the school's unpleasantness.

Whenever summoned to the school by the head, Justin's mother, a recovering drug addict, sits quietly with her head down but Mark, the father, is belligerent and hostile, openly praising his son for his attacks on the others.

'That stuck-up Felix needed taking down a peg or two. I'm proud of you for standing up for yourself.'

The boy's been excluded several times, but the school always takes him back again later. There is no other intervention to help him. One day he'll be told he's used up all his chances with us and he'll become someone else's problem.

Kaylee is different. She's undersized for her six years, and a timid child whose hunched and cringing body language makes her an easy target for the bullying she receives. Justin wears expensive clothes and designer trainers but Kaylee spends most of her time in ill-fitting, cheap cast-offs. Not only do these clothes make her conspicuous amongst her peers, they are rarely washed and anyone getting close to her is subjected to an unpleasant, stale odour reminiscent of musty pencil shavings and a hint of urine. None of her classmates want to sit beside her and the distress in her eyes, when they say bluntly that she stinks, is gut-wrenching. Social Services have looked into it but say that her mother is doing her best and showing signs of improvement. They argue that it's better for her to live in a bit of squalor with her family than to be taken into care.

Kaylee scuttles over to catch up and falls in step beside me. She doesn't look up when I greet her but, after a while, I feel her hand catch mine and hold it lightly and I let it rest there. School policy discourages any physical contact with the children but to reject this unexpected interaction would be unthinkable.

'It's a lovely day, isn't it?'

She nods solemnly, but we carry on in silence.

I offer another opening. 'I bet you're looking forward to the summer holidays.'

There's a slight tug in my hand and a quiet, 'No.'

I don't know what to say and I'm dithering over the words when the small voice at my side continues.

'Can I stay with *you*, Miss?'

'Well, when we get to the pool you'll have to sit upstairs with the others. I'll be with Mr Ford by the water.'

'No, Miss.' Her voice is louder, more urgent now. 'I want to stay at your *house*.'

We stop, oblivious of the excited, chattering pairs continuing on without us, and I turn to Kaylee and bob down so our eyes are on the same level. Hers are enormous in her grubby little face.

'You can't stay in *my* house, Kaylee,' I make the words as kind and soft as I can but instantly she reverts back to looking down at her feet. 'Can you tell me why you're so sad?'

There's a slight shake of the head.

'Perhaps I can help? Would you like me to talk with—'

Before I can finish her eyes flash up at me and she tugs hard on my hand. 'No! No, you mustn't tell.' Her unexpectedly loud voice alarms her and she quickly covers her mouth with her other hand.

'It's all right, Kaylee. I just want to help. You can talk to me.'

She studies me for a few seconds and then carefully removes the hand from her mouth and whispers, 'If you tell him he'll be angry. Please don't tell him I asked.'

'Who will be angry?' But I've seen the way Mark Johnson treats his little daughter and she confirms my suspicions with a whispered 'Daddy.'

I'm out of my depth here and there's some jostling going ahead of us that needs my attention. I take her shoulders in a firm grip and wait until she looks at me.

'Listen, Kaylee. We have to keep up with the others now, but I do want to help. Can we have a chat when the gala's finished?'

Her withdrawal is tangible and I feel a helpless guilt. There's a loud yell from one of the boys in front and I grab her hand and tug her with me.

'Come on. Let's catch up with the others before they do something completely crazy.'

We run together and she's breathless when we stop.

'Kaylee. Please let me help you.' Her eyes remain downcast and I've lost the moment. School breaks up for the summer at the end of the day and I want to talk with her before I report the situation to Ginny Powell, the deputy head.

'Look, when it's time to leave the gala, you wait behind and tell anyone who asks that I've said I need your help with something. OK?' I'm trying to balance a lightness of tone so as not to scare her with an instruction I need her to agree to. She keeps her eyes downcast and there's no response.

'Please, Kaylee. I'll see you later.' She withdraws her hand and follows the rest of the children to the steps. I'm watching her go when I hear my name called.

'Gwen! What the devil are you doing here?' It's Steve Ford. He's in charge of PE and this is his last gala. He retires today and I'll be sorry to see him leave.

I cross over to him and hand him the head's amended piece of paper. Seconds later he's looking at me with a mixture of sympathy and anger.

'What a bastard!' The words are spoken too quietly for anyone else to hear but there's no mistaking the animosity in them. Rumour has it that Steve had planned on staying for another five years but couldn't stomach working any longer with Ian Weston. I'm prepared to believe it now.

He runs a tanned hand over short, grizzled hair, still looking at the paper. Then he comes to a decision.

'Right. I need another body in the changing rooms to sort out the chaos in there. I'll swap you with Nia. She can do the poolside stuff.'

I'm so relieved I could hug him.

'Thanks, Steve.'

'No problem. Tell Nia to come through to me.' He folds the paper back up and rams it into the pocket of his shorts. As I turn to go, he adds, 'Listen, Gwen, if it becomes too difficult, send a child through and I'll sort something out. Promise?'

I nod and make my way through the door to the changing rooms.

Chapter 3

I survive my stint in the changing rooms at the swimming gala without any trauma. Every spare second is taken up with resolving disputes, finding clothes, assisting children struggling to dress damp and awkward bodies and consoling disappointed contestants. Perhaps Ian Weston is right and it's time for me to come out of self-imposed hiding.

When the last child has left, and we've done a sweep of the stalls for litter and lost property, I rush through to the front, scanning the throng for Kaylee. I can't pick her out anywhere. The Centre is open to the public again and I can hear excited voices coming from the pool area. Perhaps Kaylee's waiting in there for me, away from the other children. Taking a deep breath, I push open the door and step into the humid atmosphere where light ripples off the walls and ceiling and sound is bright and distorted. I can't see her anywhere and am turning to go when there's a scream from the water that catches my breath. I spin back and see a delighted youngster clambering onto his father's back. They're having a great time, but the damage is done. I'm unable to move, hyperventilating and feeling light-headed, when Steve Ford appears, takes one look at me and pulls me to the side where he sits me down onto the nearest wooden bench. He holds my head by my knees.

Gradually, I become aware of Steve's rough hand scraping the nape of my neck and his voice, coming at first from a great distance, repeating, 'It's all right, Gwen. It's all right.'

Once the crisis is over, I feel tearful and silly but swallow noisily, straighten my shoulders and turn to look up at him.

'Thanks.'

'No problem.' Then he holds out his hand and helps me to my feet. I can feel his arm lightly at my back as we head for the exit where the children have all but vanished, chattering noisily as they head back to the school for an early dismissal.

'What in heaven's name were you doing in there, Gwen?'

'I was looking for Kaylee Johnson. I need to speak with her.'

'Everyone's accounted for so she must be returning with the others.'

'Thanks, Steve. I'd better run and catch up with them.'

'I don't think so.' He pulls me round to face him. 'You're still deathly pale. No, you're coming back in the car with me. June's hospital appointment finished early so she'll make up the staff numbers Just give me a minute to gather up the last of the equipment.'

The aftershocks running through me reduce me to a weakness that prevents me from running out to find Kaylee. I sit down on the low wall outside the pool and wait for Steve. If he's quick, I'll probably arrive back at the school before her.

It takes him over ten minutes to store everything in his SUV, but then he's stopped by the pool manager who ushers him inside again and engages him in conversation for a further ten minutes. I'm on my feet and pacing when he reappears. And then we're on our way.

~~~

I'm grateful for the lift back. Steve throws glances at me but says nothing until we pull in at the rear of the school. My heart sinks as I notice that the place is practically deserted apart from a few staff cars.

'Thanks, Steve.'

'No problem. How are you feeling now?'

'I'm fine.'

'This shouldn't have happened.' He gives a wry smile. 'I'm not angry with you.' The slight emphasis on the 'you' indicates he's not forgiven the head. 'But it was a bit of a shock finding you like that.'

'You've been great, thanks. Crisis over.'

'Good. Then you can help me carry this lot into the PE cupboard.'

'Oh, Steve, I'm sorry. There's something I need to tell Ginny that won't wait. You know I'd love to help.'
~~~

'No worries, Gwen. There's other slave labour inside I can capture.'

He lopes off and I scramble down from his car and head for the entrance, rehearsing what I'm going to tell Ginny, when I hear a shout from the other side of the playground. It's Mark Johnson. Kaylee is cowering under one of the school benches.

'Get out of there. NOW!'

Kaylee doesn't respond.

'Right! You've asked for it.' He looks hot and angry, his face a dark red and glistening with sweat.

I make out a slight whimper and then he pounces, viciously snatching her out by the wrist. Then, before she can stand, he drags her across the tarmac, her little knees, shoulders and elbows scraping against the rough surface. She cries out in pain and terror and I'm spurred into action.

'Stop! Mr Johnson, stop!' I run towards them, oblivious of what I'll do once I catch up with them.

'Keep out of this!'

He starts to jog, Kaylee's pitiful body taking even sharper knocks.

'Stop this now or I'll call the police!'

'I wouldn't do that if I were you.' He looks directly at me without pausing and his eyes underline the threat in his voice.

'You're hurting her.'

'She shouldn't have hidden from me. Keep your nose out of my business, and I'll keep mine out of yours.'

On reaching his white van, on the verge by the gate, he literally throws Kaylee onto the front seat. He climbs up next to her and slams the door as I get there. I'm too late; left helplessly with my fingers splayed against the window. He starts the engine and roars off kicking up a faint trail of dust behind him.

I curl my hands into useless fists and stride back to the main entrance, colliding with Ginny, the Deputy Head.

Ginny quickly sums up the situation, tells me to follow her and we make straight for the head's office. The door is ajar and he's berating someone.

'You thought I might be interested in *you*?' The tone is vicious. 'Clear your desk. Find a job as far from here as possible. I expect your resignation by tomorrow morning. I'll give you a good reference just to get rid of you.'

'I don't understand. You've paid me compliments. I—' The voice breaks off, choked with emotion. It's Delyth.

'I flatter everyone. It makes things easier.'

The words make me flinch. He's not finished.

I should have got rid of you ages ago.' There's what sounds like the thump of a fist hitting the table and the sudden scraping of a chair. 'You've upset every member of my staff with your meddling. You've been a liability to the school. But this!' He's raging. 'This attack on my personal life This, *this*, was the last straw.'

'Please, Ian, let me explain.'

He continues; calmer now, detached, cold. 'There are discrepancies in the school accounts, I daresay to cover the cost of the ridiculous get up you've been wearing recently. Go now, or I go to the governors and request a full investigation.'

'But—'

'Get out.'

Delyth leaves, her head averted as she pushes past us. I catch the sympathy in Ginny's gaze as she watches her leave and self-disgust swamps me at how long I've kept myself in the dark about the true nature of this man.

Five minutes later Ginny has convinced Ian Weston that we have to make an official complaint about Mark Johnson. He phones Social Services whilst I write out a statement. I think of Kaylee's confession that she doesn't look forward to the holidays. It's ironic that for both of us school provides a welcome respite. *I* know what to expect over the coming weeks but realise that I've introduced a worrying level of uncertainty and disruption into that little girl's life. It's likely that she will be removed from the family, even if only temporarily. How will she cope if she's placed with an unfamiliar family or in a home with loud, boisterous children? What awaits her at the hands of her father if she's returned to him? In short, have I just made a grim situation worse?

~~~
~~~

Today's surges of adrenaline have drained me and I just want to go home and curl up somewhere. Please, Granny, be asleep when I get back.

No such luck.

'Where have you been? I've been calling you all day?'

I crouch down so our faces are level. 'Sorry, Granny. I was working and my phone was switched off.'

'Well, what's the point of having the blasted thing if you can't use it?'

'You know I can't chat when I'm at school.'

She may be in a wheelchair but she still manages to do an impressive version of a flounce.

'I didn't want a chat. I needed you. It was very important and you just ignored me.'

'You have your alarm pendant if it's an emergency.'

'It wasn't an emergency. But it was very important.'

I let my breath out slowly and speak calmly when I'm ready.

'What did you need me for, then?'

'How should I know? That was ages ago. You just don't care about me, do you? Here I am, unable to get around, and you go out having a good time. It's no fun being left here on my own.'

Her voice is rising as her anger and self-pity build. I try to defuse the situation.

'I'm sorry, Granny. I know it's horrible not to be able to get around like you used to and—'

'Fine words and no parsnips buttered!' She isn't to be derailed. 'After all I've done for *you,* I'd have thought a little consideration would have been in order. But no. You don't give me a second thought.'

'That simply isn't true.'

'Don't you take that tone with me! I expect a little respect and understanding. Is that too much to ask? Is it? Is it?'

Her eyes are flashing angrily and if I don't come up with a suitable intervention, she'll have a full-blown tantrum.

I kneel down next to her and take her hand. She holds it rigid in protest. 'I'm here now and I'll make you a snack in a minute and then we can have a natter and watch some television together. Who Cares Wins is on tonight.'

Her hand relaxes in mine and a little of the tension between us seeps away.

'What would you like to eat? There's some of that nice cheese you wanted. I could make you a sandwich.'

'No. I don't like it anymore.'

'All right.' I ignore the petulant response. 'There's some soup left over from yesterday.'

'No. I don't want soup.'

'That's fine.' I need to hit on the right suggestion promptly before the grumpiness reasserts itself. 'It's been such a hot day, hasn't it? There's a tub of ice cream in the freezer and we could have a bowlful with a few fresh strawberries from the planter in the garden.'

She makes a grunting noise that I take for assent.

I could do without this today.

Chapter 4

Whilst Granny tucks into her food, I go back to the kitchen, take my phone out of my bag and switch it on. I have yet more missed calls and messages from Catrin. I suddenly feel worried. Please may nothing bad have happened to her or the family.

I tap in her details and she responds in seconds.

'Gwen! Where have you been? I've been trying to reach you all day.'

'Sorry, Cat. It's just been crazy busy. What's the matter? Is Nansi okay?'

'Nansi's fine. She has two teeth now and I have the bite marks and slobber to prove it.'

'Awwww!'

'Don't you 'awww' like that. Wait till you have a six-month-old. They may look angelic on the outside, but they've got a whole arsenal of sneaky weapons at their disposal.'

'Don't believe you!'

'Gwen,' she switches to her serious voice, 'have you read any of my messages yet?'

'No. I was worried about you and Nansi.'

She groans.

'Look, you need to go onto Facebook. Delyth's been busy.' There's a sudden wailing in the background. 'Nansi's just whacked herself with her teether. I'll ring you back.'

I go to my laptop in the corner and in less than a minute the screen fills with a picture of me in the pub looking into Ian's face and holding his hand. I feel physically sick. Delyth must have followed us and taken the incriminating photo.

I drop my head into my hands. Everyone has seen this. It's been posted to do the most harm and I'm the collateral damage. No wonder the others were giggling and whispering. I'm mortified to think that people have seen this and assumed that I was having an affair with my boss - with a married man. Dernant is a small place. People will now have an opinion about me based upon this. I am condemned by one posting of a misleading snapshot. They say a picture can paint a thousand words –how can I erase them? I can't.

I steel myself to click on Delyth's list of friends and a groan escapes me as I see the avatar of Lynette Weston, Ian's wife. I remember the cut on his cheek. Did they fight over this bit of spite? Why would Delyth do such a thing? His vicious words to her this afternoon come back to me and the new dress and makeup suddenly make awful sense. She's used this to make trouble with Lynette. She must have convinced herself that he would return her affection. I can afford a moment's sympathy for someone more deluded about the man than I was.

The opening of the front door brings me abruptly to my feet. It's Becky again. I paste a smile onto my face.

'Hiya, Becky. I didn't realise it was so late.'

She's looking closely at me, her eyes narrowed. Then she closes the distance between us and puts a hand on my shoulder.

'You've seen that Facebook thing, haven't you?' I simply stare at her and grimace as I try to hold back the stinging in my eyes. She pulls me to her and holds me tightly for a few seconds after which she pushes me back and gives me a little shake.

'Don't let it get to you, Gwen. Anyone who knows you can see that you're not drooling over that bastard. You just look puzzled and surprised.'

I snatch at this tiny ray of hope.

'Can you really see that? Will others understand?'

She gives a short laugh. 'Some will. Many know enough about Ian Weston to fill in the missing pieces.' Her head shakes. 'And there's plenty who know how Delyth Parry has been throwing herself at him.'

I feel momentarily brighter but come back to the "*Some* will", and sag again. 'But most people will believe this is a nasty little affair?'

Becky knows better than to gloss it all over.

'You know how it is, Gwen. Nothing much happens here and we all like something to gossip over. I've enjoyed a good gossip and I bet you have, too. Does it matter if some unimportant people think the worst?'

'Yes. It does.' I shrug helplessly. 'I know it shouldn't, but I hate knowing that some people think the worst of me. Even if it's complete strangers, it still feels creepy and horrible.'

‘You have to let it go, Gwen, or it’ll take you over.’ She shakes her head. ‘Believe me, I know what it’s like to have people making assumptions and pointing the finger.’

Her mouth is set in a hard line that reinforces the bitterness of the words.

‘I’m sorry, Becky. I had no idea. You’ve never said.’

‘No.’ She waves my concern away with her hand. ‘It was about someone else. Someone in the family. But it still felt like a personal attack and I desperately wanted to put everyone straight.’ She looks me in the eyes. ‘You can’t tell people what they don’t want to hear. It’s a waste of time and effort which you could be spending on the more important people in your life.’

What she’s saying makes sense, but I can’t hold back the injustice I feel at being branded this way. I cringe as I remember some of the newspaper articles I’ve read where innocent victims have been pilloried. I’m struck by the realisation that the first thing that comes to my mind about those hounded people is the accusations. Even though I don’t believe the smears I can’t erase them, not even when the truth comes out. The victims must live with this knowledge. And I now have ‘depraved’ tattooed on my public persona. I am uselessly, pointlessly angry.

The ringing of the doorbell penetrates my gloom.

‘I’ll get that, shall I?’ Becky offers, as I make no attempt to move.

I shake my head to clear it. ‘No, it’s all right. I’ll go.’

‘In that case, I’ll go and see how her ladyship’s doing.’ She gives me an encouraging smile and heads off along the corridor.

I open the door. It’s Cat.

‘Hi. I’ve brought essential supplies!’ She brandishes two bottles of wine and a huge box of chocolates. ‘You’d better let me in quickly. My reserves of strength are fading fast. Superman only had to face Kryptonite; he’d have surrendered long ago if confronted by a teething six-month-old.’

I stand back to let her pass.

Cat dumps her stuff on the table and turns to face me.

'Let's have a look at you.' She holds my upper arms and looks closely at me for a couple of seconds before releasing a gentle sigh.

'Hmm. Not as bad as I expected but still in serious need of treatment. I'll get the glasses.'

I watch, dumbly, as she returns with two wine goblets that she places next to the chocolates. Then she raises the bottles.

'Which do we start on?' She holds them up in turn. 'Red or white?' She waits for an answer and I'm stirred into action.

'The white. We'll save the red for later.'

'Well said.'

~~~

Within five minutes we're sitting at the table, glasses already emptying. The box of chocolates is placed diagonally between us and I'm on my third before she speaks again.

'That's better. I'm beginning to feel almost human. Now, what are we going to do about you?'

I hold the glass to my lips and shake my head, miserable.

'Oh, Gwen. If you could just see your face. You remind me of when I first met you all those years ago.'

I look up at that.

'Don't talk rubbish, Cat.'

'I'm not. The teacher stood you at the front of the class and told us we all had to be nice to you. You were all freckles and impossibly white skin, your red hair was tightly plaited and you looked tiny. Adrian Flint sniggered and your huge eyes flew to his face and the grief he saw there stopped him in his tracks. It stopped all of us. We didn't need to know what had happened; we recognised in you some of the pain that all children suffer trying to cope in an uncharted world.'

'This is nothing like that,' I grumble uncomfortably.

'Good.' There's satisfaction in her voice. 'I'm hoping to put some perspective on the situation.' Her voice drops. 'You've been through much, much worse, my love.'

I smile then. She's managed to hit home.

'What would I do without you, Cat?'

'What would Nansi do without her favourite Godmother?'

'I'm her only Godmother.'
~~~

‘See, that makes you even more important.’

‘Thanks, Cat. But what am I going to do about all of this?’

‘What do you want to do?’

‘Make it go away. Wind back time.’

‘Honey, if I could do that, I’d be lying on a chaise longue being fed peeled grapes, someone else massaging my feet whilst a hunky band of musicians played my choice of music.’

‘But it’s not the truth about me! I’d never fool around with a married man. You know that.’

‘I do know that. I was the one who picked you up from the car park ten minutes later, remember? And the people who matter will know it too. The rest you can forget about.’

‘That’s what Becky said. But I can’t ignore this. It’s horrible. It’s…’ I search for a strong enough word to convey what I feel but nothing’s forthcoming.

‘It’s unfair? Cruel? Humiliating?’

‘Yes. Exactly.’

‘Listen to me, Gwen. My mother was a firm believer in the ‘serenity to accept the things we cannot alter’ philosophy. You deal with the stuff than can be dealt with and let go of the rest.’

‘She was a lovely woman, your mum.’

‘She was, wasn’t she? And she adored you.’

‘The feeling was mutual.’

‘She tried to intervene on your behalf many times, but your grandmother refused to listen.’

‘I could do with her here now.’

‘I know, honey, but you have to ignore the things the old bat says.’

‘I do. I do try, Cat, but it’s so hard sometimes.’

‘It’s a shame you came back here.’

‘I had no choice. Not after all that she did for me.’

‘All that she did? She took out her anger on a five-year-old, that’s what she did.’ Cat’s voice rises.

‘Shhh!’ She’ll hear you.’

‘Good. She’s made your life hell and you accept it. I don’t have to.’

I look nervously towards the door.

‘Don’t, Cat. Please!’

She holds my gaze in a hard stare for a moment. 'You know, for an intelligent woman you can be incredibly dumb sometimes.' Then she smiles. 'However, I'm not going to fall out with you tonight. Tonight, we are going to be merry!'

My glass is topped-up to the brim and she chuckles as I lower my mouth and bring the wine down to a safer level. I'm not much of a drinker and I'm already beginning to feel the effects as my skin warms and my body relaxes a little.

'How's that clever big brother of yours doing? I haven't seen him in ages.'

'Still at Forsters Browning and enjoying life in the fast lane.'

'Still with Zoe?'

''Fraid so.'

'Grrr!'

'As if you aren't totally, completely, utterly in love with Dean!'

A dreamy expression crosses her face.

'I know. Married eight years and still daft as ever.'

'I used to think you'd end up with Gethin and then we'd be sisters.'

'So did I. I'd watch him protecting you in the school yard. One cruel comment and he'd make them sorry. Didn't matter how big they were. He was just like a handsome knight and I longed for him to come to my rescue.'

I laugh at this.

'You certainly tried hard enough. Remember that time you pretended to be stuck on a branch by the stream.'

'Don't! It makes me blush even now.'

'You were calling out,' Gethin! Gethin, help me!' in a weak voice. He was too intrigued by that glossy beetle to hear you. But he did hear when the branch snapped and you fell face down in the mud.'

'Neither of you were particularly sympathetic to my plight, I seem to recall.'

'We probably were, for a couple of seconds, until you staggered to your feet and Gethin called out 'Swamp monster!' You were so affronted you put your hands on your hips and started to stomp towards us. Even you found it funny after that.'

'So I did.' She traces a finger over the chocolates. 'But it wasn't so funny when I got home.' The chosen chocolate is popped into her mouth.

'Come off it! Your mum only pretended to be cross. She found it so funny she had to wipe her eyes on the hem of her apron.'

There's a sudden knock on the door that snaps us out of our reverie and brings me to my feet.

'Expecting someone?'

'Nope.' There are few visitors here and we're both intrigued to see who it is.

It's Ben. He's dressed in a blue shirt and denims and his face is partially hidden by a huge bouquet of flowers.

'Hi, Gwen. I hope I haven't come at a bad time.'

'Not at all. Come in.' I usher him through and try to send Cat a quelling look when I catch the impish delight in her eyes.

'Ben, this is Catrin, a good friend of mine. Cat, this is Ben, our new neighbour.'

'Hiya, Ben. Nice to meet you.' Cat stands and shakes hands with him. 'What magnificent flowers!'

Ben glances at the cellophane-wrapped bundle and presents it to me.

'These are from Atticus as a heartfelt thanks for rescuing him this morning.' I take the arrangement of exotic flowers and briefly bury my face in the sweet-smelling blooms.

'And this,' he continues as I raise my head again, 'is from me by way of an apology for making you late for work this morning.' He holds up a bottle of Châteauneuf du Pape.

'I can't take this, Ben!' I'm a little flustered by the gesture. 'All I did was terrify your lovely dog into submission and then rudely abandon you.'

'That's not how either of *us* recall it.' His eyes have friendly crinkles radiating out at the sides. 'Please, take it.'

I'm dithering when Cat's hand snakes out and seizes the bottle.

'Thanks, Ben. Why don't you help the poor girl out of her dilemma by sharing the problem bottle *with* us.'

Ben tips his head to one side, waiting for my response.

'Of course! That's a perfect solution.' It *does* sound appealing.

'Well, if you're sure? I wouldn't want to force my company on you.'

'It's our pleasure. How better to show one's neighbourliness than drinking the neighbour's wine!'

'I'll get another glass.' Catrin nips through to the kitchen but not before I've seen the triumphant expression on her face. I've lost track of the times she's tried to play matchmaker. I recognise the signs.

Chapter 5

We sit together at the table and Cat leads the conversation.

'So, Ben, what brings you to Dernant?' She softens the interrogation with a genial smile but I feel uncomfortable on his behalf.

'I'd love to tell you it's the beautiful countryside, the proximity to beaches and the peace. The true answer is rather mundane, I'm afraid – it's work.' He pulls a face. 'Not the poetic answer you were hoping for?'

'On the contrary,' Cat seizes her opportunity. 'I can ask you about your work without appearing too intrusive.'

'Cat!' I'm appalled at her effrontery and expect Ben to retaliate. There's a momentary silence, where my heart appears to stop, and then he's laughing. It's a full, hearty laugh that brings those attractive crinkles to prominence.

'I can see you're a girl who doesn't beat about the bush. I like that.' He takes a sip of the expensive wine before continuing and I realise I'm keen to hear his answer.

'I'm an architect. I create bespoke buildings for clients but I also like to design affordable, green housing. One of the developers here has seen some of my work and I've agreed to deliver plans for three separate estates in the county.'

'So, are you planning on staying here or is this just a temporary stop?' Cat's brazen probing appals me but Ben seems unfazed by it.

'Who knows? I've bought the house rather than renting it, if that helps at all, but I've lived in four different places in as many years.'

Cat opens her mouth, no doubt to fire something else at him, but he turns to me.

'Have *you* lived in Dernant long?'

I'm a little flustered by the unexpected question.

'Only a year. Well, that is to say, I've been back for a year.' I'm horribly tongue-tied. 'I used to live here when I was younger.'

'In Dernant or this house in particular?'

'Here.' I realise I haven't answered the question. 'I mean, in this house.' My cheeks feel warm and I'm back to being a shy teenager exhibiting a woeful lack of social skills.

We turn as the door to the corridor swings open. Becky is standing there. She has her phone in her hand and she looks anxious as she nods towards the others.

'Hiya.' She looks at me. 'Gwen, could I have a quick word?'

'Of course.' I'm relieved to be able to leave the awkwardness I've created behind me as I follow her out of the room. I know Becky well enough now to recognise that something serious has happened and I close the door quietly behind me and beckon her away from it, towards my grandmother's room.

'What's the matter?'

'I've just had a call from my sister. I'm sorry, Gwen, but I need to leave right now. Is that all right?' She's agitated and her distress is barely below the surface.

'Of course. Go. Go now.'

'Edith's in bed, she's had her medication and I've left her with her Agatha Christie audiobook playing but she isn't asleep yet.'

'Becky, go!' I push her back towards the door. 'I can cope. You go and help Julie.'

'But—'

'No buts!'

She falters for a second then stands straighter.

'Thanks, Gwen. I appreciate this.'

I physically propel her into the kitchen where she musters a weak smile before saying goodnight and leaving.

I put the backs of my hands to my face to check the heat and decide it's safe enough for me to return to the sitting room.

'What was that about?' Cat's in a probing mood tonight. I'm saved from saying anything in front of Ben by the sound of something falling and Granny yelling with alarm before bellowing my name. I raise my eyebrows at Cat who sends me a sympathetic look.

'I'm sorry, Ben. I have to go and see what's happened.' He rises courteously as I prepare to leave. 'I may be some time. Sorry.'

'No worries. Is there anything I can do to help?'

'No. Thanks for the offer but this is one of those things best left to me.' I flash a quick smile at him and head for Granny's room.

~~~

I rap on Granny's door before entering. The room is lit by the Tiffany lamp on the bedside table. A disembodied voice from the CD player next to it is declaiming something about 'little grey cells' but Granny is pushing herself away from the light and grunting with the effort.

'What's happened?'

'Blasted thing!' She's panting and I can tell from the squinting of her eyes that's she's in some discomfort.

'What's happened, Granny?'

She sags back on one elbow and points a wavering finger towards the table.

'That! There!' When she's upset she can't think or talk in anything other than single words. I follow the rough direction of the finger and, as I move to get closer, my foot kicks something that clunks against wood. Bending down I see that her water glass has fallen to the floor and then I notice the spreading darkness on the sheet by the pillow. My heart sinks. Despite my gawky responses I was enjoying Ben's company and now I'll have to strip the bed and remake it, all the while trying to pacify a now rather damp and disturbed grandmother.

'Come on, Granny. Put your arms around me and we'll get you onto your chair for a minute.'

It's not as easy as it sounds, but after a deal of lifting and straining, she's safely ensconced where she can watch me change the bedding, giving me advice and criticism in equal measure.

Once the bed is sorted, I turn my attention to her nightdress but the summer heat has already dried it and so all that's left is
~~~

to hoist her back onto the mattress and put the fresh duvet in place.

'I'll put your Agatha Christie back on for you.'

A bony hand catches at my wrist.

'Could you read a bit for me, instead?'

Her sudden mellowness is unexpected. I'm torn between my desire to get back to the others and this opportunity to spend-some gentle time with my grandmother. I know I don't truly have a choice because I'll regret passing up these unexpected moments of affectionate togetherness.

'Of course. What would you like?'

'Some Jane Austen would be nice, don't you think?'

'What about Emma?'

'Yes, I'd like that very much.'

Granny's short-term memory problems are becoming more of an issue. I have read the first few chapters of Emma to her repeatedly but each time is like the first for her. There are other things, such as music, that she takes great pleasure in re-discovering. The downside to this, and it is a dreadful one, is the re-experiencing of all the recent bad things that she has forgotten. Every time she is told again that a friend has died it hurts as much as it did the first time. It is horrifically cruel; nature playing with her emotions like a cat with a mouse.

I take the book out of the drawer by the bed and start to read.

~~~

It isn't long before her body relaxes into sleep and I quietly slip the book back and return to the sitting room. I'm not surprised that Cat is there by herself. Not surprised, but a little disappointed. Cat doesn't look sad, though, and her gleaming eyes betray her excitement.

'Ben's gone.'

'So I notice.'

'But we had a nice chat whilst you were out of the room.'

'I'm not sure if I want to hear this!'

'Don't worry, I didn't say anything untoward.'

'Forgive me if I find that hard to believe!'
~~~

'Brownie's honour,' she gives a salute and rounds it off with a smirk 'However, the nice Ben *did* ask if you and Granny lived here on your own. I told him that supporting your grandmother made you practically a hermit these days and that you didn't have a boyfriend at the moment.'

'Cat!'

She leans forward. 'But he smiled, Gwen. He was delighted. I can pick up on these things and he was definitely happy to hear it.'

I don't know whether to scold her or dance her around the room. It's probably down to the unaccustomed wine but I feel a buzz at the news and grin back at her.

'Go on, then. What happened next?'

'I said that it was a shocking waste of a talented, lovely, beautiful lady.'

'Cat! You didn't!'

''Course I did. You didn't expect me to lie, did you?'

Curiosity gets the better of my amused indignation.

'What did he say?'

'Now *that* would be telling.' She wags her finger at me and laughs as I grab a cushion and threaten her with it.

'Cat!'

'Okay, okay. I give in.' She falls back onto the sofa, giggling. 'He went quiet for a few seconds and then he said "That's just the impression I got this morning". Then he said he'd better get back as he still had stuff to unpack for tomorrow.'

I don't reply but Cat starts to giggle again, pointing out that I'm clutching the cushion to me in an embrace. I thwack her with it and then flop down beside her.

'What would I do without you, Cat?'

'Mmm, I know. I'm amazing, aren't I?'

We sit in a companionable silence until Cat suddenly sits upright.

'I meant to ask about Becky. What's happened?'

'It's Julie again, but I didn't ask her any questions. I don't suppose she'll know much herself yet.'

I nibble the edge of my finger. I'm worried about Becky. Her sister Julie was diagnosed last October with multiple sclerosis. It's the relapsing remitting type of MS that comes and goes. Becky dropped everything then to help her with her two young children and we were both relieved when the episode faded and left Julie fairly unscathed.

The mood switches to a sombre one.

After a brief silence Cat says, 'Fingers crossed it's a false alarm, or over with as quickly as it was the last time. Julie's so lucky to have a sister like Becky.'

'So am I. Well, okay, she's not my sister, but you know what I mean.'

'I do. She's brilliant with your grandmother. She doesn't take any nonsense from her, unlike someone I know.'

'It's not the same, Cat. We all went through a terrible time, Granny especially, and I *need* to help her. You must be able to see that.'

'I do understand, Gwen, but I'm seeing it through a more objective lens and it makes me mad when she gives you such a hard time of it. It wasn't your fault.'

I open my mouth but before I can get a word out, she throws her hands up as if to fend me off.

'Don't say anything or you'll spoil the mood. You've no idea how a short break away from your own child can make you so unbelievably happy.' She glances at her watch. 'Oh no! How did it get so late? Nansi will think I've abandoned her!

'What happened to the 'short break to happiness' theory?'

'Just wait till you have your own. Then you'll understand how they mess with your logic.' She stretches and rises to her feet, yawning. 'I'll head off before Dean collapses. Children mess with time, too – one hour with a teething child bears no relationship to an hour on the clock.'

We hug and I see her to the door.

'Thanks for everything, Cat. I feel much less paranoid now.'

'That's my girl. Speak to you tomorrow.'

I watch her go down the road until she's out of sight before closing the door. Looking affectionately at the half-eaten chocolates and the three wine bottles, I trace a path down the neck of Ben's expensive offering, still more than half-full.

I wonder if I can use it to lure him back again.

~~~
~~~

I clear up the mess and have just switched off the light in the sitting room when there's a sudden pounding on the front door. My first thought is that Cat's forgotten something but she has a distinctive rap. I put the chain on the door before I open it. Instantly, a hand wraps itself around the opened edge and the toe of a trainer tries to force its way through the gap at the bottom. I'm so startled, a scream escapes me and I take a step back and pray that the chain will hold.

'Let me in!' It's Mark Johnson. 'You and I need to have a word.'

I'm shocked into a silence that makes him push and thump at the door.

'Open this bloody door now or I'll kick it down.'

I swallow a couple of times and compose myself before trying to reply. I hope that the quaking of my body isn't transmitted to my voice.

'Go away, Mr Johnson.' I sound calm and reasonable.

'I'll go when you agree to take back your lies about me and my kid.'

I keep silent.

'Do you hear me?' He throws his weight against the door and I flinch with each blow. 'You tell them that you made a mistake. You tell them that you realise now that I was helping Kaylee to her feet after she'd fallen over. You'd got the wrong impression.'

'We both know that isn't what happened. Now, I'm going to count to three and if you're still here I shall call the police.'

'Just try it and see what happens.'

'Are you threatening me, Mr Johnson?' My voice is still calm even if the rest of me is rigid with shock.

'You don't seem to get it. I'm not *asking* you to do this, I'm *telling* you, and if you don't there will be …' he pauses, 'consequences.'

'Consequences, Mr Johnson? What you're doing now is hardly helping your case. Leave, or I call the police.'

The hand stills on the door. I hear the clock tick unnaturally loudly in the sudden quiet before he speaks again.

'Yeah? So, I can't be seen having a go at you. Doesn't mean I can't convince you, one way or another, *Miss*

Meredith, and if you don't get my kids back to me you'll find out just how convincing I can be. You don't want this to end in tears. *Your* tears.'

I'm struggling to find a suitable response when he comes back with another attack.

'I've seen the photo, you little whore, so don't pretend you're better than the rest of us. They've taken my Justin and I want him back. *You* are going to get him back for me.'

Despite the shock of his verbal assault, I register the fact that he hasn't mentioned Kaylee.

'I'm calling the police now.' I move further away and as I reach for my mobile his hand and foot disappear leaving the door hanging slightly open. I'm desperate to close it but can't be sure that he's not still there, waiting. I tiptoe across towards the hinged side. I can't hear anything. I take another step until I'm close enough to touch it, pull my hands back and smack it shut.

I'm so shaken that it's several minutes before I recover from the unexpected confrontation and walk to my bedroom. It occurs to me that he might still be outside waiting, watching. I draw the curtains tightly together in the dark. I want to brush my teeth but the idea of walking into the bathroom, where the blind may be open, is too much of a challenge so I hurriedly change into my sensible long nightie, huddled over in case he can somehow see into the room.

Sleep is a long time coming. My brain throws up details of the day in a disturbing jumble of unpleasantness from which there's no escape. I'm also hypersensitive to sounds and twitch when the owl hoots, when Bramble noisily asserts her territorial rights and when something scurries through the bushes under my window. These are all noises familiar to me that wouldn't normally register on my consciousness.

At about two in the morning, I hear a dog barking. It occurs to me that it's Atticus and I find the thought strangely comforting. I drift into a deep sleep.

Chapter 6

A ringing at the front door drags me awake. It's 8 o'clock. I wrap my robe around me and stumble blearily towards the persistent din. I hesitate slightly, an after-effect of last night's unwelcome visit, and leave the chain on, just in case. When I peer round the gap, I can see Lisa, the young, rather immature, carer.

'Sorry, Lisa.' I release the chain and open the door. I forgot to remove the chain last night.'

'The chain? What chain?'

She clearly hasn't encountered the problem. 'Is there an issue with the key safe?' I look at the metal box attached to the outside wall and tap the code on the numbered keypad. The panel pops open revealing the key compartment – complete with key.

'Oh, yeah. No, there's no problem. I just couldn't remember what the number was.'

'It should be in your notes.'

'Yeah, I know. But it's so hot already and this bag weighs a ton so I thought it would be easier just to get you to open it instead.'

'That's fine today,' I concede as nicely as I can muster, 'but when I'm at school, for instance, I'm not here and my grandmother can't make it to the door herself.'

'But you *are* here, aren't you? I mean, it's the holidays so I didn't think it would matter.'

'Yes, I *am* here today, but I might have left for an appointment or to meet friends.'

'Oh, yeah. I didn't think of that. Sorry.'

She does look genuinely contrite and I am aware that my mood is coloured by yesterday's events.

'It's not a problem, Lisa. Come on in. I'm not sure if my grandmother is awake yet.' I don't add that if I were a betting woman, I'd lay odds on her having heard that relentless ringing.

Lisa stops as if she has something else she wants to say.

'Is there another problem, Lisa?'

'Nah. It's all right. It's just…' She stops.

'Yes?'

'Well, it's your car.'

'My car?'

'Yeah. Reckon you want to take a look at it.' She puts her head down so I can't make out her expression and scurries away into the house.

I was so tired yesterday, I'd left my car in the driveway instead of tucking it away in the garage. It was a mistake. Someone has sprayed red paint on its worn, white bodywork. 'Home Wrecker' is sprayed the length of one side. I walk round, stunned, and read 'Slut', 'Whore' and worse. I stand with my back to the road, unable to tear my eyes away from the ugliness in front of me. There's a tightness in my chest and I'm trapped in a world where nothing else exists apart from this mutilation. I don't even register the excited dog dancing at my knees until a hand touches my shoulder. I spin round in shock, to meet Ben's puzzled gaze.

'Sorry. Didn't mean to startle you, I was just going to ask…' He doesn't finish. His eyes are now on the car. 'What the—!'

Now I see it from his viewpoint, and acute embarrassment stains my skin and renders me speechless.

He bobs down at my feet and touches the tyre. It's flat. They're all flat.

Something snaps inside me.

'I've got to hide it.' I put a hand in my pocket to get the key. It's only then that it hits me that I'm still in my thin wrap. A further surge of embarrassment hits me physically in the stomach and this time I can feel my colour drain away.

'Steady.' Ben's low voice reaches me as he takes my elbows in his hands, supporting me. The wave of nausea passes and I pull myself upright and away from him.

'Thank you. I'll get my keys.'

He holds me back by the wrist and speaks in a quiet but firm voice. 'Sorry, Gwen, but that's the last thing you want to do.'

I try to focus on his face.

'But I have to get rid of it.' It comes out as a desperate whisper.

'Do that, and you might damage the wheel rims.' I look down at one of the tyres. I can see a deep slash in the side of it. Ben adds, in that same, calm way, 'And you don't want to destroy any evidence that the police need to catch the sick person who did this.'

'But people will see.'

'Does that matter so much?'

I run a dry tongue over drier lips. 'Yes.'

'Come on. You need to go inside and recover from the shock. He takes my arm and pulls me around the side of the car that has 'Home Wrecker' emblazoned across it. He reads it and his hand clenches on my arm. I'm more or less propelled to the front door. I sense a definite withdrawal.

'Will you be all right? I can stay with you until you're feeling stronger.'

He makes the offer but his tone is polite, discouraging.

'I'll be fine, thank you.'

He leaves with a curt nod that wounds my already stressed sensibilities.

I turn in the open door at the sound of a vehicle slowing down to a stop outside. It's Mark Johnson in his van. He holds up his phone and it's clear from his movements that he's taking several shots of my car. He looks in my direction and a smile corrupts his lips only to die as Ben approaches him. The van jerks as he revs the engine and speeds away. Ben clicks his fingers by his leg and Atticus instantly comes to heel, following him obediently across the road towards home.

Inside, I dress as quickly as I can with fingers that have become clumsy and unresponsive. Then I make two phone calls. The first is to the police, who say they'll come round when they can. The second is to Rob Oldworthy, a mechanic just two miles away in Cranston. I've come to know him well during the last year, one of the consequences of owning an aging vehicle. He promises to be with me by early afternoon and suggests I drape a sheet or something over the car to cover the graffiti.

Then I hide away in my room, trying to control the waves of emotion assaulting me. I feel shame above all else, even though I have done nothing to feel ashamed of. When I picture the car, now under cover, I see it as it is and as others will be seeing it, and their imagined judgements overlay my own.

~~~

The police arrive less than an hour later. Detective Inspector Preece is a stout man in his fifties wearing an ill-fitting brown suit and scuffed shoes. He is already perspiring in the morning heat and periodically runs an index finger under his collar as if to loosen it a little. Detective Sergeant Stafford is in his late twenties. He's a natty dresser with a cocksure manner that instantly grates on my already raw emotions.

After the introductions are made, we go outside to look at the car. DS Stafford sweeps the sheet aside with a matador's flourish and I wince to see the stark words again. They walk around, silently, both of them hunkering down to inspect the damage to the tyres. Stafford takes a multitude of pictures from different angles, presumably as evidence. I stand silently to one side, praying that they'll soon be finished so I can conceal the obscenities before any more people witness them. But this is Dernant. During their ten-minute examination several cars pass by, slowly, all the occupants looking in the direction of the drive. Word is already out.

'When do you think this was done, then?' DS Stafford asks the question without taking his roving eyes off the hideous words.

I look from him to another car driving past too slowly and DI Preece intervenes.

'I think it would be better to discuss this inside. Put the cover back on, Stafford.'

Once inside again, I offer them tea; a reflex gesture which seems both natural and bizarre. Then we sit at the kitchen table and Preece begins the questioning whilst Stafford takes notes.

'Right, Miss Meredith. This is obviously very upsetting. Has anything like this happened before?'

'No.' I shake my head to stress the point.

'No. All right. And you don't know when it happened?'

'No. I didn't look at it between arriving home at about 4 o'clock and getting up this morning.'
~~~

'Right. And is there anybody else here who might have seen or heard anything?'

'There's only me and my grandmother here. She rarely leaves the house.'

'I see.' He takes a sip of his tea. 'So, we're looking at a window of, say,' he does the calculation, 'Sixteen hours?'

'That's right.'

'Well, it looks like you've seriously upset somebody.' He takes another sip. 'Who might that be?' His body language remains relaxed but his keen eyes are probing my face and the sense of shame hits me again and I look down to hide my face from him.

'Miss Meredith?' He expects an answer and I know, as I give it, that my character is being assassinated by my own words.

'Possibly Ian Weston.'

'And who's he?'

'He's the head teacher at the school where I work.'

'Ah. So you're a teacher are you?'

'No. I'm a learning support assistant. I help the teacher in the classroom with the children who need more support.'

'I see.' He gives me a kindly smile. 'So why would this Ian Weston want to do this to you?'

What do I say? How can I defend myself? He's waiting and I have to say something.

'We had a bit of a disagreement.' This sounds tame even to my ears. 'Well, it was more of a fight, really?'

Stafford suddenly looks much more interested, but Preece continues in the same calm, probing manner.

'A bit of a fight? Could you tell me some more about that?'

'It was nothing. Just a misunderstanding.'

Stafford can't contain himself. 'Must've been one hell of a misunderstanding for him to have done that to your car!' He snorts and Preece quells him with a practised look.

'So, what was this fight about?'

'We went to The Tudor Arms on Monday after school. He wanted to discuss a scheme he was working on to help our struggling children.' I look directly into the eyes of the quiet man sitting opposite me. 'Only it seems…' I search for the words. 'It seems he thought I would be willing to er, you know, …er… have an assignation with him.' I can feel Stafford's mocking grin and my cheeks flame in response.

'And why would he think that?' Preece continues his steady questioning.

'I don't know! I've never given him any encouragement.' I'm desperate for him to understand. 'I thought he was genuinely interested in me because of my work in the school. We'd laugh about things sometimes but nothing more.'

'I see.'

I'm not sure that he does see.

'Honestly. I've never thought of him as anything other than my headmaster.'

'You're a lowly LSA. Must be flattering to have a headmaster show an interest.' Stafford's sneering gets under my skin and I bang my mug down angrily, scattering puddles of coffee over the highly polished surface of the table. I excuse myself to grab some kitchen roll to soak up the spillage and am aware of both men following my every movement. I stand by the table with my arms folded defensively across my chest.

Preece motions me to sit again and then we resume.

'Let's re-cap then, Miss Meredith. You went to the pub with Ian Weston and he suggested you have an affair?'

'Yes.'

'So, talk me through the rest of the meeting.'

'Well, I told him he'd got the wrong impression and I left.'

'And that made him so angry he came here in the night and sprayed your car?'

I look down again. This is so difficult, like exposing the contents of your underwear drawer to the eyes of strangers.

'Not quite. He followed me out to the car park.' There's a pause whilst I choose my words. 'Then he reached for me and I slapped him.'

'Ah.' Preece nods. 'How did he respond to that?'

'He was furious and said he'd make sure I regretted it.'

'You think this is his way of getting back at you?'

'Yes.'

He taps the side of his mug.

'Why would he write 'home wrecker'? From what you say he's quite prepared to play away. Isn't the phrase more like something a wife might say?'

'Lynette!' It comes out as a hoarse whisper. 'I hadn't thought about that.'

'Did you tell his wife?'

'No.'

'Did you threaten to?'

'No. But I think she knows.'

'And why would you think that?'

'Because of the photo on Facebook.'

Stafford leans forward again, poised.

'What photo, Miss Meredith?' Preece is still calm but I detect an excitement beneath the surface.

'I… we…well, we were followed by the school secretary.'

'Followed, you say?'

'Well, that's what it looks like. I mean she was at the same pub.'

'And were all the others in there following you, too?' I'd like to throw the remaining coffee in my mug over DS Stafford but I'm in enough trouble as it is. I scowl at him.

'Miss Meredith?' Preece draws me back with a quiet prompt.

'Delyth, the school secretary, took a photo of us on her phone and posted it on Facebook.'

'It would help if we could see this photograph.'

I'm aghast but have to comply. This is going very badly. I fetch my laptop, fumble my way to the Facebook page and swivel the screen so that both men can see it.

Stafford lets out a quiet whistle and Preece says nothing for an awkwardly long time. Finally, he speaks.

'And you say that there's nothing going on between the two of you?'

'Yes. I mean, no, there isn't. You have to believe me.'

'You can understand why people would find that hard to believe? You're holding hands and gazing into each other's eyes.'

'No, I'm not!' I'm furiously angry. 'He's holding my hand and I'm confused. Can't you see that?'

Preece studies the screen for a while longer.

'Why would this secretary… What's her name?'

'Delyth. Delyth Parry.'

'Why would this Delyth follow you and then post this on Facebook?'

'Because she's jealous. She's in love with him and wants to make mischief between him and his wife.' It all sounds ridiculous and I'm struggling to cope with Stafford's smirk. 'Ask anyone, they'll tell you.'

'So, the wife or Delyth might have done this?'

I consider the idea. 'Yes.'

He leans back in his chair and stares absently for a few moments. Eventually his eyes return to mine.

'Right. So, Ian Weston, his wife or his secretary might be responsible for this?'

I nod, miserable.

'Is there anyone else? Anyone you can think of who might hold a grudge against you?'

An image of Mark Johnson pulling Kaylee across the playground comes into my head.

'Miss Meredith?'

'It's probably nothing.'

'Go on.'

'One of the parents. I reported him to the deputy head. Yesterday. At the end of the day. He'd dragged his daughter along the ground.' The words come out in staccato bursts. 'A formal complaint was made to Social Services. They've taken his children away. He came here last night and tried to force his way in. He told me I'd regret it if I didn't retract my statement.'

Stafford releases another of his little whistles. 'My, you have been busy!'

This time Preece ignores him and purses his lips, his face still as he runs through my account. He sits upright and looks directly at me.

'All right, Miss Meredith. It seems to me that you've rattled the cages of quite a few people. I can go round and question them all but I'll be surprised if any of them admit to what's happened. Perhaps Mrs Weston might, and to be honest, I think she's the most likely candidate, but what do you expect her to do?'

I hadn't thought about it.

'I don't know. Pay for the damage, I suppose.'

'And what if she admits doing this but refuses to pay. What then?'

'Well, I could take her to court.'

'You could. You could. And the court might find her guilty and make her compensate you, but I can't say if it would be worth it.'

'What do you mean?'

'You'd have your day in court, but then so would the local paper and anyone else from the community with nothing else better to do on the day. Think about it.'

I do. I think about all of this coming out on an official basis and the thought horrifies me. Preece knows that I've understood. He gives me another faint smile.

'Tell you what. We'll go round to Mrs Weston first and if she confesses, we have two possible options, one that she compensates you or one where she's defiant and stands her ground. If she goes with the latter option, we'll make it very clear that she'll be in a great deal of trouble if she tries to do anything else to you. What do you think?'

I nod, tears standing in my eyes at the unfairness of this.

'And if she denies everything we'll go ahead and question the others. We'll see if they can account for their movements during that sixteen-hour window of opportunity.'

I've remembered something.

'It's less than that. A friend came round last night. She left at about eight-thirty and we'd have noticed the car then.'

'Have you got that, Stafford?'

Stafford writes something in his notebook.

'Yep.'

'Okay.' Preece fishes a small card out of his breast pocket. 'This is the number where you can reach me if you think of anything else.' I take it with fingers that tremble slightly.

I'm showing him out of the door when he turns back to me.

'Try not to let this get to you, Miss. I have a daughter about your age and I'd tell her the same thing. It's really not worth you wasting any more time on this nastiness. Whoever's done this will be facing their own demons, believe me, so don't think they've got away scot-free.'

I'm touched by this unexpected reassurance and hold my hand out to him. He takes it in a firm grip and shakes it briefly. Then he turns to Stafford.

'Come on, you. We can't hang around here all day.' Stafford can't hide the scowl that leaps to the surface. He follows his superior down the drive and his body language speaks volumes about the resentment he carries.

I close the door.

I can't settle to do anything until Rob Oldworthy shows up to take my poor car away.

Chapter 7

I'm twitchy and anxious, jumping up at the sound of any approaching vehicle in the hope that it's Rob come to take away my problem. There's a slow trickle of cars eager for a glimpse of excitement. I want to rail at them, all the while aware that last year I was amongst the crowd of people who gawped as a garage burned down in the road next to ours. It *was* exciting seeing the fire brigade turn up and watch first-hand as they saved the house next to it. But now I wonder how it must have felt for the owners hearing the excited chatter from the gathered throng, phones out to record the drama, whilst their home was at risk.

A car pulls up near the driveway and I hear a door open. It doesn't sound like Rob's truck, but I go to the window anyway.

It's someone wearing a thin, mustard yellow cotton hoodie with a matching cap. The eyes are hidden behind sunglasses that glint a metallic red. The arrogant stance gives him away. It's Ian Weston.

It's an incongruous look and all the more disturbing because of it. I've never seen him in anything other than a smart suit. I grip the window sill and watch him stride towards my car. He drags off the cover and my hand flies to my mouth. The movement must have registered because he turns in my direction. Then he points two fingers towards those hidden eyes and back at me. The gesture chills. Then he uses the same fingers to drag slowly across his throat. His stare pins me like a butterfly and I'm still frozen in place as he turns, returns to his car and drives off.

I'm left standing, useless, when another car slows and the driver gawks openly at the stark graffiti. I race outside and struggle to re-cover the offending words. The material slips and snags, and desperation makes my breath come in sobs of frustration. This living nightmare grows darker by the minute and my sense of vulnerability grows with it. I return to the house and tug the curtains closer together; a flimsy barricade to the increasing unpleasantness.

~~~

In the early afternoon I hear whispers and giggling near the house. I cross to the side window and catch sight of a group of young teenagers creeping up by the bushes that edge the drive. One of them says, 'Just do it! Go on, take it off.'

'But what if she catches us?'

'She won't. Anyway, what can she do?'

'She could call the police.'

'Yeah, and tell them what?' He affects a stupidly girlish voice, 'Oh, officer, help me. Someone's in my drive.'

'Quick!' This time it's one of the girls. She hisses, 'I've got my phone ready. Hurry up!'

I throw open the door just as a lad reaches a hand out to grab the sheet.

'Run!' Someone raises the alarm and they scatter like rabbits. A short distance away, they stop and in between the gasping for breath there's relieved laughter and more giggling. I close the door on the sounds which are drowned out by Granny demanding to know who's stolen her glasses.

At a little before three, the welcome sight of Rob's trailer appears reversing up the drive.

'Hiya, Gwen.'. He peers under the sheet and drops it back instantly. I see the sympathy in his eyes. 'That's some sick person what's done that, Gwen.'

'You're telling me, Rob.' I take a deep breath. 'What can you do?'

He scratches his thick, greying hair with oil-blackened hands.

'It's a busy time for me at the moment, what with that accident in town last week, an' all. Tell you what, I'll take it away now and I'll do the bodywork when I can but it'll take a while, I'm afraid. You'll have to cough up for the tyres and the paint but I'll do the work for nothing.'

He knows how strapped for cash I am and I don't pretend that I can afford to give him the payment he deserves.

'Thanks, Rob. I'm truly grateful.'

'You helped my Sally's girl with her reading and you wouldn't take nothin' for that so I guess it's only fair, ain't it?'
~~~

He raises my defaced car onto the back of his trailer leaving the sheet in place. Then he straps it down, making sure that nothing will be revealed on the trip to his workshop. It's the innate goodness in people like Rob, Cat and Becky that reassures me that I'm dealing with a tiny, unpleasant minority. It's still not enough, though, to take away the shaky feeling at my core.

~~~

Granny is having one of her quiet days and sleeps a lot. It couldn't have come at a better time, but experience tells me it will be at the expense of some serious challenges tomorrow. I take a concerned call from Cat, who's heard about the car through the grapevine and needs some convincing that I'm coping with this new problem. Later, after Granny's last carer has departed, I curl up on the sofa with the remote control and skip through channels on the TV. It must be the stress of the last couple of days coupled with a lack of sleep but I drift off.

I'm in my dream, stretching in desperation for the ball, when something rouses me and I look up groggily. My racing heart rate has me on edge. The TV is still on, a gleaming car winding along deserted roads to upbeat music, and I conclude that I've been woken by a loud advertisement. I click the remote to turn it off and stretch to restore life to sluggish muscles.

Then I hear it.

It's a rustling coming from the shrubs at the side of the house. If this were a normal day, I'd shrug it off, but today has been anything *but* normal and I'm instantly taut, ready to tune in to the next sound. A few seconds later and I hear it again. I've homed in more closely on the direction.

Feeling foolish and wary in equal measure, I creep forwards until I'm half a step away from the glass. The japonica bush beneath the window is picked out by the rays of the sinking sun. As I take the last half step, the still foliage erupts into a pitching and flailing mass that makes me rock back on my heels. Before I can retreat, a black cat springs out onto the lawn followed by Bramble. I watch as Bramble sees off the intruder and then I let the nervous laughter come to the
~~~

surface. I'm cross and relieved. This petty vendetta has blown out of control thanks to my spineless response. I'm not a weak person. I deal with some very difficult children and their belligerent parents. However, I'm forced to acknowledge that I avoid confrontation and unpleasantness to a woeful degree. I need to get a grip on myself.

I open my laptop and turn to the person I hold dearest in the world.

Within seconds the Skype link is made and there's Gethin. Dear, vibrant Gethin.

'Hiya, little sis. How's things?'

'Fine.'

But he's picked up on the slight hesitation.

'What's the matter? Come on, tell your big brother and he'll sort it for you.'

'It's nothing.'

'Oh yeah? Well, you tell me what's going on and I'll give it a rating between nothing and something.'

I hesitate, very briefly, before giving in and telling him everything from the meeting with Ian to the cats erupting onto the lawn. He listens quietly, apart from some choice swearing over the defaced car, and when I've finished he remains silent for a few seconds. He looks older, somehow, than he did a few weeks ago and his eyes have dark smudges under them. He chews his lower lip, something he's always done when faced with a problem, and then he looks directly at his webcam.

'Ok. The way I see it, the threat is probably close to nothing but the upset it generates is very much something. The head can't do a great deal to you without upsetting the school governors, his wife can't do anything more without the police taking action, and this Mark Johnson chap risks permanently losing his children if he steps too far out of line. He's a bully and doubtless sounds worse than he is.'

'That's what I think. I just needed someone to make it clear.' I properly smile at him and the huge weight that's been bearing down on me eases magically. 'Thanks, Gethin. I owe you.'

'Glad to help.' He looks down for a moment and when he looks up again there's an unfamiliar, tired expression in his eyes that squeezes my heart.

'What's wrong with *you*?' I ask, concerned. 'You look dreadful.'

He runs his hand over what looks like stubble on his chin and I can see other things, now that I'm looking for them. His shirt is crumpled and there's a stain near the collar. This is not like my high-powered, smooth-dressing brother. There's something else – there's a large, pale rectangle on the wall behind him.

'What's happened to your TV?'

He glances behind him and when he turns back there's a rueful twist to his lips.

'Zoe.'

'Zoe?'

'I s'pose I'd better come clean and tell you.'

I wait expectantly for him to continue. 'Well?'

'The TV.' He looks to the side as if searching for the right words. 'It...er…it got damaged.'

'How?' I'm not going to let him get away with that as an explanation. He suddenly straightens his shoulders and he grins at me.

'Zoe threw a huge, lead crystal paperweight at it.'

I'm lost for words.

He carries on, 'We had a fight. We've had lots of fights recently, if I'm honest. Anyway, we had one of those silly disagreements, over nothing, that got out of hand, she aimed for my head, hit the screen and left. Actually, 'stormed out' might be a better description.'

'I'm so sorry, Gethin.'

'Don't be. I'm coming to terms with it and, you know, I realise now that it's for the best. We were becoming more and more miserable in a stifling relationship. It was affecting every part of our lives.'

'Maybe all you need is a break from each other.'

'Nah. It's not going to happen. Zoe's gone home to her mother and I've been nursing my wounds here. But now I feel liberated. Does that make any sense?'

'You're not just being brave?' I'm relieved to see the huge smile that properly creases his face.

'I'm actually feeling better now than I have for ages. I just didn't know it until a few minutes ago.'

'Sure?'

'Certain. Absolutely certain.' He leans back in his chair and looks much more like the confident brother I know. 'Now, what else is new in Dernant? How's Granny?'

'She's…' I try to find the words, 'She's losing it, really. She can't walk on her own now, her eyesight's poor and her memory is very unpredictable. She forgets stuff or sometimes the things she remembers bear little resemblance to what actually happened.' I smile weakly, 'And you can imagine the effect that has on her temper.'

'Oh, Gwen. I'd no idea it had got so bad. How are you coping?'

'Fine.'

'Now the truth, please.'

'Not so fine. But her carers are good and help keep me sane.' My smile fades and I look steadily at the screen. 'I think we have to face up to the fact that she may need to move to a home in the future.'

'No! We can't do that! It would kill her, Gwen.'

'I'm hoping it won't happen until she's lost touch with reality and no longer appreciates her circumstances. The carers have broken it to me that eventually she's going to need more support than they can give her. She's not a well woman, Gethin.'

He looks down and when I see his face again there's no denying the pain there. I try to lift his mood again.

'However, I don't know how much of this is just put on at the moment to get the attention she craves. We both know how crafty she can be. To be completely honest, I came back to collect something last week and I could have sworn I heard her walking to her chair as I opened the door.'

'No!'

'It's pretty much impossible now, but it's what she used to do when I first came back here. She'd pretend to be totally helpless but I'd catch her in the kitchen at night reaching up to one of the cupboards where she'd hidden her Jelly Babies. Or I'd see her at the back door bending down to pick up Bramble.'

'Cunning old devil!'

'You're telling me! But she does have genuine issues now and the decline is noticeable. We'll have to face up to them sometime.' As the pain crosses his face again, I feel compelled to add, 'I'm sure she'll be fine for a while yet. Forget I said anything. We don't need to make any decisions until things definitely deteriorate.'

'I should be with you, helping you.'

'Don't be daft. You have your Big City things to do. We're all very proud of you here.'

'You shouldn't be.'

'What's that supposed to mean?'

He comes to a decision.

'I've been pretty stupid, Gwen.'

I wait for him to elucidate.

'I got done for speeding last year.'

'Carried away by your beloved Porsche, no doubt.'

'Something like that. I got some points on my licence. But after one of my blow-ups with Zoe, I was so angry I went out and drove like a madman. The police pulled me over and I've been banned for six months.'

'You idiot! How will you cope?'

'This is the bustling metropolis, Gwen. There's a huge variety of public transport on offer. It's not like two-buses-a-day Dernant. Anyway, I've had a word with the boss and he says I can work from home for a while until I get myself sorted. The six months will pass very quickly.'

His doorbell sounds in the distance.

'Sorry, Gwen. I'd better get that. Love you.'

'Love you, too.' I blow him a kiss and we disconnect.

I do love my big brother but I worry about this break up with Zoe. They had seemed like a match made in heaven, to me at least. But thinking about it, Gethin has let slip little things recently about her extravagance and partying and I can now see the toll it's been taking on him. At least he has his job. He was always the clever one at school who sailed through the subjects that I found taxing, particularly maths. He has a head for figures and a quick-wittedness that segued neatly into a career with Forsters Browning where he effortlessly moved up the ranks to become one of their best investment bankers. When I asked him what the job entailed, I lost him after the first couple of sentences but sat and listened, bursting with pride, as he continued, his dark eyes flashing with pleasure. He doesn't come back to Dernant very often but when he does the place seems lighter and brighter with him in it. Granny dotes on him. She always has. He's her golden boy.

Just chatting with him has smoothed my ruffled feathers and as the tension eases from me, tiredness sweeps in to take its place.

My watch tells me it's gone midnight and I get to my feet to head for bed when a tapping at the patio doors takes me unawares. I turn to look and gasp. Someone is standing there wearing a Scream mask.

I reach out for the back of the chair to steady myself. When I look up again, I can't stop watching as it starts to slowly rotate in my direction, its black cut-out eyes terrifying in their unresponsiveness. I feel for my phone in my pocket and there's a small card next to it. It gives me the strength I need to break free and I make a dash for the corridor, racing to the end to lower the blind on the window there. Then I take the card and phone out of my pocket and call DI Preece.

~~~

The call has gone through to Stafford who makes no bones about the fact that he believes this could have waited until the morning. With bad grace, he says he'll be with me in fifteen minutes. I cower away from the uncurtained patio doors. When the knock comes, my trembling fingers fumble at the chain, checking it's in place before opening the door a crack. I know it's Stafford but I'm so rattled I make him show his warrant card before letting him in. He's not happy.

I direct him towards the patio. 'He's over there.' The whisper sounds dramatic in the dead quiet of the night. Stafford goes through on his own and then I hear a bark of unamused laughter.

'Come through, Miss Meredith, and face your demon.'

I'm reluctant, even with Stafford there, but I steel myself to approach him. It's only when he steps to one side that I see it.
~~~

I can't control a sudden intake of breath. He's still there, his head moving slowly from one side to the other.

'Is *this* your intruder?'

The contempt in his voice slaps some sense into me. I can see, now, that there's nothing below the mask. There's nothing behind it. I draw closer, arms wrapped tightly around my body.

'You've dragged me out of bed to rescue you from something that's escaped from a children's party.' He unlocks the doors and steps outside, his flashlight bright against the darkness it leaves behind. 'Come here.'

I hesitate.

'For heaven's sake, woman, come here and see the truth for yourself.'

I follow him out to the shadows that dance violently to the movement of his light.

'See?'

My eyes track upwards to the string caught in the Virginia creeper that covers the brickwork. Dangling from it, the empty mask slowly turns. I shudder.

'But I saw him! He was there. He must have heard me make the call to you and has run off.'

'Really?' The drawled comment doesn't conceal the contempt behind it. 'So, what was he wearing? Jeans? Trainers? Shirt? Hoodie?'

Now that he pins me to the details, I have nothing.

'I don't know.' My voice is quiet. 'It was dark. I was frightened.'

'You don't know. Now there's a surprise.'

Bewildered and humiliated I look down at my bare feet. Stafford hasn't finished with me.

'Do you want to give an official statement, Miss Meredith, or shall we put this down to hysteria and move on with our lives?'

I clench my hands into tight fists and bite back the angry words that I know will achieve nothing.

I concede defeat.

Chapter 8

The sun is warm on my back and I'm giggling as Gethin throws the ball again. It's much too high and although I strain to reach it, all I can do is follow its course far over the sparkling water. It surfaces before bobbing tantalisingly beyond our reach. My distorted voice fills my ears.

'Mummy! Daddy! Get it back! Quick!'

I hear my mother, happy and reassuring. 'It'll come back in a minute. Build a sandcastle while you're waiting.'

'No! It's going away!'

'Don't be silly, pumpkin. If it doesn't come back, I'll buy you a new one.'

'It's my Kermit ball. ***Please****, Mummy,* ***please****!'*

'I promise you can choose any ball you want if this one doesn't come back.'

'No! I want this ball. I don't want any of the others.' I hear my childish voice plead and whine.

I'm upright in my bed, breathing rapidly and drenched in sweat. My pulse races in my ears, and my hands are trembling. I reach for my glass of water and gulp it down. The alarm clock tells me it's nearly 6.30. The bright light shimmering behind the curtains promises another hot day and, now that the panic is subsiding, I give myself a pep talk. Whatever happens today has to be an improvement on the last twenty-four hours. I can spend some soothing time in the garden and perhaps, later, read one of the many books I have stacked up in my room.

I've convinced myself, and within ten minutes I'm back in the kitchen, dressed and ready for action in my gardening kit of old jeans and paint-splattered t-shirt. I've just grabbed my gloves, secateurs and kneeling mat when Granny's voice pierces my little bubble of happiness.

'Gwen! Gwen! Where are you?'

I put the gardening tools down by the back door and make my way to her room accompanied by a non-stop summoning.

'Here I am, Granny. What's the matter?'

'What did you say?'

I raise my voice slightly, 'What's the matter, Granny?'

'Nothing's the matter. Should it be?'

I open the curtain a little to let some more of the sunlight penetrate the gloom of the room.

'Turn that light off! It's hurting my eyes.'

The curtain is pulled back across a little and I move to her bed. Her moist eyes are focused on my face and I take in the confusion and pain that's evident in the increased furrows on her forehead. She was always strong and sturdy, never overweight–she was too self-controlled for that–but firm, robust. Her recent lack of appetite has taken its toll; the skin on her face is slack and loose, pulling on her features and exposing the outline of the skull beneath. The deep lines of dissatisfaction on either side of her mouth give her the appearance of a ventriloquist's dummy and I feel a surge of anxiety.

'Let's sit you up.'

She lets me haul her up the bed but not without a barrage of complaints. Once propped up on the banked pillows she needs several seconds to recover before she can speak again. I offer her some painkillers but she waves her hand angrily. Eventually, the words come.

'I know what you're doing.' She waves her hand again as she rallies her strength to continue. 'You just want to shut me up.' Another pause. 'Well, I *won't* have it!'

I catch hold of the agitated hand and try to still it. The map of raised blue veins can be felt more clearly now and I use gentle strokes. It doesn't work.

She snatches it back.

'Why have you put the light on? You know I can't sleep with it on.' She bangs her hand down on the quilt, wincing as the jolt fires through her arthritis. 'It's all right for you. You can stay up as long as you want but I need to go to sleep. Leave me alone.'

'Granny—'

'Go away. I'll see you in the morning.'

I hesitate. Then I cross to the window and draw the curtains tightly together, returning the room to its gloom.

'Goodnight, Granny. I'll see you later.'

As I pull her door quietly shut behind me, I know that the gardening will have to wait. She's having a bad day and I'll need to stay within earshot until her carer comes.

During the next hour and a half, I hear her restless movement punctuated by groans of pain. I'd love to smooth away her troubles but our relationship makes her resentful of my attempts to help her. We're trapped, both of us, in a bond not of our own making. This woman has fed me, clothed me, helped me with my homework and protected me – all of it voluntarily and unstintingly. But she can't find it within herself to dredge up any real, lasting affection for me.

I do have memories of her tickling me until I begged for mercy, cuddling me and wrapping me in a squeeze of a hug. But those are distant memories. Everything changed and I was the one who changed it. With Gethin it's different. Gethin is loved, truly loved, and he can make her face crease into a genuine beam of pleasure that completely transforms her. I've tried for years to generate one of those smiles. I'm still trying.

~~~

At 8.20, Lisa arrives. My irritation mounts at her noisy fumbling with the key box and, in the end, I stride across to the door and fling it open. I'm exasperated by the girl and annoyed with myself for allowing such a trivial thing to get under my skin. I twist my face into what I hope resembles a welcoming smile and usher her in.

'Thanks.' She sidles past me into the hallway. 'There's something wrong with your key thingy. It's not working.'

I step outside, tap in the number and open it. Lisa shrugs.

'Well, dunno what the problem is but I've been trying for ages.'

I secure the key again and face the young woman whose lips show the beginnings of a pout.

'What number were you using, Lisa?' I manage to keep my voice calm and friendly despite feeling anything but.

'The one you gave us. 3351.' She's belligerent and I'm struggling to maintain my equilibrium. I force my clenching teeth apart.
~~~

'The number's 3551.'

'That's what I said.'

'No, Lisa, you said 3351.'

She gives that shrug that so annoys me. 'Well, whatever. I'd best get on and get your grandmother sorted.'

I watch her go and release my unwarranted aggression in a sigh that might be loud enough for her to pick up. I don't really care.

Five minutes later I'm opening the patio doors. There's a piece of A4 paper on the ground and I pick it up and turn it over. It's a simple drawing in broad red marker pen of a round face with a tear falling from its single eye. I shudder. I can't put it into words, or even coherent thought, but there's something disturbing about it. I crush it into a ball and drop it in the dustbin. I have to stop over thinking things and rein in my paranoia.

What I need is a gardening workout and there are plenty of weeds to choose from. It doesn't take long for the tension to seep out of me. There's something intrinsically soothing and satisfying in the simple task of clearing away the unwanted growth to make way for the burgeoning flowers. It's an almost automatic process and the clean air and the birdsong lift my spirits and shut out the harsh realities of my life.

There's a fluttering beside me as my bold little robin puts in an appearance. His colour's muted now after a busy season rearing two broods of chicks, but he hops across until he's barely a foot away and cocks his head from side to side, glossy, beady eyes following my movements. I dig my trowel into the next section and turn over a worm that wriggles in knots for the few seconds it has before it's seized. The chicks must still be dependent because he flies away with it, returning within minutes to wait for the next bounty.

I'm digging down to remove a stubborn dandelion root when I become aware of a scampering sound that heralds the arrival of Atticus. The robin takes off with a flurry of aggrieved 'tic' calls as the collie bends down on its speckled forelegs and drops a grubby looking tennis ball by my hand, looking from it to me and back again, repeatedly, in the hope that I'll get the message. I remove my glove and pick up the slobbery item.

‘Delightful, Atticus. Just delightful.’ I throw the offending ball as far as I can down the garden and am on my feet and ready to capture him as he returns, ears flapping and tail whisking in large circles.

‘Come on, then. Let’s get you back home.’ I hook a finger into his collar and lead him down the path to the open side gate, where we meet Ben.

‘I’m sorry. He seems to think this is an extension of his hunting grounds.’ Ben sounds friendly enough but there’s a hint of formality that wasn’t there the other evening. I’m annoyed by it and by his behaviour yesterday. I pass Atticus over.

‘Don’t worry. He’s no bother.’ Atticus looks up at me with eyes that beg for some fuss and I comply automatically, briefly rubbing his head. ‘Well, I’d better get on.’

I straighten and Ben hesitates as if to say something, but I’ve had enough criticism over the last couple of days. I go back through the side gate and close it behind me.

~~~

Granny is sitting in front of the TV when I come back inside. The volume is uncomfortably loud, but that hasn’t prevented her from drifting into a fitful sleep. I wash the soil off my hands and am making myself a cup of tea when there’s a ring on the doorbell. Granny stirs but doesn’t wake as I rush to prevent whoever it is from ringing again.

It’s DI Preece and he’s mercifully on his own.

‘Good morning, Miss Meredith. I wondered if I could have a quiet word.’

He follows me through to the kitchen, glancing at my sleeping grandmother as we pass.

‘Would you like a tea or coffee?’

‘No thanks. It’s just a quick visit to fill you in on our progress,’ he gives a rueful smile, ‘or lack of it.’

‘Ah.’ I can’t hide my disappointment.

‘I’m sorry but Ian Weston and his wife both swear that they spent a cosy night in together.’

Granny moans and we wait in silence until her breathing indicates that she’s still asleep.
~~~

'Delyth Parry says she had an early night, and as for Mark Johnson, he swears that he drank himself into oblivion and his wife corroborates his story.' I must look as miserable as I feel because he continues, 'We've made it clear that this is being taken seriously and I don't think there's a likelihood that you'll have any more harassment.'

I look into his bloodshot eyes and want him to know that I appreciate his coming here promptly to reassure me.

'Thank you.' I give him a wobbly smile.

'Stafford tells me that you gave yourself a scare last night.'

I toy with contradicting his version of events but common sense prevails.

'I'm sorry. I thought there was someone here and I panicked.'

'Sure?'

'Yes.'

'Okay. I know how upsetting all this has been, but it's almost certainly one of those heat-of-the-moment affairs and things will settle down. My advice is to put it behind you and ignore any ignorant comments. You're young; you have your life ahead of you. Enjoy it.'

He holds out his hand and I shake it.

I show him to the door but as he leaves, he has one more thing to add. 'I'm going away for a few weeks but if you have any more trouble or queries then ask for DS Stafford and he'll come round.' He adds, in an attempt to mollify me, 'I know he's a bit brash but he's learning and he's got a sharp mind there underneath the smooth exterior.'

I'm prevented from giving an opinion as a quavery voice calls out, 'Gwen! Gwen! Where are you?'

He gives me a sympathetic look and leaves.

'Gwen!' She's cross and her raised voice induces a coughing fit.

'It's all right, Granny, 'I soothe, bobbing down next to her and offering her the glass of juice from the table at her side. She waves it away with one gesture and then grabs at it, gulping down mouthfuls that leak from her lips in careless rivulets. I try to mop them up before they reach her blouse but she slaps my hand away.

'Stop fussing!'

'I'm just—'

'You're making me spill my drink.'

I wait for her to finish. She thrusts the almost empty glass at me and I take it but before I can move away, she's grabbed my wrist.

'What time it is?'

'It's about 10.30.'

'Well, where's that wretched girl with my breakfast? She should have been here ages ago.'

'She came earlier, Granny. She got you ready and gave you some food.'

'Don't be ridiculous! I've not seen anyone today.'

'You've been asleep and you're not properly awake yet. You'll remember in a minute.' My attempts at defusing the situation fail miserably.

'I'm *quite* awake, thank you, and I tell you I've not had my breakfast. You don't know. You weren't here.'

'Granny, Lisa came earlier. If she hadn't, you wouldn't be up and dressed.'

I watch her brain struggle with that one. She won't give way on this, even though we both know the truth. She *has* to be right these days and won't rest until she thinks she's won.

'I got ready myself.' She searches for something to say to back up this ridiculous statement. 'Then I came through with my walker and sat down here.' Her eyes momentarily flicker in triumph.

These pointless battles are exhausting for both of us but I give way, as I do now, because her mind *is* failing and her advancing dementia erodes her personal skills letting her behave in a manner that would have been unthinkable a decade ago. Her social compass has swung full circle taking her back to the egocentric, uninhibited behaviour of a young child. I gently disentangle her loosely clasping hand.

'Would you like me to get you something to eat?'

'No. I'm not hungry.'

'Something to drink, then?'

She considers this for a moment. 'Tea. Not too hot. And don't put lots of milk in it either.' She starts rummaging amongst the cushions. 'That blasted girl's stolen the remote control.'

'No, she hasn't. It's no use to her. It's probably slipped down the side.'

'I saw her looking at it. I bet she's put it in her bag.'

I put the glass down and do a rapid frisking of Granny and the chair and produce the missing item from under her right leg.

'Here you are.'

'Where was it?'

'It had worked its way under your leg.'

'Stupid girl! Why did she put it there?'

I hand it over without further comment and leave her pushing the buttons.

~~~

The rest of the day passes uneventfully enough. Cat phones to see how I'm doing and is angrier than I am over the lack of resolution. I just feel weary about the whole thing. It feels like my life and who I am has changed overnight. Even though there's nothing left to see, occasional cars still slow down as they approach the house, the occupants craning their necks as they pass. A couple of times I've made the mistake of doing some work in the front garden and my appearance has generated muted excitement and pointing. I keep well into the background now.

My misery is compounded by my financial woes. Since returning here, I've had to give up my reasonably paid job as a multilingual advisor for Krantz Industries and accept the considerably lower pay of a learning support assistant. I don't have to pay rent, but I contribute a large chunk of my meagre salary for our food and a share in the heating bills. I also spend quite a bit taking Granny to appointments, buying the extras she needs and stocking and maintaining the garden. I'm beginning to recognise the difficulties I'll be facing until I get my little car back and, whilst I'm incredibly grateful to Rob Oldworthy for offering to do the labour free of charge, the cost of the tyres alone is going to stretch my budget to breaking point.

Granny is obstreperous and awkward during her waking hours and I struggle to hang on to my calm and sense of
~~~

humour. Twice today I've had run-ins with her that have ended with me muttering under my breath the things I really itch to say to her face. I remind myself that most of this is down to her creeping illness but the personal attacks are difficult to take at the moment. I know the point is coming where she'll make the accusation that she's managed to hold in since I was nine years old.

It was my birthday and she'd let me invite friends round for a small party and had provided a sumptuous spread for us. Some of the other parents were there and when one of them joked about needing a drink to get through the experience, Granny had found a half-empty bottle of brandy and a full one of sherry. Before long, the adults were making more noise than we were.

After all the farewells and balloon waving, the house settled into its usual calm and only Gethin, Cat and I were left. Granny had stayed in the kitchen with her good friend Joyce, the near-empty bottle of sherry between them.

'Let's ask Granny if we can go to the park.' Gethin was still buzzing from the brightly coloured fizzy drinks he'd been guzzling and there was still at least another hour of daylight left.

Cat and I thought it was a great idea and we trooped towards the kitchen with as much decorum as we could muster. As we arrived at the doorway, Granny's slightly slurred voice carried to us, loud and bitter.

'I can't help it, Joyce.'

'Shhh, Edith! Keep your voice down.'

Joyce's words had the desired effect but we were close enough to hear the next exchange.

'I hate her, Joyce.'

'This has to stop right now, Edith.'

'She took my boy, my Peter, away from me.'

'This has to stop now, Edith. This irrational hatred of yours is damaging that little girl. She needs your love.'

'I'm doing everything I can for her. She's the image of her mother; she'll survive. It's Gethin who needs me. He's the one who's really suffering. If *she* hadn't been born none of this would have happened. I'd still have my Peter.'

Gethin drags me backwards. He pulls me through the house and out into the road where the three of us stand facing each other in silence. Cat and Gethin are pale and shocked; I'm still processing the poisonous words. It's Gethin who rallies first, taking my arm and shaking it.

'She doesn't mean it, Gwen. She's drunk. She's just a miserable old bat who doesn't know what she's saying.'

I'm still incapable of movement and he pulls me into a fierce bear hug. I can feel his heart pounding through my thin party dress and I suddenly need to get away. I struggle free and make for the woods and when I finally run out of steam, Gethin and Catrin are there with me. Their silent support makes a difference and I let them comfort me as I sob out my distress.

Granny never spoke to me directly about my parents after that and her attitude to me remained unchanged – responsible, supportive but ever so slightly distant. And once I was aware of her feelings, I could never be completely at ease with her again. Nor could I ever diminish the power of that vicious outpouring. The open wound has never healed and neither has my stupid need to try to compensate her for the damage I'd done in one thoughtless, careless, self-absorbed moment.

Chapter 9

'Mummy! Daddy! Get it back! Quick!'

I hear my mother, happy and reassuring. 'It'll come back in a minute. Build a sandcastle while you're waiting.'

'No! It's going away!'

'Don't be silly, pumpkin. If it doesn't come back, I'll buy you a new one.'

'It's my Kermit ball. ***Please****, Mummy,* ***please****!'*

'I promise you can choose any ball you want if this one doesn't come back.'

'No! I want this ball. I don't want any of the others.' I hear my childish voice plead and whine.

'Okay. No need to cry. I'll get it for you.' She rises gracefully from the towel beside my father, brushing grains of sand off her slender body.

But I know what's to come and the scream builds in the pit of my stomach as she splashes into the deeper water and starts her slow, powerful crawl towards the ball, Kermit's bobbing face mocking her approach.

For the third day on the run, I wake in a dream-filled terror.

I sit at the kitchen table watching the sun blaze above the green horizon. Summer's never been my favourite season. Its heat and humidity suck the strength from me, and the pale skin that accompanies my red hair makes me wary of the damage caused by the sun's rays. The level on my too expensive bottle of factor 50 tells me that I'm going to have to buy another one soon. Granny loves the heat. She likes to bask like a lizard and would happily coat herself in cooking oil to give her skin the kind of tan she still associates with luxury holidays in exotic places. Cat tells me it isn't easy smearing sunscreen on a toddler; it has to be a doddle compared with coating a hostile and uncooperative grandparent.

It's tempting to go back to bed and just lie there in the darkened room but I'd rather busy myself with housework to try to keep unwelcome thoughts at bay. The sitting room is restored to Granny's expectation of neatness in no time and I reach over the sofa to pull the curtains open. For a second, my eyes are blinded by the bright light, which is why I don't see it immediately. There's a piece of A4 paper stuck to the glass about half way down. Taking up the space is another simple drawing with an eye done in red with thick marker pen. A teardrop is falling from it.

My skin prickles with shock and fear and I move backwards into the centre of the room, never taking my gaze off the piece of paper. I don't know why I find it so frightening but my gut tells me that this simple sketch is a warning. Its effect is innate and completely out of proportion. It occurs to me that someone could be watching, wanting to see my reaction, and I turn on my heel and check that no one is at the opposite window. This is ridiculous. I stride back across and study the drawing. I tell myself that no one's drawn an image of me with a stake through my heart or hanging from a gibbet. This is an overreaction. The carer's due today at 7.15. I'll wait until she arrives and then I'll go outside and remove it. Simple.

Claire arrives at the appointed time. She's older than most of the carers and I think she struggles physically with the job, but she makes up for it with her kindness and patience. If Granny refuses to cooperate, Claire will try to persuade her perhaps a couple of times and then will quietly capitulate. To her credit, any time saved is spent in conversation with Granny who usually appreciates the undivided attention.

I slip out of the front door and am stunned into immobility. The Madonna lilies from the flowerbed beneath the window are scattered on the narrow path along with clods of earth. At first, I wonder if Atticus is responsible, but as I approach for a closer look, I notice that the bulbs have been crushed and mangled. It's the sort of damage that would be done by someone grinding a heel on them. The paper on the window is openly mocking and I snatch it off, holding it by the edges as if I'll be contaminated by closer contact with it. I'm annoyed with myself and fold it twice and stuff it into my jean's pocket. That's better. My petty triumph at dealing with the paper is undermined by my panicky scanning of the area, searching for signs of the culprit. I see no one and go through to the back garden to get a bucket and bristle brush to sweep up the mess.

It doesn't take long. I turn the lilies out onto the compost heap with a gentle care that I know is ridiculous but I can't help myself. They've been desecrated and I want to protect them from any further degradation. I pick up the rake and return to smooth over the bed. When I've finished, I turn to face the garden that slopes down gently to the road. It's been so dry that I'm not surprised to see brown patches appearing. That's when I recognise the shapes. A word has been written with weedkiller in letters at least two feet high. There's no need to go to the fence at the bottom to read it. WHORE is developing for everyone to see.

That sensation of being watched ripples over me and my eyes search for confirmation. He's almost unnoticeable, unmoving under the shade of the trees lining the pavement. I can't see the eyes behind the dark glasses but I know. I know he's been there, waiting. Ian Weston in his mustard yellow cap. He turns to move away, the light from his lenses flashing red from the sun. I can't control the shudder that convulses me.

I'm still staring in his direction when a white van draws up outside and Mark Johnson leans out and takes some pictures with his phone, before shouting,

'You haven't withdrawn that statement yet. If you know what's good for you, you'll sort it now or this is going to end in tears. *Your* tears.' Then he gives an unpleasant grin that curls into a scowl as he roars off. When I look up again, Ian's gone.

The fright that I feel is outdone by the anger that courses through me and I run back to the shed, grab my spade and fork and return to the damage. The spade won't cut through the dry turf and so I stick the fork in and use that to try to turn over the offending letters.

The sun's already hot and within twenty minutes I've hardly made any headway, the sweat is dripping off me and my mouth's dry. It's so tempting to retreat to the cool of the house but another car slows to have a gawp and I'm spurred into continuing.

A soggy tennis ball lands at my feet.

'Not now, Atticus. Home!'

He picks it up and drops it again, this time making a little whining noise of appeal. Then footsteps cross the road and Ben Pascoe appears.

'Atticus, heel!' Atticus lies down on the ground beside me. 'I'm sorry. He just made a beeline for here.'

I stop and stare at him, too hot to speak. He stares back and then I watch his eyes go from me to the fork to the hideous letters still visible in the closely cropped lawn.

He says nothing. It annoys me and I turn away from Atticus and spear the ground with the fork and try to wrench more dry sod up to cover my humiliation. I'm on automatic pilot, spearing, twisting, turning, and I don't care what he thinks.

His hand on my shoulder comes as a shock and I pull back, freeing myself from his touch. He stands in silence for a couple of seconds, then he starts to speak in a calm and quiet voice.

'Gwen, you look done-in. Go into the house and get something to drink and I'll do this.'

'No. It's all right. I'm fine, thank you.'

There's a muttered curse before he tries again.

'Look, you don't want people to see this, I understand that, but you're in need of a break. Let me do this while you rehydrate.' He adds, 'Please.'

I bristle, ready to throw his offer back in his face, when I hear another car approaching and I know that I need his help.

'Thanks. I'll be back in a minute.'

'Take as long as you need. Have a shower and put on some sunscreen. I'll be fine here with Atticus to help.'

Atticus wags his tail and I can't hide the wry grin that creeps up on me.

'I'm sure he'll provide exceptional support.'

After several glasses of water, I go through to the bathroom where my reflection grimaces back at me. My face is red –no, it's a throbbing puce. My hair is plastered to my scalp and I'm coated in earth that's smeared into dirty streaks over me and my clothes. I'd intended going straight out again but concede that a rapid shower and change of clothes makes sense.

Ten minutes later I'm slathering on the factor 50 and ready to return to battle. Atticus comes to greet me as I emerge from the garden gate at the side of the house and I give him a bit of fuss as he romps along beside me.

Ben looks up at my approach and gives me a nod of approval. He's done more than half of the patch.

'Thanks.' I struggle to find something appropriate to say. 'It would have taken me hours to get this far.'

'No problem.'

He's using the spade so I pick up the discarded fork and go to work on the other side of him.

'Leave it, Gwen. I'm almost finished.'

'I can't stand here and do nothing while someone else sorts out my problem.'

'Don't they say something about a problem shared?

'That's why I have this fork. To share.' I push it into the ground and stand on the shoulders to wiggle the tines in deeper and he shakes his head and goes back to using the spade.

Within quarter of an hour, we're finished and there's now a rectangular bed in the middle of the lawn. I'm dreading coming up with an explanation for Granny but it's such a relief to have removed that hideous slur.

I hold my hand out. 'Thank you, Ben. I really appreciate you doing this.'

'Glad to help.' We shake hands in some kind of silent pact but he hangs onto mine and turns it over, studying it.

'Those blisters look nasty. Do you have a first aid kit?'

'It's nothing.' I try to pull my hand away but he increases his grip.

'Your hand's raw. It needs antiseptic and dressings.'

'It's not that bad…' but my voice tails away. He's right. I hang my head. I'm sore, hot and exhausted and it can't be eight o'clock yet.

He takes my other hand. 'This one's not so bad but it must hurt like hell.' He sighs before adding, 'I've a kit over the road. I think I unpacked it last night.'

'No. It's all right. I have one here.'

'Come on then.' He lets go of my hands and heads for the front door.

'What are you doing?' Even to my ears it sounds challenging and graceless.

He turns back again. 'I'm going to clean and dress your hands.'

'There's no need. I'll do it myself.'

A small huff of exasperation escapes him. Then he speaks carefully as if to a small child. 'Gwen, both your hands need to be cleaned and dressed and it'll be much quicker and easier if you'll let me do it with my two undamaged ones. Five, maybe ten minutes and then I'll be out of your hair.'

'I'm sorry.' I've become a small, rebuked child. 'Thank you.'

~~~

We stop to remove our filthy footwear at the entrance and he follows me through to the kitchen where a panting Atticus has already taken up a place by the fridge, eyeing the cat flap with suspicion.

'Bramble!' I spin round but there's no sign of her anywhere.

'Sorry. I completely forgot about your cat.'

'Not a problem.' I shut the door through to the sitting room and click the lock on the flap. 'There. All safe.'

'I'm not used to cats. It just didn't occur to me to check first.'

'No harm done, Ben.'

There's silence for a while and it's not one of those comfortable ones that you read about. Then he straightens.

'Right. Let's get these hands sorted. Where's your first aid kit?'

He scrubs his hands while I grab a clean towel from the rack above the Aga and put it on the counter beside him. Then I cross to the Welsh dresser, take the green tin from one of the drawers and place it on the table.

'You soak those hands and I'll sort out the antiseptic and dressings.'

There's one of Bramble's empty bowls on the floor and I take it to the sink, run cold water into it and put it down in front of Atticus. He laps so energetically, splashes form in a wide ring about it. I chuckle, and go back to the sink, filling it
~~~

with warm, soapy water. When I look up again, Ben is staring at me, and I think I can see a hint of a smile on his face. He pats the kitchen chair next to him and I obediently go across and sit on it. Then he takes my right hand and places it on the table, palm side up.

The blisters have burst and some of them are seeping blood. I'd been so desperate to obliterate the obscene writing that I'd worked through the pain but now the sensation is making itself known and I suck my lower lip between my teeth and clamp down on it.

Ben speaks quietly. 'I didn't appreciate the extent of the damage. This must hurt like the devil.'

I shake my head and release my lip. 'It's just a few blisters.'

'Well, let's get some antiseptic onto them and then see about covering them up. I'll try to be as gentle as I can.'

He opens an antiseptic wipe and dabs my damaged palm. For someone with such large hands he has a remarkably light touch.

'I'm afraid some of this is down to me.' He continues dabbing at my palm which is now on fire. 'That shower will have softened the skin allowing things to get this bad.'

I shake my head. I'm trying to keep the pain hidden and don't trust my voice. He picks up the cream and applies a coating that quickly brings the fire down to a smoulder and then he fixes a clean white dressing in place.

'Right. Time to do the other one.'

He takes my left hand and studies it. Mine is pale and tiny in comparison with his.

'These don't look so bad. They're still raw but they're not bleeding.' He starts to dab at them. 'I think you'll get away with some plasters on these.'

I say nothing, watching as his hands continue to work methodically and efficiently. There's something soothing, almost mesmerising, about the process and it comes as a surprise when he announces, 'There. I think that'll do.'

'Thanks. You were right. It was quicker and easier this way.' I don't know what else to say and that familiar gaucheness overcomes me. 'You've obviously done this sort of thing before.'

'I've a younger sister who was always getting herself into scrapes.' His mouth tightens into a straight line and he busies himself putting things back into the green tin.

The kitchen door opens and Claire bustles through.

'Right. Well, that's me finished, Gwen.' She notices the two of us sitting together and adds, 'Sorry, I didn't realise you had your young man here.'

'He's not!'

'I'm not.'

Our response is instant and she simply nods and carries on as normal.

'Well, your grandmother's comfy. She wouldn't have a shower but she's had a good wash, eaten most of her breakfast and she's watching TV now.' She heads for the door and turns to add, 'Don't forget she has an appointment with Dr Kumari at 4.30 this afternoon.'

A groan escapes me. 'Thanks, Claire. It'd gone completely out of my mind.'

'It ain't surprising, my dear, after all the …er…' The words drift off and I appreciate her tact but squirm at the knowledge that she's aware of what's happened. 'Well, I'll leave you to it then.' She takes another couple of steps and then stops again. 'Will you be able to get her there? Without your car, I mean?'

I can feel heat flame my face. 'Yes. Don't worry. We'll be fine.'

'There we are then. I'll see you again on Tuesday. Bye.'

Ben hands me the tin and I cross to the dresser and replace it in its drawer. I stand with my back to him, giving myself time to recover from this latest blow. How am I going to get her to the surgery without my car? Can I afford two taxis?

I turn back to Ben. 'Many thanks for all your help. If there's anything I can do to repay you, please let me know.'

It's a dismissal and he knows it. He clicks his fingers at Atticus who chooses to obey him and crosses to his side. But he's hesitating.

'What will you do without your car this afternoon?'

'I'll get a taxi.' I've made my voice light and assured. 'It's not a problem.'

'Good.'

He heads towards the door, Atticus lolloping faithfully at his heels, but he pauses and then comes back. 'Look, I need to book myself in with a medical centre and I may as well do that today as I have to be in town this afternoon anyway.'

'No. It's all right. We'll manage.'

He runs a hand around the back of his neck. 'Are you always this obstinate?'

I'm stuck for an answer. Part of me is bristling at the accusation while the rest of me is shouting that his help in this would be a godsend.

'Gwen, I'm going into Cranston later. It would be no bother at all to give you and your grandmother a lift to the centre. It's up to you.'

I swallow my pride, audibly. 'Thank you. It would be a great help.'

He gives a nod of his head. 'Right. If I come round at about four will that give you long enough?'

'That would be perfect.'

'And I'll come in to the centre on my way back from dropping off some plans at the office, sign up and drop you back home again.'

I open my mouth to protest, notice the humorous challenge in his eyes, and meekly thank him.

~~~

Granny's entrenched in her favourite chair in front of the TV, watching Downton Abbey and nibbling on some custard creams that Claire has left for her on a plate. I don't want to derail the calm and consider going into the garden and doing a bit of therapeutic weeding but my hands are smarting and I don't want to risk making the dressings grubby. My unfinished book is on the arm of the sofa and I'm just reaching for it when there's a clattering sound behind me followed by an explosion of anger.

'Damn and blast! What fool put them there?'

The plate and the remaining custard creams are scattered on the carpet. I bend down to pick them up and the grumbling rumbles overhead like thunder trapped in a valley.
~~~

‘Stupid woman! I told her not to put them there. Now look what’s happened. They’ve gone everywhere. What a waste. They’ll have to be thrown out. Ought to be docked from her wages. And I just fancied those ones and now I’ll have to do without.’

‘It’s all right, Granny. There’s the rest of the packet in the kitchen if you’d like some more.’

There’s a considered silence.

‘Do we have any of those chocolate chippy thingies?’

‘Yes.’

‘I’ll have those instead.’

‘Would you like another cup of—’

‘Shhh!’ She points at the screen. I take the hint and go to find the choc chip cookies.

~~~

When Ben raps on the door, we’re ready for him. I’ve explained to Granny that we’re getting a lift with our new neighbour but she’s taken aback when she sees him.

‘Who’s this?’ The challenge is underlined by the slight quaver in her voice and I bob down to her level.

‘This is Ben Pascoe, Granny. He’s moved into the Morgan’s house over the road.’

I go to stand again but she pulls me back down and asks in a carrying whisper, ‘What’s he doing here?’

‘Mr Pascoe is giving us a lift to the surgery for your appointment with Dr Kumari.’ I can see her trying to make sense of the words and pull myself upright to make the formal introduction. ‘Mr Pascoe, this is my grandmother, Edith Meredith.’

He bends over her, offering his hand. ‘Very pleased to meet you, Mrs Meredith.’ He’s wearing that crinkled smile of his and I watch her response. She softens.

‘Good morning. I’m afraid I didn’t catch the name.’

‘Ben Pascoe, Mrs Meredith. May I give you a lift into town for your appointment?’

His smile’s still there and to my immense surprise she rustles one up of her own.

‘That would be very welcome, Mr ….er…’
~~~

'Ben, Mrs Meredith. All my friends call me Ben.'

'Thank you, Ben. You're very kind.'

I'm so taken aback by the exchange that I let Ben wheel her down to his car. He opens the front passenger door and I take her arm to help her to her feet. She struggles to rise, leaning heavily on me before dropping back again and I'm working out the logistics of the next move when Ben hunkers down next to her.

'Would it be all right if I carried you, Mrs Meredith? It's a bit tricky getting into the front.'

She beams at him. 'That would be fine, Bill. Thank you.'

Ben lifts her with apparent ease and has her strapped in before I've finished folding the chair, which he takes from me and places in the boot.

The journey is remarkable for the change in my grandmother's demeanour. She still plays the grand dame but there's a simpering quality to it. My Granny's flirting!

'This is a lovely car, Bill. It's much more comfortable than Gwen's. Have you had it long?'

'I'm glad you like it, Mrs Meredith—'

'Edith. You must call me Edith.' She pats his hand and I can't hide my amusement until I catch Ben watching me in the rear-view mirror. His eyes are twinkling and my grin returns.

Chapter 10

The surgery is heaving with people, many of them elderly. I check us in with the receptionist who tells us to take a seat without even looking up to acknowledge our presence. There's an empty plastic chair next to the aisle, which is ideal. We sit together in silence at first. Granny's hearing is not very good and so any conversation against background noise has to be undertaken at a level that makes privacy impossible. I'm hoping against hope that she'll sit quietly until we're called. It's a vain hope.

'Isn't that Eve Evans?' It's hardly low enough to count as a whisper.

I pretend to be busy searching for something in my bag.

'Gwen.' It's punctuated by a rap on my knee. 'Isn't that Eve Evans?'

'Shh, Granny.' I squeeze her hand and give her a cheery smile as I search for possible distractions.

'It *is* Eve Evans.' Her indignation with me turns up her volume and I'm braced for whatever comes next.

'You know. Eve Evans. Her husband ran off with that stupid girl in Tesco.'

'Hush, Granny, *please*.'

'Don't you hush me, my girl!'

'Look, I've found some mints in my pocket. Would you like one?'

I hold the packet in front of her just as she's drawing breath to speak again. Miraculously, she's diverted by the sweets and I remove one. Please let it buy me enough time to come up with another strategy! The room is strangely quiet. I risk a quick scan of the faces, most of which are turned in our direction. I'm sure my grandmother's floor show has been welcome entertainment, but the knowledge that I'm now perceived in the same light as the stupid girl in Tesco does nothing to lift my spirits, and I can feel the familiar heat coming off my cheeks.

Eve is called in next and I sag back in my seat.

A young mother arrives with two small children, signs herself in and takes a seat opposite us. Her children make no attempt to obey, or even listen to, her threats and bribes to behave themselves. She takes out her phone and I can hear the tinny music accompanying a game that she plays with adept thumbs. Within a couple of minutes Thor and Rihanna are playing with the automatic doors. When they tire of that, they start chasing each other up and down between the rows of seats, their high-pitched shrieks impossible to ignore, knocking into people as they go.

Granny is incensed.

'You two!' she bellows. 'You two, sit down and behave yourselves!'

They stop and stare back at her. Then they run to their mother who wraps an arm around each of them and glares at us.

'Who do you think you are, shouting at my kids?'

Sometimes, my grandmother's faltering brain will draw her away from conflict in one of her rambling *non sequiturs*. Not this time. I'm braced for the comeback.

'Your "kids",' the distaste for the term couldn't be clearer, 'are hooligans.'

'Mind your own business, you old bag. They're just little kids. Can't you bear to see others enjoying themselves?' She clutches the smiling children closer and adds, 'Cow!'

I feel the stiffening in Granny's demeanour. She's not finished.

'If *you* don't rein them in, I'm sure someone else *will*.' I'm shocked by the clarity of her words; she's fully in control.

There's total silence in the room and I sense everyone tuned in to the cabaret.

'How dare you? Just 'cos you're so old you can't remember what it was like to be a child don't mean you should take it out on others.'

'It's not the children's fault.' I know there's more to come. 'It's yours.'

There's a gasp and a definite ripple of interest across the room.

Thor and Rihanna are grinning now, delighted to be the centre of attention.

The mother's so angry she gets to her feet, her phone clattering to the floor between us. She moves to sweep it up and the rage is clear in the slitted eyes, tense posture and the ugly set of her mouth. I stand, too, though I've no idea what I'm going to do.

Granny's furious but in a controlled way that's more frightening than that of the wild and bristling woman confronting her. 'You ignore those children and let them run riot. In another couple of years, they'll be treating you with the same contempt.' She emphasises the next words. *'We can all see it.'*

The woman clutches her phone to her chest and her gaze sweeps the faces turned towards her. Whatever she sees causes her to falter. She looks behind her at her openly mocking children and her free hand clenches. Then the fight seems to go out, deflating her like an air bed with a slow puncture.

'You ain't worth the trouble!' she hisses, and struts back to her seat with her head held high in defiance. Her arms gather Thor and Rihanna to her side again, but her knuckles are showing white.

'Edith Meredith. Edith Meredith to Room 3, please.'

I take the brake off the chair and wheel Granny away from the arena. As we pass people, I'm aware of some nods of approval in her direction. I feel a pang of sympathy for the woman we leave behind us. None of us know anything about her situation and I doubt that attacking her will achieve anything positive. I send up a silent prayer that she'll be gone by the time our consultation is finished.

~~~

The waiting room is half empty when we re-emerge and Ben is filling in a form at the reception desk. I'm amused to see that our monosyllabic and brusque receptionist can turn on a charm offensive when motivated by the presence of a personable young male. She's leaning forward and making comments in an unusually breathy voice. I push the wheelchair to a space by the door and wait.

It had been a fraught meeting with Dr Kumari, doubtless exacerbated by the earlier skirmish with Thor and Rihanna's mother. When Granny was irritable and snappy with him and
~~~

then complained about waking repeatedly in the night, he glanced at me with some sympathy and suggested a supply of sleeping tablets to help the situation. There were mutterings of dissent, but she let him prescribe them anyway. The offer had been made before, mainly, I suspect, for my benefit, but it seems unethical to drug her so that I can have a good night's sleep.

The afternoon has been exhausting and her head now lolls to the side, her mouth open and her eyes shut.

I hear Ben thank the receptionist for her help and then he's standing in front of us.

'Everything all right?'

'Yes, thanks.'

'Do you need to go anywhere else? The pharmacy, for instance?'

'No. We're fine. Granny's prescriptions go to the pharmacy here in Cranston. I'll collect it with her other medication in a couple of days.'

'Anywhere else? I'm finished for the day and it'd be no trouble if there's anything you want to get while you're out?'

There's a pause as I run through the things I need and balance them against the funds I have at my disposal to actually purchase them. 'No. I'm fine. Let's take Granny home.'

I stand and grip the handles of the wheelchair, forgetting about my blisters and unable to hide a grimace of pain.

'Let me do that.'

'I can manage.'

'I'm sure you can. But you don't want to start those blisters bleeding again. I'm simply suggesting that for the next few minutes you entrust your grandmother to me.'

I relinquish my hold and take a step to the side. 'Thanks.'

He moves into place and smoothly negotiates the doors and the ramp while I follow behind sneaking a look at my hand. There's blood beginning to seep through below the middle finger, marking the pristine white of the bandage. I hold my arm against my side, annoyed with myself for this demonstration of weakness.

Granny's so tired she barely stirs as Ben transfers her to the front passenger seat, and then we're heading back to Dernant. I fill the conversation vacuum.

'How are you finding Pembrokeshire?'

'Honestly?' There's a rueful grin on his face.

'Honestly. Warts an' all.'

'It's so laid back I want to shake some immediacy into people. I'm not used to the mañana attitude I keep coming up against.'

I can't hold back a chuckle at this. 'It's been commented on before.'

'I'll pass on something that needs to be forwarded to the right section and when I go back the next day it's still in the in-tray.'

'You'll adapt. There's something quite soothing about the pace of life here.'

'I don't feel especially soothed at the moment.'

'Give it time.' One of his eyebrows lifts ironically and I add, 'The important things are dealt with speedily. Sometimes this means that things considered less important can be leapfrogged and bumped back a bit.'

'And who does the prioritising?'

'Ah. That's a bit trickier. Let's just say it makes sense to treat people here with a friendly respect. An aggressive response is generally counterproductive.'

'So no rants, rages and threats?'

'Not unless you have masochistic tendencies.'

His laugh fills the car and I relax back against my seat and smile in response.

He looks at me in the rear-view mirror. 'I will confess to finding definite upsides to the place. The scenery here is spectacular and the beaches are some of the best in the world.'

I nod and turn my head to look out of the window. His phone rings and I look back as he clicks a switch on the steering wheel to answer it.

'Hi, Callie. How's things?'

'Ben. Ben I… Oh, Ben he's…' It's the voice of a young woman and she's too distressed to continue.

'It's all right, Callie. I'm here. What's happened?'

'He's…he's…'

'Callie, calm down. Tell me what it is. Whatever it is, we'll work something out. You're not alone. We're all here for you, you know that.'

There's a sniff followed by a noisy blowing of a nose and then Callie tries again.

'I've had a letter from the solicitor. Ben, Paul's demanding equal custody of Ellen and Jay. He wants them every alternate week and half the holidays as well.' The voice breaks again. 'I can't bear it. They're my life.'

Ben's face tenses in concern and the pain I see there shocks me.

'Listen, Callie. Leave this with me and I'll see what the situation is. Okay?'

Her voice comes back dispirited, heavy with defeat. 'The solicitor says there's nothing to stop him. He's not hurt them in any way and he has a right to maintain his relationship with them. He has rights!' Anger prompts an outburst shocking in its venom. 'He wants them to spend time with *her*. He says that she's looking forward to being a second mother to them. A second mother! The home wrecking bitch! She's taken him and now she's taking them as well.'

'Look, Callie, I'm in the car at the moment. I'll ring you from the house in a couple of minutes. I promise I'll do everything I can to help.'

He disconnects the phone and his mouth is set in a formidable line. He glances at me in the mirror. He's angry and I sense that some of that anger is directed at me.

He pulls up outside our house, has the wheelchair out of the boot almost before my feet are back on the ground, and returns to the front to slip my grandmother, still sleeping, from the car to the chair. Without speaking, he pushes her up the drive to the front door where he applies the brake and steps back.

'I have to go now.'

'Thanks, Ben. You've been a great—'

He lowers his head to mine. 'I'm sure you had no idea of the potential damage to anyone else, and I get that. I know how caring you can be, but it's often the innocent who pay the price for a thoughtless act.'

I'm too shocked to respond.

He strides off and leaves me with an abruptness that chills my blood. I shudder, straighten my shoulders and push Granny into the house.

Chapter 11

Granny keeps up her barrage of confused complaints until the evening carer prepares her for bed and she drifts off with her painkillers into an exhausted sleep. It's that time of the day when the colour begins to leach out of the landscape and I draw the curtains, make myself a mug of tea and snuggle down into the armchair to read my book. It's a good book. Cat recommended it to me and I was two-thirds of the way through it before the end of term. Now I struggle to lose myself in it. I read a page and the text is meaningless. My brain won't let go of that image of me in the pub with Ian Weston, or DS Stafford's smirk or Ben's reaction to the writing on the car. Or Ben's last words to me.

I make several attempts to carry on reading but it's pointless. After an hour, I place the book on the small table by the comfy chair and go into the kitchen. I'm at a loose end and consider making a hot chocolate but it's too muggy and humid for that. Cat bought me some bath bombs for Christmas and I still have a few left. They're supposed to be soothing and relaxing and never did I feel more the need to be soothed and relaxed.

Five minutes later, I'm perched on the edge of the bath watching it begin to fill. Damp swirls of steam are already forming above it and I drop in one of the bombs and get up to fetch my nightie and wrap. I manage the few steps to the doorway when I'm brought up short by a thunderous banging coming from the other side of the house. Seconds later the sound has moved and I realise that it's someone beating against the windows, going systematically round the house. It's so loud, the fabric of the house reverberates with it. The corridor I'm in is arranged like one of those old-fashioned trains with compartments coming off to the right. At one end is a spare room, then the bathroom, then Granny's room, my room and finally the unused guest room. There's a small window at each end of the corridor and I flinch as the pounding reaches the one by the spare room. I follow the noise helplessly as it makes its way along the line of rooms. I become aware of my cringing body language. When it reaches the other side by the front door, I spur myself into action, racing to the entrance and flinging the heavy door open to confront the perpetrator.

It's quiet. There's no one there and I step onto the driveway and peer to each side. The light is murky grey rather than midnight black and it's too difficult to make out any details. But it's quiet. No rustling. No movement of any kind. Even the trees are static in the still air. I take a step to the right, ready to check the rear garden, when a car pulls up in front of the house.

The passenger door opens and a familiar voice says, 'Thanks, Mrs Lewis. You're a star.'

'My pleasure, Gethin. Pop round sometime for tea and a chat.'

'Be careful what you wish for! I might just oblige.'

She laughs and my wonderful, reassuring, *surprising* big brother turns, drops his bag, and holds his arms out to me.

'Gethin!' It's all I can say as I run at him and let him pick me up and swing me in a circle.

When he puts me down something rustles in the undergrowth on the other side of the road and I spin round to look, hand at my mouth. Gethin tunes into my fear and puts a steadying hand on my shoulder.

'What is it? You're like a highly-strung whippet.'

I can't bring myself to turn back from the disturbed shrubs so he has to lean over my shoulder to hear me. 'Someone's just been round the house banging on the windows.'

His hand tightens. 'Who?'

'I don't know. I'd just stepped outside moments before you turned up. There was no one there.'

He follows my stare. 'And you think they're hiding over the road?'

'I don't know, but there was a rustling sound just then and I …'

I feel him straighten behind me and then he forcibly turns me and pushes me in the direction of the house.

'Right. You go inside and lock the door and I'll go and investigate.'

'No! You can't. What if they're in there?'

'That's the whole point.'

'But you might get hurt.'

'No. I'm too much of a coward for that. I'll just make a lot of noise, look bigger than I am and scare them off.' He gives me another little push. 'Now go.'

'No. I'm not going in on my own. I'll wait here for you.'

He hesitates and then lopes across the road. It's so dark I can't make him out anymore. All I can hear is the crackle of dry leaves and the snapping of twigs. He returns and shrugs.

'Couldn't see anything. Let's get you inside.'

He grabs his bag and we're in the doorway when we both notice something on the floor. He stoops to pick it up and says nothing for several unnerving seconds. Then he hands it to me.

It's a simple line drawing of a face with one eye and a crudely drawn tear below it. It's done in the same thick, red, marker pen. I turn it back and forwards several times but I know there'll be nothing else.

I'm still staring at it when Gethin's head turns in the direction of the corridor. 'What's that noise? It sounds like water.'

I can hear it, too, and suddenly realise what it is.

'Oh no!'

I push past him and run towards the steam curling from the bathroom. Water is slopping over the rolled edge of the bath and there is already a layer on the floor that threatens to bridge the carpet runner in the doorway. I wrench the taps shut and gaze at the chaos before me. Gethin stands in the entranceway, taking in the scene.

'What on earth…?

'I was going to have a bath and completely forgot about it.'

It's beginning to feel like one of those 'last straw' moments until he turns to me and says, 'What's that *awful* stink?'

Everything seems to be extremes of emotion at the moment and I start to laugh helplessly. He tiptoes through the layer of water and stands in front of me, half-amused, half-anxious.

'Well?'

I bring myself under control. 'That *awful* stink just happens to be a very expensive, beautifully fragrant bath bomb.'

His face relaxes and he pulls me to him in one of his bear hugs. 'Whatever it is, it still stinks!'

It's so good to be held secure like this and I give myself up to it, happy to stand protected within the circle of his arms.

'It's good to be back.'

'It's good to have you back. Very good.'

'How's Granny?'

I struggle to free myself. 'Granny! I'd forgotten all about her. The banging will have terrified her.'

He follows me to her door and I'm praying that she hasn't been calling for me. An image flashes in my head of her tangled in bedclothes as she tries to escape and I open her door in panic. We stand on her dark threshold and I'm plucking up the courage to turn on the light when a loud snore erupts from her bed. My eyes have adjusted to the gloom now and I can make out the familiar lumpy form beneath the duvet, rising and falling in time to the noisy accompaniment.

'Doesn't seem overly terrified to me,' Gethin whispers in my ear. We back out and creep towards the kitchen where I giggle, like a schoolgirl, with relief. I'm aware that my brother is watching me closely and, although there is a smile on his lips, the hazel eyes reflect his concern. He pulls out a chair by the table.

'Sit down and I'll make us some tea.'

'No. I'll do that. You've only just got here. You must be exhausted after your journey.'

He ignores me and propels me towards the chair and pushes me down onto it. '*I'll* get the tea. I've been sitting for hours and am looking forward to stretching my legs for a bit.'

I sink back gratefully and rub a hand over my neck, aggravating the blistered skin. 'You've convinced me. Don't suppose you can remember where everything is, though.' He responds to my teasing by swiftly opening the relevant cupboards, filling the kettle and joining me at the table whilst waiting for it to boil.

'I'm sorry, Gwen. If I'd known the trouble you were in, I'd have come straight away. It's a pain not having the car but at least the train was quick and not overcrowded.' He looks sheepish. 'I've done something else really, stupidly stupid.'

'What?' I lean forward. 'You've not had another fight with Zoe, have you?'

'No. Don't worry. Zoe and I are past history and all that's left is the disposing of our shared assets. It should be straightforward. All the stuff in poor taste is hers and the rest is mine.'

'So, what else have you done?'

'While I was on the train, someone pinched my wallet containing all my cards and a bit of cash. I had it in the hip pocket of my jeans…' He grimaces as I throw my hands up in despair. 'I know, I know. It was daft of me. Someone jostled me and apologised profusely whilst someone else seized the moment – and the wallet.'

'What have you done about it?'

'The sensible thing. I've cancelled everything and new cards will be on their way as soon as the banks have sorted stuff out at their end. Sadly, they'll go to my place which leaves me in a bit of a predicament financially.'

'I don't have much spare but we'll manage. At least you won't go hungry.'

'Thanks, little sis, but there's some cash in my bag that I'd put aside for emergencies and I should be able to manage on that.'

The kettle clicks itself off and he rises to make the tea. Now that the crisis is over, the recent lack of sleep makes itself felt. My eyelids are heavy and it takes a major effort to sit forward to take the steaming mug placed in front of me. Before I can pick it up Gethin slides it away.

'What you need now is bed, my girl. Come on.' He stands by my side and hauls me to my feet. A jaw-clicking yawn escapes.

'But I haven't made your bed.' The words are distorted through further suppressed yawns.

'I can deal with that. This was my home too, remember. Come on. Let's get you tucked in and we can sort all of this mess out in the morning. Okay?'

I nod, incapable of speech. Within five minutes I'm in my room and in my bed. I haven't washed or brushed my teeth but I don't care. I sleep deeply for the first time since my run-in with Ian Weston.

Chapter 12

I patter through to the kitchen and Gethin is there before me, reading yesterday's paper at the table. He's sitting the way he used to as a child with his feet wrapped around the front legs of the chair. I feel a surge of love for my brother and move forwards to drape my arms over his shoulders and clasp my hands across his chest. He twists his head to look back at me and one hand comes up to mine and gives them a squeeze. Then he taps them lightly and gets to his feet.

'Sit down, Gwen. Do you want tea or coffee?'

'I'll get them.'

'No, you won't. I've a freshly brewed pot of tea.' He points to the old teapot, which he must have dug out from the back of one of the cupboards. 'And there's a cafetiere on the hob with at least enough for two cups.'

He's put out a bone china cup and saucer for me and I'm touched by the gesture.

We chat about amusing incidents from our past as we share toast and marmalade but, when we've cleared the table, his face becomes shadowed and serious.

'We need to do something about these,' he holds up both of the red-eye pictures, 'and the thumping on the windows.'

Now that he's here they seem much less menacing and I'm tempted to say we should just ignore them, but I can't quite suppress a shudder and I nod my assent. I fetch the card I was given with DS Stafford's contact details and, after a bit of rehearsing what I need to say, I dial the number. He's not there so I leave a message. Then Gethin suggests we walk around the house in case there's any evidence to be seen. Although it's not quite 8 o'clock the sun is warm on our backs and the parched ground reveals nothing.

'It's like concrete,' Gethin mutters, clearly disappointed.

'What were you hoping for? Size 13 boots with a large and unique bit of damage to the tread?'

'Something like that, I suppose.' He gives me one of his twisted, rueful smiles and we continue to cover the whole garden until we're back by the side gate.

Someone is muttering outside the front door and I know instantly what I'm going to find when I round the corner.

'Good morning, Lisa. Can I help you?'

'It's this bloody— oops, sorry. It's this stupid, *stupid* key thingy.'

'Show me what you're doing.' I'm patient.

Lisa raps the side of the key safe in temper and then talks through the stages.

'First I lift this flap.' She does so. 'Then I tap in the number. Three, three.-'

'Stop! That's where the problem is, Lisa. The number is three, ***five***, five, one.'

'That's what I said.' She's indignant.

I take a deep breath as I think how to get round this.

'Okay, Lisa. I think perhaps you heard me say three, ***three*** once and now it's fixed in your head. I'm sorry about that.' No, I'm not, but I need to sort this any way I can. 'But we need to remember that it's three, ***five***. Do you know anyone who's 35?' I'm met with a blank stare. 'Do you know anyone who lives at a number 35?'

'*Which* number 35?'

'*Any* number 35.'

There's a significant pause.

'Yes! My Auntie Sylvie lives at 35 Windsor Lane. She moved there when she married my Uncle John but—'

'There we are then,' I break in before she can tell me their full life-stories. 'So, all you have to do in future is remember 35 goes at the beginning.'

'Oh, yeah. Thanks.' She picks up her bag and only then does she notice Gethin. Her face lights up in a way that I can only describe as predatory.

'Hiya. Who are you, then?'

There's a faint twitching at the corners of Gethin's mouth as he offers his hand and declares formally, 'I'm Gethin. Gethin Meredith. Pleased to meet you.'

Lisa is so overwhelmed she gives a tiny bob as she shakes his hand. Then she blushes blood red and I feel more kindly disposed towards her. She *is* very young.

~~~
~~~

We're in the sitting room chatting about Cat and her family when Lisa appears with Granny at her walker. Their full attention is focused on the chair in front of the television and I go over to help Lisa guide Granny down into her favourite spot.

'There now.' Lisa twists her head round so that it's in the line of sight of her charge. 'I'll be off then.'

Granny grunts without looking at her and Lisa turns to take her leave. She stops mid-spin when she sees Gethin.

'Oh! Hi. I didn't see you there.'

Gethin smiles kindly at her and she remains poised for flight before throwing a blushing, 'Perhaps I'll see you tomorrow?' in his direction. She leaves and the room is now quiet apart from the rummaging noises Granny makes as she searches for the remote control. Gethin crosses over to her and bobs down by her right leg. She detects his presence and her eyes search his face. Then her face cracks into a tremulous smile.

'Peter! Peter, you've come back to me.' She holds her arms out. 'Come here, my lovely boy.'

Gethin looks desperately at me for guidance. I move in front of her and take her hand, clasping it gently.

'Granny, this is Gethin. You remember Gethin, don't you?'

Puzzled eyes turn to meet mine, struggling to make sense of what I've just said.

'Gethin?'

'Yes, Granny. My brother, Gethin. He's come to stay for a few days. He said he wanted to see his favourite Granny.'

We watch, a little apprehensively, as her brain processes the words. Suddenly her face radiates happiness.

'Gethin! Gethin, come nearer. I can't see you properly over there.'

He leans across and kisses her cheek and I see all the morning's tension seep from her, making her look younger and more vital.

I get to my feet and go out to the garden to give them some space to catch up. Some of the bedding plants are looking straggly now, and I do some much-needed deadheading. I prune and tidy, accompanied by the ever-present robin. The pressure inside me has eased since Gethin's arrival and I lose myself in the task, taking pleasure from the process and its end result.

~~~

Gethin joins me over an hour later. His eyes are sad and I take his hand and lead him to the bench on the other side of the rectangular fishpond and wait for him to speak.

'I didn't realise how much she's deteriorated over the past couple of years.' He sighs deeply. 'She doesn't seem to remember anything of my last visit and all she talked about was things I'd done as a child.'

'Some days are better than others but the deterioration is undeniable. It's the cruelty of memory loss. The most recent stuff is amongst the first to go.' I give his hand a squeeze. 'She was delighted to see you, though. I've not seen her so happy in ages.'

'I've left you to shoulder this on your own, haven't I? I'm sorry, Gwen. I've been so wrapped up in my own small worries, I've not given your situation a second thought.'

'Don't be daft. If I'd needed you here, I'd have called you and I know you'd have come running. Fretting over the past helps no one.'

There's a silence as we both process this last sentence and its ramifications. Gethin squeezes *my* hand. 'Try to remember that, Gwen. I've been saying it for years but you don't listen to me. Listen to yourself, eh?'

A car pulls into the drive and we walk round to the front as DS Stafford is exiting his rather low-slung car. He studies us closely before making an approach, holding his hand out to Gethin and awaiting an introduction. I am irritated that he has no apparent intention of shaking *my* hand, but I comply with protocol.

'DS Stafford, this is my brother Gethin. Gethin, this is DS Stafford who was looking into the damage done to my car.'

Already they are squaring up to one another. They are both in jobs that involve high levels of testosterone and I suspect that each considers himself the Alpha male. We agree to talk in the garden so that Granny isn't disturbed and DS Stafford starts the conversational ball rolling.
~~~

'So, you say that someone went round the house banging on the windows.'

'Yes. That's right.'

'And this would be when?'

Even his raised eyebrow has the power to annoy me.

'About 10.20 last night.'

'I see. And you say this banging was loud?'

'Yes.'

'And on all the windows?'

'Yes.'

He turns to Gethin. 'And were you in the house when this took place?'

'No. I arrived just afterwards.'

There's a pause during which the two men stare at each other.

'And did you bang on the windows as a joke, perhaps?'

'No. I'm not in the habit of terrifying my sister.' He's riled and it shows.

'Strange you should arrive just as the banging occurred.'

I raise my voice in case I'm overlooked altogether. 'He had a lift home from the station with Vera Lewis. She dropped him off just after I ran out of the house.'

'I see.' He seems almost disappointed. 'And were you in the house on your own, Miss?'

'No. My grandmother was here.'

'And what did your grandmother make of the noise?'

I falter. This feels like a trap. 'She was asleep.'

'So, the intruder didn't bang on *her* window?'

'Yes, he did. But-'

'He banged on her window but she didn't hear it?'

Gethin doesn't wait for me to answer. 'She's on medication and sleeps very soundly.'

'I see.' Two simple words that drip with enough inference to inflame both of us.

'Now listen here. I don't know what you're implying but Gwen had a fright last night and you seem to be—'

'I'm simply establishing the facts, sir. Your sister says that someone went round the house banging loudly on the windows, but there's no one can corroborate this because you weren't here and the only other person who *was* didn't hear it.'

I put my hand on Gethin's arm to calm him. The muscles under my fingers are bunched and taut. I press harder and when I catch his attention, I give him the merest shake of my head to warn him off. He backs down.

'Well, Miss, without any actual evidence to go on there's not a lot we can do.' He shrugs carelessly.

Gethin's arm grows steely again. He says curtly, 'And what about the drawings put on the window and through the door? Can't you see the threat in that?'

Stafford replies smoothly, 'As I haven't seen these drawings, I can't make any comment on them at all, can I?'

Gethin strides to the house and returns less than a minute later with the pieces of paper, which he thrusts towards Stafford. Almost immediately they're handed back.

'Looks like a child's drawing to me. You said you worked in a school with that head teacher.' He looks at me with his smirking eyes and I want to hurt the man. 'Well, I daresay it's a gift from one of your pupils.'

'No.' I shake my head angrily. 'This isn't the work of a child.'

'And you know that because?'

'Because, well,' I chew my lip. 'Because this isn't the sort of thing a child would draw.'

'So you've never seen a child draw a face with an eye on it?'

'Of course, I have. I work with young children'

'Well then, how can you say this couldn't have been done by a child?'

I'm so angry and so twisted in knots by his unreasoned logic that I can't answer him.

Gethin intervenes. 'Can you guarantee that this *was* done by a child?'

He's got the better of Stafford and I know that this servant of the law has only one interest now and that's to get back at me for losing this battle.

'Well, there's nothing I can do at the moment. I can't stay here discussing this. There's been another crime committed in Milford that I need to attend to. Feel free to call if there are any *significant* developments.' He turns on his heel and leaves us.

I look up at Gethin's face and need to defuse the rage I see there.

'Well, that went well, didn't it?' I say it lightly and he gives the faintest of smiles in response.

'I think it's time you reported him to his superior.'

'There's no point, Gethin.' I'm angry, too, but I daren't show it. I can't face the idea of another confrontation with the man 'Anyway, what could he actually do? There's no proof, no evidence and he can hardly go round the village asking people if they drew the 'childlike' eye.'

Gethin glowers a little longer and then his shoulders relax and he drapes an arm across my shoulders.

'You're right, of course. It just makes my blood boil to see him so contemptuous and dismissive of something that was meant to frighten you.'

'But you're here now. It's all over.'

Chapter 13

After a pleasant evening chatting about old times with Granny and Gethin, I go to bed early to catch up on some much-missed sleep.

Granny's screams bring me instantly awake and I rush into the corridor just as Gethin appears at the bathroom door with dripping hair and wrapped in a bath sheet.

'What on earth's that?'

'It's Granny. Something's spooked her.' For a split second I think back to the previous night's window banging, but it's obvious that Gethin hasn't heard anything untoward either. Then I'm panicking. What if someone's broken into her room? Without knocking, I burst into the darkness and flick on the bright overhead light. Granny is clutching the duvet to her chin and she's looking in frantic darting movements around the room. Gethin has come in behind me and I ask him to check the windows as I perch on the bed and cover one of Granny's hands with my own.

'It's all right, Granny, we're here.'

Her eyes are huge in her crumpled face.

'Granny, I'm here with Gethin. You're quite safe.'

Gethin points to the locked windows and shakes his head.

'I think you've had a bad dream-'

'It *wasn't* a dream! It wasn't. He was here.'

'Who was here?' I'm using my most soothing voice but it does nothing to ease her agitation.

'I don't know. But he was here. He had a light and was shining it.' She's still scanning the room and the hand under mine is shaking. 'He was going through the drawers.'

I glance at the big chest next to her bedside table. Nothing looks out of place.

'There's no one here. Look – Gethin has checked behind the curtains. Everything is as it should be.'

Gethin's clearly upset by her distress and perches next to her on the bed, lifts her other hand and kisses the back of it.

'I'm here now, Granny, and you know I wouldn't let anybody hurt you, don't you?'

Her eyes leave mine to settle on his.

'Gethin?'

'That's right. I'm staying here for a few days. Remember?'

'You're staying? That's lovely.' She gives him a fond smile and he kisses her hand again. A drop of water splashes on to it. 'Why is your hair wet?'

'I was showering in the bathroom when you started screaming as if the hounds of hell were after you.'

'Did I?'

'Yes, you did. But everything's fine. You get your beauty sleep and we'll have breakfast together in the morning.'

'I'd like that.'

He bends forward to kiss her forehead and she looks relaxed and content. She's possibly forgotten the scare already. We wish her goodnight and leave her with her bedside light on.

Out in the corridor again, Gethin looks tired and worried. He speaks his fears. 'Do you think there really was someone in her room?'

'Now who's being daft? You saw for yourself that the windows were locked and the only other way in would be through her door and we were both here so quickly we'd have noticed someone fleeing the scene.'

He looks round in a full circle.

'Gethin, she's naturally paranoid. She accuses all the carers of stealing from her. She accused one of them last month of taking that huge oil painting of Manorbier Castle at Dawn. She'd forgotten it was in the dining room and when I showed it to her, she then accused the carer of hiding it there.'

'Sure?'

'Certain.'

'Okay. I'll get dressed and I'll give the house a quick once-over to reassure myself.'

I try to stifle a yawn. For the second time since his arrival, I'm propelled to my room and I gratefully curl back up in bed and drift straight off again.

~~~

It's nearly nine o'clock when I resurface, refreshed and happy. I throw on a light cotton top and calf-length, floaty skirt and go straight through to the kitchen where Gethin and Granny
~~~

are sitting next to each other tucking into boiled eggs and toast.

Gethin looks up at my approach.

'Morning, sleepyhead!'

'Hiya. Looks like a nice breakfast.'

'We've got a place here for you, plenty of toast and there's a pan on the hob awaiting your egg.'

I sit down and take one of the slices of toast.

'I just fancy some toast this morning. But I'd love a cup of coffee if there's some left in the pot.'

'One cup of the finest Arabica coming up.'

The coffee aroma is strong and heartening. I always find the taste a little disappointing in comparison, but it's still more than satisfying.

Granny is scraping out her eggshell.

'Did you sleep well, Granny?'

'Like a log. Isn't it wonderful that Gethin's here?'

'Yes, it is.' I smile fondly at both of them and Gethin smiles back.

The day feels full of promise and I have a second slice of toast, covering it liberally with bittersweet marmalade. Gethin remembers something.

'That Lisa girl said to remind you that Granny's prescription needs picking up.'

'Hell! I meant to collect it yesterday but completely forgot about it. We're short of one of her pills and Monday'll be too late. I'll go this morning.'

It occurs to both if us at the same time that I don't have a car at the moment.

'How will you get there?'

I glance at the kitchen clock. 'The bus goes from Bishop Road at 9.50. If I leave now, I'll be in plenty of time to catch it.'

He pushes his chair back. 'I'll go.'

'No, there's no need. I know where to go and they know me. I'll go and you can keep Granny company.'

He wavers but Granny tugs on his hand.

'Let's go and sit in the garden for a while. I can catch up on all you've been doing at school.'

He's nonplussed and looks to me again for guidance. I smile gently back and give a slight shrug of my shoulders. His face relaxes.

'That would be lovely, Granny. You finish your tea and toast and then we'll sit in the shade and chat.'

I leave them together, grab my shoulder bag and go.

~~~

Vera Lewis is in the front snipping away at her compact rose bushes with some well-worn secateurs. She comes to the gate when she sees me and smiles warmly.

'Morning, Gwen. Another beautiful day.'

'It is, Vera.'

'You must be thrilled to have Gethin back. It was fortunate that I was picking up Sally from the same train or he'd have had to walk. He hasn't changed at all, has he! Your grandmother must be so delighted to have him back for a while.'

'She's over the moon. You know how fond of him she is.'

She hesitates before saying in a rush, 'We were so sorry to hear about all that nonsense the other day with the car and the stupid gossip stuff.'

My smile wobbles a little. 'Thanks.'

Her hand comes over the top of the gate to take my wrist and squeeze it affectionately. 'Some people are just downright malicious but you needn't pay any heed to those spreading these rumours. Those of us who know you, treat them with the contempt they deserve.'

'That's very kind of you to say so.'

'I didn't know whether to mention it or not, but I didn't want you thinking that we'd been taken in by any of it.'

'I appreciate it. You've always been the best neighbours anyone could hope for.' I glance at my watch. 'I've got to go! Sorry.'

I give a wave and then I'm running down the lane, my skirt billowing behind me. As I arrive at Bishop Road, the bus is just visible as it disappears around the bend. A few seconds earlier and the driver would have noticed and stopped and waited for me. We may not have many buses, but the service
~~~

is friendly and not run on the strict lines of a more efficient system.

My skin pricks with heat and already some of the shorter curls are sticking to my clammy face. There's nothing for it but to walk the mile and a half to Cranston.

I'm touched by Vera's attempt to reassure me. I'm sure that her relationship with Rachel has caused maliciousness in the past and quite possibly still does so. I can more fully appreciate what the two of them have been through now. However, she's made me aware that I'm the subject of lurid speculation and if Vera knows about the 'stupid gossip stuff' then so does all of Dernant and probably half of Cranston, too. I feel suddenly very vulnerable and exposed and wish, momentarily, that I'd let Gethin collect the prescription.

I walk briskly on, my gaze fixed on my sandaled feet. A car passes, slows and then starts to reverse back towards me. It's Ben Pascoe. He leans across the passenger seat, opens the window and calls out to me.

'Can I give you a lift?'

I remember his brusqueness the other day and my jaw clenches. 'No thank you. I'm fine.' I wait for him to pull away but he stays put.

'There's nothing between here and Cranston and it's an awfully hot day for a yomp.'

'I'll be fine. It's not that far.'

I hear him sigh. 'Gwen, I have a nice car, a spare seat and air-conditioning. I also have a fine line in weather conversation.'

A drop of sweat trickles between my shoulder blades and my face is probably as red as it feels. I glance at my watch. If I don't arrive in Cranston soon, I'll miss the last bus back.

'You have air-conditioning?'

'I do. Guaranteed to get you to your destination cool and collected.'

'In that case…' I lean down and give him a grateful grin before getting into the front seat.

He waits for me to buckle up and then we're on our way. The chilled air blowing through the vents is bliss and I turn my head slowly from side-to-side, basking in its freshness.

When I open my eyes again, Ben glances at me, a smile on his face.

'Better?'

'Much, thank you.' I feel shy and gauche again and several seconds pass as I search for a safe comment to make. Just as my mouth opens a phone rings and he clicks a button on the steering wheel to answer it. A woman's voice fills the car.

'Ben? It's your grandmother.'

'Hello, Grandma. Everything all right?'

'Yes. Probably. Maybe…'

Ben sighs faintly. 'What is it, Grandma?'

'Well, I've had a call from someone who says my computer has a problem and they can sort it for me.'

Ben is instantly alert. 'What did you do?'

'Nothing!' She's indignant. 'You told me not to agree to anything like that without checking with you first and I told them that.' Then she sounds anxious. 'Was that right?'

There's a barely perceptible release of breath before Ben speaks again. 'That's great, Grandma. Well done. What did they say?'

'They said that they were experts and could sort it out without my having to trouble you but I said I wanted your advice first.'

'Excellent. That's a perfect answer. How did they respond to that?'

'They said they'd ring back later after I'd spoken to you.'

'And you didn't agree to anything?'

'Of course not. I'm not stupid, Ben.'

'Sorry, Grandma, I just needed to check that they hadn't tricked you in any way such as asking for your password or something.'

'There's no point asking me for that. I haven't a clue. Your mother has set it so it all starts up automatically.'

'Great.' He's silent as he follows two Lycra-clad cyclists around a sharp bend. Then he says, 'I've got to go now, Grandma. I'm in the car.'

'Okay, dear. I'll speak with you later. Lots of love.'

'Lots of love to you, too.'

There's a click and the connection is cut. There's a rueful twist to his smile.

'Sorry about that. She's been plagued by calls from opportunists.'

'Tell me about it!' I mutter angrily. 'My grandmother was worried sick a couple of years ago when she was told that her bank account had been accessed by someone and they needed her details to put a stop to it.'

'She didn't tell them, did she?'

'No. She was already having trouble with her memory back then otherwise she'd have told them everything.'

We pass another cyclist, this one going flat out, head low, knees pumping. Ben carefully negotiates past him.

'Where have all these racers come from? I've never seen so many in one place.'

'They're practising for Ironman Wales.'

'The triathlon?'

'That's the one. Swim, cycle and run impossible-sounding distances within set time limits. They close the roads for the day of the competition itself, but for weeks beforehand, keen competitors are here familiarising themselves with the 112 mile bike circuit.'

'Respect!'

'I know. The whole thing's supposedly good for the tourist industry here but it's a little frightening for holidaymakers when suddenly confronted by several cyclists on an abruptly-narrowed rural road.'

Ben steers his way carefully past two more riding abreast, before speaking again.

'How's your grandmother now? There seemed to be some upset the other night.'

'She's fine at the moment. My brother Gethin has come home for a while and she adores him. I've left the two of them chatting away about the past whilst I pick up her medication from the pharmacy.'

'You sound very fond of your brother.'

'I am.' I can hear the warmth in my voice. 'He's always been there for me. Granny was the most elated I've seen her for over a year when she saw him yesterday. He's the most important person in her life now and this visit will do wonders for her.'

'You don't mind that?'

'Mind what?'

'That she cares for *him* so much?'

I'm puzzled. 'No. They've always got on well. I have a…' I pause, searching for the word, '…a different relationship with her. I annoy her a lot of the time; he makes her happy. It's a special talent, making people happy.' I can't quite keep the wistfulness out of my voice. 'Gethin has it in bucketloads.'

We've arrived at the decorated sign announcing Cranston's twinning with Montgris and as we approach the high street, a car indicates to pull away from the kerb and Ben slips into its space.

'I don't believe it!' I'm openly admiring. 'Have you any idea how hard it is to get a parking space here in the summer?'

'Some of us are just born lucky, I guess.' He flashes one of those warm, crinkly smiles at me and all the awkwardness between us evaporates.

'I could give you a lift back if you weren't planning on staying long yourself. I've not got a lot to do here – just a quick business call and a trip to the post office.'

Now it's my turn to smile happily. 'I'd love that. Thanks. I just need to go to the pharmacy and I could do with a few stamps myself. I could meet you outside the post office?'

'Great.' He flicks his wrist to look at his watch. 'Is half-an-hour too soon?'

'That would be perfect.'

'Half-an-hour it is, then.' He tips his head in assent and crosses the road, dodging a brewery lorry. I watch him go and am aware that I'm still smiling. He reminds me a little of Gethin, I suppose; both of them, confident, clever and kind.

My wheel of fortune is turning.

Chapter 14

At the pharmacy, I wait by the food supplements shelf while the assistant sorts out my grandmother's prescription. Two women are standing at the end of the aisle and something about their body language makes me look in their direction. They are staring at me with their heads almost touching and it's clear I'm their topic of conversation. For a moment I'd completely forgotten about the Facebook posting; now I'm humiliatingly aware of it and I turn away, to study the range of vitamin supplements on offer with a determined fascination. To my horror I hear a familiar voice bearing down on me.

'There she is!' It's Mrs Sweeting, well-known busybody and moral voice of the community. She comes to a halt behind me and I am mired in misery as I turn and look up into her scowling face. A more timid friend waits in the background as the inevitable assault is launched.

'I have to say I'm most surprised, Miss Meredith. Most surprised and disappointed in you.' Her ample bosom heaves as she continues. 'You are in charge of innocent, developing minds and to throw yourself at Mr Weston like that is wicked. Have you no shame?'

'It wasn't like that, Mrs Sweeting.' I'm ready for a fight.

'Nonsense, girl! I've seen the evidence for myself. Bridget showed me the photograph and I told her that it was my duty to bring the matter up at the next governor's meeting.'

'Mrs Sweeting, whatever you imagine happened, didn't. I appreciate your concern for my moral welfare but you don't understand the situation, nor do you have any right to make these erroneous assumptions about me.' I close the distance between us. 'If you continue to spread these rumours, I shall have little option but to sue you for slander.' Before I launch into an over-the-top tirade, I notice the abnormal stillness in the room. Everyone is facing in my direction and listening intently. There's a mixture of embarrassment, interest and delight and I don't know how to handle it. Then one of the assistants calls my name and I walk through the still-silent throng to the counter.

‘Here you are, Miss Meredith.’ She gives me a kind smile before turning a colder expression on the others, some of whom shuffle nervously. Conversation starts up again, overly animated and studied, and I’ve had enough. I walk swiftly to the exit with my head held high and what I hope is a confident expression on my face.

Back on the pavement again, my body loses its rigidity. I clutch the large bag of prescription medicines to my stomach in an attempt to still the churning there. This is new to me and I’m ill-equipped to deal with it. The bell on the clock tower strikes the hour and spurs me on to my meeting with Ben at the post office.

I’m passing the alleyway just before it when a hand shoots out and drags me off the pavement, slamming me back against the wall. I’m stunned into silence and stare blankly at the contorted face of Mark Johnson. I’m so close I can see the pores in his swarthy skin and the breath on my face smells of beer.

‘I’ve been waiting for you to do what I said.’ He’s angry. ‘Why haven’t you told them yet?’

I stare mutely back at him. He hasn’t finished. ‘They’ve still got my boy and I want him back. *Now!*’ The last word is uttered so violently, flecks of spittle strike my cheeks and I flinch. I try to free my hand but the effort angers him and he grabs both wrists and pins them to the brickwork above my head. The movement pushes my breasts forwards and his gaze drops to them. I squirm but this simply brings a leer to his face.

‘You don’t seem to be getting my message. I hold you responsible and I’m going to make you pay for every minute my Justin is away from me.’ He transfers both my wrists into one hand and the other one comes down to squeeze and fondle, then he pushes himself against me and I can feel his arousal as he drops a brutal kiss onto my mouth, grinding his wet lips against me.

A shadow hits us and Mark pulls back, smiles at a stunned Ben and lets go of my wrists. ‘See you later, darlin’’ With that he swaggers off.

‘I’m sorry.’ Ben’s voice is tight and angry. ‘I didn’t realise you were otherwise engaged. I’ll see you back at the car.’

I'm still struggling with the shock of what's happened and his censorious tone is the last straw.

'You think I welcomed that… that *mauling*! You make me sick with your ridiculous, high-handed opinions.' The pitch of my words is rising and I'm powerless to stop it. 'Leave me alone! I've had enough of all of you. I've been judged and found guilty but *I've* done nothing!' He's still standing there. 'Go away!' I'm losing control, and then the nausea comes to the surface and I bend over and retch until I've emptied my stomach.

When I drag myself upright again, Ben is standing closer to me and I can see his concern. He stretches a hand out towards me and I knock it away.

'Don't! Don't even *think* of touching me.'

'Gwen, I—'

I don't let him get any further. 'Leave me alone. If you come any closer, I'll scream. I mean it.'

I stagger past him onto the bright street and make my way quickly and a little unsteadily down the hill to the river where it flows sluggishly past the assorted commercial buildings opposite. I walk along the path until I come to a bench where I sink down in the far corner, tuck my feet up, wrap my arms around my legs and stare at the water without noticing it. There's a pressure building inside but I daren't cry to ease it – I'm spectacle enough already.

~~~

Revulsion courses through me in shuddering ripples. The memory of Mark Johnson pressing his aroused body into mine, the grabbing of my breast and the foul grinding of his mouth against my lips are so real I'm still experiencing their horror. I feel him, smell him, hear him. I see his leering, sweaty face and my stomach protests, making me clutch my knees more tightly into me. I'm also scared. What if I come across him again where there aren't people to protect me? How far would he go?

In between this assault on my senses, I see images of Ben Pascoe and his shocked, reproving expression. This is not the first time he's found me wanting and there won't be another
~~~

chance. In his eyes, and those of others, I'm a brazen marriage wrecker who selfishly pursued a decent man and seduced him away from his delightful family. Anyway, I don't want anything more to do with Ben. He's hurt me deeply and I'm not going to give him the opportunity to do so again.

I'm so tired and rattled by the events of the last few days that, for the briefest of moments, I consider telling Social Services that I was mistaken about Mark's treatment of Kaylee. But the idea is dismissed before it's fully formed. If he can make *me* feel like this, what must it be like for his little daughter?

When I came back to care for Granny, the claustrophobic atmosphere almost reduced me to panic attacks. Then a generous care package was set up funded by a trust fund and I was able to leave the house for a few precious hours each day, enjoying the freedom and companionship that the school provided. What happens now? If I return it will be to nudges and innuendo and unspoken criticism. Is there any other work I could do? Nothing that will allow the flexibility I need for sudden emergency visits home and nothing in the area that won't foster the same crushing response I now face. Then there's the financial situation. The repairs to the car will suck up my last, puny reserves of money. I'm ensnared in a net of lies that is growing tighter and more painful by the day and my inability to claw a way out of the situation has brought on a tension headache that throbs with the heat of the midday sun. If I'm to make it back to Dernant, I need to leave now whilst I still can.

I stop clutching my knees and am putting my feet back on the ground when a movement to my left catches my eye and I see Ben Pascoe. He's pushing himself upright from his position against the wall and watching me. Has he been there all along? What does he want? He moves cautiously towards me and there's uncertainty in his expression. When he arrives at the bench, he speaks so quietly the words are almost lost against the backdrop of squabbling birds vying for the bread being thrown to them by a family with young children.

'Gwen. How are you?'

I don't answer. I can't. I'm too distressed and angry.

He stands silently for a few seconds and then he holds out the large, pharmacy bag.

'You dropped this.'

I don't remember dropping it, only Mark Johnson clawing at me and Ben thinking I was enjoying it. I still can't speak but I put a hand out to take the bag and hate the fact that my fingers are trembling and try to still them by pushing the bag firmly against my chest. I'm still looking down when his voice continues, very gently.

'I'm so very sorry, Gwen. Please believe me.'

I hear what he says but can't bring myself to look up from the rigid fingers clasping the paper bag hard against me.

'I couldn't see you properly and completely misjudged the situation.' I see his extended hand in my peripheral vision but remain frozen.

'Then I saw your eyes huge with shock and horror and realised what I'd just witnessed.' He sighs. 'Is there anything I can do to try and make things right between us?'

I shake my head, miserable and horridly close to the tears I'm desperately holding back.

Then he sits at the other end of the bench, facing me.

'What I saw sickens me to the stomach and I can understand your distress at the mistake I made. If you can't forgive me, can you at least let me help you in any way that I can?'

I hear myself swallowing noisily. But I'm unable to reply. My fingers are automatically pleating and unpleating the top of the bag and my headache is pounding.

'Gwen? Please let me help you.' The softly-spoken voice is almost my undoing but I manage to contain my tears.

'I've behaved appallingly and would do anything to take back my words. But it's not possible, is it?'

He's right. My spine stiffens and I shake my head. It's time I took back control of this situation instead of passively rolling along with it. I stand and face him properly.

'You don't know me, Ben. You've made several assumptions that I find particularly distasteful and I think it's best if we agree to keep a respectful distance from each other.' My voice sounds calm and firm with no hint of the internal wobble that whirls inside of me.

The extended hand is withdrawn and he looks disconcerted. He rubs the back of his neck and then says more briskly, 'Let me take you to the police station and then I'll give you a lift home.'

'The police station?'

'To report what that – that lout did to you.' His anger surfaces and this time I'm the one who's calm and collected.

'There's no point.'

'Of course, there's a point! He assaulted you.'

'It's my word against his.'

'But I can back you up.'

'No, you can't. The police will ask you what you saw, and because you're a decent person you will have to tell them the truth.'

'Which is exactly what I'm proposing to do!'

I feel depressingly in control now. 'When they ask you what you saw you will have to answer that it looked like some passionate clinch.'

'It wasn't. The bastard was molesting you.'

'So why didn't you intervene?' I'm composed. I know where I'm going with this.

'Because I thought—' He breaks off and shakes his head.

'Hearing you confirm what you *thought* you saw simply paints a more lurid backdrop to what's happened and only makes my situation worse. Can't you see that?'

He's silent and I can see him wrestling with an inner conflict that makes a muscle tic in his cheek.

I've had enough and speak more forcefully.

'I don't want the police to know anything about this. They already see me as some kind of predatory scarlet woman and this will only serve to reinforce that view.' I can hear my building resentment and give him a hard stare as I recall his brusque dismissal of me after reading the scrawl along the side of the car. He believed that I was a home wrecker then, and I've had enough of people who pre-judge and condemn on appearances. 'Thank you for bringing this to me,' I hold the bag aloft, 'but I'd better be getting back now.'

I've gone perhaps half a dozen steps before he overtakes me and stands in my way.

'Gwen, I can only reiterate how sorry I am. You may not believe me, that's your prerogative and I don't blame you after the crass way I've behaved. However, I do beg you to do the sensible thing and let me drive you home.'

'The sensible thing?'

'I'm going home now, you're ready to go home now, and I have a car that can easily accommodate both of us. You look exhausted and it's a long, hot weary trek back.'

'I can walk.'

My petulant tone exasperates him. 'Look, you can punish me all you want but there's no need to do this to yourself. You're not one of those 'cut off your nose to spite your face' people, are you?'

I want to snap back but he's right. To refuse to travel back with him would be childish and stupid.

'Okay,' I concede.

He falls into step beside me and we walk silently to his car where he holds the door whilst I tuck myself into the seat with the large paper bag perched on my knee.

~~~

It's a silent journey and I'm relieved when the car pulls up outside the house. The thumping in my head is so bad I feel nauseous and I don't know how I'm going to face Granny and Gethin.

Ben seems to have the power to tune into my thoughts. 'You could tell them that the walk into town has been too much in this heat and you need to go to bed for a bit.' The suggestion is a good one.

'Thanks.' It's all I can manage and he comes round to open the door and help me out of the car.

Before I leave, he says, 'I am truly sorry, Gwen.'

I hurry up the drive away from him and Gethin opens the door as I raise my key to unlock it.

'There you are!'

'Is everything all right? Nothing's happened to Granny has it?'

He ushers me in. 'No. No, she's fine. That Lisa girl's been here and she and Gran have been sparring with each other.'
~~~

I'm aware of his searching look and drop my gaze before it. 'Are *you* all right?'

'Yes. I'm fine.' I move to pass him but he puts a hand on my arm and turns me to face him again.

'Something's happened. Tell me.'

'Nothing's happened. I'm just hot and have a blinding headache.'

'Is it to do with that new neighbour? I saw him drop you off.'

'No. I'm fine, I tell you. Ben simply gave me a lift back to save me a trek in this heat.'

'He hasn't tried it on with you?' There's an edge to his voice that I need to blunt.

'Of course not! He's just a neighbour. We've never so much as held hands. Does that satisfy your curiosity?' The words drop more harshly than I intended into the uncomfortable atmosphere developing between us. 'Please, Gethin, it's been a long day. I missed the bus into Cranston and if it hadn't been for Ben, I'd still be on my way back now.'

He holds his hands up. 'Okay. I didn't mean to throw my big brother weight around. I care about you, you know. It's been us against the world for so long I sometimes forget that you're all 'growed up' and can fight your own battles now.'

'And I'm sorry for being a bit snappy. You know how I hate this stifling heat.'

'Yeah. It's your red-hair. I should make allowances.'

I give him a wavering smile, battling the pain that is pressing outwards against my skull. 'I ought to thump you for that remark but, fortunately for you, I'm feeling too rough. You'll be okay to keep an eye on Granny for a couple of hours, won't you? She'll probably sleep or watch the TV.'

'Sure. Off you go.'

I pass the bag across to him. 'Here's Granny's medication. Leave it on the desk and the carers will deal with it.'

He takes the bag but then his eyes narrow as he stares at my shirt. I follow his gaze and realise that Mark has left three, faint, grubby fingerprints on the white background

'Did Ben do that?' It's a growl and I panic as I try to dredge up an excuse. But Gethin knows me too well to be fobbed-off with one of my pathetic lies. I take a deep breath and tell him about Mark Johnson grabbing me and embroider the tale a little with Ben coming to my rescue.

The rage I see makes me anxious. This time I'm the one putting out a restraining hand.

'Gethin, leave this alone. I've already explained to Ben that telling the police will only reaffirm their image of me as a sex-mad man-eater and I just want to put it behind me. If you so much as *approach* Mark Johnson you'll just make things worse for both of us.'

He says nothing at first, jaw set and fists clenched. I place myself directly in his line of sight and try a reassuring smile.

'Please, Geth. This isn't the school yard. You've always protected me and you know what a difference it made when we were younger. But this wouldn't be a scrap between schoolboys; this would be something that would bring the law down on your head and feed the flames of the hateful rumours about me.'

He looks away. 'I can't bear to see someone get away with hurting you, Gwen.'

'I know. But if you let Mark Johnson suck you in with his poison, he's the only one that'll win. *Please* let this go.'

His shoulders flex and then he turns back and pulls me into a fierce hug. He mutters, 'All right, Gwennie. You win.'

I put my arms around his waist and lean into him. Grateful for his support. We stand like that, unmoving, until a bellow from Granny tells us that someone's lost the remote control, she's missing her very favourite programme and nobody cares.

Chapter 15

Sunday, and it's going to be another scorching day.

Gethin's still asleep and I'm going from room to room, hesitating in front of the curtains before pulling them open with a flourish that's at odds with the tremble in my hands. The patio doors are the last ones at the side of the house and I pull back the right-hand one. Nothing. I reach out for the other curtain but whether it's a sixth sense or a build-up of adrenaline, I can't bring myself to open it. I grip the fabric and will myself to get on with it; rip it back like a plaster on a child's grazed knee. I can't. This is ridiculous. I do several countdowns to force myself to take action, but I chicken out at the end of each one. I'm still standing like that when I hear Gethin's yawn as he comes into the room.

'Morning, Gwen. How did you sleep?'

'Really well. Knowing that my big brother was in the house melted away all my irrational fears.'

'Perhaps I should stay a bit longer.'

'No.' Guilt washes over me. 'No, Geth. I didn't mean that. Honestly. I'm fine.'

'I know you, Gwen.' He comes across and gives pulls me in for a hug. 'You pretend that everything's fine and let things pile up until they're too much for you. I've let you down in the past when I should have been more supportive. You wouldn't have had that breakdown if I'd been there for you.'

'You promised not to tell Granny.' I'm pleading. Pathetic.

'Of course not. I gave you my word. Hell, Gwen, you *know* there's no need to hide it as if it's some character failing!' He stands back, exasperation evident in his rigid stance. 'You've got to stop putting everyone else first. You'll fight for others but you never fight for yourself.'

'I did once.' The words fall heavily between us. 'My selfishness changed our lives for ever.'

'Gwennie, stop this. You were a child.'

I push against him. I can't look him in the eye. 'Please, Geth, let it go.'

'No.' He's quiet but firm. 'I'm proud of what you've achieved and how you've coped here with Gran.' He tilts my chin up so that I'm looking into his troubled eyes. 'But you've been through so much and I don't want to see you hurt like that again.'

'You're not your sister's keeper, Geth.' I try to inject a self-confidence and composure into the words. Then I pull away and head for the kitchen. 'Tea or coffee?'

He's looking at me with wary eyes but he replies with a matching lightness. 'Coffee, please. I can't think straight until I've had my caffeine fix.'

He joins me at the counter and holds up the copper pig. 'I've always loved this.'

'I know.' I say, measuring out the coffee. 'It's so round and chunky it practically begs to be caressed whenever I pass it.'

'Remember that day I tried to pick it up?'

'Granny almost had a fit. I never knew whether she was worried about the pig or the potential damage to your feet.'

'It became a challenge after that. I'd sneak in here and try to lift it. Who'd have thought something so bright could weigh so much. Heaven knows what it's worth now.'

I'm getting down the cups from the cupboard when he moves away, saying, 'I'll open this curtain. Let the day in.'

The back of my neck prickles. I *know.* The cups rattle together as I place them on the table.

'What the—'

It's there. Stuck to the window. A red eye with one tear drop. I must have made some noise or movement because he's there with me in an instant, pulling out a chair for me to collapse onto.

'It's all right, Gwennie. It's all right.' But I hear the quiver in his voice and know that it isn't.

Gethin pours the coffee and adds sugar to one of the cups before passing it to me.

'Here. Drink this.'

Despite the heat of the day my fingers are stiff and cold and I wrap them around the cup and take sips of the sweet drink. It helps. Gethin is watching me closely.

'Thanks, Geth. Don't know what got into me. It's only a drawing.'

'Do you have any freezer bags? I'll pop it inside one in case there's fingerprints.'

I take one from the drawer and go with him to the door. It's only when he slides it open that I realise the significance of the eye and step out onto the patio, searching for the damage.

Gethin's sealing the bag when he spots it. It's Granny' statue of a little boy holding a water dish. It's on its side. The pieces of its head are scattered around like stone petals. I drop to my knees beside it and I'm aware of two sounds; my moans of grief and the panting of a dog.

Atticus bounds across but when he reaches me, he simply lies down and puts his head in my lap.

Ben joins us moments later.

'Atticus! I'm sorry, Gwen. He just—' His voice dies as he takes in the scene. 'What's happened here?'

'You must be Ben Pascoe. I'm Gethin Meredith, Gwen's brother.' I'm annoyed at Gethin's ready acceptance of the man, but I did credit him with rescuing me from Mark and so I just have to put up with it.

I watch them shake hands. Atticus licks my fingers and the action releases me. I run a hand over his back, the silky warmth therapeutic. Gethin helps me to my feet and the three of us go back into the house and I find a bowl to give Atticus a drink while Gethin tells Ben, in tight, angry sentences, about the eye drawings and the damage they've heralded. Ben is all too aware of the car and the weedkiller incidents. When he looks at me, I think I see shame in his face for the way he's treated me. Maybe it's just pity.

The coffee restores my equilibrium and I feel ready to face up to things.

'So, what do we do now?'

Ben is firm. 'You inform the police.'

'That's what I've been telling her. She won't hear of it in case it makes things worse.'

'*She's* in the room, you know.' My hackles are raised. Perhaps it's because of the truth in what Gethin's saying. 'If we take this to the scathing DS Stafford, I know what he'll say.' Both men move as if to remonstrate with me but I verbally slap them down. 'This is directed at me, and I'm the one suffering the collateral damage. Stafford will say that the eye is a child's token of some sort and the statue could be down to any number of perfectly innocent reasons.'

'Gwen, we're on your side here—'

'Then listen to me, Geth. Try to understand my position in all of this. This is *my* reputation that's being shredded. This is *my* pain.'

Ben leans back in his chair and threads his fingers behind his head, his brow furrowed. Atticus puts a grey-flecked paw on his knee and I see some of the tension leave his master who absently reaches down to pat his dog's head and rub his shoulders.

'I don't like the viciousness behind these acts, Gwen.' Atticus leans in for more fuss. 'What if they escalate?'

'If something else happens that we can prove is deliberate, then I'll be there beating a path to Stafford's door.'

A sigh escapes Gethin. 'Okay, Gwen. If that's the way you want it. We'll log the details of this incident and keep the drawing safe. But anything more and I'm reporting this.'

'Fine.' I force a smile that evaporates at Ben's next comment.

'What are you going to do with the smashed statue?'

'Oh God! Granny. What do we say to her?'

Gethin's response is quick. 'We'll tell her that she gave it to me and I have it safe in my garden.'

'She'll never believe that. Grandad gave it to her on their silver wedding anniversary.'

'I know. But she's already forgetful and I'm sure I can convince her. Remember that time I stole your ice cream and blamed it on a passing dog? By the time we got back to the car you were sure that's what had happened.'

'You thug! You've kept that quiet all these years.''

'I might have got away with it, too, except Gran had seen the whole thing. She was livid. I was sent to my room as soon as we got back. She came up later and she cried. She actually cried.'

'I reach out and give his arm a squeeze. 'I don't remember that at all.'

'No. She kept it all quiet but it was a pretty effective form of punishment, I can tell you.'

I forget that Ben's there until he gets to his feet.

'Well, I'll leave you two to it, but if there's anything I can do please let me know.' He looks directly at me. 'Promise?'

I cross my chest. 'And hope to die.'

The attempt at humour falls flat.

'I'm a shout away, Gwen. There's no need to take any risks.'

'I'll keep an eye on her, Ben. Thanks for the support.'

There's the briefest of hesitations and then he's gone.

'Right, Gwen. Let's get rid of the evidence.'

We carefully put the remains of the statue into a stout rubbish bag and store it in the shed.

~~~

Lisa is on the morning rota and surprises me by unlocking the door on her own. I resist the urge to praise her lest it be seen as patronising. She's seven minutes late but you can't have everything.

Gethin gets out his laptop and works at the kitchen table. I retreat to the garden, telling myself to ignore the newly-created space in the corner. Within a few seconds the robin is down and I give the first real smile of the day. I envy Ben's connection with Atticus. Granny has a strict no-animals-in-the-house rule, but perhaps one day I'll be able to have a proper pet of my own. As if aware of my thoughts, the tiny creature hops onto my gloved hand and I hold my breath in wonder. He's so close I can see the magical detail in his tiny feathers. This is a privilege and compensates for much of the unpleasantness of the morning. He drops down to the ground again and I laugh and dig my trowel into the dry earth until another worm appears. This one is eaten on the spot and I spend another ten minutes working around the plants, digging deeper than necessary to keep a steady supply of wriggling food coming.

Lisa calls to me as she leaves. She hasn't given Granny her shower because she didn't want one and she's not eaten all of her breakfast. I hold an exasperated sigh inside and watch her leave.

Granny isn't happy.

'Stupid, stupid girl!'

'She's young.'
~~~

'That's no excuse.' She's searching for more ammunition. 'She isn't gentle like that Betty woman.'

'Becky.'

'That's what I said. Becky. Do you take me for a fool?'

'Why don't you sit in front of the television and I'll put something on for you to watch?'

She ignores me. 'And she steals things.'

'I'm sure she doesn't, Granny.'

'Are you accusing me of lying?' The anger is building. I sense we're heading for temper gusting at the top of the Beaufort scale.

'Of course not, Granny. Sometimes she moves things around and then they're missing for a while.'

'She's stealing from me. Think I can't see her going through my things? This morning she went through the drawers in the bedroom. Take a look if you don't believe me.'

Gethin joins me. 'Is there a problem, Gran?'

There's a puzzled expression on her face.

'Peter?'

He bobs down next her. 'Hiya, Gran. It's Gethin. You remember me? Gethin, Peter's son.'

'Gethin.' She's trying the word out. She says it several time before it falls into place. 'Gethin! Come and give your poor old granny a hug.'

Fifteen minutes later he's back in the kitchen and I can hear Downton Abbey in the background.

'Well done,' I say. 'Potential crisis averted.'

'My pleasure.' He comes closer and drops his voice. 'Do you think there's any truth in her accusation of Lisa stealing from her?'

'I very much doubt it. She's always claiming that things have been nicked only for them to reappear later.'

'Right. It's just…it's just that I don't think I trust the girl myself.'

I'm troubled enough by his concerns to go through to the bedroom and check the drawers. Everything seems in order, but someone has definitely gone through them. The piles of clothes are disturbed and they weren't like that yesterday when Granny asked me to find one of her brooches to pin to her blouse. It's unsettling. I've ignored her previous claims about Lisa and dismissed out of hand her fears about someone being in her room with a torch.

We decide to resort to some sneaky checking up on Lisa's activities tomorrow. People refer to being sick to the stomach, but that's how I feel. There's a horrible roiling there and I push my fist against it to try and ease it.

~~~

When the door opens in the evening, I'm surprised and delighted to see Becky there.

'Becky! I didn't expect you back so soon? How's your sister?'

'She's doing okay.'

She smiles. Normally one of her smiles can light up a room but this one falls flat and doesn't reach the pain in her eyes.

'I'm sorry, Becky. It must be so hard for you.'

'Oh, I'm all right. It's best I keep busy at the moment. I'm no use to her hanging around the house.'

'Come and have a coffee. There's some in the pot.'

She hesitates and turns towards the door. 'No. I'd better get on. Keep going, and all that.'

Nothing more's said. It troubles me. She looks exhausted and unhappy and I'm aching to help her, but she clearly doesn't want to talk.

I go through to the kitchen, reach for the coffee pot but decide against another belt of caffeine and make myself a ginger and cardamom tea instead. Gethin's tapping away at his keyboard and I stand looking out at the fields. The sun is lower in the sky now, glazing the branches of the trees in a rose gold. I tell myself how lucky I am to be living in such a beautiful place. I've had some setbacks in the last few days but they can't compare to the devastation of knowing that a younger sibling is facing a brutal, terminal illness.

Gethin closes his laptop and stretches. 'Fancy coming for a stroll?'

'Oh. I don't know. What about Granny?'

'How long will her carer be here?'

'Forty minutes.'
~~~

'So, we go as far as the bridge and back. Twenty-five minutes maximum.'

I so rarely get out these days that the notion takes me aback. Then I realise how stupid I'm being. It's a great idea.

'Done. I just need to slip on some sandals and I'll be ready.'

Just being out of the house like this, with no other purpose than to enjoy the experience, raises my spirits in a way I couldn't have imagined ten minutes ago. The fierce heat of the afternoon has given way to a comfortable warmth that kisses the skin rather than searing it. Vera's partner, Rachel, gives a friendly wave as she wobbles past on her bike and I try to remember when I last rode a bike. It's not good to delve back into the past and I pull my thoughts back to the present.

Gethin's watching me, a gentle smile on his face.

'When did you last go for a walk?'

'I honestly don't know. Ages, anyway.'

'Will you try to go out, even if it's only for five or ten minutes, every day? You can choose a time when Gran has someone else with her.'

I'm chewing my lip, certain there must be some hurdle that can't be overcome. It occurs to me that I'm overthinking things. A calm settles and I return his smile.

'Sounds like an excellent idea.' I put a hand to his shoulder and at the last minute give it a push and sprint away. 'Last one to the bridge loses!'

He still manages to beat me but we stand together, bent over to ease more oxygen into our burning lungs, and then we're laughing. It's so very good.

Gethin stands at the wooden railing and looks down at the brook known locally as Stinky Ditch. The ground on which we're standing resembles more of a lazy hump in the road than anything as grand as an architectural structure and I follow Gethin to stare down at the meagre trickle of water that flows sluggishly through the tangle of greenery, old bottles and a shopping trolley that lie in its path. Gethin bobs down, searching for something in the crisp leaf litter at our feet, and pops back up again with a twig in each hand. We play Pooh sticks like we used to do, but nothing manages to come through the other side and we declare it a draw before heading back home, arm-in-arm.

Chapter 16

We're ready for Lisa in the morning. Gethin has marked a five-pound note with a tiny red smiley face and left it on Granny's dresser partly hidden by one of her medicine bottles.

When she arrives, I struggle to greet her normally and am afraid that my face reveals our covert machinations. Lisa, however, breezes through the house as normal and it's not long before we hear Granny bellowing at her. This subterfuge makes me uncomfortable. I know we're doing it for a good reason, but in some ways it seems as dishonest as the crime we're hoping to uncover. Well, Gethin's hoping it works; I'm praying that he's got her wrong and she won't rise to the bait.

I'm pacing, jittery with coffee and anxiety, when she comes through to get the folder that contains details of all that's been done during her visit. Gethin slips out of the kitchen and when he returns there's a triumphant expression on his face.

He goes straight across to Lisa and asks her, in a conversational way, if she can swap his five pound coins for a note. She gives him the besotted look of a devoted puppy, fishes a note out of her pocket and hands it to him.

Gethin studies it in silence. When he speaks the words are quiet and unhurried but to the point.

'You've stolen this from my grandmother's room.'

The change in Lisa is instant. No longer the devoted acolyte, she's spiky and goes straight on the offensive.

'How dare you! I haven't touched anything. You take that back or I'll get the police on to you for… for… for telling lies about me' She's squaring up to him, getting in his face, but he remains calm.

'Tell me where you got this note from, then.'

'My mum gave it to me this morning to go and buy some milk for her on my way home from work.'

'Let me show you this, Lisa.' He produces his phone, clicks the screen. 'This note was left on the dresser next to my grandmother's bed.'

'So? There's thousands, *millions,* of five-pound notes in the world. Just 'cos I've got one, doesn't give you the right to call me a thief.’ Her finger’s starting to jab at his chest but Gethin ignores it.

‘Let me magnify this corner here, Lisa. See that smiley face?’

She falters. This can’t be going the way she expected it to. Her forehead creases as she stares at the red mark. ‘Yeah, I see it. So?’

Gethin shows her the corner of the note that she’s just given him.

‘See, Lisa. I put that smiley face on there this morning and took this photo as proof. This *is* that note.’

She’s staring through him. I can almost see her brain trying to find an escape route. Then all the fight leaves her in a rush and her shoulders slump.

‘It…I didn’t mean…I was just going to borrow it. Honest. I was going to bring it back tomorrow. On my mother’s life.’

‘Lisa, this is serious.’ Gethin’s unruffled. My stomach’s churning in horror at what’s unfolding. He continues, ‘You’re a thief and a liar.’

‘No! Not really. *Please*, Mr Meredith, it isn’t how it looks. They pay me minimum wage for this and that’s not enough for me to live on. It’s hard work and some of the people can be really nasty.’ She glances at me and mutters, ‘Sorry.’

‘But this isn’t the only thing you’ve taken, is it?’

She blinks and her mouth works before she manages the softest ‘No’.

‘No. You’ve taken things more valuable than this money. You’re going to have to pay for that.’

Tears have pooled in her eyes and I can’t bear this any longer.

‘Gethin, could I have a word?’

He looks surprised, as if he’s forgotten I’m there. I lead the way to the other side of the room and drop my voice to a whisper.

‘She’s admitted it, Gethin. She’ll not do it again.’

‘I’ll make quite sure of that.’ His whisper is more of a growl and Lisa reaches for the edge of the table and grips it as if to support herself.

‘Honestly, Geth. You’ve scared her.’

'She's been stealing from Gran. She deserves to be scared. A trip to the police station will round things off nicely.'

'No!' I've forgotten to whisper, and drag my voice down again. 'I don't want the police involved.'

'Don't be silly, Gwen. She's a thief and deserves to be punished.'

'She has been, Geth. Look at her. She's shaking so badly I think she might collapse. I don't want to call the police. Let's just leave things as they are.'

He grips my shoulder and speaks more quietly.

'She's been stealing things. You can't ignore this, Gwen.'

'But I don't want to involve the police.' The scared little girl has surfaced and I'm afraid I'm going to cry.

'All right. How about this? We don't inform the police but let her employers know what's happened.'

'But she'll lose her job, Geth.'

'Gwen! What if she's been doing it to someone else? What if we say nothing and someone else suffers? How would you feel then?'

I hang my head. I'm ashamed at my lack of courage. I want the problem to go away and if turning a blind eye could do it then that's what I'd been willing to do. However, he's right. I have a duty of care to the other people she visits and can't ignore this for their sake.

'Okay. I'll tell her employers. But no police. I really can't bear to see Stafford or anyone else again at the moment.'

He just stands there in silence, his grip tightening on my shoulder. When he lets go, I'm braced for his decision.

'Fine. We'll do it your way.'

He goes back to Lisa who immediately confesses to taking small sums of money on other occasions and a pair of earrings that she declares Granny has no use for now. That does anger me but she's quickly apologetic and promises to return the earrings tonight.

Gethin brings things to a close.

'Right, Lisa. I wanted to call the police but my sister has suggested we simply inform your employers and leave the police out of this.'

I watch the conflicting emotions chase across her face as his words slowly filter through to her.

'Thank you. I'm very sorry and—but you can't tell Cranston Care! They'll sack me.'

'Sorry, Lisa. You're getting away lightly as it is. At least you won't have a criminal record around your neck.'

She opens her mouth to speak, closes it again, and I watch the tears fall. I hate situations like this and a part of me aches to console her. The rational part of my brain acknowledges Gethin's sensible handling of a distasteful encounter. It's true. Lisa's betrayed the trust of a vulnerable woman suffering from dementia. It would be immoral not to inform her employers. I wish life were black and white and not this distressing murky grey. I wish I had the courage to face up to this kind of unpleasantness instead of hiding from it.

Gethin seems as unsettled as I am by the experience and says he's going out for a run. He returns an hour later and he's obviously overdone it. Sweat is dripping from his flushed face onto a T-shirt that clings to him and appears several shades darker than it was first thing.

When I approach him, he holds up his hands to ward me off.

'Better keep your distance, Gwen. I'm none too fragrant. Stupid to go running at this time of day when the weather's as hot as this.' He crosses to the sink, turns on the cold tap and lets it run over his head, turning his face repeatedly to drink straight from the falling water.

I grab a towel and hold it out to him when he's finished.

'You're a star, my little sister.'

'You're an idiot, my big brother.'

He grins. 'Guilty as charged.' He chucks the towel back to me. 'I'd better get out of these stinking clothes.'

'Have a shower. Or there's plenty of hot water and you could have a long, lazy bath. You can have one of those bath bombs that made such an impact on you the other night.' I smile innocently.

He wrinkles his nose in disgust. 'If I weren't such a gentleman, I'd make you pay for that remark.'

'No, you wouldn't.'

'Think not?' He walks towards me, fingers on both hands wriggling manically. 'Want to be tickled?'

I shriek and he chases me round the kitchen, both of us giggling as we did when we were children.

'What's going on in there?'

Granny's voice cuts through the merriment. I make our pax sign and head for the sitting room to make peace with her, too.

~~~

The three of us sit out on the patio later under the shade of a large umbrella. Granny's hungry after her ignored breakfast and so we have a simple snack of sandwiches accompanied by cherry tomatoes and strips of the cheese that she likes. It's consumed in a companionable silence broken occasionally by Granny's requests for pepper or mustard, or her complaints about the freshness of the bread and the blandness of the tomatoes.

I'm startled by the ring of the doorbell. Gethin must sense my anxiety.

'I'll get that.'

Before he can push himself away from the table, I'm on my feet.

'No. You finish your food. It'll be the postman.'

I flash a warm smile at him and hope he doesn't see through to the pathetic creature hiding behind it.

At the door, I pull my shoulders back and adopt what I assume to be an aura of competence and self-confidence. In keeping with this new persona, I swing the door open, ready to face trouble head-on. What I do face is Joyce, Granny's friend.

'Joyce! Oh, this is a wonderful surprise! We didn't expect you back for a week or so yet.'

The deeply etched lines on her face crease into one of her affectionate smiles and I step back to usher her into the house.

'Lovely to be back, Gwen. Don't get me wrong, it was a blessing to be there to welcome my great-grandson home, and everyone made such a fuss of me, but it's a comfort to be back in my own territory.' Her rubber-tipped stick takes her weight as she negotiates the step. 'It's like taking off a corset and being able to let it all hang out again.'
~~~

She used to be taller than me, but age has shrunk her skeleton, twisting it so that now we're on a level. The scent of talcum powder and sun-warmed apples linger after she's dropped a kiss on my cheek.

I love this woman.

'How's Edith?'

'Fine.'

'No, I mean how is she really?'

We face each other in the hallway.

'She's about the same, Joyce. Good days and bad. I don't think there has been any significant change since you've been gone.'

'Good. I'm glad to hear it.' She reaches out a hand to touch my cheek. 'So why are you looking so done-in, my pet?'

I pull back and her eyes narrow. 'You can't pull the wool over my eyes, Gwen, so tell the truth and shame the devil.'

'It's nothing, Joyce. A misunderstanding that's caused a bit of nastiness online. That's all.'

She isn't going to be easily derailed, but I have a distraction up my sleeve. 'I forgot! Come through, come through! We have a visitor.'

I lead the way, walking at a pace that is a compromise between my normal one and the slow one that irritates her as patronising. Gethin turns at our approach and is instantly on his feet.

'Joyce! How delightful to see you.'

She totters, a little breathless now, towards the chair he's pulling out for her next to Granny. 'Thank you, Gethin. Didn't expect to see you here. Thought that fancy company you work for couldn't spare you.'

He chuckles and gives her a quick peck on the cheek. 'Can I get you something to drink? Tea?'

'Tea would be most welcome, thank you.'

Granny becomes aware of the disturbance and swivels round to see what's going on. I watch the confusion in her eyes.

'Joyce?'

'Hello, Edith. How have you been?'

The confusion is still there. She recognises Joyce, but I suspect her sudden appearance has thrown her and she has no idea if her friend's been there all the time or not. Joyce must have come to the same conclusion and grips Granny's hand. 'I've just got back this very minute, Edith. I've been away visiting the family in Norfolk. I'm a great-grandmother now and so you'd better treat me with some respect.'

The transformation in Granny's face is magical. The dour expression melts away, a genuine smile softens her features and I catch a glimpse of the pretty woman she once was. Regret squeezes my heart at the part I've played in creating the bitter lines around her mouth.

Joyce sends us away, saying that the two of them will be fine and to take advantage of the situation to do whatever we want. Gethin and I are heading for the kitchen when something drops through the letterbox onto the floor. It's a piece of folded paper towel and as I unwrap it, a pair of earrings fall into my palm. They're the stolen drop pearl ones The paper towel has 'dont tell Im begging you' scrawled across it in a green felt pen that has bled into the fibres like fungus. I'm unaccountably hurt by the association of these precious items with today's upset. Gethin puts an arm across my shoulders and steers me through to the kitchen.

We're sitting opposite each other sipping ice-cold apple juice when Gethin makes a restless movement that I know from old means that he wants to say something but isn't sure how to frame it.

'Go on,' I say. 'Out with it.'

'Am I really that transparent?'

'Yeah. Sometimes.'

'Well,' he runs a finger through the condensation on his glass, 'it's just that all the unpleasantness this morning has got me worried.' He doesn't take his eye off his drink.

'And?'

'And,' he stares at me with troubled eyes, 'I've remembered that Gran keeps her jewellery in boxes hidden around the place. What if other pieces have gone, too?'

I reach across and clasp his hand. 'Stop worrying, Geth. There's almost nothing left.'

'What!' He pushes back from the table, making the drinks clatter on its surface.

'Calm down. I don't mean nothing left in the sense of disappeared or stolen. Once we knew that there was a dementia developing, her solicitor convinced her to stow her valuables in some safe deposit boxes. All she kept were a few things that she calls her trinkets. Her Fabergé set is hidden above her wardrobe along with some sentimental stuff but most of the really valuable stuff is in the bank vaults.'

'Thank God for that!' His relief is obvious. 'I thought for an awful moment that they'd been stolen too, or that she'd been swindled or things had become so difficult she'd had to flog them.'

'Nope. All that was sorted over a year ago.'

'Well, that's a relief.' He takes a long swig from his glass. 'Is it still Jennings, Crabbe and Hunter?'

'It is. They've been remarkably good with her. They even sorted out a trust fund to cover her enhanced care costs and the upkeep of this place. Everything is paid for automatically and there's plenty invested in that to keep her comfortable for as long as it takes.'

'What if there's an emergency?'

'I go to JCH in my capacity as trustee, explain the situation, and they sort it. Not that there's been anything except for an issue a few months ago with the washing machine.'

'Okay. So that's Granny sorted. What about you? How are you coping, financially?'

'Well, living here my board and lodgings are taken care of, so to speak, and I have my salary at the school for anything else.'

'Is it enough?'

I'm so stunned by the question I can't form an immediate answer.

'Look, Gwen, I doubt you're being paid more than the legal minimum wage.'

'But, as I explained, that's really just pin money. Everything else is taken care of.'

He gives a short, sharp bark of laughter. 'Pin money? Come off it, Gwen. Granny and the house are well taken care of. But what about you? Your clothes are, quite frankly, shabby and you had to catch a bus when you needed to get to Cranston the other day.'

'I've got a car.

'Ah, yes, your car. Where is it?'

I feel miserable, as if I've been found wanting.

'It's at the garage.'

'That's my point. It's *still* at the garage. If my car was covered in graffiti, I'd have it back within twenty-four hours; forty-eight, tops. Or I'd have a replacement. Where's yours? You can't afford to pay for its prompt return.'

'Rob's doing it as a favour.'

He slams a hand down on the table with a suddenness that makes me flinch.

'If I weren't tied up in this feud with Zoe, I'd buy you a new one. I should have stepped in years ago.'

'I don't want you to buy me anything, Geth. Or to "step in". You're always bailing me out and it has to stop.'

'Have you any idea how frustrating, how frankly bloody *irritating* it is, when you adopt that self-effacing mantle of yours.'

I stare at him, horrified by this unexpected attack.

He sighs and runs a hand over his face. When he next speaks, he's regained his composure. 'I'm sorry, Gwennie. Really, I'm truly sorry. It just makes me mad that you feel like you always have to atone for the past. You were five. It's time to let it go.'

'I can't.'

I take my glass over to the sink and pour away the contents. I need to be busy. I have to do something to distract me from that aching hollow inside.

I'm aware of him standing behind me. He gives my shoulder a squeeze.

'I shouldn't have spoken to you like that. Forgive me?'

'There's nothing *to* forgive, Geth.'

'There is, but I don't want to make things worse so I'll shut up. I *am* sorry, Gwen.'

His mobile phone on the table rings. He ignores it.

'Hadn't you better get that?'

'It'll just be nonsense from the office. I'll phone them back in a minute.' He turns me round to face him. 'Look, I need to get on with some work, but why don't you go for a walk? I think it'd do you good to get away from here for a little while.

Gran has Joyce and if there are any problems I'll come and track you down.'

I put the empty glass on the draining board. 'Thanks. That sounds like a wonderful idea. Sure you won't come, too?'

'I'd love to, but work awaits and I'd better face up to it.'

~~~

It takes less than ten minutes to change into a T-shirt and shorts, slap on some sunscreen and top it all off with my battered sunhat. I can't remember the last time I was completely free to simply do what I fancied without considering anyone else.

The air hums with heat, but the trees provide a gentle, dappled shade that helps to counter it. I realise that I'm walking like I always do, with a brisk sense of purpose, and so I make a determined effort to rein myself in and slow to an unaccustomed saunter. It feels abnormal and wholly natural at one and the same time. Most of the houses here are screened by shrubs and fences, but each driveway offers a peek into the private grounds of our fellow villagers. They're all immaculate, even those carefully designed as informal cottage gardens. I used to find gardening a chore, but now I do it almost compulsively. I don't know if it's because I love the process itself or if it's because it provides a break from the claustrophobia of being trapped in the house with Granny.

A rambling rose, escaping the confines of its own plot, trails over a fence and the scent is exquisite. It's nothing like those you buy in supermarkets with their perfect, identical shapes. This is the real thing – irregular in form, but all the better for that, and with a heady perfume that no house freshener can come close to.

With each step my shoulders seem to loosen and my breathing eases. There's a sense of contentment that I refuse to chase away by analysing it. I've drawn level with the spot where we tried to play Pooh sticks yesterday and I'm rooting around in the gutter for a bit of twiggy wood to chuck in, when I hear it. It's the sound of rustling vegetation and the crackling of undergrowth.
~~~

Instantly I draw back and look up and down the road. Nothing. The sound continues. It's coming from Stinky Ditch. The hairs rise on the back of my neck as I search for an escape route. Could I outrun Mark Johnson or Ian Weston? The irrational panic is taking hold when a new sound comes to me. It's a dog whining and it's accompanied by the splashing of water.

I lean over and my pent-up breath leaves me in a sigh of relief.

'Atticus! What are you doing?'

The whining increases and I can see his struggling hindquarters that move in conjunction with the discarded shopping trolley. He's trapped again.

'Okay, Atticus. I'm coming.'

The whining is interchanged with excited yelps as I make my way down the side of the bridge, skittering on the dried mud and stopping where I can get a better view of his predicament.

He appears to have trapped his collar in the grid of the trolley and no amount of cajoling makes any difference. I'll have to free him myself. He's only about six feet away, but it's six feet of bramble and nettles. I should have worn jeans, a long-sleeved top and my gardening gauntlets.

His predicament impels me forward and after an initial attempt to tread down the vicious greenery, I give way to its superior vigour and simply wade through, murmuring words of encouragement in between my own yelps of pain.

'What have you done, boy? Let's see.' A long, pink tongue laps at my fingers as I try to work out how to free him. The disc from his collar has threaded itself through the twisted metal and there's not enough leeway to free it.

'Okay, Atticus. We'll take this off you and see what we can do once you're free.' I unbuckle the collar and Atticus expresses his gratitude by flinging himself at my crouched position, knocking me backwards into the sluggish water as it trickles past a fresh cluster of nettles. In an instant my previously untouched face is tingling and smarting.

Now that the collar's off him, there's enough give to manoeuvre the name tag free and I re-fasten it around his neck. I get to my feet and Atticus stands obediently to heel, waiting with an air of expectation for the next step. There's nothing for it but to brave the thorns and stings once more but I manage to grab a handful of dock leaves and when we're up on the bridge I rub them hard into the nettled bumps on my arms, legs and face.

'Come on, we'd better get you back to your master.'

I'm praying that Atticus won't see Bramble on the other side of the road and end up flattened by a passing car. However, he lollops along beside me, tongue hanging out of the side of his mouth, and he looks every inch the faithful, obedient hound.

When I approach Ben's drive, I notice that the gate hasn't been fastened by the metal clip at its top and there's an Atticus-sized gap at its side. After he's safely on the right side of it, I follow behind him, closing the gate firmly. I make my way to the front door, Atticus bounding around in wild circles. As soon as Ben appears, the daft mutt squirms at his feet in delight and I can't hide my grin at his antics.

Ben is wearing chinos, an open-necked shirt and a puzzled expression.

'Gwen? Is everything all right?'

'Yes. Everything's fine. I went for a walk and came across Atticus in Stinky Ditch.'

'Stinky Ditch?'

'It's that trickle of water under the hump in the road near the village sign.'

'How did Atticus end up in…Stinky Ditch?' He's smiling now.

'Your gate was open.'

'That'll be the postman. The scrawny one just slams it and leaves. I'd better have a word with him.' He stops and the puzzled look is back. 'What on earth have you been doing? You're *green*.'

A swift glance reveals the streaks on my arms and legs caused by the dock leaf juice.

'Blame your loveable dog. He got his name tag caught in an abandoned trolley and I had to trawl through some nettles to get to him. This entrancing colour is a by-product of nature's cure.'

He takes my hand to get a better look at my arm. The breath catches in my throat and I'm transfixed as his gaze switches to my face. His expression is unreadable; a combination of concern and something more intense. I come to my senses and snatch my hand away.

'Gwen, that must sting dreadfully.' His voice is low and resonates somewhere deep inside me. 'You're covered in nettle rash and scratched all over as well.'

I squirm with embarrassment.

'It's nothing. Just a few brambles that were added into the equation.'

He runs a finger over one of the deepest scratches, smearing the beads of blood. A shudder ripples through me and I take a step back.

'Really, Ben, it's nothing.'

He doesn't say anything but I can tell from that tic in his cheek that he's struggling to find the words. The air is charged and I'm caught between an irrational urge to draw closer to him or to make a run for it. Stupid! I'm already up to my stinging neck in trouble and I don't need another complication in my life. I give Atticus a rub behind the ears and turn away, throwing a casual 'see you' over my shoulder.

I'm almost at the gate when he catches up with me.

'Gwen, let me thank you properly for your trouble…and pain.' His eyes are sparkling now, teasing, and I feel a growing response in mine.

'A simple medal will do, Ben. 'For Valour' would probably cover it. Maybe a small ceremony at Buckingham Palace. Nothing fancy.'

'I was thinking more prosaically, I'm afraid. How about a picnic tomorrow?'

'A picnic?'

'Yes. You know the sort of thing. I bring along a rug, a hamper full of delicious food and something chilled to drink. You provide the delightful company.'

I'm silent. I've told myself to keep clear of this man. But I can't remember going on a picnic. It sounds quirky and fun. He's waiting for a response. I make my decision.

'I'd love that, Ben. As long as there's real lemonade. There has to be real lemonade or there's no deal.'

'Real lemonade it is, then.' There's an easing of the tension between us and I feel happiness bubbling up.

He fusses Atticus as he adds, 'How about midday?'

The fizzing almost bursts on the surface when a sobering thought beats it back down again.

'Oh, I can't. Gethin's going into town to see an old friend and I can't leave Granny.'

'Right. I see.' Atticus leans against his leg and looks up at him with adoration in his eyes. 'Well then, let's take Granny on a picnic.'

I stare at him whilst my brain spins through the ramifications of taking Granny out of her comfort zone. She might love it. I think she *would* love it.

'Do you mean that?'

'I do. I'd consider it an honour if you and your grandmother would accompany me on a picnic tomorrow. And I promise to include lemonade.'

'Done!' We shake on it and that bubbling is back.

He adds, 'We could go down to the beach.'

'No!' The word drops like a stone between us. It sits there, ugly and brutal as I work on another response. 'The beach is difficult with a wheelchair and there's no shade. We could go to the Bishop's Palace in Lamphey.' I try to tamp down the wheedling note. 'It's a beautiful old ruin with places to shelter from the sun and the area is walled and safe for dogs. Atticus would love it.'

There's still a hint of puzzlement in his eyes and I wonder if I've spoilt the moment, but he nods and says, 'That sounds like a great idea. Lamphey it is. Is fourish okay for you? It means we're not out in the midday heat.'

I didn't realise that I'd been holding my breath and I set it free. 'That'll be perfect. I'll go and break the news to Granny.'

'Good. Is there anything in particular that I need to bring for her?'

'Can you rustle up a thermos of strong, sweet tea?'

'I can.'

'Then all will be well if there's tea, sandwiches with the crusts removed and something sickly sweet to finish off with.'

'Done.'

I'm positively bouncing back home on my wet and grubby trainers when a movement catches my eye. Someone is striding away down the road, head bent, mustard yellow cap flickering in the light filtering through the trees. I jog up our path, to the safety of the house.

~~~

I tell Gethin about the picnic plans and he behaves as only a big brother can.

'Oooh! Do I detect the stirrings of romance?'

'Don't be daft. We're taking Granny for a break.'

'If you say so, Gwennie. If you say so.' He clutches his hands to his heart and flutters his eyelashes.

I punch him on the shoulder and then we're laughing like idiots.

Later, I go into the garden and breathe in the scent of the jasmine near the patio doors. There's something strange about the clematis growing along the yew hedge between us and the field. As I approach it, I can see that the petals are dropping and the leaves are twisted and brown. It's dying. Someone has cut the stems of the plant just above ground level

If I hadn't moved the dead foliage with my foot I'd never have noticed the grubby paper bearing the fading image of a weeping eye.
~~~

Chapter 17

I'm determined not to let any unpleasantness spoil my day and so I don't mention the vandalised clematis to Gethin and I've shoved the scuffed bit of paper into the back of the drawer where I keep my old-fashioned, cotton nighties. Cat's always teasing me about them. She wears vest tops and shorts in bed and can't understand why anyone would choose to wear something that covers them from head to toe. Perhaps there's something about being enfolded in the familiar fabric that makes me feel safe, protected – even loved, perhaps.

There's the sound of a key in the front door and Becky walks in. She gives a cheery smile but there are dark bruises of fatigue under her eyes.

'Morning, Becky. You don't look like you've slept well.'

'You know how it is.' She gives a shrug. 'Anyway, with Lisa gone, I've been put on a morning and afternoon rota and so I won't have to keep switching my body clock with night stints.'

'How's your sister?'

Her lips briefly compress into a tight line. 'She's finding things hard at the moment but we're all crossing our fingers for a good outcome.'

'I'm sorry.'

'Don't be.' The response is gruff. I suspect she's trying hard to keep her emotions in check. 'I'd better get on.'

After Becky's left, I explain to Granny about the picnic. She vacillates between delight, suspicion and confusion. This could be a delightful patch of colour in her humdrum life or a terrifying, inexplicable void of distress. Worried about how she'll behave, I roam the house looking for things to take with us to please or amuse her if I sense a tantrum rising.

When Ben rings the bell, I'm jittery with nerves. His eyes narrow.

'Is everything all right? Your grandmother's not been taken ill?'

I'm struggling to respond when another thought strikes him.

'There hasn't been another incident?' His voice is low and urgent.'

'No! No, everything's fine.'

'You're strung out like a fiddle. What's happened?'

'Nothing, Ben. Honestly. It's just that I'm not sure how Granny will cope today. The only time she goes out now is with the group that organise respite trips and Joyce goes with her and…' I tail off, unable to keep my concern buried.

'It'll be fine, Gwen. If your grandmother's unsettled, we'll simply move on to somewhere more familiar.'

I look down at my feet. I'm terrified that he's going to suggest the beach again. There's a pause and then he speaks to my bowed head.

'How's this then? If she's forgotten about the trip to Lamphey, or doesn't want to go, we have the picnic here instead, in your garden.'

His reasonable calm brings me perilously close to tears. I clear my throat before raising my gaze to his and responding.

'That's a great idea.' I give him a smile that he's quick to return. 'Let's go and see what she says.'

Granny's watching a programme about antiques as we cross the room to her. She looks startled when she notices Ben but she clicks the remote to turn off the set and turns to look at him.

'I know you.' It sounds like a challenge.

'Yes, Mrs Meredith. We met a couple of days ago. I'm Ben Pascoe from across the road.'

We both wait as she processes this information, her eyes inwardly focused as she struggles to make sense of the situation. Then she snaps to attention, a triumphant gleam in her eye.

'Of course. You took me to the surgery in your nice car. How lovely to see you again.' She's reverted to grand dame mode and holds her hand out to Ben. Without any hesitation he takes it and drops a kiss onto her fingertips. Granny's almost purring with pleasure when he straightens up again. She stuns me by adding, 'You're going to take me out for a picnic.'

'That's right, Mrs Meredith.'

'Edith,' she says, flapping her hand coquettishly, 'I told you to call me Edith.'

He breaks into a warm smile that has us both grinning like besotted teenagers.

'Shall we go then, Edith?'

'Lead on…' She hesitates.

'It's Ben, Edith. It would make me happy if you'd just call me Ben.'

'Ben.' It's as if she's trying out the unfamiliar name. Then she sits to attention, points towards the door, and calls out, 'Lead on, Macduff!'

I catch Ben's delighted response and my cheeks feel stretched tight with pleasure.

With Granny safely ensconced in the front passenger seat, we set off. We turn left out of the village and Granny pipes up.

'Where did you say we're going?'

'The Bishop's Palace, Edith'

'Lovely. It's a while since I was last there.'

Ben looks at me in the driving mirror. 'So, what should I know about this place?'

I open my mouth to reply but Granny beats me to it.

'Oh, it dates back to medieval times. Of course, it's just a ruin now. Bishops then were like royalty. We're not talking vows of poverty, here. They liked their earthly pleasures.' She gives a coarse chuckle.

My mouth is still open, this time in amazement.

'So, this really was a palace.'

'Yes, Ned, it was. Grand buildings and lots of staff to look after not only them but the guests, the animals and gardens. There were four fish ponds, I believe, plus a deer park that would have provided venison to supplement their diets.' She breaks off. 'Look, a squirrel.'

She's pointing at a sign that's almost obscured by ivy but I can't make out any creatures on it. She settles back against the car seat and I see her contented smile in the wing mirror. Less than five minutes later we arrive in Lamphey.

~~~
~~~

Ben turns down the lane towards the Bishop's Palace. There's a couple of walkers with dogs but no other cars and he's able to park directly opposite the entrance. Within minutes, Granny's back in her wheelchair, Ben has a large rucksack on his back, Atticus is at his heels and we're within the enclosure. The grass is neatly trimmed and there's no difficulty pushing the wheels across its surface.

Sizeable remains of the old buildings stand in varying stages of disrepair. There's a small internal gatehouse that's largely intact and the two big halls are till there, but as hollow skeletons having long lost their roofs. The rest of the buildings are now mainly reduced to a few grey walls patched in ochre, green and silver lichens. The effect is strangely tranquil. One of these walls is throwing a large patch of shade. I head for it. 'Right. I think that spot will do wonderfully.'

Once there, I watch as Granny takes in her surroundings. Her expression looks a little wistful. I bob down next to her.

'Are you all right, Granny?'

I'm completely unprepared for what she does next. She rests the palm of her hand against my cheek and says, 'This hasn't changed at all, Gwen. I used to come here with your grandfather. He called it our own little bit of heaven.'

My eyes are prickling and I squeeze them shut to try and hold back the tears; I can feel my mouth distort with the effort.

'Are you crying? Don't be silly, girl. You always were such a strange, sensitive little thing.'

She takes her hand away but I know I'll feel its treasured presence for a long time afterwards.

Atticus is let off the lead and is clearly delighted with his new-found freedom. He races around from one bit of stone to another, only pausing to inhale the diverse scents along the way. He races across towards Granny carrying a stick he's found somewhere. She draws back in her chair and I step forward to reassure her just as Atticus drops the stick in her lap. Ben is running towards us, alarm clear on his face. Then her hand comes out and rubs behind the dog's ears and he drops his chin onto her knee, staring up at her with his big, doting eyes.

'What a good girl,' she croons. 'Good dog.'

Ben and I exchange relieved glances

'Lovely Flossie. Who's a good girl, Flossie?'

~~~

I remember Flossie. One morning I came downstairs and Granny was cradling Flossie in her arms. She was sobbing and I was shocked. Granny wasn't someone who showed her emotions. Joyce was there, too, with her arm around shoulders that shook with grief.

'That's it, Edith. Let it out.'

I'd been playing with Flossie the day before. She'd been running around with me like she normally did. This limp creature in her arms bore no relationship to the dog I knew. Her eyes were shut but there was blood on her face. Granny's hands had blood on them, too. I couldn't tear my eyes away from the horror but they travelled further along Flossie's body and I gasped. Her tail was gone.

'What are you doing here? Get out!' The words were distorted with tears but the anger was clear.

'Go on. Get out!'

I still couldn't move.

'Go away!' The pitch rose to something resembling a scream. 'Do as you're told! This is your fault.'

'Edith!'

'It's true.'

I ran. I kept on running until I reached our den in the garden. When Gethin found me, I was shuddering so badly I couldn't speak. He simply gathered me into his arms and rocked me, making soothing noises until I fell asleep. When I woke up, he was still holding me but his cheeks were wet with tears that he couldn't hold back.

'It's going to be all right, Gwen. It's going to be all right.' It was like a mantra. But it wasn't all right. It never could be.

~~~

The memory sends a shudder through me but I ignore Ben's silent query and put on my cheeriest voice.

'Let's get the food out, shall we?'

‘Food?’ Granny’s antenna has tuned in on one of her favourite topics. ‘That sounds marvellous. Have you brought anything sweet?’

‘Ben’s prepared our picnic. I’ve no idea what he’s brought. It’s a mystery and an adventure, isn’t it?’

‘I’m not sure if I like mysteries.’ Her brow wrinkles as Ben kneels down next to her and unzips his backpack.

‘I hope there’s something here that you’ll like, Edith. If not, you must give me some suggestions for next time.’

He clicks his fingers at Atticus who behaves like the perfectly-behaved hound that he isn’t and goes and sits patiently behind his master.

‘I’m sure everything will be impeccable, er…Ted. Yes. This is going to be splendid.’

Ben produces several packages from a rucksack that seems to have the capacity of Mary Poppins’ carpetbag.

‘Now what have we here?’ He opens a foil parcel that contains piles of neat sandwiches, cut into triangles and with crusts removed. ‘What would you like to start with, Edith? We have smoked salmon, cucumber, or cheese and pickle.’

The choice overwhelms her and he repeats the options, pointing to each stack in turn.’

‘Salmon would be nice, I think.’

‘Good choice, Edith.’

‘Thank you, Ted. Are there any bones?’

‘No. I checked very carefully.’

He places two of the dainty morsels on a small plate and passes it to her. She has a tentative bite, chews noisily for a few seconds and then announces that it’s delicious.

Granny samples the full range on offer, eating with gusto and rhapsodising over the ‘perfect’ sweet tea poured from a thermos. He’s remembered the lemonade and there are mini sausages, strips of ham rolled around soft cheese, and finger-sized slices of tortilla. He’s also remembered to bring seasonings and mustard. There’s even a bowl of sliced strawberries with optional clotted cream, and tiny raspberry cupcakes to finish. The event is more successful than I could have imagined. I chuckle when Atticus makes happy sounds of contentment as Ben sneaks leftovers in his direction.

Granny, full to bursting, falls asleep grasping half a cupcake. I crouch down to remove the pieces and Ben offers me a hand to help me to my feet. Once upright, he doesn't let go but tugs me across towards the nearby gatehouse, Atticus bouncing along beside us.

We stop in the shadow of the old building where we have a clear view across the grass towards my sleeping grandmother. She looks small and peaceful, nothing like the stubborn and wilful monster of the last few years.

'Penny for them.'

'Sorry?'

'Penny for your thoughts. You look enchanted by something.'

'Enchanted?' He's studying my face intently, a gentle smile softening his features. I don't know what to say. Then I'm giggling.

'What is it? What have I said?'

'Well, I could offer some beautiful responses to do with the setting and its beauty, but the true answer is that I'm amazed at your taming of my dragon of a grandmother.'

He looks in her direction.

'Dragon? Never. Edith is as sweet a lady as I've ever come across.'

I'm about to make a cutting response when it occurs to me that I'm being horribly disloyal to the woman who gave up so much for me. I'm also appalled at how heartless I must sound and, in that split second, I see myself through Ben's eyes and the little that he knows of me. The recollected shock of his reaction to my home-wrecking reputation chills me. My happiness evaporates. I snatch my hand from his and stride back towards our picnic area. I've only covered a short distance before he catches up with me, turning me around so that we face each other.

'What just happened then?'

'Nothing. We ought to be heading home now.'

'No. One minute everything was fine and then you shut down. Froze me out.' He's studying me closely and I wriggle in his grip. Instantly, I'm released. 'I'm sorry, Gwen. Whatever it is I've done, I'm sorry.'

'No.' I'm shocked. 'No, you've not done anything. It's me.'

'I need you to explain. Please.'

'It's me. You don't know me. You think I'm a homewrecker. I'm the sort of heartless bitch who pokes fun at the woman who gave up everything to raise me and Gethin.' The words are tumbling over themselves. I can't help it. Nor can I help but see the horrified expression on Ben's face.

I turn again and head for Granny and safety but he appears in front of me, solid and determined. I feel the anger and hurt draining from me and I want to curl up on the closely-cropped grass.

'Gwen, tell me what's going on. What's all this about? You know I don't believe that social media nonsense about you and the head teacher.'

'You *did*.' I sound sulky, resentful. There's a silence broken by the discordant mocking of a pair of magpies.

When Ben speaks again, he's calm but insistent. 'I'm sorry, Gwen. I'm truly, genuinely sorry for my crass behaviour. I don't normally go round making snap judgements.' His next words are quietly spoken; a shared confidence. 'I've been really worried about my little sister. She's going through a hard time at the moment. She has two young children who mean the world to her but her husband's moved in with another woman. The court has said that he has equal rights to see them. This means that she loses them for that time. They're her life and she isn't coping well at the moment.' He runs his hand round the back of his neck. 'It all seems so unfair.' He reaches for my hand, 'And then I took out that unfairness on you.' He laces his fingers with mine. 'Forgive me?'

His grip is firm, reassuring. I told myself I wouldn't give him another chance to hurt me but there's something so reassuring and attractive about him that my barriers tumble.

'I'm sorry, Ben. I'm the idiot here. And I'm sorry for spoiling the mood.'

'Then let's recapture it. Come on, let's simply enjoy the moment.'

Atticus chooses that moment to push between us and drop his stick at our feet.

I reach down to pick it up but Ben's hand clasps my wrist.

‘Leave that. I’ve brought something better.’ He slips the rucksack off his shoulders, opens a flat pocket at the front and removes a red Frisbee ‘Ever played piggy-in-the-middle with a dog?’

For the next fifteen minutes we skim the disc at each other while Atticus races from one side to the other trying to intercept it. It doesn’t seem to bother him that he rarely gets a chance to catch it; the chase is all. It’s a delightful rough and tumble experience. The sun is still high in the sky when Ben scrapes the back of his hand against the rough wall. He’s only skimmed the knuckles but I insist that we’ve had enough and add, between gulps of air, that it’ll give me a chance to replenish my deprived lungs.

We retreat to the shade thrown by one of the tall ruins and sit with our backs against the stone wall, Atticus lying between us, panting. Granny is in sight and still sleeping and everything seems uncomplicated and calm. If only things could stay like this.

‘We must do this again, Gwen. Soon.’

My happiness is complete. I haven’t scared him off and he wants to see me again. Please don’t let anything spoil this moment.

‘I’d like that,’ I say lightly.

‘Good.’

He unzips a side pocket on his rucksack. ‘I almost forgot!’ He removes something on a broad, striped ribbon. I know this isn’t the palace you specified, but I think it’s the perfect one to present you with this.’

He places the ribbon around my neck. There’s a plastic, gold-coloured medal hanging from it with the words For Valour inscribed in black ink. I hold it closer to get a better look. There’s also a simple sketch of Atticus and I realise that the perimeter is a ring of twined nettles and brambles with a dock leaf at the base. I’m so touched I can’t speak. As I smile at him his image blurs.

‘I didn’t mean to make you cry, Gwen.’

‘I’m not,’ I mumble. ‘I’m just so happy!’

He scoops a stray tear onto one of his fingers. Then he pulls me to him in a comforting hug that I don't want to end. It's Atticus rising between us, that breaks us apart.

Ben laughs. 'Atticus, I could throttle you sometimes!' Atticus promptly rolls onto his back and wriggles as he waits for a vigorous tummy rub.

The next minutes pass beyond time as we chat about bland nonsenses in our pasts. He tells me about his decision to go into architecture, I mention working as a multi-lingual advisor for Krantz Industries before coming back to help Granny.

'*Multi* lingual. Sounds impressive.'

'Not really. Most of it involved translations of pretty boring technical stuff.'

'So, how many languages do you speak?'

'Three or four.'

'Three or four! Fluently?'

'Not wholly. But when you're translating stuff, you can always look up things in dictionaries or online.'

'I think I detect some unnecessary modesty here.' His awe makes me chuckle.

'Honestly, I'm competent but if Atticus could read a dictionary, he could do it.'

'Was it all written stuff or did you have to explain things in person as well?'

'Well, sometimes, yes. A delegation would come across and I'd meet and greet and then interpret for both sides.'

'I knew you were hiding your light under a bushel. Don't try to tell me you did that with a dictionary in one hand.'

I'm ridiculously pleased with his response.

He goes still for a moment before saying, 'You gave up a job you obviously loved to care for your grandmother. I got you so very wrong didn't I?'

I feel a connection flare between us as he covers my hand with his.

'Gwen, I'd really like to get to know you better.'

Atticus leaps to his feet and looks across towards the wheelchair where Granny is waking up. It's enough to break the spell and, the connection lost, I head back to her before she's properly awake.

‘It’s time for us to go home now, Granny. All right?’ Her eyes are still unfocused. ‘It’s been a lovely picnic here with Ben but we need to get back.’

She says nothing but there’s no panic or displeasure there.

When Ben drops us off he tells Granny that he hopes we can have another outing very soon.

The blood sings in my veins. Not even the harsh cackle of a low flying magpie takes the edge off my delight.

Chapter 18

I wake from a deep and dreamless sleep, still cocooned in the happiness from yesterday's outing. I pull back the curtains and look out at the clear, bright day and open the window to inhale the scents from the garden. This is how life is meant to be. I stretch like a contented cat. The sound of Gethin humming tunelessly to himself in the kitchen makes me smile. I select some fresh clothes and head to the bathroom for a quick shower, before following the coffee aroma to its source.

'Morning, Geth. Did you have a good time with Andy?'

'I certainly did. Andy brought along Huw and Dave as well and we had a great time mulling over the old days.'

'It must be at least a couple of years since you saw any of that crew.'

'Yeah, but you know how it is with old friends. What matters is the shared past. Time is irrelevant.'

His phone rings. 'Sorry, Gwen. I'd better deal with this.' He goes out into the garden and I rescue the coffee pot and pour us both a cup.

The front door opens and Becky appears. She's not due for another hour yet.

'You're very early. There's coffee in the pot, if you'd like some.'

'That'd be marvellous, Gwen.' She lowers her heavy bag to the floor and joins me at the table. 'My first call of the day was cancelled just as I arrived at the house. I thought I'd come here as I was in the area anyway.'

'Come on, sit down. I've not really seen much of you recently.'

'Snap! That's another reason why I came straight here.' She draws closer to the window. 'I see your brother's still here.'

'Yes. He's been given permission to work from home for a while.'

'I'm glad. You could do with some emotional support with all this going on.'

I put the mugs on the table.

'How's your sister doing?

'There's not much change but everyone's rallying round which makes it easier.' She leans forward. 'But enough of that. What about you? How are *you* coping now?'

'I'm getting over it. You were right. It's just one of those storms in a teacup and I need to focus on the things that matter to me.'

'That's what I like to hear.'

Gethin comes into the kitchen.

'Apologies, Gwen. There's a problem at work. Oh, hi.' He comes up short and then flashes a broad grin. 'It's Becky, isn't it?'

His phone rings again and he glances down at the screen, mutters something under his breath and apologises before heading back out to the garden.

I'm just about to make a comment when my mobile rings on the counter.

'Sorry. I'd better see who that is.'

There's no one there. I say hello a few times and then hang up.

She pulls a face. 'Not the most talkative type.'

I laugh. 'I expect it was someone who realised they'd dialled the wrong number and I picked up just as they disconnected.'

Whoever Gethin's talking to is making him angry. I can't hear the words, he's obviously trying to keep the volume down, but the tone carries and the body language is unmistakable. I'm glad I'm not in a testosterone-fuelled job.

It's while I'm pouring the coffee that my phone rings again.

At first, I think it's another wrong number but then I become aware of faint noises in the background.

'Cat? Is that you?'

Becky's looking amused and mouths, 'Not again!' Cat is known for her accidental key pushes.

'Sorry, Becky. You'd better cover your ears. I'm about to whistle in the hope she hears it.'

I've taken a lungful of air but before I release it in a high-pitched warning, a rasping sound comes through clearly, followed by the unmistakable sound of someone breathing. Then a distorted voice says, 'I'm watching you.'

My fingers fumble as I press the red button to disconnect the call. I put the phone down on the table.

'Gwen?'

I'm unable to look away from the display.

'Gwen? What's going on?'

'It's a crank call.'

'What? Heavy breathing?'

'Says he's watching me.'

'Who?'

I look at her then. 'I don't know. They've made the voice hoarse and unrecognisable.'

It rings again. It's a number I don't recognise. I should have registered that fact earlier.

I let it ring.

We stand together for what seems like ages and when it finally stops, it's Becky who pulls me out of my stupor.

'Well, do you remember the number?'

'No. I didn't think.' I push away from the table and take a notepad and pen out of a drawer on the Welsh dresser.

'Did you get any impression at all who it might be?'

I shake my head. 'Nope. It might not even be a man.'

It rings again and we both jump, releasing the tension in nervous laughter. I copy down the number. Then I sigh and pick the phone up.

'What are you doing?'

'I don't know if this is the same number. I might be blocking someone from Cranston Care.'

I answer, holding the phone a few inches from my head as if it's contagious. Someone's saying something and so I put it to my ear.

'…wear that nightdress for me.'

This time, I turn the phone off and drop it onto the table as if it's contagious.

'Gwen?'

I shudder. 'He said something about my nightdress.'

Becky spends a few seconds staring blankly into the distance and then snaps to attention.

'Okay, you just need to block the creep—'

'How did he get my mobile number?'

Gethin comes into the kitchen.

'Sorry about that, ladies. Business calls and all that.' He crosses to the hob and lifts the empty coffee pot.

'Yours is in the mug next to it.'

He must have picked up on the atmosphere because he's straight across.

'What is it?'

I shake my head.

'She's had some anonymous calls. Someone saying they're watching her.'

His surprise is obvious, as is the anger that sweeps in to replace it.

'Who is it? Tell me. This harassment has gone on long enough. I'll drag him down to the police station myself.'

He picks up my mobile phone. 'He rang you on this?'

'Yes.'

'But how did they get your number?'

Becky's frown deepens. 'That's what I just said.'

We both watch, mute, as Gethin switches the phone on again and starts to scroll through the log.

'Do you recognise the number?'

He holds the phone in front of me and we all jump when it starts to ring. Gethin clicks the button to answer it. Becky and I watch as he clicks through to something and the blood drains from his face.

I hold my hand out but he ignores it and so I lunge for it and wrest it from his hands.

Becky looks over my shoulder as I scan the screen. It's a photo. It's of me and it must have been taken this morning as I looked out of the window. My arms are stretching up, and my mouth is slightly open and curved in a contented smile. Although I'm fully covered by my nightdress, the knowledge that there's only that thin layer of material between me and whoever's watching, makes me feel unclean. Underneath the picture, in bold text, are the words "You know what I want".

I sink clumsily onto one of the chairs. This can't be happening.

It's Becky who recovers first.

'Right. You need to block this number immediately. Then you need a new sim card and only inform those who need to know, what your new number is.'

I stare at her. She raps my arm.

'Do it! Block it now!' I'm still uselessly looking at the screen when she adds, 'This was taken this morning?' Becky gives me a little shake when I don't respond.

'Yes. Oh God! Someone was out there watching me!' I swallow hard to control the rising nausea. 'If I hadn't had a shower first thing I'd have undressed in my room and…and…'

I can't go on.

'Good.' Becky's brisk and business like. 'Things could have been worse. *Much*, worse.'

Gethin gets to his feet and comes across. He looks older.

'Someone's out to get you, Gwen.' His voice lowers to a growl. 'Whoever it is, they'll have to come through *me* first.'

His anger pushes some sense into my numb brain.

'It's all right, Geth. Becky's right. It could have been a lot worse and no real harm's been done. Wobble over.' I sound as bright as I can. 'I walked into this one, but thanks to you and Becky, the damage barely registers. I'll get a new sim card and that'll stop the creep in his sorry little tracks.'

'Do you mean that?'

'Of course.' I hold in a shudder at the memory of someone waiting in the field to take that picture of me.

Then he groans.

'Geth?'

'Those calls I've had this morning, they're from work. They need me in the office for a couple of days. I'll phone them back and tell them I can't make it.'

'You'll do no such thing! I'll be fine here.'

'No. I can't leave you like this.'

'Don't be ridiculous. I'll just be super cautious until you return.'

'No answering the door?'

'Not unless it's someone I know and trust and it's daylight.'

'No working in the garden on your own.'

'Agreed.'

'Oh, I don't know, Gwen.' He sighs. 'I don't like to leave you.'

‘I know. But this is just a bit of spite. The only thing hurt is my reputation – and that’s already been well and truly mangled.’

He’s not convinced.

Becky makes a suggestion. ‘What if I were to come across and stay here overnight until you come back? Would that reassure you?’

‘You’d do that?’ he asks.

‘For a friend as good as Gwen? In a heartbeat. We can watch TV and eat ice cream.’

‘Now you’re talking! As long as I get to choose the ice cream.’

Becky grins. ‘Of course – just as long as it’s salted caramel.’

Gethin reluctantly agrees to Becky’s plan. He sorts me out with a new phone card and I phone my contacts to let them know about the change. Cat is, if anything, angrier than I am and insists on coming round.

Cat and Gethin do their best to distract me and I pretend to laugh along with them and adopt what I hope is a carefree attitude. I’m aware of their exchanged glances but we all go along with the charade and by the time Cat has to return to Nansi, I’m feeling brittle enough to snap. I crave the chance to simply crawl away. Gethin is so solicitous I have a ridiculous urge to scream and rage. I’ve been down this road before and I know where it can end. So, unfortunately, does Gethin and I have to muster up all my resources to convince him that I’m fine and that I’ll be safe here with Becky.

~~~

When Becky appears with her overnight bag, I breathe a little more easily. Her calming presence should convince Gethin to catch the late train from here that connects with the last one for London. I need him to go. I can’t bear his concern. It eats away at my confidence and undermines me.
~~~

Gethin picks up his bag. I hold my breath, willing him on, but he puts it down again and pulls me in for one of his fierce hugs.

'I can stay, Gwen. Work will somehow manage without me.'

I push him away. 'Go!' It comes across more aggressively than I intended. I lower my voice and fix a smile on my face. 'Go on. I've Becky here, Ben across the road and Cat and Dean are a phone call away.'

'Sure?'

'Certain.' He pastes on a smile of his own. 'Okay then. I'll be back in two days. Call me whenever you want.'

'Of course.'

'Promise?'

'Promise.'

He grabs his bag.

'And I don't want you standing in the doorway waving me off.'

'Gethin, your train leaves in fifteen minutes. Go!'

He goes.

There's a silence that hangs over the house following his departure and I shiver.

'Cold?'

'No. Just glad that Gethin's agreed to go.'

'He cares. It must be wonderful to have someone looking out for you like that.' She sounds wistful. 'Have you eaten anything?'

'Cat forced a cheese omelette down me before she left.'

'Would you like me to rustle up something else?'

'No. Honestly, I'm fine.'

Becky's mouth twitches in a sardonic smile. 'Really?'

I consider bluffing it out but there's a welcome difference between her gentle query and Gethin's overbearing concern and I give a wry smile.

'I know it's silly but I can't shrug off the unpleasantness – the knowing that someone's watching me.'

'Well, I'd be more worried if it *didn't* bother you.'

I grin. 'I suppose when you put it like that…'

She pulls out the chair opposite me and sits down, her hands clasped loosely on the table.

'Do you know who's doing it?'

I shake my head. 'Sadly, there's a queue of people with a grievance against me.'

'Impressive!'

I laugh at that. It's a relief to view it a bit more objectively.

'So, who's first in the queue?'

'My amorous head is a likely candidate, but DI Preece thought that the damage to the car was more likely to be the work of his wife.'

'The two of them'll get over it. From what I've heard, Ian Weston's philandering reputation is common knowledge. I can't fathom why Lynette stays with him.'

'What do you know about her?'

'Not a great deal. By all accounts she has a serious drink problem but I suppose that's one way to numb the pain of infidelity.'

'Poor soul.'

'That poor soul may have defaced your car, remember.'

'I'd rather discover that she'd done it as an act of misplaced retribution than someone else had done it cold-bloodedly to destroy me.'

'So, who else is in your queue?'

'The father of two of the children at the school.

'Why him?'

A sigh escapes me. 'It's complicated.'

'I can cope with complicated if you speak really slowly and use simple words.'

I laugh at that. 'You know full well that I'm not belittling your intelligence.'

'Go on then.'

'There was an incident. The last day of term.'

'Yes?'

'He has a little daughter and she's frightened of him.'

'How do you know that?'

'Because she told me on our way to the swimming gala. She asked if she could come and live here.'

Becky's hands clench. 'Poor wee dab.'

‘I know. She was hiding under a bench when he came to pick her up at the end of the day. He dragged her out and pulled her along the playground floor all the way to his van.’

Becky gasps and the tendons in her hands stand out; white strings of anger.

‘What happened next?’

‘I told the school and he was reported to social services. They took the little girl and her brother away later that afternoon.’

‘And you think this man is doing this to punish you?’

‘Perhaps.’ I shrug. ‘He wants me to retract my statement so that he gets the kids back.’

‘I thought he didn’t care about the little girl?’

‘I’m not sure that he does. But he does care about his son.’

Becky sits back in her chair and closes her eyes. Then she gives a quick shake of her head.

‘So, what’s the situation with the children now?’

‘They’re in care.’

Becky takes a deep breath that she lets slowly releases. She’s looking distressed. ‘Is that the best place for them? Won’t the little girl find that worse? What about their mother?’

‘She’s a recovering drug addict.’ I register the spasm that crosses Becky’s face. ‘I think she loves the children but she’s a lost, timid woman who’s no match for her bully of a husband.’

‘Still, wouldn’t it be better for the girl to be in her own home with a mother who loves her than in the alien and noisy environment of a care home?’

‘I’ve asked myself that same question, but—’

Before I can finish the sentence there’s a pounding on the door. Instinctively, I leap to my feet and move further back from the noise, my eyes never leaving the door.

Becky starts to move towards it.

‘Gethin said not to open the door after dark.’

She looks as if she’s going to argue with me when a familiar voice calls out, ‘Gwen, it’s Ben. Open the door!’

Becky flings the door open.

His face is ghostly in the moonlight and Atticus is crouched at his feet.

'Gwen, it's Gethin.' He puts out a hand as if to hold me back, 'He's okay, but someone's given him a bit of a beating.'

Chapter 19

I don't know how long it takes for his words to register, but then I'm in front of him.

'Where is he? Tell me, Ben. Where's Gethin?'

He steadies me with a hand under my elbow. 'It's all right, Gwen. I called for an ambulance. They're with him now.'

'Ambulance? Oh God!'

His grip tightens. 'I don't think he's seriously hurt. He'd been knocked unconscious but he opened his eyes when I reached him.'

I tug my arm from his hand, push past him and run out of the door. The strobing lights direct me to the huddle down the road and I'm praying desperate, broken prayers as I race towards it.

Gethin's being moved to a stretcher and I reach him as they lift it. I call his name and the paramedics halt, letting me see him.

There's blood trickling down from a cut on his temple. His eyes are closed and I'm suddenly terrified, frozen in fear. I can't talk. I can't move.

Not again, the words whisper in my head. Please, not again. I can't bear it. Please.

Ben takes my arm, 'It probably looks worse than it is.' The words are meant to reassure me. I've heard words like that before. I don't trust them.

'Are you a relative?'

I look at her and try to speak. Ben puts an arm around my shoulders and says, 'This is his sister, Gwen Meredith.'

Gethin opens his eyes, stares at me and then turns his head away.'

I recoil as if he's slapped me.

'Okay, Gwen,' the paramedic continues, 'we're taking him to the hospital to be checked over but we haven't found anything that gives us cause for concern. Do you want to come in the ambulance with him?'

I nod and accept a hand up into the back of the vehicle as he's strapped securely in place.

~~~

The journey to the hospital passes in a blur. In my peripheral vision, blue flashes reflect off buildings and signs as we pass them. The accompanying bursts of the siren, to move traffic out of the way, crush my heart. It's a struggle to breathe as I watch the monitor that converts Gethin into a digital array of lines and blips. He moves and says something against the mask on his face, trying to remove it with one of his hands, and I'm struggling to undo my seat belt when I'm told firmly that I'm to stay in my place and let them get on with their job.

At the hospital, they wheel him in and I'm told that an outbreak of MRSA means that I have to stay behind in the waiting area where the bright light hurts my eyes. I'm staring at the circulating pixelated messages on the sign above the reception door when someone sits in the seat next to me and takes my hand. It's Ben.

'How are you doing?' His voice is low.

I've no idea how to reply. The familiar panic and surreal nightmare is so close that I'm frightened for me as well as him. What will I do if Gethin leaves me, too? I turn to Ben.

'What happened? Who did this to him?' I'm insistent. *'Tell* me, Ben.'

His eyes are steady and his fingers interlace with mine.

'I don't know, Gwen. I was out with Atticus. He began to growl and tugged me over to that old rhododendron by the footpath.'

His hand is crushing mine but it's a welcome force, anchoring me in reality.

'I tried to move on but Atticus stood his ground and then I heard a groan.'

My free hand covers my mouth, holding in the terror that's threatening to spill out in unpredictable waves. Ben pulls the other hand to his chest and holds it there.

'I shone my torch into the darkness and found Gethin curled up. He wasn't moving but his eyes were open. That's when I called the ambulance.' He gives a grim smile. 'Once I knew he was in safe hands, I came to tell you. Forgive me.'

'Forgive you?'
~~~

'The whole way over here I've been furious with myself for breaking the news to you so clumsily.'

I look at him properly for the first time and can see the distress in his face. It brings me back from the self-centred brink.

'You've been wonderful, Ben –kind and supportive. I'm sorry to come across as a bit...' I pause, '…a bit unhinged.'

'You're allowed to be upset, Gwen. But I do honestly think Gethin's going to be fine.'

'Did he say anything?'

'No. He recognised me though, I'm sure of it.'

One thing's been disturbing me and I twist in my seat to face him full on.

'Why did he turn away from me?' There's a despicable wobble to my voice. He knows what I'm talking about.

'I think he didn't want you to see him like that. I think he was protecting you.'

Oh God. The nightmare continues. It rolls around, sometimes in the barely perceptible distance, but my fear never fully leaves me.

'Seriously, Gwen. You don't need to put yourself through this worry. Wait until we hear from the medical staff and we can take it from there.'

His calm and composure break through and the impending hysteria is pushed back and contained. He said "we" He said, "*we* can take it from here". I'm not alone.

'Thanks.' I muster a smile. 'I apologise for the overreaction.'

'No need.' He bends his head closer to mine. 'Let's face it, you've had a rough week. You're allowed to be a bit upset.'

'A bit, perhaps. Not full-blown end-of-the-world hysterical.'

'Hardly that.'

I attempt a smile but he doesn't know that my words are unpleasantly close to the truth. However, he's right. There's no point getting worked up about an unknown quantity and I surreptitiously do my breathing exercises to bring me back on an even keel. I'm pleased with my success until I'm shocked upright.

'Gwen?'

'Granny. I forgot all about Granny!'

'She's fine. Becky's staying with her. Everything's under control.' I sag back again, relieved but feeling foolish. I repeat to myself that everything's under control and I simply need to keep things together.

He brings down the hand that's been holding mine to his chest, but he doesn't let go of it and we sit together quietly, waiting for news.

A couple of uniformed policemen approach the reception and are buzzed through. I wonder if they're here for Gethin. They're back again less than five minutes later and leave.

Ten minutes pass and guilt gets the better of me.

'This has been really great of you, Ben, but I'm fine now and you can leave me here.'

'I'm happy to stay.'

'But it's late and you've already done more than enough for us.'

'I'll stay.'

I don't make any more objections and simply whisper, 'Thanks.'

Time moves on in the jerky hands of the clock on the wall. We sit mainly in silence but it's not unpleasant and I feel in charge of my emotions again. After an hour or so Ben offers to get a drink from the vending machine. My hand feels cold when he lets go of it but the hot coffee's welcome. When we've finished, he disposes of our empty cups in one of the bins and I'm reassured when he returns to his seat and takes my hand again.

His next words come as a jolt to the system.

'Back at the ambulance, you said "not again". Have you been through something like this before?'

I stare at him. I can't dredge up a response.

He fills the gap. 'I just wanted you to know that I'm here for you. I'd like to help.'

I feel overwhelmed.

It's a massive relief when he says, 'It's all right if you don't want to tell me. I'm not prying. Just remember that I'm here if you need a friend.' He stretches and looks at his watch and continues, his expression now light and casual. 'My younger brother was always getting into scrapes. We spent ages in our local hospital waiting for X-rays, stitches or plaster casts. Once, his small super-bounce ball slipped through the stairgate that was there to keep Callie safe. He wriggled his arm in beyond the elbow to retrieve it and was stuck fast. Imagine the scene in the waiting room: our mother holding Callie, me looking embarrassed, and then Simon wearing a stair-gate.'

The image makes me chuckle and we revert to companionable small talk and silence.

After three hours, I can feel the anxiety creeping back in. 'What ifs' start to crowd my mind and I have an urge to pace that I'm struggling to control. Every time someone comes through the door into the waiting room a surge of fear strikes me.

But then the next person through the door is Gethin. I run to meet him but he puts up a hand to hold me off.

'No hugs, Gwen. I'm too sore.' He softens the words with a brief grin. White butterfly strips grip his temple and the opposite cheekbone, and his lower lip is puffed up and scabbed.

The nurse beside him holds out a paper bag.

'Here's your medication, Mr Meredith. Take things easy for a couple of days and contact us if you have any new symptoms.'

He thanks her and we head for the exit in silence. Gethin walks slowly and his movements are stiff and careful. I want to help.

'Is there anything I can do, Geth?'

'No.' He says it without looking at me.

I feel the pressure of Ben's hand briefly on my back and I look up at him. He smiles and then moves ahead of us.

'I'll get the car and bring it round to the front. There's no rush, so take your time, Gethin.' Then he lopes through the foyer and out of the automatic doors. I walk slowly, keeping pace in the same way as I do when accompanying Joyce. I can sense the frustration in his every painful step.

When we leave the building, it's dark and there's that unnatural quiet that descends when most of the population are asleep. Ben's car is already waiting and he nips round to the front passenger side and holds the door for Gethin who winces as he twists into the seat and I stand helplessly and watch. I feel useless and redundant.

Ben opens the rear passenger door and I muster a smile and slip inside the car. As I'm doing up my seatbelt, I notice movement in the shadows by the entrance. It's someone wearing a hoodie. I crane round in my seat as we pull away and he moves into the light. It's just a stranger; his lit cigarette glowing faintly.

The return trip is a silent one. I'm bone weary and no longer able to control the thoughts that chaotically run through my brain. Broken snippets of the events of the last few days flit in and out quite randomly and there's no making sense of it all. For the first time in years, I'm afraid that I'm losing control and am about to fall into a dark, bottomless pit. Part of me wants to scream to release some of the tension; part of me knows that *that* very scream may trigger the fall.

Ben brings the car to a smooth halt at the top of our drive and in moments he's holding the car door wide for Gethin who makes small grunts of protest as he pulls himself upright and onto his feet.

I clamber out, tear my gaze away from his measured progress and rush to the keysafe to remove the key and unlock the door. I'm standing inside holding it open when I look over the road. Is that someone on the other side watching us? I look at Ben and Geth but they're facing into the house and when I turn back again there's no one there.

I close the front door and, as I do so, Becky appears wearing pyjamas and a robe. She looks at Gethin and smiles. 'They let you out then.'

'Yep.'

'Looks like you could do with some beauty sleep.' She stands to one side, and her comment eases the tension. But there's something I need to know.

'Is this my fault? Is it another warning?'

'For heaven's sake, Gwen! Why must it always be about you?' Gethin snaps.

Ben slips an arm across my shoulders. 'She's just worried about you.'

Geth sags a little and turns back towards me. 'I'm sorry, Gwen. I didn't mean that. You know I didn't. I'm just sore and angry and the pain killers are wearing off.' He gasps and holds a hand to his side. 'Things look worse than they are. I've been thoroughly checked over and have nothing worse than a bit of concussion and a couple of bruised ribs. Once they settle down, I'll be fine.' He manages a crooked smile. 'Get some sleep; you look worse than I do.'

Becky steps in front of him. 'Need a hand?'

'Nah. I'm fine, thanks.'

'What about your medication?'

Gethin hands her the bag. 'I don't know what's in there, but if you could winkle out something to deaden the senses, that'd be welcome.'

'I'll give you a head start. Off you go.'

The mood has lightened again and I want to keep it that way. Becky peers at me, 'I think I agree with your brother. You do look in worse shape than he does.'

'Thanks. Your charm and tact could do with a polish.'

'That, my friend, will cost you extra. Want a hot drink?'

'No. I'm fine.'

'Then I strongly recommend bed before you keel over.' She takes a couple of steps and stops to add, 'Sleep for as long as you need. I'm here until eleven.' She opens the paper bag and checks the contents as she moves towards the kitchen. Once she's running the tap, Ben turns me round to face him. 'You do look done-in. You should listen to Becky and get some sleep.'

Now that it's all over I feel drained and can only manage a nod in response.

'And don't worry about Gethin. He's going to be fine.'

Another nod.

'And don't forget that I'm here for you whenever you need me. Okay?'

A double nod and I manage a genuine smile.

Then he pushes me towards the corridor. 'Go on. Bed.'

Chapter 20

'Mummy! Daddy! Get it back! Quick!'

I hear my mother, happy and reassuring. 'It'll come back in a minute. Build a sandcastle while you're waiting.'

'No! It's going away!'

'Don't be silly, pumpkin. If it doesn't come back, I'll buy you a new one.'

'It's my Kermit ball. ***Please****, Mummy,* ***please****!'*

'I promise you can choose any ball you want if this one doesn't come back.'

'No! I want this ball. I don't want any of the others.' I hear my childish voice plead and whine.

'Okay. No need to cry. I'll get it for you.' She rises gracefully from the towel beside our father, brushing grains of sand off her slender body.

But I know what's to come and the scream builds in the pit of my stomach as she splashes into the deeper water and starts her slow, powerful crawl towards the ball, Kermit's bobbing face mocking her approach.

Something's wrong.

I'm wrenched back to reality. My clock tells me it's 8.30. I've overslept. After last night's hysteria, I'm determined to regain my self-control and keep things in perspective. My breathing eases and the trembling stops.

I can't bring myself to open the bedroom curtains after yesterday's intrusion and so I grab some clean clothes and lock myself in the bathroom to change away from possible prying eyes.

Becky's standing by the patio doors. Her face is picked out by the sun and it shocks me to see the distress there. She gives a start when she notices me and adopts a convincing smile.

'Hiya, Gwen. How are you feeling now?'

'I'm fine, thanks. But how are you? You looked upset. Is it your sister?'

She hesitates and then says, 'She's doing okay.' Any further enquiries are cut off when she adds, 'I had a quick check on your brother but he's sleeping peacefully. I'm guessing he'll have a sore head for a couple of days and feel a bit sorry for himself but there's no lasting damage done.'

'Thanks, Becky. You've put my mind at rest.'

'I could see how worried you were last night, but there's no point in fretting over stuff you have no control over.'

'I've been hearing that same mantra a lot recently.' I manage a rueful chuckle.

'There's usually more than a germ of truth in the old sayings. You feel things deeply and you let them get to you.'

'No more than anyone else.'

'I'd say significantly more than most people. Take that little girl you were talking about yesterday.'

'The one from school?'

'That's the one. Most people would wash their hands of a situation like that once it had been taken over by social services, but you're still thinking about her in that care home, aren't you?'

'A bit, yeah.' I'd geared myself up to be positive and cheerful to compensate for last night's wobble and this isn't helping. I head for the kettle. 'Cup of tea?'

'Of course. But don't think I'm not aware you're changing the subject.'

'And I thought I was being subtle.'

'About as subtle as your grandmother.'

'Ouch!'

She moves across and leans against the counter, studying my face. 'Come on then. Out with it. Why don't you want to talk about her?'

'I don't know. Maybe because I don't think I can do anything to help.'

'So, what's the problem? She's no longer at home with her brute of a father.'

'I know, but I can't help but think of her in the completely alien environment of a children's home with streetwise kids who she'll find intimidating.'

'You said that you think her mother—' Whatever Becky was going to say is interrupted by a bellow emanating from the direction of Granny's room.

'Wretched woman!' Becky looks mortified. 'Sorry, Gwen, that was unprofessional but she's going to wake Gethin.'

It's the last part that gets to me. Is Becky interested in my brother? The thought's a pleasant one.

We rush off together to do some damage limitation. It occurs to me as I reach Granny's room that we're going to have to come up with a strategy to hide Gethin's injuries from her.

~~~

Becky deals with Granny and insists on making me my breakfast, too. She's offered to stay the night as originally intended but as Gethin's here I tell her that there's no need. She takes me up on my offer of staying when things are on a more even keel and we can have a proper, carefree, girly night. I'll be seeing her again in a few hours, anyway, as she's down as Granny's afternoon carer.

After she's gone, I make a cup of tea and tap gently on Gethin's door. There's no response so I increase the tap to a knock. When there's still no response, I sneak open the door and approach the bed. He's asleep. His injuries are less shocking now that I know what to expect and he looks young and vulnerable. I'm wondering whether to leave again, when he moves his head and peers at me with groggy, unfocused eyes.

'Just brought you some tea.' I whisper the words and prepare to leave but he catches my arm and holds me back.

'Thanks, Gwen. How are you doing?' The words are a bit slurred.

'I think you'll find that you're the one in bed with concussion.'

'You're the one who had all the worry.'

'I'm fine.'

'Honestly?'

'Honestly.' I realise that I mean it. I've come through the worst and the sky hasn't fallen in. 'Is there anything you need?'
~~~

'You could pry a couple of those painkillers from the packet and hand them to me. I'll wash them down with the tea and then go back to sleep.'

'Good idea.'

I leave, quietly shutting the door behind me, and it feels like I've reached a turning point. I haven't gone to pieces and just that knowledge is enough to make me feel I can cope with whatever life chooses to throw at me.

Granny's watching the television and I grab my gardening gloves, open the patio doors and start to work on the garden.

I begin with the clematis. The dying tendrils are easily removed and join the shrivelled lilies on the compost heap. I'd been so upset by that mean piece of vandalism but I have things under control today. The dead plants are a shame but I can replace them in time with new ones. Things go on.

The next task is weeding around the pond. I start on the far side and my robin is a permanent feature. He bobs around hoping for food and several times he puts himself between the trowel and the weeds and I pull back just in time. He flits from the ground to my hand, flicking his tail and I find myself chuckling out loud at his antics. The power of positive thinking.

~~~

Granny seems settled and is clearly having one of her better days. I make her lunch and we eat together in comparative harmony. When she's finished, I expect her to want to return to the television. She looks towards the open patio doors. 'Are you going to be working in the garden again?'

'Well, I'd started weeding the edge of the pond and I'd quite like to finish it.'

'I was thinking it might be nice to sit outside for a while.'

'Okay. I'll get your wide-brimmed hat and the sunscreen.'

She tuts but it's lacking in venom and ten minutes later she's in her wheelchair and asking to be put closer to the pond where she can watch me weeding. I expect the usual barrage of criticism but she sits quietly in the main and makes genial comments about the flowers, the fish and the hot summer
~~~

we've been having. I'm enjoying the cessation in hostilities when the robin appears and perches on my gloved hand.

'Gwen! Look! I think it's a robin.'

'It is. Isn't it incredible?'

Without thinking, I bring my hand nearer to show her but the robin stays put, unfazed, and Granny's delight makes me grin.'

'So tame!' She chuckles. 'And you know just how handsome you are.' She stiffens and sits upright, causing the robin to utter a tic of warning as it flies down to the ground. 'Where's Gethin? Shouldn't Gethin be here?'

'He's had to go back to work in London for a few days.' As soon as the lie slips out, I know I'm committed to it. She grunts in response and then falls into silence.

I continue to prise the weeds from the baked ground and become aware of the slow, steady breathing that tells me she's drifted off into sleep.

I manage another half hour and am arching my back to ease the stiff muscles when there's a squeal of tyres followed by a thud and the sound of breaking glass. I drop the trowel and rush through the side gate to the front. Trevor Richards often leaves his car on the road outside their house and it's clear that someone's crashed into the rear of it. The driver is young, embarrassed and fully apologetic. As far as I can see, there's not a great deal of damage and the glass is from one of the sidelights. Trevor's body language goes from spiky rage to laid back resignation and I'm relieved that at least nobody's been hurt. I offer to get a dustpan and sweep up the glass whilst they exchange insurance company details.

As I head back to the house, I see Ben walking down our drive. He raises his hand in a wave and I wait for him to catch up.

'Hi, Gwen. How's things? I just knocked at the door but there was no answer and I didn't want to risk waking your brother.'

'Gethin's out for the count but I think he's going to be fine.'

'And how are you?'

I think back to my near-hysterical behaviour yesterday and feel a flush of embarrassment. 'I'm fine, Ben. I've had a lovely afternoon in the garden with Granny and I'm just getting something to sweep up the glass from the prang up the road.'

'I thought I'd heard something.' He squints as he looks towards the incident where the only sign of anything amiss is the two men crouching down intently examining paintwork.

'It's minor stuff; no one hurt, no major damage done.' I'm pleased that I have everything under control and hope this will compensate for my helplessness last night. 'Would you like some tea? A cold drink?'

'A cold drink sounds perfect.' He follows me as I make my way up to the open garden gate and I'm almost through it when I hear her.

'Help! Help me!' The words are faint but the fear resonates. I run the last few yards and what I see stops me in my tracks.

The wheelchair's on its side, the upper wheel is turning slowly in the still air. Ben sidesteps me and it's then that I notice Granny. She's face down by the fishpond, hauling herself backwards, her feet scrabbling against the ground. Her hair is dripping wet. Ben is hunkered down on the ground next to her as I try to make sense of what I'm seeing. Then I'm there, too.

'Granny! Oh my God, what's happened?'

'Get me up! Get me up!'

Ben responds in that calm, soothing way of his. 'We need to check that you're not hurt—'

'Just get me up from here!' It's close to a scream and she's doing her best to push herself upright.

We each take an arm and begin to raise her, slowly and carefully, and when she's standing between us, she points at the upturned chair.

'Who did that?'

'Shhh, Granny. It's okay. We've got you.'

'I don't understand.' She's looking around with wild eyes, the pupils are large, reflecting her shock. 'What's going on?'

I turn to Ben. 'Have you got her?' He nods and I let go and pull the wheelchair upright. I reach down to release the brake. It's not on.

'Gwen?'

Ben's still supporting her. I manoeuvre the chair next to him, holding it steady as he lowers her carefully into it.

'You're safe now, Granny. We've got you. Let's get you out of the sun.'

She's silent, slouched to one side, eyes sweeping from left to right. I notice that she's holding on to Ben's hand and he's bending down, crooning soft sounds into her ear.

Once inside, I grab a towel and blot some of the water from her hair and face. Her top is drenched, too. She must have tipped headfirst into the pond and it's a miracle she was able to pull herself to safety. She sits quietly, docile, for a few minutes and then she grabs my wrist and speaks in a hoarse voice.

'Someone tried to kill me!'

'What do you mean?' I kneel next to her.

'I was in my chair.' She peers at me. 'You weren't there.' A coughing fit prevents her saying anything more and Ben gently releases her hand and goes to get a glass of water. She has a few sips and then pushes it away, splashes disappearing into the sodden fabric of her top.

'I was watching the fish. Someone crept up on me.' She cranes her neck, swivelling round in the chair, eyes startled. 'He tipped up my chair. I fell into the pond.' She swallows noisily. 'He tried to kill me.' She's clutching my arm in a painful grip.

'Who tried to kill you, Granny?'

'*He* did.'

'*Who*?'

'How do I know!'

'Did you see his face?'

'If I saw his face I'd know, wouldn't I!' She mutters, 'Stupid girl.'

I find her irritation reassuring.

Ben tips his head to one side, motioning me to join him.

'We need to call a doctor to check her over.'

'Of course. I'm not thinking clearly. I'll do that now.'

He holds me back. 'Shouldn't we call the police as well?'

'I don't know, Ben.' My mouth's dry but I force the words out. 'The brake wasn't on. Perhaps this is my fault.'

He's silent for an agonising second or two. Then he gives a brief smile.

'Have you ever left it off before?'

'No.'

'Then it's unlikely, isn't it? Wouldn't that be something that you do automatically now; a reflex action?'

'I don't know. I guess so.'

'And what about this stuff about someone pushing her in?'

'When we first found her, she was surprised to see the wheelchair on its side. I'm not sure this isn't her paranoia asserting itself.'

'But what if it isn't? What if someone did try to push her into the pond?'

I shiver, the glad certainties of the morning slipping away. 'Wouldn't we have noticed if someone had been here?'

'What if we didn't?'

'But that would mean that someone was watching us, waiting for an opportunity…' My voice dies away. Then I whisper, 'But someone *has* been watching us, haven't they?'

He nods, his concerned eyes scanning my face. I wonder if he's waiting for me to have a meltdown and the thought is enough to make me snap out of the weakness I feel and view the situation as dispassionately as I can.

'I'll phone for a doctor to come over and I'll let the local police know about the situation.' I can't stop the shudder that rocks me as I contemplate another bout with someone like Stafford.

We both spin round when we hear someone at the door. It's Becky.

'Have I missed something?'

I have an inexplicable desire to laugh.

Chapter 21

Becky takes over, composed and professional, and a doctor from the surgery is with us within half-an-hour. He pronounces Granny to be fine apart from some minor grazes to her hands and chin and relative normality is resumed.

I go repeatedly over the scene, unable to form any conclusions. Could Granny have stood on her own and knocked the wheelchair over? I think it's unlikely but it's not impossible.

Once I've considered all the innocent scenarios, I have to contemplate the ones I'd rather not confront. Could this have been a deliberate attack? If so, to what end? Would Ian Weston really sink so low as to take out his anger with me on an innocent, elderly woman? I can't answer that question. I remember his gestures about watching me and slitting my throat.

What about Mark Johnson? He's made it clear that he expects me to change my story about the playground incident so that he can get his son returned to him. I think back to his assault on me in the alley in Cranston and shudder. Could this attack be a warning shot? Does he think that I might be persuaded to retract my statement to protect those dear to me? Would he realise that therein lies my Achilles heel? In fact, could either of them be responsible for the attack on Gethin last night? I simply don't know.

Something occurs to me and I go out to the pond. I scout around the small perimeter and then kneel on the edge, peering into the depths. I'm slowly moving my hand through the pond weed when Ben appears beside me.

'I've brought you some chilled apple juice.' He stops. 'What are you doing?'

'I'm just looking for something.' I try to make the words nonchalant and throwaway but Ben persists. 'Did your grandmother lose something when she fell? Can I help you look for it?'

'No.' I stand and brush bits of grit off my knees. 'It's nothing.'

There's an audible intake of breath and then he says, 'So what is this 'nothing' you were looking for?'

'Really, it's nothing.' I look at him, and that quiet determination of his makes me uncomfortable. The longer I hold off telling him, the bigger an issue I'm making of it.

'It's just me being silly.'

'Gwen, none of the things that have happened recently strike me as silly.'

'Seriously. It's nothing of value.'

'Yes?'

'Oh, all right!' I sound petulant. 'I just wondered if there was one of those eyes here.'

'Those eyes? Oh, *those* eyes. The warnings.'

'I just thought, if I found one here then I'd know it hadn't been an accident.'

'I see.' To his credit, he doesn't make any disparaging comments. He puts the glass of juice down on the paving slabs, goes around to the opposite side of the pond and starts to slowly sift through the weed the way I'd been doing.

We're both lost in the search when a shadow falls over me. It's Gethin.

'Good God! What on earth are the two of you up to?' I hold out a hand and he helps me to my feet, wincing as he takes some of my weight. 'Becky's just filled me in on Gran's tumble.'

'She hasn't seen you, has she?' I'm panicking. 'I told her you'd gone back to work for a few days.'

'Calm down, Gwen.' He holds a hand against his ribs and takes a controlled breath. 'I'm not completely clueless. From what I've heard from Becky, Gran has had trauma enough for the day.' He looks down at the pond. 'What *are* you doing?'

Ben doesn't prevaricate. 'We're looking to see if someone's left one of those eye drawings. It might prove that this was a malicious act and not an accident.'

'Ah, I see.' Gethin squints against the sun, then he closes his eyes completely. 'Could we carry this on in the shade? I think my head's about to shatter.'

Ben stands, too. 'You do look a bit green around the gills.'

Gethin attempts a smile. 'Actually, if you don't mind, I'll go back to my bed for a bit.' He takes a couple of controlled breaths as I watch him, anxious. His scabbed lip curls momentarily. 'I think it's best for all concerned if I hang onto my stomach contents.'

He leaves, his stance rigid and I want to help him but know intuitively that he wouldn't welcome it.

Ben comes round to my side of the pond.

'He'll be fine.'

His ability to tune into my thoughts is a little unnerving. 'Am I really so transparent?'

'Those big green eyes of yours give you away every time.'

I stare up at his face and we're so close, I can see flecks of amber amongst the brown of his. I'm not sure if I'm breathing. The world has reduced to Ben's eyes. Nothing else exists. I can't break away. I don't want to break away.

Then his pupils are so close, they've entered mine and all I'm aware of now is a light kiss on my mouth. My eyes close and I savour the building wonder of the moment. His hands cup my face and I respond to the deepening pressure. I'm reduced to sensation.

When he pulls back I feel amazed and bereft. I open my eyes and he's smiling. I can't define the smile exactly but there's an element of delight and surprise there that I'm sure must mirror mine.

He's about to say something when the doorbell punctures the moment. I give myself a little shake and go to answer it. I'm grinning broadly.

The grin disappears. It's Stafford.

'Miss Meredith.'

'You'd better come in.' I stand to one side and he steps into the house. He scans the surroundings. I suppose it's something that he does automatically.

'What can I do for you, sergeant?'

'Two things. I need to speak with your brother and I'd like to have a friendly chat with your grandmother.'

If the chat with my grandmother will be friendly, what's the one with Gethin going to be like?

'They're both in bed.' No niceties; I've lost all social skills where this man's concerned.

'I see. I'd still like to see them. Could you show me to your brother's room?'

'Why?'

'I'd just like to verify some things with him, that's all. Nothing for you to worry about.'

I feel patronised. Ben materialises by my side. I don't acknowledge him but his very presence bolsters mine.

I'm considering waking Gethin and bringing him through to the kitchen when I realise that if I do that there's a risk of Granny seeing him and the damage to his face.

Stafford scrutinises Ben. 'Would you be Ben Pascoe, by any chance?'

'I would.'

'So, you're the one who came across Gethin Meredith last night after the attack.'

I don't know how I hadn't put the two and two together and made the obvious four. He's following up on the assault. Much as I dislike Stafford, I'm keen to see justice done for my brother.

'Let me go and see if he's awake.'

Gethin groans when I tell him about Stafford but agrees to see him in his room.

'Do you want me to help you sit up?'

'You're fussing, Gwen.'

'Sorry.'

~~~

A couple of minutes later the four of us are gathered in Gethin's room. He's propped up on three pillows and it reminds me of one of those deathbed scenes in old movies and I vacillate between an inclination to giggle …or weep.

'I understand you took a bit of a beating last night,' Stafford says, his gaze sweeping round the room.

'It was nothing.' Gethin tries to shrug it off and sits forward but the effect is spoiled by a gasp of pain.

'Doesn't look like nothing from here.' Stafford is studying him with the same intent look he gave the inside of the house.
~~~

The words of DI Preece come back to me about him having a sharp mind underneath the smooth exterior.

'Two of our constables came to the hospital to take your statement but apparently you said you couldn't remember anything and so it would be a waste of police time.'

'I did, and it is.'

'Perhaps you'd allow me to be the judge of that.' The animosity still buzzes between them and I no longer feel so confident about Stafford being here to bring Gethin's assailant to justice. 'Tell me what you remember?'

'I've already told you!' The anger must hurt because one of his hands clamps down over his ribs. 'I saw nothing. I heard nothing.'

'Were you attacked from the front or behind?'

'I don't know.'

'Well, give the question some thought. Was someone waiting for you or did they follow you?'

'I don't know.'

'It's not a difficult question. At some point, you were hit. Did you see it coming or were you hit from behind?'

'Look, I don't want to talk about this. It happened. Nothing was taken. It's over as far as I'm concerned.'

Stafford simply stares at him for several long seconds. When he speaks again, I think I detect a sneer.

'You summon me because of a child's drawing, yet an actual assault isn't worth my time. *You* might not be concerned, Mr Meredith, but what happens if the next time it's an elderly neighbour? What if it's your sister?' He leans over him. 'Don't you think you owe it to others to at least try to help us prevent this happening again?'

The fight goes out of Geth. He sags back and for the first time I appreciate how much the last few days have affected him. He's physically aged. He looks drained and I'm frightened by the defeat in his eyes. The blame I feel is almost unbearable. A hand slips over mine and I feel the reassurance of Ben's grip.

Gethin speaks, the words flat and lifeless. 'I'm sorry. I'm not being deliberately obstructive.' Then his eyes meet mine and I see guilt and pain in them. 'Gwen's been through the mill recently and I didn't want to add to her troubles.'

'You think the attack was linked to the earlier incidents?'

Gethin clearly can't bring himself to utter the words. He just nods.

'It hasn't occurred to you it was a mugging?'

'Nothing was taken. I still have my wallet and phone.'

'Perhaps the appearance of Mr Pascoe was responsible for that.'

Stafford glances across at us and I'm aware of those hawkish eyes lingering on our joined hands. 'So, let's keep an open mind, shall we, and go back through the events of last night. Tell me *everything* you remember.'

Gethin reaches for the glass of water by the bed, grimacing at the simple movement, and then he lies back and fixes his gaze on Stafford.

'I'm not hiding anything. I genuinely don't know who attacked me. They must have come at me from behind.'

'They? There was more than one?'

'I don't know! All I remember is a blow to the back of my head, the ground coming up to meet me and then being kicked in the ribs.'

'Can you describe the shoes?'

'No. I felt the blows rather than saw them. Then I must have lost consciousness for a moment. Next thing I know, Ben is bending over me.'

Stafford casts another glance over us. 'And how long have you known Mr Pascoe?'

'Just a few days. He moved into the house opposite us about ten days ago, I think.'

Stafford deliberately lingers on Ben's hand covering mine before tracking up to my face. 'And you've known this man for only ten days or so, Miss Meredith?'

'Yes.' The unspoken inference stings. I hate this man, and I try to wriggle my hand free from Ben's to put some distance between us, but he holds on. I don't know if I find that frustrating or comforting.

Stafford addresses his next comment to Ben. 'And how well do you know these two, Mr Pascoe?'

'I think that fear and danger have a way of bypassing the normal social niceties, don't you? I'm aware of Gwen's predicament and I find the attack on Gethin a disturbing development.'

He's calm and collected and Stafford simply looks at him in silence. Just at the point where I feel I have to say something, anything, to fill that silence, he speaks again.

'I agree. Very disturbing.' His eyes narrow as he scrutinises Ben's face. 'Could you run me through the events of yesterday evening as you saw them?'

'Of course.' His response is measured, unhurried and cool. 'I went out with Atticus, my dog. I can't tell you the exact time but it was getting dark. Atticus pulled me across to the rhododendron bush. I was trying to move him on when I heard a moan.' He looks across at Gethin. 'By the time I arrived he was opening his eyes and I think he recognised me. I phoned for an ambulance and as soon as it arrived, I came here to let Gwen know.'

'Did you see anyone else?'

'No one. Though I think I might have heard someone running in the distance.' He adds, before Stafford says anything, 'But I can't be sure. It was more an impression than anything definite. I can't describe it any better than that. I've nothing specific to go on. I might have invented the notion to fit the scene. I'm sorry.'

'Can you explain how you came to injure your hand?'

The question startles a gasp of shock out of me. I'm beyond astonished. 'You surely can't be suggesting that—'

'It's all right, Gwen. He has every reason to ask.' Ben is still calm, unfazed by the insinuation. 'I scraped it against a wall the day before yesterday, playing Frisbee with Gwen and my dog.'

Stafford arches one eyebrow in my direction.

'It's true! I was there. I saw it happen.' My response is the antithesis of Ben's composed one. I decide to keep my peace. The slight curl of Stafford's lip is enough to reel my emotions in.

He turns back to Gethin.

'Can you think of any reason why someone would want to hurt you?'

'Of course not. I think it's obvious that…' His voice peters off and his eyes lock with mine. He looks wretched.

‘It’s obvious that…?’ Stafford continues to probe.

Gethin tears his gaze away from me and faces his inquisitor. His next words are so quietly spoken, I find myself leaning forward to catch them.

‘I think this was to get at Gwen.’

Ben clasps my hand tightly. I don’t know why I’m so shocked by Gethin’s words. I’ve suspected it from the start, but to hear him utter them hits home. I’m grateful to have Ben beside me. Without him, I’m afraid I’d be a pathetic heap on the ground.

Stafford turns his gaze back to me but what I see there surprises me. Is that a hint of pity in his expression? Is it possible that the sneer has been replaced by the slightest softening of his stance? Or am I simply seeing what I want to see?

‘One final thing, Mr Meredith. Can you tell me the extent of your injuries?’

‘The hospital say that I’m just a bit bruised and concussed. Nothing’s broken and I’ll be fine.’

‘I’d say you were either very lucky or someone knew exactly what they were doing.’

The words disturb me.

~~~

When Stafford’s finished with Gethin, he follows us into the kitchen.

‘Right. About this other incident concerning your grandmother, can you fill me in on the details?’

I cross my arms over my chest. ‘We were together in the garden. I was weeding by the pond and she fell asleep.’ I look at his face but his features give nothing away. ‘I heard a crash on the road outside and went to see if I could help.’

‘Tell me about this crash.’

‘It was just a young lad who’d clipped the back of a car parked on the road. There was very little damage and I offered to brush up the glass—’ I realise something. ‘Oh! I didn’t get back to them.’

‘I expect they’ve coped somehow.’ My hackles rise again at the dry comment, then I continue.
~~~

'When I came back, I met Ben – Mr Pascoe – who'd just been to the front of the house to see how Gethin was doing. We both came in through the side gate and heard my grandmother calling for help.'

Stafford directs his next question at Ben. 'And how long were you with Mr Meredith?'

'There was no response at the door so I left without seeing him.'

'No response?'

'No. I didn't ring the bell in case he was asleep. When I didn't get an answer to my knock I started to leave, which is when I saw Gwen returning to the house.'

Stafford's eyes narrow in a disconcerting way. 'And you heard nothing inside the house?'

'No.'

Stafford goes to stand by the open patio doors. 'And your grandmother was out here when you returned?"

We join him and I shiver as I look towards the pond. 'Yes. Her wheelchair was on its side and she was lying on her front trying to move backwards from the water.' I know I have to add another detail. 'The brake was off.'

'Ah.' My words appear to give him some wry pleasure. 'Careless. So, what makes you think this is a police matter?'

I hesitate. This man makes me so unsure of myself. It feels as if everything I say condemns me further in his eyes. 'She was in a bit of a state and when she first saw her chair. She wanted to know what had happened to it. Then, later, she said that someone had tried to kill her.' I look down for a minute to hide the anxiety I feel. 'When we asked her what had happened, she just kept on repeating that someone had tried to kill her. Mr Pascoe said we ought to report it just in case it was true.'

'Do *you* think someone tried to kill your grandmother?'

'I honestly can't say. She has dementia and that can make her a bit paranoid sometimes.'

'I'd better have a word with her.'

'Please…' I put my hand out to touch his arm but snatch it back before I make contact. 'Please be careful with her. She won't know who you are and may not remember the incident at all. I don't want her to be upset all over again.'

'You do have a very low opinion of me, don't you?'

Fortunately, Becky walks into the room, preventing me from answering. She stops when she realises I have company.

'Oh, sorry.'

'It's all right, Becky. This is Detective Sergeant Stafford and he'd like to have a word with my grandmother about this afternoon. How is she?'

Becky gives Stafford a passing smile before turning back to me. 'She's fine physically apart from a couple of scrapes to her face, but I think the incident has knocked her back a bit. She doesn't seem to remember anything about it and so we've not discussed it.'

Stafford faces her. 'Is she awake?'

'Yes. I was just about to bring her through so she could watch some television.'

'I'd like to have a quick word with her. There's no need to tell her I'm here.'

Becky hovers, uncertain. She looks to me for confirmation and I give a brief nod of assent.

A few minutes later, Granny arrives in her wheelchair. The marks on her face are thankfully faint but she's sagging in the chair. The experience has taken it out of her.

Stafford steps forward and, before I can make any introduction, bobs down and places a hand over hers.

'It's a pleasure to meet you, Mrs Meredith. How are you doing?'

The usual acerbic inflection is absent, replaced by a clear but gentle tone. Granny is immediately flustered and looks for help. Before I can come to her aid, Stafford continues.

'This is a lovely house and garden you have here, Mrs Meredith. I can see how much love has gone into them.'

Granny looks puzzled but her wary expression has relaxed a little.

'Thank you, Mr… er…'

'It's Owen, Mrs Meredith. I was just passing and wanted to say hello.'

'Owen? Yes of course. I remember you now.'

Stafford doesn't bat an eyelid. 'It's such a lovely day. Would you like to sit in the garden with us for a little while?'

He turns to Becky. 'Perhaps you could bring us a cup of tea?'

Again, Becky looks across at me and I shrug helplessly. I have no control over the situation.

Stafford stands and suggests, in that quiet persona that he's adopted, that I push my grandmother out towards the pond. He precedes me and stands with his back to the pond watching her face.

Ben stands behind me. Perhaps he appreciates that two unfamiliar faces would be too much for her.

Stafford indicates with subtle movements of his hand that I'm to keep on pushing her towards the water and it's only when we're close to where I'd left her earlier that she stiffens.

'That'll do, Gwen.'

I sense an easing of the tension in all of us but I'm aware that her eyes are darting around and she's no longer listening. Stafford bobs down again.

'Is everything all right, Mrs Meredith?'

She doesn't even look at him. She's locked somewhere inside her head. Perhaps her tired brain is trying to make sense of things that refuse to line up in a sensible manner.

Stafford tries again. He raises a hand and gently touches her chin. He's broken through and she stares at him, confused again.

'You've scratched your face, Mrs Meredith. Does it hurt?'

She processes the words and, after a significant delay, her right hand comes up and strokes the skin around her mouth.

'Did you have a fall?' The probing continues.

'A fall? Did I have a fall?' Her voice is querulous.

Stafford still wears that concerned smile and waits. Granny looks in my direction.

'Have I had a fall? Why didn't you tell me? This isn't good enough, Gwen!'

Stafford rises and holds out his hand to her. She accepts it with an automatic social response and they shake briefly.

'It was a pleasure meeting you, Mrs Meredith. I'll leave you to your lovely garden.'

Granny smiles politely and they part company.

I follow him out to the front of the house.

'Thank you for not upsetting her.'

There's a brief hesitation before he says, 'I'd advise you to watch over her more carefully in the future.'

It feels like a curt and brutal dismissal.

Chapter 22

It's 4.30 am. I wake suddenly and am instantly alert. Has Granny called out? I rush through and open her door but nothing seems amiss. Her snoring has a settled, reassuring rhythm and I close her door and stand outside it.

Once my breathing is more under control, I go and get dressed and pad on bare feet through to the kitchen.

It's been three days since Granny's 'tumble' (as we're calling it). She was confused and bewildered the first day. There was an unusual lassitude about her, and she had difficulty standing, balancing or holding things. Most of the time she just sat in her chair, ignoring the television and showing no interest in eating.

My guilt was overwhelming and I couldn't get Stafford's last comment out of my head. Cat, Ben and Geth joined forces to convince me that it was unlikely that I'd left the brake off, and even if I had, it wouldn't have caused the chair to topple that way. They took me into the garden and experimented, taking it in turns to play out different scenarios with the wheelchair. I'm not sure how it happened, but the others resorted to more and more extreme suggestions that, in the end, had us giggling and did help to lighten the darkness I felt inside. More importantly, we couldn't replicate the outcome, which left us with the options of either Granny having done something we hadn't considered, or that someone had deliberately tipped her into the pond.

I've kept such a close eye on her since, that she's expressed her irritation at my presence. 'For heaven's sake, girl, stop fussing and flapping!'

I didn't appreciate just how relieved I'd feel to be on the receiving end of some snappy criticism.

Yesterday, she was back to her old self. I'm still keeping an eye on her, but trying to do so less intrusively. No one will harm her while I'm watching.

There's been no more maliciousness during the last couple of days. No damage. No teardrop eyes. No silent phone calls.

I walk through to the sitting room and open the curtains at the patio doors – without flinching. It's still dark and silent out there but there's a peacefulness to it.

Today feels different, calm. I feel calm–well, calmer. I pour myself a glass of milk, sit in one of the armchairs and look across to the east where a wash of light glows on the horizon, triggering a riot of birdsong.

I rest my head back and drift off to sleep.

~~~

The crash of splintering crockery wakes me. I leap to my feet and rush to the kitchen. Gethin's standing by the Welsh dresser, shards of broken china scattered in an irregular arc at his feet. My sudden appearance startles him.

'Good God, Gwen! I didn't know you were up. You almost gave me a heart attack.'

He's looking a bit better today. The swelling's gone down on his lip and the cut on his temple is largely hidden by his hair. Physically he looks better, but there's been a jitteriness to him that wasn't there before the attack. Sometimes, when I sneak a look at him, his expression is angry; sometimes he looks scared. I suppose that real life isn't like fiction. People don't shrug off acts of violence and carry on regardless. Real people are shaped, albeit temporarily perhaps, by their experiences, and a random attack must make an impact.

He groans as he bends down to pick up the pieces and I push in front of him.

'Let me do that. You make us something to drink.'

He pulls himself upright. He forces a smile that doesn't touch the stark look in his eyes. This is my confident, happy-go-lucky brother and he has me worried. He gives my shoulder a quick squeeze.

'That sounds like a fair trade to me.'

I clear up the mess and stand next to him while he busies himself with the cafetiere. He ignores me. There's something troubling him; he's chewing the undamaged part of his lip.

'Gethin?'

'Mmm?'

'Can I help?'
~~~

'No. The coffee's almost ready.'

He's wilfully misunderstanding me. I'm certain of it.

'You know what I mean, Geth. There's something you're not saying and it's worrying me.'

He places both hands on the counter and leans forwards onto them for a moment. Then he straightens and faces me.

'Work still need me back in the office for a couple of days.'

'So?'

He releases a sigh. 'So, I can't go and leave you here.'

'Of course you can!'

'Gwen, someone's been making your life a nightmare and may have tried to hurt our grandmother. I can't just walk away and leave you.'

'Don't be ridiculous! You're not well enough to go back to work yet.'

'They're pretty much insisting I go back for a meeting they've set up.'

'Tell them you've been attacked. They'll understand.'

'No way am I telling them that. I don't want them speculating about the circumstances.'

'How long would you be away?'

'Two days at most.'

'Geth, I can hold things together for two days. Perhaps Becky can stay overnight.' I search for other reassurances. 'And Ben's only over the road and I've got his number in my phone on speed dial.'

'I don't know. You've come so far and I'm worried that this is going to set you back again.'

I speak before he can throw any more excuses in my path.

'Don't be daft! I'm fine. If anything bothers me, I'll pester the delightful Stafford.'

He gives a genuine smile at that.

'If you're sure?'

'I'm certain.'

He sighs again, but this time it's obviously in relief. All right, you've convinced me. 'I'll let work know that I'll be there tomorrow.'

The phone rings a few minutes later. It's Cat.

'Hiya, Gwen. Nansi and I are on our way to town to do some shopping. Is there anything you need?'

'Apart from an unexpected windfall and global peace?'

She chuckles.

'I was thinking more along the lines of toilet roll and chocolate.'

'Nah. I'm fine, thanks. Give Nansi a big slobbery kiss from me.'

'My pleasure. We'll drop in and see you later.'

'Looking forward to it.'

~~~

While Clare is busy with Granny, I grab a moment to deadhead the roses. The scent of the lavender as I brush past it is heavenly and the day feels good. I'm reaching up to remove one of the faded blooms when a flurry of wings alerts me to the presence of the robin just before it alights on my hand. It cocks its head from side to side and I say, 'All right then. Let's see what I can dig up for you.'

I turn round and am surprised to see Gethin and Ben standing next to each other in the doorway.

'You see, Ben. She can charm the very birds from the trees.'

'She's pretty charming herself.' Ben's reply makes me grin, but I'm delighted by the compliment. There are days when all feels right with the world, and this is one of those days.

~~~

In the early afternoon, Cat turns up with a sleeping Nansi in her car seat. I usher her into the kitchen and position the door to the sitting room so that I can keep an eye on Granny while affording us some protection from the volume of the show she's watching.

When I turn back to Cat, she's positively fizzing with excitement. I offer her something to drink but she won't hear of it.

'No! No time for that. Sit down and let me tell you all the gossip! She grabs my arm and pulls me down next to her, dark eyes flashing with excitement. 'You won't believe this!'

'Go on, then. What won't I believe?'

'Guess!'

I try to think of something but she can't wait.

'It's Ian Weston!'

I shrink back in my chair. She pulls me forward again.

'Wait until you hear it, you silly goose! It's all good stuff.'

'Go on then.'

'Well, you remember Sara Hughes?'

'Sara with the voice of an angel and the vocabulary of a navvy?'

'That's the one! She married that estate agent in Narberth. Their home's fabulous. I went there once with Emma and they have an entrance hall with a chandelier. You should see the kitchen—'

'Ian?'

'Ian? Oh yes, Ian.' She brings her head closer to mine. 'Well, Sara is a friend of Izzy Fielding.'

My blank look prompts an explanation.

'Izzy Evans, as was. You know! Parents own a large farm out Broadmoor way. Married Steve Fielding.'

I'm none the wiser. She laughs and moves back a bit, studying me.

'Honestly, Gwen, your lack of local knowledge appals me!'

'I apologise. Now, where do Sara and this Izzy woman fit in?'

'Izzy just happens to be a friend of Lynette Weston.'

'And?'

'Let's just say, never has the cost of a Vanilla Spice Latte been such good value in terms of returns.'

I lean forward now, keen to hear what she's found out.

'Izzy told Sara that she and Annie were with Lynette Weston that evening when she came across the Facebook thing.'

A chill creeps down my backbone. I'm not sure if I want to hear any more of this. But Cat rushes on.

'Lynette had been drinking heavily, she has been for ages now, apparently, and she went ballistic! She wanted to come straight over here but Izzy and Annie kept pointing out the trouble she'd be in – "Head teacher's drunken wife in assault" sort of thing – and that she needed to sober up before she did anything.'

I'd like to stop listening but there's a fascination in the horror that I can't resist.

'Anyway,' Cat continues, 'Ian comes in later, she lays into him, pulling his hair and kicking and scratching him in front of the others and he beats a hasty retreat in his car.'

The words conjure up an image of the cut on his cheek. I shiver, but Cat is racing on at full throttle and doesn't notice.

'Several flagons of coffee later, and Lynette disappears at two in the morning. They think she's in the toilet but then they hear her car drive off. Izzy and Annie guessed she was coming here and quickly followed her. By the time they arrived she'd already let rip with a can of aerosol paint she must have got from her garage. They managed to stop her from lugging one of your potted bay trees at your front window, bundled her into the passenger seat of her car and Annie drove her home.'

For some reason the only thing I can think of to say is, 'Poor Lynette.'

Cat looks at me, head on one side. 'You're a strange little thing, aren't you? Most people would want her to pay for what she did to you.'

'From what I've heard, she's been suffering these infidelities of his for years.'

'Sara says the Facebook thing was the last straw as far as she was concerned.'

'Does Lynette hate me?'

'Well, yes.'

I wince.

'But she hates him more. At about three in the morning she heard him creeping in. She went out to his car looking for proof of an affair but all she found was a weedkiller spray on the front seat.' Cat makes a flourish, 'And that, m'lud, is the evidence for the prosecution.'

'So now we know.'

'We do, indeed. Sara has also told me that Lynette's kicked him out and her friends have persuaded her to check in for rehab. It's just possible you've inadvertently done the woman a good turn.'

'Thanks for that, Cat. It's a relief to know who did it. You're a good friend.'

'That's nothing! Oh boy, wait till you hear the next bit!'

'There's more?'

'Oh, yes!'

'Go on then. I'm all ears and apprehension.'

She chuckles, a full, throaty chuckle that makes me smile in response.

'Did I mention that Sara is the niece of Kitty Ellis?'

'The wife of Alun, Chairman of the governors?'

'The very same.' Cat smirks. 'You're going to love me for this next bit.'

'I love you anyway, you know that, but don't let me stop you.' Her excitement is infectious.

'So, Sara goes to see her aunt who has something top secret that she has to promise to keep to herself. You'd think Kitty would know Sara better by now, but she must have been bursting to tell someone.'

I'm suddenly afraid that I'm not going to like this; that it's something to do with my conduct. She draws closer again.

'Delyth, went to Alun, confessed that she'd borrowed £75 from school funds to get a plumber to fix her sick mother's boiler and thought that the head had known about it and agreed to it but that now he was using it to blackmail her into leaving.'

I can't control the gasp that escapes me. 'We heard him, Cat. The deputy head and I heard him threaten her.'

'Well, Alun appears to have been infuriated and welcomed the opportunity to get rid of your Mr Weston.'

'He's not *my* Mr Weston!'

'Sorry, Gwen. Figure of speech. No need to go all bristly on me.' She gives my arm a conciliatory pat. 'Alun's had complaints about Ian's bullying and there's been rumours of romantic "liaisons".'

I groan.

'Okay, yes, he's seen the Facebook photo. And it's not the image the school wants associated with their married head teacher.'

'I'm never going to escape this slur, am I?'

'But Alun's also heard about the damage to your car and the forcing you to go along to the swimming gala. According to my source, you're more sinned against than sinning.'

'It still rankles, Cat. I'm sin-*free* in this respect.' I fold my arms.

'*Listen* to me Gwen! Ian was told that a full investigation was going to be instigated into his conduct and the blackmail allegation.'

'I can't bear it, Cat! I really don't want to be dragged through all of this.'

'Shhh! Let me finish. According to Kitty, one of Ian's friends runs several academies abroad. Ian offered to resign with immediate effect if Alun agreed to give him a good reference for a job there.'

I'm reeling from all the information that she's thrown at me. 'Is there going to be an investigation?' My voice rises. 'Am I going to be dragged in front of the governors and be accused of having an affair and have that damned Facebook picture thrown at me? I really need this job, Cat.'

'Gwen! You're becoming hysterical. Calm down! Listen to what I'm saying.'

She waits for me to comply. 'Better?' I nod. 'Good. Then I'll summarise things as simply as I can. Are you listening?'

'Yes, Cat.' My reply is deceptively meek and she pats me on the head.

'*Good* Gwen. There's a good Gwen.'

I growl. She giggles and leans closer again.

'Gwen, Alun *wanted* Ian Weston out. Ian has given him the ammunition he needed. Alun agreed to give Ian a good reference to get rid of him.'

She peers closely at me. 'Are you still with me?'

'So, if Ian hands in his notice and leaves, that's the end of it?'

'Already gone.'

'No!'

'Yep! Handed in his notice, packed up and left within an hour. A few weeks ago, he'd booked a cruise for him and Lynette to prove to her that he was a changed man. Well, yesterday he went on the cruise. On his own.'

I'm beyond speech.

'Knew you'd be pleased!'

'Are you sure about all of this?'

'Gwen, this information has come almost from the horse's mouth.'

I collapse back in my chair, working through everything she's said.

'So, if I have this straight, Ian's now on a cruise and won't be returning. Lynette's getting rehab and I'm not going to be dragged in for humiliating questioning.'

'That, my friend, is the situation in a nutshell. Apparently, Delyth will get a slap on the wrist and a written warning for borrowing school money.

The full impact of what she's told me hits home and I let out a whoop of delight that startles Nansi from her sleep. Moments later, I'm holding her on my knee, blowing raspberries into her neck and tummy while she chortles with delight.

Gethin comes through to see what all the noise is about. Cat gives him a summary of the news and we sit together in a haze of delight, passing the adorable Nansi between us. Even my no-nonsense brother seems smitten by her and comes in for some teasing from Cat.

'Wouldn't you and Zoe like your own one of these?'

He freezes for the briefest of seconds. Cat doesn't know that Zoe's left him and I'm trying to think of something to change the subject when Gethin gets in first.

'You've got the day off tomorrow, Gwen. Why don't you and Cat have some fun together?'

'You didn't tell me, Gwen. Is this one of Granny's respite trips?'

'It is–but I didn't know if she'd be up for it after…' My voice dies away but Cat steps in with her determined voice.

'That's brilliant! And now that Weston's gone you can let your hair down and have some fun.'

'There you are.' Gethin agrees with her. 'You, Cat and Nansi can have a riotous time while some of us sit in a blistering hot office in the city.'

Cat's grin turns to a pout. 'Sorry, Gwen. I've just remembered, Dean's mother's coming and we've arranged a full itinerary that takes in several teashops, the park and at least two garden centres.'

'It doesn't matter. I can catch up on some housework and finish that book you gave me.'

Gethin sighs. 'Doing some fulfilling housework sounds like a perfect way to spend a day of freedom.' His sarcasm bites. 'Give me strength!'

I'm trying to think of a witty riposte when there's the welcome distraction of a knock at the door. I flee Gethin's accusing stare and go and answer it.

It's Ben.

'Hi.' It's all I can think of to say.

He smiles. 'I was passing and thought I'd pop in and see how things are going.' I usher him and he notices the others. 'Greetings, all.'

'Hiya, Ben! Come and meet my little rug rat.' Cat's eyes positively gleam with pleasure. I brace myself. 'Nice timing! We have a problem and I think you're just the person who can solve it for us.'

'Problem?' He's looking at me intently. 'Not your grandmother?'

Cat's in charge now 'Nothing like that. Come over and take a seat.' She taps the chair next to my vacated one. 'Would you like some tea? Coffee?'

He raises a quizzical eyebrow and I shrug. I know when I've lost control of the situation.

Ben sits as instructed. 'How are you doing, Gethin?'

'Fine. The headache's gone and I'm only properly aware of my ribs when I do something extreme.'

'Good.' He turns to Nansi. 'And who do we have here?'

Cat hands her over. 'This is Nansi. Say hello to Ben, Nansi.'

Ben holds her with an expertise I put down to his being an uncle. While Cat makes the tea, he raises such delighted chortles from Nansi, they turn into hiccups just as Cat puts a mug on the table and relieves him of his twitching charge. There's a brief silence and then Cat's off again.

'Hey, Ben, Gwen's grandmother has her monthly day out with a respite group tomorrow. It's a chance for Gwen to have a break and do something frivolous.'

'*Not* housework,' adds Gethin, fixing me with an amused look.

'Sadly, I can't go with her because my mother-in-law's coming. What are your plans for the day?'

'Cat!' My horror only serves to make all three of them laugh. Ben rests an arm along the back of my chair and turns to face me.

'As it happens, I have some plans to draw up that I can do tonight which leaves me at a completely loose end tomorrow.'

'Ben, I'm sorry. This ambush is unforgiveable.' I send a quelling look at my treacherous friend who Cheshire-Cat-grins back at me 'There's no need for this. I'm looking forward to some quiet catch-up time.'

Ben clutches his chest. 'Ouch! You'd rather spend some quiet time here than accompany me, at a loose end, somewhere else? I'm wounded!'

'I didn't mean it like that—' I don't get any further. There's no point. I wouldn't be heard above the laughter.

When things are calmer, he asks where we should go. He says that Freshwater East beach sounds good. Cat steps instantly into the breach.

'Why not go to Folly Farm? They're part of an endangered species breeding programme as well now. It has everything – cute farm animals, giraffes, a mini fairground. It's got loads of things to do, they serve food and there's plenty of shady places if it gets too hot.'

'Sounds good. What about you, Gwen? Could you bear to spend a day at Folly Farm with me?' He adds, 'Think before you reply. I have an extremely fragile ego.'

I scan the three expectant faces in turn before giving my response.

'Well, if you put it like that, I'll have to say yes. I don't want your damaged ego on my conscience.'

'Folly Farm, it is.' Then he leans over and drops a quick kiss on my lips.

I can still feel that tingling touch when everyone's gone.

I'm standing in the garden under the stars, breathing in the scent of jasmine and honeysuckle.

All's right with the world.

Chapter 23

It's 7.30 when I surface naturally from sleep. Sunlight is seeping past the edges of the curtains and I remember that I'm going to Folly Farm with Ben. It feels ridiculous, grinning broadly on my own, but I can't help it. I'm so looking forward to my day out.

The contents of my wardrobe are few and far between and so I select the same floaty skirt that I wore on that disastrous trip into Cranston. However, I can't bring myself to wear the white top. I've washed it twice now but I can't shake off the memory of Mark's grubby fingerprints. I choose a green short-sleeved T-shirt instead and push all unpleasant thoughts away.

Gethin's in the kitchen putting his laptop into his backpack. He looks up as I approach and tips his head in the direction of the kettle.

'There's at least one mugful of recently made coffee over there.'

I grab a mug and am pouring the dark nectar into it when I notice him put on his baseball cap.

'You're not leaving already! I thought your train didn't leave for another two hours yet.'

'I decided to take the earlier one. I figured that if I go now, I'll miss some of the rush-hour chaos.' He's chewing his lip again. 'You will be all right, won't you?'

'I'll be fine. I'm out for most of today with Ben and you'll be back tomorrow night.'

'It doesn't stop me worrying about you.'

'Well, it's time you did. Anyway, everything's settled down now. Ian's left and Mark's not darkened our doorstep for days.'

'What if he turns up at night again?'

'I have Ben on speed dial, remember?'

He twists his wrist and checks his watch. 'Okay. But be careful. No taking chances, and I expect a reassuring Skype call from you this evening.'

'Will do.'

He slides his backpack onto his shoulders.

‘I’ll be off then. Enjoy your day out. It’ll do you good to have some fun for a change.’

‘I’m looking forward to it.’

‘I can tell! Your grin’s bigger than your face.’

He turns at the door. ‘And I don’t want to find any penguins in the bath on my return.’

‘Agreed.’ I’m about to add, ‘Nothing more dangerous than a bath bomb’ when it occurs to me that reminding him about that night doesn’t help my case.

Then he’s gone.

~~~

Joyce arrives whilst Granny’s having her breakfast. She usually accompanies her on these respite days out and I think it does them both good to escape their normal routines for a bit. They’re off on a trip to Aberystwyth and not due back until 5.30 which gives me a dizzying sense of freedom.

‘How’s things, Gwen?’

‘Pretty perfect.’

‘*That* good, eh?’ Her face wrinkles with mischief. ‘Do I detect matters of the heart in that cat’s-got-the-cream expression of yours?’

‘Am I so obvious?’

‘My lovely, I’ve known you all your life. You wear your heart on your sleeve.’

‘Is that a bad thing?’

‘Sometimes. Sometimes it makes it easier to be reached and damaged or broken.’ Her smile takes the slight sting out of the words. ‘But I wouldn’t have you any other way. I know far too many people who hide their true, unpleasant colours behind a benign mask.’

Becky wheels Granny through from the kitchen.

‘There we are, Mrs Meredith. All fed and watered and ready to take on the wildest west of Aberystwyth.’

Granny gives a harrumph in response but I can see the pleasure behind it. She and Joyce have weathered so much together and I’m aware of the fun that bubbles up from my grandmother when in her company.
~~~

Becky picks up her workbag. 'I've arranged to be here for their return, Gwen, so I'll be back by 5.30 at the latest.'

Her exit coincides with the arrival of the specially adapted van that's taking the group of giggling pensioners on their supported day out. I'm waving them off when Ben crosses the road.

'All safely on their way?'

'Yes. They're just like schoolchildren on these trips. I've provided some snacks but I'd lay odds that Granny's already examining hers and will have started on them within the next five minutes.'

He laughs and adds, 'When do you want to leave?'

'How about ten-ish? I don't think Folly Farm's open before then.'

'Ten-ish it is. I've given Atticus a thorough workout but this means I can give him another one that'll make him positively *beg* to be left in peace.'

'Make sure you don't wear yourself out in the process. There's 120 acres of Folly Farm to explore.'

'In that case, I'll restrict my energy output to throwing our battered Frisbee as far as I can. Atticus'll be a panting heap by the time I'm finished with him and dreaming of his bed in the cool of the utility room.'

'Poor dog.'

'That *poor dog* leads a better life than I do.'

'I'll not have a word said against him.'

'That's very kind of you considering your painful experience in Stinky Ditch.'

I laugh at that. 'Well, I'd better go and sort things out inside. See you at ten.'

'Looking forward to it, Gwen.'

He gives me one of his crinkly-eyed smiles and heads back home.

~~~

The mantle clock is chiming ten when Ben's car stops outside the house. Twenty minutes later, we've pulled into the massive car park and are following others to the entrance.
~~~

Ben insists on paying. He says it offsets his guilt when he remembers the injuries sustained releasing his daft mutt from the trolley. I put up a token resistance, but I'm secretly relieved that the money I'd put aside on this jaunt can now be put towards some more sunscreen and kept in reserve for things like a taxi to take Granny to the surgery.

I approach the brightly coloured map board and ask Ben where he'd like to go first. He comes to stand next to me and I tap on the barn. 'Most people are heading here. It's perfect for getting close to some farm animals.'

'What's this?' He points to 'Cwtch Corner' in the barn. 'I don't think I'll ever get a handle on your lack of vowels.'

'On the contrary, we're less miserly with them. We have seven vowels to your five. Ours includes a w, which is usually pronounced oo, and a y which is usually an uh sound.'

He turns back to the board. 'So, this is 'Cootch' Corner?

'We'll make a native of you yet!'

'It would help if I knew what it was I was actually saying. What's a 'cootch'?'

'It's a word you'll find on key-rings and fridge magnets in all the tourist shops. It means a hug or cuddle.'

His eyes positively twinkle with merriment but all he says is, 'Cwtch. I like it.' Then he takes my hand. 'Come on. This way.'

'Where are we going?'

'I thought it'd be good to see some giraffes.'

'But they're right over the other side of the park.'

'Exactly. Most people will start at the beginning. If we go to the end, it might be less busy.'

'I like your thinking.'

We cut across in a zigzagging diagonal and I don't know whether I'm breathless because of how fast we're walking or because I'm holding his hand.

The giraffes are in an enclosure with zebra and antelope but Ben tugs me over to a wooden walkway that leads upwards to a covered area called Giraffe Heights. We have the space to ourselves and as we look on, one of the giraffes ambles across the yard to a tall pole that has leafy branches attached at the top. We're on a level with its head. I'm fascinated as I watch a long, black tongue helping to grab the shrubby bits of foliage.

Ben murmurs, 'Amazing!' and I watch in entranced silence. A few minutes later it turns towards us and for a few precious seconds it comes right up to the observation platform, close enough to touch. I'm scared to break the spell, worried that if I reach out with my hand I'll frighten it off. But then it ambles back the way it came. Instantly, I regret the missed opportunity.

'Don't worry. We'll come back again and you'll have another chance.'

His words almost wind me. 'How do you *do* that? How do you know what I'm thinking?'

'It's easy. You have an expressive face.' His face draws closer to mine as he adds, 'I wouldn't take up poker, if I were you.'

And then we're kissing. Like that time in the garden, I'm lost in the giddy sensation and it's only when he pulls away that I realise we're no longer alone. A large family group joins us and Ben moves to the side to let one of them with a stroller get up to the front.

We're back at paddock level when Ben says conversationally, 'You do know, of course, that those horns on their heads aren't really horns at all?'

'They aren't?'

'Nope. They're called ossicones.'

'I'm impressed. How do you know that?'

'Because I'm very intelligent and … it says so, on this board.'

I tut and shake my head. 'Your true colours are beginning to show!' And then we're off again, this time to the penguins.

I don't think it's possible to watch a group of penguins and not smile. There's plenty of glass walls so that we can see them cut through the water in their tank, but on land, every movement seems unwieldy.

'I expect you knew that a group of penguins is called a waddle,' I announce casually. 'And that pebbly area there is to stop them getting bumblefoot.'

'What's bumblefoot?'

'I haven't read that far yet.'

He laughs. 'Touché.'

'Miss! Miss!'

It's two of the children from the school. They run towards me as their parents stand and watch. I let go of Ben's hand and bob down to their height.

'Hiya, you two. Having a good time?'

'What are *you* doing here, Miss?'

'I'm having a good time, too.'

'Do you like penguins?'

'I do. In fact,' I lower my voice to a whisper, 'don't tell anyone, but I *am* a penguin.'

Their eyes grow huge and then Sophie says, 'She's just joking, Aaron.'

'Joking am I? Have you never been chased by a penguin? I'll give you a five second head start.'

It's only when I start the slow count that they understand the game. They give little squeals of amused terror as I waddle after them with my arms firmly tucked to my sides. When they reach their parents, I stop and give them all a wave before joining an amused Ben.

'We'd better read a bit more of this board. Don't want my favourite penguin getting bumblefoot.'

~~~

After a chaotic spin on the go-karts, we head for the Big Wheel. A short queue has formed but we don't have to wait long to be seated in one of the carriages and every few minutes we're raised higher as the next carriages are filled. When we're waiting at the very top, Ben tips up my chin and this time the kiss is deeper, more intense. I'm lost and simply give myself up to the experience. It's only when the carriage sways as it moves on another stage, that he draws back and there's a rueful expression on his face.

'I think it might be for the best if I limit myself to fairly chaste pecks for the time being.' He holds the front of his T-shirt between finger and thumb and fans his chest with it. 'We'll not be welcome back if our ardour melts their nice Ferris wheel.'

I'm still too stunned to speak and he leans forward and draws a gentle hand down my cheek. 'You feel it, too, don't you? That power pulling us together?'
~~~

‘I didn’t know it could be like that.’ My voice sounds husky.

‘Maybe neither of us has found the right person before.’

There’s another jolt and then the wheel starts turning.

‘Come on, let’s admire the view.’ Ben takes my hand again. ‘I’m looking forward to spending as much time with you as possible, Gwen Meredith.’

I didn’t think it was possible to be so happy.

We sit together watching the magnificent Pembrokeshire countryside roll out beneath us. Even when Ben points out the sea sparkling in the distance, it does nothing to dampen my pleasure. I send up a silent prayer of thanks to Cat for her part in this. Sometimes things just feel *right*.

After the wheel experience we grab some food at The Hungry Farmer. The place is quite full with excited children, the babble of noise forming a backdrop that provides us with privacy to talk freely.

We chat about nothing in particular for a while and then Ben apologises.

‘I prejudged you and I’ll never forgive myself for that.’

‘Don’t be daft. You weren’t to know that I wasn’t a man-eating vamp with a predilection for head teachers.’

It occurs to me that all of that unpleasantness with Ian is in the past. It was a transient bit of nothing. I feel free of it now.

Ben continues. ‘It was because of Callie. It’s no excuse, I know, but she’s having a hard time and I took her situation out on you.’

‘Forget it, Ben. I do understand. She’s your little sister and you feel protective of her. That’s natural. I’d leap in to protect Geth. That’s families for you.’

‘It bothers me, though. If circumstances hadn’t thrown us together, I might never had got this chance to know you better.’

‘Well, here we are and that’s all that matters.’

‘I know.’ He pauses. ‘I think this Callie business has hit me harder than I thought. She’s the youngest in the family and she’s been spoiled by us. When she announced that she was in love and was going to marry Paul, we all tried to tell her that it was too soon. She wouldn’t have it. Within six weeks of meeting him she was thumbing through the wedding magazines, as much in love with the experience as the man, I think.'

'I heard an agony aunt once suggest that all brides should be married in boiler suits. There's an element of sense in that.'

'Yeah. Well, once Ellen and Jay came along, Paul was the doting father but he turned his romantic attention elsewhere and now she faces losing the children for half of their lives.'

'I'm sorry, Ben. I don't think there's anything I can say to help.'

'I shouldn't be burdening you with this. I just wanted to explain my despicable behaviour.'

'Water under Stinky Ditch.'

He laughs at that. 'I'll never, ever, forget that image of you covered in bumps and scratches and a streaky green. I think it was then that I realised that I needed to know you better.'

I raise my glass of water. 'To Atticus and Stinky Ditch!'

We clink glasses and he looks serious again. 'I decided a couple of years ago that I wasn't going to put myself in Callie's situation. It takes time to really understand someone and know if they're the right person for you. I'm looking forward to getting to know you, Gwen.'

I look down and busy myself with my Mediterranean salad. I've had a wonderful day and I'm not going to spoil it by fretting over future revelations. I ask him what we're going to do next and he studies the app on his phone before grabbing my hand and pulling me to my feet.

'Come on. I think a turn on The Golden Gallopers is called for.'

~~~

The Golden Gallopers is the name for the old-fashioned carousel in the funfair part of the farm. We climb aboard our brightly painted horses and the ride picks up speed. I'm laughing with delight, when I catch a glimpse of a mustard yellow cap among the crowd. The breath catches in my throat and I twist round trying to see the face beneath it. I spin past the same place several times but it's gone. As the ride slows, I search the crowds but there's no sign of it.
~~~

Ben holds a hand out to help me alight and when I turn to look behind me, he asks, 'Everything all right?'

I drag the flicker of fear back under. 'Yes. I thought I saw someone I knew but I must have been mistaken.' It's foolish to let an overactive imagination spoil the mood and I hook my hand around his arm. 'Where to now?'

'Now, we're going on The Caterpillar.'

The Caterpillar is one of those rides where the open carriages go at increasing speed round an undulating track. I follow Ben into one of the carriages and he puts an arm across my shoulders as we set off. I'm laughing out loud as we go faster and faster, the force pushing me into his protective hold. It's simultaneously thrilling and carefree and I feel truly alive for the first time in years. When we reach the optimum speed, the long cover comes down over the top, plunging us all into darkness and I have that childish sadness at knowing that the experience is nearly over.

I clamber out afterwards on wobbly legs and Ben laughs and kisses me.

'Have you any idea how enticing you look with those riotous red curls and that radiant smile?'

I feel the smile stretch even further at the compliment.

Before we leave, Ben suggests we grab a coffee and we go to the booth near the entrance. It has Cwtch Coffee written above it and after he's ordered our drinks he says, 'Well, that's the coffee taken care of. Now for the cwtch.' He pulls me in for a cuddle and I feel secure, safe, loved.

'I think I'm getting to like the sound of this strange language of yours. You must teach me some more words.'

He tickles my ribs and I pull away, giggling and squirming until I manage a gasped 'Stop!' and the delicious torment ceases.

'So, my little mine of Welsh information, what's 'stop' in your melodic language?'

'Ooooh! Straight in at the deep end.' I put a hand on his arm. 'I'm not sure if you're ready for this level of complexity yet. Want to try something easier?'

'Nope. I've made my decision. Let me have it!'

'Don't say I didn't warn you.' I give a dramatic pause before announcing, as seriously as I can, 'Stopio.'

He mimics me. 'Stop-ee-oh'? Seriously?'

'Yep! Think you can cope with that one?'

My punishment is another tickling.

On the way out through the gift shop, Ben stops and buys a cuddly penguin, which he presents to me.

'Something to cwtch when I'm not around.'

I hold it tightly next to me and when we reach the car, he goes to the passenger side and opens the door for me.

I hesitate, a little surprised by the gesture.

'I know. It's not the norm now, but everything feels fresh and new and this just seems right, somehow, for our first proper date.'

Pleasure coils inside me and I simply smile and slip into my seat, clutching my penguin.'

Half an hour later, Ben drops me off outside the house, saying he'll come back once he's given Atticus his freedom. I wave him off and take the key from my small crossbody bag as I approach the front door.

It's as I insert the key into the lock that my skin prickles with the sensation that all's not right.

When I open the door, what I see confirms it.

Chapter 24

Drawers from the antique bureau in the hallway are lying haphazardly on the floor, which is strewn with papers. Shaking, I step cautiously forward and glance through to the kitchen. More chaos. Drawers and cupboard doors are open and their contents spill out on to every surface.

Granny keeps our father's signed cricket bat in a corner of the sitting room but now it's lying on the floor in front of me. I pick it up, transferring the penguin under my arm, and creep through the doorway. I walk soundlessly on the toes of my sandals but my heartbeats are so loud, I can't be sure they won't give me away. The house has an empty, dead feel. The only sounds are those pulsing inside of me.

I stand in the middle of the room and slowly scan it.

My laptop's missing from the table. The shelves next to it had a framed photograph of my parents on their wedding day. It's gone. My stomach lurches. The pain I feel at the loss is crippling.

I retrace my steps to the driveway, still holding the bat. I can't clear my head to think rationally and simply stand for a while.

I take my phone out of my bag and call the police.

Then the notion that someone might be watching sears through the chaos, and I scan the road for signs of anyone lurking in the shadows. No one.

~~~

It's Becky who arrives first. I'm still standing in the driveway and I fill her in on the situation. There's now an issue concerning what we're going to do with my grandmother on her return as I've been told we can't use the house until it's been checked over. It's at this point that Ben appears with an excited Atticus who bounces across. My hand automatically fusses him. Ben comes up to me and points to the cricket bat in my other hand.
~~~

‘Planning on a quick innings before Granny arrives?’

I watch him as his eyes take in the open doorway and the mess visible just inside it.

‘What’s happened?’

‘We’ve been burgled.’

He says nothing for a few seconds, then he exhales slowly.

‘Have you called the police?’

I nod. ‘The house was still locked when I came back. I unlocked the door and found the house ransacked and some things missing.’

‘You definitely locked it?’

‘Of course!’ I’m a little narked at the question. ‘I’m one of those neurotic people who check and double check things like that.’

‘What about the back door and windows?’

‘I know they were all closed when we left. The police are on their way and I’ve been told not to go back into the house or do anything that might contaminate the crime scene.’

Becky says, ‘If no one’s forced an entry, perhaps it’s someone who knows the code for the keysafe?’

I hadn’t thought of that and go to check it but Ben holds me back.

‘You can’t touch it, Gwen, in case it needs to be dusted for fingerprints.’

‘Oh, of course.’ It’s an unwelcome echo of his advice regarding my vandalised car. Now my mind is trawling through who I’ve trusted with the code that would do this to us. Might Lisa have done this in revenge for losing her job?

Becky touches my arm. ‘What are we going to do about your grandmother. She’s due back soon, isn’t she?’

My response is a blank, helpless stare.

Becky taps a fingernail against her teeth. ‘What about Joyce?’

‘Joyce?’

‘Yeah, Joyce. If the driver can drop her off with Joyce, I could go round there instead and sort her out for the night, if Joyce wouldn’t mind.’

‘I don’t know. Sorry, I’m not thinking straight. Would that work?’

'I don't see why not. Joyce is very good with her. I don't think she'd mind given the situation.'

'Could you drop off the medication?'

She gives me a rueful smile.

'It's in the house.'

I groan.

'Hang on a sec, Gwen.' Becky stands still, a frown creasing her head. Then she looks at me and smiles.

'It's okay. There's nothing mission critical that can't wait until tomorrow morning. I'll drop in first thing and if your grandmother's not back by then, I'll take the meds up to Joyce's house. Have you got her mobile number?'

I nod and take my phone out of my bag again. 'What do I say?'

Ben steps in. 'Just tell her the situation and ask if it's okay for Edith to go back with her. He raps his leg and Atticus moves to stand obediently next to him. 'I'll take Atticus home and be right back.'

My fingers are clumsy as I scroll through to find the number and click on it. There's a long wait and then Joyce answers.

'Hi, Gwen. Don't worry. We're running about half-an-hour late but we've had a great time. Your grandmother's asleep next to me.'

'We have a bit of a problem at this end, Joyce.'

'What kind of problem?'

'We've been burgled and we can't access the house until the police have finished with it.'

'Oh no! How dreadful!' She then says, more quietly, 'Nobody hurt, I hope?'

'No. It happened when we were out.'

There's silence from the other end of the call for a moment and then Joyce speaks before I can make my suggestion.

'Well, Edith can't come back to you in those circumstances. Why doesn't she come back to mine? She's so tired out, she won't be any trouble.

'Joyce, that would be wonderful. Are you sure?'

'It's already decided.'

'Becky says she can come across to yours to get her ready for bed.'

'No need, my dear. It won't hurt Edith to go to bed dirty for once and she'll not manage more than some soup after that huge fish and chip meal she guzzled on the prom.'

'Well, if you're sure.'

'It'll be fine, Gwen. Your grandmother will spend most of the time sleeping after all that food and fresh air'.'

'Love you, Joyce.'

'And I you, Gwen. Try not to worry.'

I hang up and turn to face Becky.

'Joyce has it all in hand.'

Becky is looking in my direction but I know she's not seeing me. She seems to be mulling over something.

Ben returns just as Stafford's car arrives followed by a small van. My surly policeman advances on us, a grim smile on his face, and my misery is complete.

'This is becoming a bit of a habit, Miss Meredith.' He nods in acknowledgment. 'Mr Pascoe.' He turns to Becky. 'And we've met before but I didn't catch your name.'

'I'm Becky Hughes. I'm one Mrs Meredith's carers.'

'So, which of you discovered the burglary?'

'I did. I came back about fifteen minutes ago and when I unlocked the door, I could see that everything's been rummaged through.'

'Rummaged through or burgled?'

'Burgled!' I'm snapping at him. 'My laptop's gone, for a start.'

'And the door was locked?'

'Yes.'

'Who has the key?'

'Just me. There's a couple of spares in my bedroom.'

'Are they still there?'

'I only looked in the sitting room and the kitchen, so I don't know.'

'Good.' He stops his quickfire attack of questions to point at my hand. 'Why are you holding a cricket bat?'

'It was on the floor. I picked it up in case … in case …'

'In case someone was still in there?'

'Yes.'

An exasperated sound escapes him. 'Brilliant idea. Approach an intruder with a weapon that he can take and use against you.'

His sarcasm makes me so angry I can feel it swamping the ebbing shock.

'I thought it might be better to put up *some* kind of fight. I could hardly do that without an advantage of some sort.'

He simply gives me a withering look. There's something about being wrongfooted by him that brings out the worst in me. An image of the bat whacking his shins flashes into my head but Ben puts a steadying hand under my elbow and it fades.

'Well, as I seem to be a regular visitor of yours, I've pulled out all the stops and hopefully we can get to the bottom of this unpleasantness once and for all.'

He gestures to the occupants of the van who approach carrying shiny metal cases. Then he turns back to us.

'Well, we'll let them get on with the job in hand.' He removes his notebook. 'And in the meantime, if you could answer a few questions?'

We're interrogated about our movements and alibis and he raises that annoying eyebrow of his when I tell him that Ben and I spent the day together at Folly Farm. When I ask how long this is likely to take, he replies, 'As long as is necessary. I'll let you know when you can go back in and then it would be helpful if you could give us a list of any missing items.' I nod.

'I have your mobile number. Where will you go until this is finished?'

I haven't thought that far ahead. Ben answers for me.

'Gwen can stay over the road at my place.'

That eyebrow arches again and my fingers tighten spontaneously around the handle of my father's cricket bat. Stafford's lip curls in the way that irritates me so much, 'I hope I don't need to point out that using that item as an offensive weapon could get you into serious trouble?'

He knows.

'And,' he points to the penguin, 'what did you intend to do to them with that?'

I grit my teeth and I'm still gritting them after he's disappeared into the house.

Becky says, 'Well, I suppose I'd better be off.'

She looks drained and I feel guilty for adding an extra strand of stress to her life.

'I'm sorry, Becky. You've been great, as always, and I take your support for granted, don't I?'

'Don't be daft! I'm just sorry I can't do more to help. Fingers crossed, the police will be able to match fingerprints to the guilty culprit and then we can get back to normal.'

She picks up her care bag, hesitates as if to say something else, but then carries on to her car and drives off.

Ben gently prises the cricket bat from my tense grip.

'Come on. Let's get you over the road. We could both do with a restorative cuppa.'

~~~

Ben's sitting room is flooded with light from two huge picture windows that provide a view of an established garden. It's furnished in a plain but comfortable style and some of the pieces have a patina that comes with age.

He's clattering away in the kitchen and my numb brain begins to tick over again. It throws up questions I can't answer. I don't know the who or the why, for a start. I tell myself it could simply be an opportunistic burglary, and my brain replies, 'But what about the locked door?' I know I have to stop this line of thought until I have more to go on and I try to distract myself. I'm still clutching my penguin and I get up and place it carefully on a chair where it can look out at the view. I know it's ridiculous but I can't help myself.

I wander over to the far wall and look at the pictures that are ranged there. Most of them are rural scenes; some of them seascapes. I turn away and can see that there are framed photos dotted around the room. There's what looks like younger versions of Ben in some of them. In one snap, he can only be about ten years old and he's standing with two younger children, one of whom shares such a strong resemblance I suspect she's Callie.
~~~

'That's the three of us.' He puts a tray down on the table and joins me. He traces a finger over the other boy. 'That's Simon, he's eighteen months younger than me and this,' he hovers over the girl, 'is Callie.'

She's laughing at something, carefree and happy, revealing the gap where her two front milk teeth once were. Somewhere, there must be photos of me like that. Ben picks up another framed picture from the mantlepiece. It's of a pretty, young woman with that same carefree smile. She's holding a grinning toddler by one hand and has a younger child balanced on her hip.

'That's beautiful! She's so pretty and happy.'

'That one was taken nearly two years ago. I'm not sure if you'd recognise Callie now. Since Paul left, she's changed. That bubbling personality that drew everyone to her has worn away leaving her lacklustre and subdued. She's struggling and there's not a lot that any of us can do to help her. She adores those children and faces losing them for half of their lives.'

'It must be very hard for her. And for you to see what she's going through.'

He grimaces. 'It's hard for us seeing her so miserable, but I'm also worried about the effect this is having on Jay and Ellen. To be blunt, Callie clings onto them now, smothering them with a sort of feverish love. When they go to Paul's, they return excited and happy and she's so wounded by it, she points out all their father's shortcomings in a desperate bid to undermine their pleasure. She's damaging her relationship with them and we're powerless to stop it. She sees Paul as the devil incarnate and she's consumed by a desire to make him as unhappy as she is. All she's doing is driving Jay and Ellen away from her and into his new life; the very thing she dreads.'

He turns me round to face him.

'Here I am unburdening myself on you when you have such serious things going on in your own life.' He draws me across to the table and pulls out a chair for me to sit on.

'How do you like your tea?'

'Milk, no sugar, please.'

He adds milk to both of the teas and hands me one of them. The warmth from the mug is soothing and I simply cup my hands around it. When I look up, Ben's staring at me. There's a frown crease on his forehead.

'Gwen, we need to do something to protect you properly.'

'I've been thinking—'

He holds his hand up to stop me. 'I don't want to come across as bossy or controlling but it would really reassure me if you'd at least let me install a couple of those wireless doorbell cameras.'

'Ben, I—'

He continues, more earnest now, 'They're easy to set up and they'll record the comings and goings of everyone who walks up your driveway or comes into the garden. It would give us peace of mind to know that we at least have a record of who's around. Hopefully, it would catch any new attempt to hurt you that could then be used by the police to put a stop to all of this once and for all.'

'I was going to say—'

'It wouldn't cost you anything. I can get one really cheaply through the contacts I've made through my building projects.'

'If you'd let me—'

'I need to do this, Gwen.' The words have a desperation to them and I'm touched by his concern and frustrated that he won't let me speak.

'Ben, shut up!'

I've shocked him into silence. I smile to soften the words.

'If you'd just let me get a word in edgeways.'

He looks puzzled.

'Ben, I've been thinking the same thing. I've been looking them up on the Internet and was going to ask you this afternoon if you could help me choose one.'

'You were?'

'I was.'

'Well, that's a relief. I've been wondering how to convince you. I can probably buy a couple of good doorbell cameras for peanuts. If you'd let me do that, I'd be grateful.'

'*You'd* be grateful! I think you have this all the wrong way round. I owe you.'

'No, you don't. I'm quite selfishly looking after someone who matters to me. A lot.'

His words trigger a response inside me that makes me squirm with delight. I matter to him. A lot! The still-working part of my brain intervenes.

'I'm pretty sure I can get the trustees to agree to fund it and so I'll be able to pay you back.'

'There's no need.

'I insist.'

He looks set to argue the point, and then a smile twitches his mouth and he holds both hands up in a gesture of defeat.

'Okay, Gwen. I know when I'm beaten.'

He points to the corner of the room where he's propped up my father's cricket bat.

'I honestly think it makes more sense to arm yourself with the power of technology and leave such weaponry to those with the strength to wield it.'

'Not you as well! Stafford made it more than clear that he thought I was an idiot.'

'I'm no fan of the man but, in this instance, I do think he had a point. What were you going to do if the burglar was still in the house? Whack him across the ankles and hope he'd run away howling in pain?'

My lips twitch at that. 'I wasn't really thinking that far ahead.'

'Precisely. That's what Stafford was getting at. If it was Mark Johnson, would you have been able to stop him snatching that bat off you?'

I shake my head. I remember his grip on my hands in the alleyway and my panic when I'd been unable to free myself. Ben rushes on as if he's scared I'll change my mind.

'I'll arrange for a locksmith to come out tomorrow morning, first thing, and I'll buy a smart doorbell and fix it for you. Then you'll be able to see who's on the other side of the door before you open it…' His voice tails away and the frown line's back. 'Your laptop's gone.'

I nod.

'So you'll have to use your phone.'

'Is that a problem?'

'No. Not at all. But you have some decisions to make now.'

I hadn't given much thought to my missing laptop in the tsunami of problems, but now I'm aware of all the information on there.

'Is it password protected?'

'Yes. I'm not completely stupid.'

'I'm not getting at you. You'd be amazed how many people don't bother.'

'Well, I have. It's a proper one, too, that the mystical encryptors in The Cloud told me was strong.'

'That's good.'

'And all the sites I use have different, strong, passwords.'

'Excellent!' His eyes narrow. 'Unless you keep a list of those passwords on the laptop for reference?'

I fix him with a cold stare and he laughs and throws his hands up in surrender again.

'Sorry, Gwen. I'm just trying to minimise any possible damage.'

'It's ok. I know you're trying to help.' I sit upright, back straight. 'I'd better contact the bank, and then I'll change all my passwords for my online sites.'

~~~

It takes an age waiting in queued calls to access the bank. The actual process itself is swift and straightforward and I feel an enormous sense of relief when that's been done. Then I begin the laborious process of changing all my passwords. When I sit back, sighing, Ben takes my hand and leads me through to his impressive kitchen and the back door.

'Let's take a stroll around the estate, m'lady, and you can give me the benefit of your opinion on the contents that I've inherited.' He offers me his arm, and I take it. For a moment, the illusion works but the arrival of an excited Atticus brings me down to earth, almost literally, and I'm smiling again.

'Atticus, you lovely dog! Where's your ball?'

He races down the garden and comes back with a chewed Frisbee.

'I'm afraid English isn't his first language and we're struggling to make headway with it.'
~~~

I take the Frisbee. 'This'll do.' I give it a spin and it wobbles a good distance before coming to rest on the grass. Atticus gives an excited bark, races after it and tumbles head over heels, before recovering and speeding back with it. I grin at Ben who sighs.

I sling the battered disc again and this time the speckled legs go so fast, he overtakes the Frisbee, can't stop in time, and ends up in the shrubs. I double over in laughter which is made all the merrier by Ben's anguished expression before putting his head in his hands, as he says, 'Just once, I'd love to see him as the noble dog I imagined in my head.'

'Nonsense! You think he's adorable just as he is.'

The side gate opens and I turn to see Stafford with one of the members of the fingerprint team. All the pleasure drains from me.

'Good to see you're not moping, Miss Meredith.'

Atticus bounces back and drops the Frisbee at Stafford's highly-polished brown shoes. Then he bends down over his front paws, hind quarters high, and gives excited little yelps of enticement.

Stafford is unmoved by the display. 'Just to let you know that we've finished with the house now and all we need are the fingerprints of those who've been in there during the last week.'

'Do I have to bring my grandmother down to the police station?'

His gives an exasperated shake of his head. 'This may be Pembrokeshire, but we do have some modern technology such as digital scanners now.'

I hope my embarrassment isn't written large across my face.

The man next to him says, 'If you could show us something that your grandmother's handled recently we can avoid troubling her, if that's all right with you.'

'That's marvellous. Thank you. Shall we go across now?'

'You'll need to get his as well.' Stafford points at Ben who remains implacable and good humoured.

The four of us troop across to the house. Mr Pargeter, down the road, appears to be using shears on the hedge he clipped only two days ago. He raises a hand in salute and I wave back.

My life is playing out on a live screen and I don't have the remote control.

At the entrance, I halt. The papers are still scattered over the wooden floor, the drawers now stacked one on top of the other.

'If you'll come this way, Miss.'

I follow him through to the kitchen.

'If you could just sit at the table and we'll scan your prints into this machine here.'

While he's finishing with Ben, I try to think of something that Granny will have held. Ben looks up and says, 'What about the remote control?'

I look at the technician who nods in agreement and follows me into the sitting room. The furniture may be upright but the place still looks ransacked. Drawers hang open, cupboard doors flung wide. I go to pick up the remote control but the technician calmly holds my hand back and uses his gloved one to pick it up by its edges.

'Is this the chair your grandmother uses?'

'Yes.'

'I can see that it's well-padded,' he smiles kindly, 'but it also has broad wooden arms. Would your grandmother use these?'

'Of course! Why didn't I think of that!'

'We should be able to get some prints off here.' He's bending down, looking at the wood from the side. Without changing his stance, he adds, 'If there's something else, something like a glass she drinks out of, for example, that would be good for confirmation purposes.'

The door to her room is open and it's not possible to see the carpet beneath the mounds of clothes, books and walking aids. I point at the glass on the bedside table, he nods and I back out again

Once he's finished with the glass, the technician asks if there's anything that would have Gethin's prints. In the kitchen, I find his mug still by the kettle. His notepad's under the table and I watch the man retrieve it.

When Ben takes my hand, mine feels cold inside his.

Chapter 25

Once the technician's left, I feel the hollow emptiness that descends when an adrenaline rush of excitement has passed.

'I don't know where to start.'

Ben comes and stands next to me as I stare at the chaos.

'Come on,' he says, his voice gentle. 'Let's start in the rooms that your grandmother uses most.'

I'm grateful for the suggestion.

'I think the room she's most aware of is this one with the television and her favourite chair. She's asleep for most of the time she's in her bedroom.'

'Good plan. Let's get going then.'

I scan the room.

'What do we do?'

'We start somewhere, anywhere, and see where we're taken next.'

'If we put the bookcase back against the wall, we've got somewhere to put all these books that are littering the floor.'

And so we begin.

In a surprisingly short time, we have the bookcase sorted and already the task before us seems less daunting. We work our way methodically across the room, only speaking when Ben needs advice on where to place something.

The relief at restoring order to the room is blunted by the knowledge of the things that have gone. Ben's put his phone on the table and we compile a list as we go along. Most of the missing things are decorative items that have a monetary value that exceeds their emotional worth. I give silent thanks to Joyce and the solicitor who convinced Granny to lock most of her prized things safely away. A couple of vases have been damaged. I consider repairing them with glue, but a sensible voice in my head tells me that I'd never trust them filled with water again. They go into the bag designated 'rubbish' on the floor by the table.

Every silver photo frame has been taken. I'm hoping we have the original photographs somewhere. If we haven't, how do I replace those precious shots of my parents? The faded black and white ones of my great grandparents? The playful poses of my grandparents with my toddling father between them?

'Gwen?'

I give a brief shake of my head. That way madness lies.

'I'm fine.'

'You aren't. I can understand how upsetting this is, but for a moment there you looked – I don't know, haunted? What is it?'

I shrug.

'Tell me. Please.'

'It's the photos. I don't know if we have copies.'

'Come here.' He hugs me close, saying nothing for a minute or so. Then he holds me at arms' length. 'I'm so sorry, Gwen. I can't answer that one. What I *do* know is that there's no point dwelling on something until you know the situation. Hopefully your Grandmother kept the negatives. Let's leave it for the time being and I'll help you with it later. Okay?'

I nod. Part of me acknowledges the sense of his argument but there's another part that's already grieving an unknown loss.

Ben rallies. 'We're just about finished in here. Do you want a break or shall we make a start on your grandmother's room?'

'Let's push on.'

He heads for the corridor but I catch his hand and pull him back.

'Thanks, Ben. I couldn't have done this without you.'

He simply smiles and pulls me along behind him.

Granny's room seems the most dishevelled. The floor is invisible under clothes, books, old magazines and half-used bottles of scent. I just stand and survey the clutter.

Ben nudges me. 'Why don't you start with the clothes and I'll make a few neat piles of the reading material. Catch!' He throws a winter coat at me and I'm released from my stupor. I slide it onto a hanger and immediately the task feels less hopeless.

We've finished Granny's room and I'm stretching to ease the knots of tension.

‘Had enough?’ Ben stands behind me and starts to massage my neck and shoulders. It’s tempting to give in to the soothing balm of his fingers but I know I can’t.

‘Nope. I’d like to, but I’ll not be able to relax knowing that it’s still waiting to be done.’

‘Where next, then?’

‘The kitchen.’

He gives a final roll of his thumbs into the muscle between my shoulder blade, turns me round, drops a kiss onto the tip of my nose and propels me round and back along the corridor

~~~

I feel less of an emotional response to the functional kitchen but it still hurts to see the broken shards of pottery scattered across the surface of the floor. It’s not the loss of the plates, bowls and mugs, but the recognition of the wantonness of the destruction. I’m troubled by the strength of feeling behind the damage. Someone is lashing out and I sense that these smashed remnants represent me. I recall the warnings delivered by Ben and Stafford – it was idiotic to risk exposing myself to someone full of such malice.

A knock on the door has me spin around. In an instant, Ben has put himself between it and me. There’s another knock and I can feel him tense as the door begins to open.

It’s Becky.

‘Hi there. It looked like the police had gone and I wondered if you could use some help.’

I’m momentarily robbed of the ability to speak. Ben’s breath is released in a huff of relief. Then I summon a smile.

‘That would be brilliant, Becky, thanks. We’re both wilting a bit at the moment.’

Becky takes another step forwards and she flinches when she takes in the scene in front of her.

‘I’m so sorry, Gwen. This is awful.’

‘It’s not your fault, Becky. You had nothing to do with this.’

Her eyes well up and I go across and give her a hug. She pulls away and says, her voice brisk and impersonal, ‘Come on then. What can I do to help?’
~~~

Half an hour later and I'm flagging. It all feels like an uphill slog. Ben disappears for a minute and when he returns, he has Granny's CD player and some discs in his hands. He puts them down on the table and inserts one of the discs. It's a selection of hits from the 60s and 70s, and the kitchen fills with the sound of Abba singing *Dancing Queen*. It raises a grin from all of us and soon we're singing along and moving to the rhythm. Ben suggests *I Fought the Law* as a tribute to Stafford. He laughs at my grim expression.

I can see the gradual restoration of the place as we systematically work our way through, Becky cleaning the items that have been dusted for prints, Ben putting the whole pieces in matching piles on the table and me putting them away on the shelves and in the cupboards.

Rod Stewart is belting out *Maggie May* and Ben says, 'It's strange to think of your grandmother as a young woman enjoying these.'

The words come as a shock. He's right. This is the music she grew up with, that she and our grandfather must have danced to together. The dour, unbending woman I know now, likely sang along and danced to these.

Ben's voice interrupts my thoughts. 'Come on, no slacking! We've still got the bathroom and your bedroom to do yet.'

Becky puts down a bag that makes a chinking sound of broken pottery as it touches the floor. 'Why don't the two of you go and deal with the bedroom. I can finish off here and then make a start on the bathroom.'

~~~

I've been dreading facing up to my bedroom. The drawers are open and my clothes have been disturbed but most of them are still in situ. I can't control a shudder as I think of someone handling my underwear. Tomorrow, everything will be washed at the highest setting I can get away with.

'This room seems to have escaped fairly lightly.' Ben straightens up the shelves and starts to replace the books.

I can see that one of the reasons it's escaped so lightly is that there was very little in it anyway. However, whoever did this was angry. There are small, malicious signs in petty
~~~

breakages and in books with pages mangled in their journey to the floor.

My fingers run alongside a rough groove that's been gouged across the wardrobe. It seems such a petty piece of vandalism and I snatch my hand back at the thought of its link to the person responsible for it.

The small table is on its side in the corner. I stand it upright and pick up the trinkets that have tumbled from it. Whoever did this, seems to have realised that they weren't worth very much. Everything's been left apart from the silver photo frame.

Ben stoops to pick up my Spanish dictionary and points out something on the floor by the skirting board. I can't see it at first. It's almost the same shade of white. He picks it up and it's his stillness that draws my attention to his face, with its mouth set in an angry line.

'What is it?'

He hesitates, and I suspect he'd like to hide whatever it is from me, but I hold out my hand and wait.

It's the photograph that had been in the silver frame. It's of the four of us: Gethin, me and our parents. Except it isn't of the four of us anymore. Someone has ripped a strip off the right-hand side. All that's left of me is the edge of my dress and one of my shoes.

I sway and Ben catches hold of me. This is vicious and personal. The relentless pressure is taking its toll and I'm not sure how much more I can take. I don't know who's doing this or why. The hopelessness takes the resolve out of me and I sag, miserable.

The last notes of *Stayin' Alive* drift through from the kitchen and *No Woman No Cry* starts up. Ben turns me towards him, I rest my face against his chest and we begin to sway to the music. When it finishes, we stay together. I no longer feel so distressed but exhaustion is kicking in and I don't have much left in me to give.

Ben searches my face. I smile. I know I wouldn't have been able to cope with all of this without him.

'Had enough?'

I nod and he puts the damaged photo face down on the little table. Then he leads me out into the corridor, shutting my door behind him.

We can hear clattering coming from the bathroom and look in on Becky. Dark sweat marks under her arms and across her back are testament to the effort she's been putting in. She sees us and stands, hands in the small of her back as she stretches.

'Becky, I'm more grateful than I can say.'

'I'm just so sorry about all of this. It shouldn't have happened.'

'I wish it hadn't.'

Again, I get the feeling that she's hesitating; that there's something more she wants to say. She gathers her things and leaves without saying it.

'Come on.' Ben takes my hand. 'I'll make up the spare bed and rustle up something simple to eat. Would an omelette fit the bill?'

'I'm sorry, I think I'm too tired to eat.'

'Then I'd better get a move on before you collapse.'

~~~

The omelette revives my flagging reserves of energy. It's half-past nine and I'm stretching into a yawn when Ben says, 'What are you going to do about Gethin?'

'Gethin! I promised to Skype him tonight.' I look around for my laptop. Then I remember.

Ben disappears and returns moments later with his which he puts down in front of me. He leans over my shoulder as he starts it up and puts in his password. The screen fills with an image of two young men standing next to each other, grinning at the camera. There's a strong family resemblance. I twist round but Ben is, as usual, ahead of me.

'The one on the right's my father. The other's my Uncle John.'

'They look close.'

'They were. They shared a birthdate, the same interests and a great passion for the sea.'

'Were? What happened?'
~~~

‘My uncle was killed within a few weeks of this photo being taken.’ That muscle is twitching by his jaw again. He gives a slight shake of his head. ‘Anyway, let’s get you sorted with Skype.’

Less than five minutes later, Gethin answers.

‘Hiya, Gwen. How’s things?’

He’s wearing a tuxedo and bow tie, and I’m foolishly distracted by them.

‘You’re looking very dapper tonight.’

He grins. ‘Big company do.’ He’s looking vibrantly happy, such a change from the last time we Skyped. He glances at his watch. ‘Actually, I’m running a bit late. Is everything all right?’

‘We’re fine, but the house has been burgled.’

There’s the sound of a vehicle beeping outside.

‘Hell! What next! Was much taken? Is there any damage?’

‘Nothing major.’

‘Thank God! And you and Gran are fine?’

‘Yes. No one was in at the time. It’s just a few trinkets.’ There’s more beeping outside.’

‘I’d better go and cancel my lift.’

‘Don’t be stupid. Everything’s under control here. There’s nothing more to be done.’

‘Are you sure?’

‘Scout’s honour.’

There’s more beeping.

‘Okay, Gwen, but I’ll be back tomorrow.’

‘Seriously, Geth, everything’s fine tonight. There’s no need to worry. I’m here with Ben and Gran’s with Joyce.’

The next beeping is protracted and persistent.

‘Go, Geth, before you annoy the whole neighbourhood!’

‘He looks towards the door and back again. ‘Love you, Gwen.’

‘Love you, too.’

He disconnects.

I stare at the laptop screen. It’s a relief to know that I caught him before he left, and I’m not going to pretend that I’m sad that he’s returning tomorrow. I yawn.

‘Come on, sleepyhead. Bed.’

I stumble through to a room that's lit by a table lamp beside a king size bed.

'Ben, this is your room. I thought I was having the spare one.'

'After all you've been through, it made sense for you to have the bed that I know is comfortable. The spare one is still an unknown quantity.'

I start to protest but am overtaken by another yawn that makes my eyes water.

Ben takes a shirt from the wardrobe and hands it to me. 'Go on. There's an en suite through there and I'll be in the next room so if you want anything you just have to yell.'

Then he's gone.

I put on the shirt and slide under the duvet. There's a line-dried cotton fragrance with just enough of a hint of the scent of Ben to make me feel secure. I drift off to sleep.

Chapter 26

The sun is warm on my back and I'm giggling as Gethin throws the ball again. It's much too high and although I strain to reach it, all I can do next is follow its course far over the sparkling water. It surfaces before bobbing tantalisingly beyond our reach..

My distorted voice fills my ears.

'Mummy! Daddy! Get it back! Quick!'

I hear my mother's, happy and reassuring. 'It'll come back in a minute. Build a sandcastle while you're waiting.'

'No! It's going away!'

'Don't be silly, pumpkin. If it doesn't come back, I'll buy you a new one.'

'It's my Kermit ball. ***Please****, Mummy,* ***please****!'*

'I promise you can choose any ball you want if this one doesn't come back.'

'No! I want this ball. I don't want any of the others.' I hear my voice plead and whine.

'Okay. No need to cry. I'll get it for you.' She rises gracefully from the towel beside my father, brushing grains of sand off her slender body.

But I know what's to come and the scream builds in the pit of my stomach as Mummy splashes into the deeper water and starts her slow, powerful crawl towards the ball, Kermit's bobbing face mocking her approach.

Something's wrong. She's drifting to the left and despite facing back towards the beach she's moving further away from us. Her left arm rises in the air and she calls out. 'Peter! Peter, help!'

Daddy reacts swiftly and then he's gripping me by the shoulders and shaking me.

'Wake up, Gwen. Wake up.'

I don't understand.

'It's just a dream. You're safe. I've got you.'

But it isn't really a dream. It's a re-enactment of the truth.

'Gwen, listen to me. You're having a nightmare. Open your eyes.'

This is wrong. I've lost my bearings. The bright sunlight sparkling off the waves has gone. In the gentle glow of a bedside lamp, I see Ben's troubled face.

'You're all right, Gwen. You're in my room and nothing can hurt you.'

'Ben?'

'That's right. I'm here.'

I'm still in a hybrid world between dream and reality and it takes several seconds for the real situation to come into focus. When it does, all the strength leaves me and I slump in his arms.

We stay like that for a while. I can hear him murmuring reassurances and my rapid heartbeat begins to recover. When I push myself upright, he eases himself back, watching me closely.

'All right?'

I nod.

'You're dripping in sweat. I'll get you a glass of water. I'm only going as far as the kitchen. Okay?'

I nod again.

He's back with the cool drink but I'm shaking so much I can't control it and he holds the glass steady for me. When it's empty, he places the glass by the lamp.

Next, he hitches himself onto the bed next to me, his back up against the headboard, and draws me into his shoulder.

'Tell me,' he says.

'I can't.'

'Yes, you can.' He grips me tighter. 'You were screaming about the sea and your parents. You were frightened – that frightened me.'

'Please don't do this.'

'It sounded as if something happened to you when you were a child.'

'Please.' It's a mere whisper of sound.

'Gwen, I want to help. I get the impression you're struggling with something. Please don't shut me out.'

'I don't want you to hate me.'

There. I've said it.

'That's not possible.' Then he plays his trump card. 'This is important. I don't want there to be a barrier between us. I need you to be open with me.'

I'm trapped and know a fleeting urge to run away. But he's right. There can't be a hope of a future for us if I don't tell him the terrible truth.

'All right.' I'm defeated. I tell the story, the words dropping leaden into the shadowed room.

'I was five. We'd gone on holiday. Fuerteventura. Our parents found a secluded beach and Geth and I played while they sunbathed.' I falter. Ben holds me fractionally tighter and I carry on.

'Gethin and I were playing with our Kermit ball when it landed in the sea.' I take a deep breath. 'We couldn't reach it and I begged my mother to get it back for us.'

'Go on.' The verbal nudge is quiet but determined.

'I made a huge fuss. In the end, Mummy went to get it.' My breath snags as I force the words out. 'She got caught in a rip tide, a flash rip they called it. She cried for help…'

There's a strange stillness about the room now. Ben is silent, unmoving. I continue.

'Daddy told us to stay back and he went in after her.' The noise as I swallow sounds unnaturally loud. 'Then *he* was struggling.'

My mouth works soundlessly as I try to get the next words out. 'Two brothers from the UK saw what was going on. One of them paddled out on his surfboard to help, the other went to phone the emergency services.'

Ben squeezes my hand.

'When the other brother came back with help, Gethin and I were all that was left…'

My voice breaks but I make myself carry on. 'We huddled together on the sand as the rescue party went in after them. One by one they returned with the bodies. We watched them desperately trying to breathe life back into them.'

'Dear God!' The words sound as if they're wrenched from him. Then I'm crushed against him.

I don't know how long we stay like that but there's more I have to tell and I push against him.

‘A local family took us in overnight while we waited for Granny and Grandad to come over from Wales.’ I can hear the dreadful weariness in my voice now. ‘When they arrived, we booked into a hotel for the night before the trip home. Grandad had been suffering from angina for a while and that night he had a fatal heart attack.’

I can’t go on.

Ben says nothing, just carries on holding me in a grip that’s almost painful. I’ve told him and now all I can do is wait to see how he reacts.

Agonising seconds later, when he’s still not responded. I push against him. Have I broken our fragile relationship? It’s at that point that he sits upright so that he can turn to face me.

‘I’m beyond sorry, Gwen. I can’t imagine the trauma that you’ve been through. That would be enough to destroy most adults. To go through it as a child must have added another awful level of terror and distress.’ He takes my hands in his. ‘Why?’ it’s the gentlest probe, ‘why would you think I’d hate you?’

‘Because *I* did it. *I* destroyed our lives.’

‘That’s nonsense. You were a child.’

‘If I hadn’t forced my mother to go into the sea, none of this would have happened.’

‘She chose to go. She wasn’t to know there was a rip tide. None of you knew.’

‘If I hadn’t been so selfish…’

‘Gwen, you were a child.’

Has anyone ever blamed you?’

I hang my head.

He persists. ‘Did anyone tell you this was your fault?’

‘Granny. Not to my face. But at my birthday party one year I heard her telling Joyce.’

‘Telling her what?’

‘Her exact words were, “She took my boy, my Peter, away from me”.’

‘You must have misunderstood.’

‘No. There’s not a great deal to misunderstand there, is there?’

‘Have you spoken to Joyce about this?’

'Why?'

'Because I've watched the two of you together, you and your grandmother, and she may be grumpy and ungrateful a lot of the time but I've seen a genuine affection when she looks at you.'

'You have?'

'Definitely. There was that time at Lamphey Palace when she cupped your face with her hand.'

'Gethin kept saying it didn't matter. He said I didn't mean it to happen. He said not to listen to what people were saying.'

'All this time you've carried this burden of guilt? What help did you get?'

'Help?'

'Counselling. Therapy.'

'We spoke to a woman once, but it was so upsetting, Gethin told Granny we didn't want to go back.'

'Your grandmother should have insisted.'

'She's the one I hurt most. She'd lost her son and her husband. She only agreed to take us in because there was no one else in the family.'

'I bet if you'd had proper help, you'd have come to terms with what was simply a tragic accident. I'm convinced that your grandmother doesn't blame you for it.'

'You really believe that?'

'Yes. No one could possibly not be moved by what you've been through.'

I look down at our joined hands and remember Jake.

'Gwen? What is it?'

'Jake wasn't.'

'Who's Jake?'

'We went out together during the last couple of weeks of the summer term. It was my first year at college. He was doing Sports Studies. We'd been drinking with friends and ended up at a beach.' This is so hard, but I carry on. 'I panicked. Said I wanted to leave. Jake asked me why and, maybe it was because I'd drunk too much, but I told him what I've just told you. He said he could cure me of my childish fear. He picked me up and carried me into the water and threw me in.' I register Ben's grimace 'He held me down in the waves for a few seconds and said, "See, it's only water."

When he let me back to the surface I clawed at him, apparently, and started to scream. He called me neurotic and told me to get a grip.'

There's a silence as I struggle to find the next words. They're released in a whisper.

'The screams, the waves, the memories – they were all too much. Some of the others helped me from the water but I went to pieces. I had a breakdown and was admitted to hospital.'

I'm pulled back against him and I lie limp in his arms.

'It's all right, Gwen. It's all right. It's over now.'

I'm so tired, so physically drained, I sleep.

~~~

There's that strange feeling of trying to make sense of unfamiliar surroundings when I come to. I'm in Ben's bed. Surprisingly, I don't cringe with embarrassment when I recall all the things I said. Now he knows everything. His response has given me hope.

When I next see Joyce, I'll ask her about those words that have troubled me for over a decade now. She knows Granny better than anyone.

I go through the house until I find him. He's standing at his open patio doors with a mug in his hand. He turns when he hears me.

'Morning, sleepyhead. Cwtch.' He smiles and open his arms and I cross the distance between us until I'm snugly ensconced in a clasp that's satisfyingly strong. I'm oblivious of everything else until something pushes against my knee accompanied by excited little yelps. I laugh and break away to give Atticus the fuss that he's demanding.

Ben says ruefully, 'I'm beginning to think that you've usurped me in his affections.'

A chuckle escapes me. The day feels lighter somehow. It's time to put my past in some kind of adult context and start to live my life in the sunshine instead of keeping a low profile in the shadows.

We make a simple breakfast together in the light and airy kitchen and, as I pass Ben the toast, I realise I'm in love with
~~~

him. It comes as such a shock my hand pauses midway between us.

'Gwen?' He takes the toast. 'Are you all right?'

'Yes.' *Please* let him feel the same way. 'I'm fine.'

Chapter 27

Our hard work last night has been worth it. The house looks fairly normal and it's only when you search for particular things that you realise they're no longer there. I'm surprised at how buoyant my mood is under the circumstances. The last twenty-four hours have been like that Folly Farm big wheel, turning from highs to lows and back again.

Ben has changed the lock on the door and the door cams will be delivered later today. He's had extra keys cut so that he and Geth can have one, too, and I've given Cranston Care the new keysafe code.

He spots the CD player and cases on the table.

'I'd better put these back in your grandmother's room. Hopefully, Stafford will be able to pin down who did this from the fingerprints and then you can put all of this ugliness behind you.'

He has to work on site today but before he leaves he gives me one of those kisses that fills my senses so completely, nothing else exists.

The first thing I do is load the washing machine for one of its many cycles of the day.

Becky turns up a few minutes early to make sure that she can give Granny the medication she missed yesterday and we've barely had time to talk about last night before we hear a taxi pull up. As soon as Becky realises it's Joyce, she hurries out to help her manoeuvre Granny into her wheelchair. I'm on tenterhooks. What will her reaction be to the burglary?

She doesn't seem to notice.

'Did you have a good time in Aberystwyth?'

She looks puzzled. 'What would I be doing in Aberystwyth?' she demands irritably.

Joyce smiles fondly at her. 'Someone's a bit of a crosspatch this morning.'

'I am *not* a crosspatch!'

'Did I say I was talking about *you*?'

'Of course you were. You were getting at me because I was—' She breaks off and her lips twitch. 'All right. Maybe I was a little bit of a crosspatch.'

Joyce laughs. 'Tell the truth and shame the devil, Edith.' She gives Granny's shoulder a gentle squeeze, before Becky wheels her through to her bedroom. Then she turns to me.

'Right, Gwen. Tell me everything.'

I pull out a chair for her at the table.

'Coffee?'

'Later. I want to know what's going on. It was only after you phoned that I remembered how you distracted me last time when I asked why you were looking so done in. Out with it. I want the whole, unvarnished truth, my dear.

I tell her everything, from the fuss at the pub to the burglary.

'Oh, dear child, I had no idea. You keep things so close to your chest. Is there anything I can do?'

'No. I think it's all under control now. Hopefully the fingerprint team will be able to tell us who did this and then we can put a stop to all of this nastiness.'

'What's been taken? I know we managed to persuade Edith to put most of her valuables under lock and key but there were some nice things that she insisted on keeping.'

I sigh.

'It's mainly just the small stuff that's gone including her jade pieces, plus,' I feel my spirits sinking with each item listed, 'both Cartier watches and Grandad's Rolex, her Fabergé earrings and necklace, the Apostle spoons, the copper pig and all the silver photo frames.'

She pats my hand. 'I'm so sorry, Gwen. I can imagine how hurt you must be by it all.'

'My biggest worry's Granny. What did she say when you broke the news to her?'

'Well, to be completely honest, my love, she was so exhausted after our day out, she went from anger to sorrow to sleep; all in less than ten minutes.' She gives a rueful grin. 'I *forgot* to mention it again this morning and I'm hoping it's one of those things that's not registered permanently. The place looks pretty much the same as always.'

'That's such a relief. I'll not say anything and hopefully it'll all blow over. The jewellery and watches were in a box on top of her wardrobe and she's not mentioned them since they went up there.'

'There we are then.'

I hesitate before adding, 'There's a couple of things you might be able to help me with.'

'Go on.'

'Most of the photos went with the frames. Do you know if there are spares? You know, ones of the family, my parents.' I stop in case my voice gives away my distress at losing this link to them.

Her face softens and I know she understands.

'I can put your mind at rest straightaway. After the accident, Edith struggled to cope. She didn't want you or Gethin to see how upset she was and it was really difficult for her. Her way of managing things was to tamp it all down like a smouldering fire.' A faraway look comes into her eyes and I can see her sadness. 'She had several photo albums and gave them to me for safekeeping. They were just too painful to look at.'

'I didn't know.' My voice sounds husky.

'She tried, Gwen. She really tried to protect you but she was damaged by the tragedy and some days it was a struggle for her to function even on a basic level.'

I'm thrown, and it must show.

'Gwen, she'd lost her only child and her husband in the space of a couple of days. She had to hold things together for you and Gethin and deal with all the paperwork, the inquest, the gruesome media interest. It almost destroyed her.'

This is my chance. I take a deep breath and plunge in.

'So is that why she said she hated me?'

'Hated you?'

Her brow concertinas and she looks puzzled.

'She's never hated you. What makes you think that, for heaven's sake?'

'I heard her say it at my ninth birthday party. She said, "'I hate her, Joyce. She took my boy, my Peter, away from me."'

Some of the colour drains from Joyce's face. She looks anguished and I regret telling her.

'I'm so sorry, Joyce. Forget it. I'll make that coffee now.'

She grabs my hand and pulls me back down again.

'I should have realised.' Her groan frightens me but she hangs on to my hand and continues. 'You changed. You changed and now I understand why. You became even more withdrawn and polite. There was a neediness to please your grandmother that she found irritating. Dear Lord!'

Joyce buries her face in her hands whilst I watch her, anxiously. When she looks up again, she's regained her composure.

'Oh Gwen! If only you'd said something. Edith wasn't talking about you; it was your mother. She couldn't bring herself, right from the start, to refer to her as anything other than 'she'. Edith had a blind spot where your father was concerned. Peter was her dream child. No one was going to be good enough for him and your free-spirited mother took him away from her.' She sighs again. 'Given time, she'd have come round; she *was* coming round, I think, before the accident–but afterwards, your mother became a convenient scapegoat for her.'

'She didn't hate me?'

'No. Never has. She's always had that snappiness to her but it used to be balanced by a lively sense of humour. She had a miscarriage when Peter was four after which she was told she couldn't have another child. It added a layer of bitterness to her that she struggled to keep in. After the accident, the snappiness came to dominate but the old Edith is still there, not far below the surface.'

'She adores Gethin.'

'Ah. There, I'm afraid, we have her Achilles heel. Gethin is the spitting image of his father and she dotes on him as a consequence. She can't help it. She looks on your brother and sees Peter. It's hard on both of them. Gethin found the smothering hard to take. He didn't know how to handle it.' She becomes insistent. 'But it doesn't mean she doesn't love you. The love's the same, it's the obsession that's different.' She fishes in her sleeve and produces a tissue which she uses to dab her eyes and then blow her nose.

'Joyce, I'm so sorry. I didn't mean to upset you.'

'Bless you, child. I should be doing the apologising. You've had this hanging over you since you were nine.' Her eyes fill again and she turns away and does some more dabbling with the tissue. She throws a gruff, 'Time for you to make that coffee now I think.'

~~~

After Becky's gone and Granny is sitting in her favourite chair, Joyce totters through to the kitchen.

'Is it all right if I stay for a while?'

'As if you need to ask!' I go across and give her a hug. 'Granny loves your company and it'll give me some space to get my thoughts back on an even keel.'

'There we go then. Everyone happy. Edith and I can enjoy one of our chats about the good old days, and you can get some colour back in those cheeks of yours.' She pats my hand. 'I've told your grandmother she must remember to wear her alarm pendant. I know the carers automatically put it on her in the morning, but with all of this going on, I don't like the idea of her not being able to summon help.'

'Of course.'

'I'm her first port of call and so it never matters if she pushes it by mistake.' She adds, 'Gwen, I hope you won't mind me saying this, but you've always done what you can not to upset people. I can see now that it's your way to stupidly try to compensate for things that were always beyond your control and *never* your fault, but I'm sure you're aware that there are those that take advantage of it. You need to challenge things when they're not right. Grasp the nettle, my love. It might hurt for a moment, but nothing like the agony that comes from letting the nettles in your life flourish unchallenged until they're so big you simply *can't* ignore them anymore.'

'It's a good analogy, Joyce. I wish I'd faced up to Granny after that birthday party. We'd both have benefitted from it.'

'There we are, then. You have a sweet nature, Gwen, and I don't want you hurt on account of it.'

'Sometimes it feels like my life has always been like this. It won't be easy to turn it around.'

'No. It won't. But you have that nice young man of yours to help you find your way.'
~~~

I feel the heat flare in my face, but I know I'm grinning. She taps my cheek gently and whispers, 'He sounds like a keeper, my dear.'

I laugh out loud at that. It's a laugh loud enough to disturb Granny.

'Joyce? Joyce! What's going on? Where are you?'

'Hold your horses, Edith. I'm on my way.'

~~~

The weather's turning. Clouds are clumping in the sky and a breeze is building. The cooler air is like a balm and I go into the garden and turn towards it, feeling it move the tendrils of hair against my cheeks.

I'm unbelievably relieved at the truth behind that misunderstanding all those years ago; relieved, but angry that I hadn't had the courage to ask about it at the time. All those years when I'd added another level of crippling guilt. I created an unnecessary and damaging burden and made clumsy attempts to make amends that irritated rather than soothed the one person whose love I was desperate to gain. There's a lesson here. I don't like to rock the boat or put my own interests first. I'm beginning to appreciate how foolish I've been. There's a massive difference between selfishness and martyrdom and I've been tempted to follow the sainted route for all the wrong reasons.

There's a flurry of wings and the robin appears at my feet. He's a welcome distraction.

'Come on, then. Let's see what we can find for you.'

He follows me, almost underfoot, as I remove the trowel from the shed and start to root around in the soil. It doesn't take long before he's feasting on grubs and worms and I'm so amused by his antics, I don't notice the creeping shadow until I'm under it.

I'm hauled to my feet and pushed backwards against the shed.

Mark Johnson looms over me and he's so angry I can feel it in every quivering fibre of my body. This time, I know it's gone beyond drunkenly pawing at me.
~~~

‘I’ve just been to see my Justin. They won’t let me in. He was standing behind them, sobbing. They say the hearing’s in two days. They say the situation’s changed and I’m not allowed to be with him – even with someone else in the room.’

He jabs at me with one of his fingers, punctuating the words with painful digs.

‘I told you to take back your statement. You haven’t, have you?’

I find my voice. ‘No. I know what I saw and I’m not going to lie.’

‘I want my kids back. You hear me?’ His face pushes into mine again but there’s no rancid beer in his breath; he’s stone cold sober. ‘You should know better.’

The words hit harder than the jabs.

‘*You* know what it’s like. *You* know what it’s like to lose someone. Remember how if felt when *your* parents died? Go on, remember that loss. *Yo*u can put this right.’

He’s waiting for an answer. I give the only one I can.

‘No.’

‘Try again.’ He grabs my head and shoves it against the wooden slats behind me. I’m momentarily stunned and when I open my eyes again, Mark Johnson’s flat out on the paving and Ben is standing over him.

Joyce has halted a little way from us, her feet robustly planted apart and her stick held as a weapon. ‘Are you all right, Gwen?’

I push myself away from the shed. ‘I’m fine, Joyce.’

‘I’ll call the police.’

She lowers her stick and uses it to retreat, as nimbly as she can, back into the house.

Ben turns his head to look at me. I’ve never seen that menacing expression on him before. I want to remove it.

‘Has he hurt you?’

‘No. I’m fine.’ I take a step nearer him. This is a Ben I don’t know. ‘Honestly, Ben. The cavalry arrived and no harm’s done.’

In those few seconds, Mark takes his opportunity to run for it. I hold Ben back.

‘Let him go. He’s at the end of his tether.’

I reach up to cup his face in my hands, forcing him to look at me. 'It's over, Ben. Let the police deal with Mark.'

The fight leaves him and he pulls me to him.

'I came in and he had you pinned. What if I hadn't got away in time? What if–'

He crushes me tighter to him.

'Ben. Stop this.' My voice is muffled against him. 'I'm fine. And if you hadn't arrived, I had Joyce armed and dangerous and ready to enter the fray.'

The crushing grip eases and then he holds me away from him, searching my face.

'Sure you're okay?'

'No damage done. You're here. Nothing else matters.' I take his hand. 'Come on, we'd better make Joyce a soothing cup of tea.'

~~~

Stafford listens to us recount the details and says they'll bring Mark Johnson in for questioning. However, there's little evidence of physical harm and he wasn't officially trespassing.

'Can you search his flat?' I'm desperate to get our things back but what he says next pours cold water onto my hopes.

'We already have his prints on record and there's nothing in here that matches them.'

'What about gloves? Perhaps he wore gloves.'

Stafford sighs.

'Tell you what I'll do. I can use his attack on you to get a warrant and we'll see if there's any evidence there. All I'm saying is, don't hold your breath.' As he leaves, he adds, 'And if you see him again, just give us a call. Leave the cricket bat where it is, eh?'

I nod meekly, but that hint of humour in the man raises him a little in my estimation.

About an hour later, the door opens and Gethin walks in. He looks dreadful. His eyes are red-rimmed with fatigue and there's an exhaustion to him that worries me. Even after the
~~~

beating he took, he didn't look as crushed and miserable as this.

Joyce, about to go back home, says, 'What on earth's happened to you, my boy. You look ready to drop?'

'I'm just tired, Joyce. The train was packed and then I had to call in at the police station to be fingerprinted.'

'Nonsense! I know you better than that. You look downright miserable and defeated. What's happened to you?'

'I've told you!' He snaps at her.

She studies him with narrowed eyes.

'I'd reign in that temper if I were you,' she says calmly.

He's instantly ashamed.

'I'm so sorry, Joyce. That was unforgivable. I'm fighting Zoe in court, my ribs still hurt, someone's making my sister's life a misery and now we've been burgled. It feels like a never-ending nightmare.' He gives her a kiss. 'Forgive me. I just need to get my perspective back.'

'Well, you know where I am if you want to talk.'

A vehicle pulls up outside.

'That'll be my taxi,' she says, 'so I'll get out of your hair and leave you to it.'

We fill Gethin in on the afternoon's excitement. He smashes his fist down on the table, making me jump.

'I should have been here.'

I reach across and cover his hand with mine. 'I'm fine, Geth. No one can hurt me in here. I have you and Ben as back-up.'

Ben clears his throat.

'I've been thinking, perhaps Gwen would be safer staying with me until this has all blown over.'

We both stare at him, open-mouthed. I recover first.

'I can't, Ben. I have to be here for Granny and, anyway, I have my big brother here to look after me.'

He runs a hand backwards across his scalp, making his hair stand on end.

'Gwen, I know this is your home and I can understand why you feel the need to be here, but you've no idea how anxious it makes me when I'm not with you. I can't take another fright like the one this afternoon.'

‘She’ll be safe with me.’ Gethin sounds affronted and I’m torn between dismay and humour at the two of them sparring over me.’

I go across to the sideboard and pick up a small box.

‘This arrived earlier. It’s a door cam and Ben’s going to fit it before he leaves. I couldn’t be safer if you barricaded me inside Fort Knox.’

Gethin’s lip quivers. ‘Point taken.’

‘There we are then,’ I say. ‘Panic over.’

Ben looks at the package.

‘I ordered two of them. There should be one for the back as well.’

‘That’s all that came.’ I murmur, ‘Perhaps the other one’s still at the depot.’

‘I’ll follow it up. At least we have the doorbell one.’

Once Ben’s fitted the camera, he takes a laptop out of his bag.

‘This is an old one I had for backup. I’ll connect this and your phone to the cam and check that it works on both of them.’

‘Oh, I couldn’t take your…’ I let the words drift away. I understand the reassurance this gives him and I’m grateful that he cares.

Gethin is smiling now and offers to go outside to test it. Ben and I sit with heads touching and watch him approach the door.

‘Little pig, little pig, let me come in.’

Ben pushes a button on the phone and squeaks, ‘Not by the hair on my chinny, chin chin!’

Gethin laughs and we pronounce the test a success.

Chapter 28

I don't remember having any dreams in the night and the day feels fresh and hopeful. Gethin's sitting at the kitchen table when I come through. He looks worried and that worry transfers itself to me.

'What's wrong, Geth?'

'Nothing. I'm just working on some figures for work and it's a real pain.' He runs a hand over his face.

'Can I help?'

'Nope. This one's down to me.'

'Have you had something to eat?'

'Not hungry.'

He goes back to poring over his screen.

'You ought to eat, you know.'

'You're fussing again.'

'I'm just showing my caring side. Can I make you some breakfast?'

'Gwen, I'm trying to concentrate here.'

I whisper, 'Sorry.'

He grins.

'Okay, I'd love a coffee.'

I move around the kitchen as unobtrusively as I can and place the mug of coffee on a coaster by his right hand.

'Thanks, Gwen. I know I'm being a bad-tempered bear but I do need to get this done.'

'No apology needed. I understand.'

The day feels close and the blue sky's become a bright grey that hurts the eyes. I step out onto the patio. Yesterday's breeze has been replaced by a heavy stillness. My robin must have been waiting for me. He's straight down to my feet and I give in to his appealing black button eyes and fetch the trowel. He's so keen, he sits on my hand as I turn over the soil. It feels like a tiny miracle to have this connection with a wild creature and my spirits soar. I turn when I sense movement behind me and release my hidden scream as a long breath. It's just Gethin standing at the doors with his mug in his hand, watching.

'That bird looks better fed than I do.'

'Well, you turned down my offer of breakfast, but there's plenty of worms and grubs going spare if you'd like some.'

He holds up his free hand.

'I'll pass on that kind offer.' His expression becomes serious and I feel my stomach drop away. He's looking in the direction of the pond. There's a piece of paper at the edge. We both move towards it at the same time and when I go to pick it up, he holds me back.

'No. I'll get a bag.'

While he's gone, I spot the damage. Lying just under the smooth surface of the pond, floating motionless on their sides, lie the goldfish, their colours already muted by death. This hurts more than the burglary. These were sentient creatures. A wave of nausea hits me. Something flashes in my head. I can't capture it but whatever it was has increased the unease I feel.

Gethin returns wearing a washing up glove, picks the paper up by the edge and turns it over. It's a weeping eye but there are two changes. This eye is represented by a cross, like a clown's eye, and the red pen is now a broader black one. The effect is visceral and I sense the viciousness behind it.

Gethin carefully inserts the image into the clean sandwich bag. I point to the pond. He stares at it in silence for what seems an age, and then he turns troubled eyes on me.

'Oh Gwen.' He sighs.

I clasp my hands together to stop the trembling. 'What do we do?'

'I suppose we wait, and see what happens when they find Mark.' He sounds grim. 'But I have to say, I don't like this at all.' He puts a hand on my shoulder and turns me to face him. 'You have to be careful. No risk-taking. Promise?'

I nod and then remember the door cam.

'Do you think Ben's door cam might have caught him?'

We rush through and I check Ben's laptop. There's nothing there.

Geth is looking at me again. He tips his head on one side, like my robin.

'What?'

'Nothing.' He smiles. 'Don't worry, Gwen. I have your back. Everything will be all right.'

~~~

I wander through the house. This latest setback has hit hard and I need a distraction. I want to capture yesterday's hopeful mood. Ben's laptop is still open on the table and I search for local news.

One of the items catches my attention. There's a "70s Extravaganza" taking place today in the grounds of Pembroke castle with tribute bands, memorabilia and side stalls selling everything from vintage items to local produce. The longer I look at it, the more it seems like the answer to my prayers. This is a chance for me to go out with Granny to something that I think we'll both enjoy.

I tell Ben when he drops in to see me mid-morning and ask him if he can drop me off with Granny when he goes back to work. I was expecting him to be delighted for me. I'm wrong. He's rigidly against it.

'This is crazy, Gwen. We don't know where Mark Johnson is at the moment and you're proposing to wander around where he can get to you.'

'But he can't. The place'll be milling with people.'

'Like the day you went to get the prescription, you mean?'

'That's not fair! He pulled me off the pavement.'

'And there's nowhere amongst all of this extravaganza where he could grab you? Pull you behind a stall, say, or one of the marquees?'

'He'd be stupid to do that. He's already in trouble as it is.'

'Exactly. He didn't look like a man in control of his actions that last time I saw him.'

'I promise to be careful.'

'That's not enough to reassure me.'

Gethin appears. 'What's not reassuring?'

'Gwen wants to go to this 70s thing in Pembroke Castle this afternoon.'

'Has she told you about the fish?'

I flash him a warning glance but I'm too late.

'What fish?'

'The fish she and I found less than an hour ago. Floating in the pond. Dead.'
~~~

Ben is on his feet and straight out into the garden. I follow. All my plans, my hopes for the day, lie in ruins.

Gethin comes out, carrying the new eye picture and hands it to him in its polythene bag.

I hear Ben's sharp intake of breath and know that it's only stiffened his resolve.

I try to control the wheedling note in my voice.

'Could you come, too?'

He looks at me and I can see a combination of anger and sadness in his expression.

'I can't, Gwen. There's a meeting on the site that I have to be there for. I won't be finished before four at the earliest.'

My shoulders droop. I'd formed a picture in my head of Granny and I out together, sharing some laughter. Now, my head's filled with images of dying fish and Mark Johnson's furious face. I can't see a time when all of this will be behind me.

Then Gethin comes up trumps.

'If you can give us a lift in, and pick us up afterwards, I'll go with them and keep an eye on things.'

I hold my breath and realise I'm also holding my crossed fingers behind my back, like I used to.

'Okay. It's a deal.' There's more. 'You,' he says, waggling a stern finger in front of my delighted face, 'are to stick with this brother of yours and do whatever he tells you.'

'No problem!'

'Promise?'

'Promise.'

That wheel's turned full circle.

Ben says he'll be back for us at about one-thirty and rushes back to work.

I go to Gethin and put a hand on his arm.

'Thanks, Geth.'

'You're welcome.' He looks amused. 'You do appreciate that you're now obliged to carry out any orders I give you?' He places a finger alongside his temple as if dredging up an idea. 'For instance, I have shoes that need cleaning, a shirt that needs pressing and an insatiable appetite for pancakes.'

'I need to see the small print on the contract, but I'll go and whip up some batter.'

'I wasn't serious. Though, now you mention it, pancakes sound like an excellent idea.' There's a pause during which the mood darkens. 'Keep Granny busy in the house and I'll sort out our little problem in the pond.'

~~~

At one-thirty, I have Granny ready in her chair. I've told her we're going to have a day out and she seems mildly interested. Her wheelchair's folded and ready and my spirits are soaring.

She recognises Ben and his presence seems to reassure her. Gethin and I sit in the back, enjoying the entertainment.

Ben manages to park on Main Street and insists on pushing Granny up the steep hill to the castle. Before he leaves, he exacts another promise from me to stick with Gethin and do as he says.

Then we're off.

The grounds are teeming with people, many of whom have entered into the spirit of the thing and are wearing fashions of the era. Some are clumping about in ridiculously high platform soles below extravagant flares. The weather's warm but muggy and some have donned hot pants; others look overheated in Lycra. There's laughter everywhere and five people bounce past us on Space Hoppers.

I bob down to Granny's level.

'It's a celebration of the 1970s,' I tell her.

Her expression's puzzled but she doesn't look upset.

One of the nearby stalls is covered in vintage items. I pick up something called a Stylophone. It's the size of a small transistor radio with a silver cut-out section like a flat keyboard. She holds out her hand for it.

'I have one of those,' she says happily. There's something like a stylus tucked in a groove and connected by a wire. She fishes it out and runs the wand over the keys, Her face breaks into a beaming smile as a dreadful, robotic tremolo sound issues from it. She even taps out a tune but it doesn't sound familiar'.
~~~

The stallholder tells me I can have it for £10, but that's more than I can afford. I shake my head, but can't retrieve the Stylophone from Granny who's now playing something I identify as Yellow Submarine. I shrug at Gethin who sticks his hands in the pockets of his jeans; the personification of the bored male shopper.

As she plays, engrossed, a small crowd gathers round and when she finishes, they clap enthusiastically. For a second, that confused expression is back, and then she's revelling in the attention.

She thanks them graciously for their applause, plays the chorus again and they join in, raucously, before giving her another clap and moving on, many of them to the stall it came from.

I manage to wrest it from her grasp and hand it back to the stallholder. He pushes it back at me.

'You keep it, Miss Meredith,' he says. 'Looks to me as if it's found who it was looking for.'

I don't know what to do. The pleasure it's given Granny is worth the asking price many times over and it feels wrong not to pay him. I'm also thrown by his use of my name.

'That's very kind of you, but I can't accept.'

'Course you can. Anyway, it's not for you, it's for that pretty lady next to you.' He directs the last words, louder than normal, at the intended recipient and she looks fit to burst with happiness.

'That's very kind of you, young man.' She holds her hand out again and I return the object of her affection to her.'

I turn back to him. 'Thank you. I don't have my purse with me. Do you have a child at the school?'

He nods. 'I don't get along to parents evenings and the like but our two little girls think you're the bee's knees.'

'In that case, I'll make sure to pay you back when term starts again.'

'You can't pay for a gift. And anyway,' he leans forward, 'look at all the custom you've sent my way.'

I laugh and thank him again, before rejoining Gethin who looks unimpressed with the situation. He takes over the pushing of the wheelchair and he stiffens when the tinny refrain from Yellow Submarine starts up again.

'Oh Gethin, if you could see your face!' I fall against him and the humour of the situation gets to him, too, and soon we're strolling along together with our electronic troubadour providing the accompaniment.

I daren't point out the lava lamps or other gadgets in case she forms the same attachment to them. It's a bit akin to dealing with a toddler in the sweets aisle of a supermarket.

One of the tribute acts starts up and the air is filled with Abba's Dancing Queen. Granny stops playing and looks up.

'What's that?'

'It's a group. They're going to play Abba songs.'

'Well, they're dreadfully loud!' She scowls and I'm wondering whether we should move somewhere quieter when I notice her foot is tapping in time with the music. Geth grins at me and then we sit on the grass on either side of her wheelchair and give in to the experience.

It's a lovely afternoon. Granny drifts off to sleep at one point, but wakes refreshed to join in with the Rod Stewart set. When Ben turns up, she's singing along to Sailing and I wish I'd captured the amazement on his face.

When the act finishes, I kneel down in front of her and tell her it's time to go home now.

'I've had such fun, Gwen. Can we come again?'

I kiss her cheek. 'Next time they come here, I'll make sure we have front row seats.'

'That would be lovely. You've made me very happy, Gwen. I know I take you for granted sometimes but I do appreciate you.'

She swivels to the side.

'Ned! You're here, too. How wonderful.'

'I'm your chauffeur, Edith. I'm afraid it's time to leave now.'

She yawns. 'Yes. You're probably right.'

We head back across to the entrance and I turn round for one last look and spot a mustard-coloured cap which bobs to the right and out of sight. I shiver. Then I remonstrate with myself. I bet there's hundreds of the things out there. I've had a wonderful afternoon and I'm not going to let myself needlessly spoil it.

On the way back, we all fall into a contented silence. That might explain Ben's shock when the strains of Yellow Submarine start up next to him …

Chapter 29

Granny's sound asleep by the time we pull up outside the house. I gently extricate the Stylophone from her grasp and Gethin and Ben put her in her wheelchair and push it up to the front door. Becky's already seen us and lets us in.

She picks up a box from the hall table and whispers, 'This was waiting on the step.'

It has G Meredith written in block capitals across the top and it's obviously been dropped off rather than posted. I reach for it, but Gethin intervenes.

'That could be for me.'

I watch him remove the paper. When he opens the cardboard, he takes a step backwards and drops the box at his feet. He's gone deathly white and Becky goes to him and takes his arm. I reach down and in my clumsy haste, I knock the opened package over. A blue ball bearing Kermit's face rolls out, dislodging a newspaper cutting.

'Tragic End to Holiday' is the bold headline, and in a slightly smaller font, 'Family Suffers Triple Tragedy. Children Orphaned'.

Ben pulls me back and turns me round, burying my face in his chest. The only sound comes from Granny's gentle snores and the faint whisper of the ball rocking against the wooden floor.

Becky says, 'Come on, Gethin. Come and sit down.' She's being professional but I can hear the shock in her voice. I pull away from Ben and look at my brother. He's still very pale. I don't know what to do. I remember Mark Johnson saying that I should know better, that I knew what it was like to lose someone, and I'm sure this is his brutal way to remind me. I go back into the hall, Ben sticking close to my side, and I bend down to pick up the ball. It's not the same as our one. The blue's wrong and someone's crudely glued a picture of Kermit to the surface. I put it down on the little table and stoop to pick up the photocopied newspaper articles. Before I can read them, Geth comes through and snatches them out of my hand.

'No, Gwen! Leave it.' He crumples them in his right hand. 'Don't give whoever did this the satisfaction of knowing how much it's upset you.'

There's a knock on the open front door and Ben automatically draws me back against him. It's DS Stafford.

'I just called to give you an update,' he scans us, 'but can someone first fill me in on what's happening here?'

Neither Gethin nor I seem able to speak and Ben steps into the breach.

'Someone left a package on the step addressed to G Meredith. It contains items relating to a tragedy that the family suffered years ago. It's come as a bit of a shock, as you can see.'

I find my voice.

'Yesterday, when Mark Johnson attacked me in the garden, he made reference to me losing family and that I should know what he's going through and retract my statement.' I run my tongue over dry lips and add, 'This must be down to him.'

Granny stirs in her wheelchair and Becky goes to her but Stafford quietly calls her back.

'Miss Hughes, if you could just wait there for a minute.'

For a moment, I think I see panic in her face, and then she's calm, sensible Becky again. Stafford continues.

'Well, there's no sign of Mark Johnson and a search of his flat failed to reveal any of your stolen property. However, in the course of our enquiries we did discover that Miss Hughes, here, is none other than the sister of Mark Johnson's wife.'

I look from him to her and back again.

'She can't be. Her sister's called Lisa. She's seriously ill. Tell him, Becky.'

'Gwen, I'm sorry. This has nothing to do with me. I swear—'

'You can swear all you like, Miss Hughes, but that doesn't take away the fact that your other sister is Mrs Mark Johnson.'

'Becky?' I'm sinking under his words.

'Gwen, you have to believe me, I'd never—'

Stafford interrupts again.

'Miss Hughes, it would help us enormously if you were to accompany us to the police station for a chat.'

She looks like an animal trapped in a corner.

Stafford extends an arm to guide her towards the door. At the last minute she says,

'You must believe me, Gwen. I'd never do anything to hurt you.'

And then she's gone.

I feel hollow.

I'd like to run away and hide but not even that's an option. I hear myself say, 'I'd better get Granny ready for bed.' The words come out flat and toneless. It's exactly how I feel. I've gone beyond terror and entered a monotonous world of basic survival. I've been here before. I just need to work through this and I'll come out on the other side when I'm ready.

I see Ben's troubled face, but not even he's reaching the real, protected, me.

'What can I do to help?'

'Nothing. I'll be fine.'

I approach the wheelchair but he's there before me.

'Do you want to take her to her room?'

I nod. 'Yes please.' I smile and hope it doesn't look as plastic as it feels.

Once inside, I thank him and tell him he can go now.

'I'm here, Gwen. Don't lose track of that. I'm here for you and will help in any way I can. Understand?'

I nod my head but don't look him in the eye. I'm coping and his attempts to penetrate my protective coating aren't welcome.

Granny's so exhausted after our day out, she's compliant and it takes me less time than I expect to have her sorted and back asleep in her bed. I switch off her light and go through to the kitchen. Ben and Gethin are sitting at the table. Ben must have brought across the bottle of whisky that's sitting between them. I remember the bottle he brought round after Atticus got stuck in the cat flap. I can't work out when it was, but it seems like a very long time ago now.

He stands and pulls out a chair for me but I shake my head.

'Sorry, Ben. All I want to do now is go to bed.'

'Okay.' He kisses the top of my head and I walk steadily through to my room. I didn't think the day could possibly get worse.

But it does.

I open my door but stay rooted to the spot. It's there, stark against the white of my pillow.

My robin. Rigid. From the doorway, I can see that his eyes are missing. I hear my moan above the sound of racing footsteps.

Ben pushes past me to see what's wrong, and then he's back, blocking my view with his body. His powerful grip grounds me in reality.

But I don't feel safe.

Chapter 30

I wake from a dream-drenched sleep. Gethin had persuaded me to take one of Granny's sleeping pills. While succeeding in knocking me out, it's left me hazy and muddled. I see the box that Becky handed to us, Gethin's white face, and my little robin.

The door-cam recording had revealed someone in a hoodie leave the box on the step. The face is hidden but he's the same build as Mark Johnson.

Gethin had disposed of the robin for me. I didn't ask how. It's better not to know.

I ought to get up and face the day but it's such a struggle to move limbs that are leadenly unresponsive.

There's something prickling away in the background of my mind. It feels like there's something I'm missing.

A warbling version of *Yellow Submarine* brings me to my senses. I haul myself out of bed and throw on yesterday's clothes. Will Cranston Care have sent a replacement for Becky? Her betrayal hurts. I trusted her. Did she go into my room and put—I stop myself going further down that route. The old greyness is descending and I need to apply my relaxation techniques to keep it at bay.

But first, Granny. She's sitting by the silent television, showing off her skills to Clare who's making all the right, kind noises.

I walk quietly behind them and enter the kitchen. Immediately, Ben is on his feet and asking how I am.

I fend him off with an upturned hand and sink down on one of the hard chairs. There's a silence broken by Gethin asking if I'd like a coffee. While he makes it, Ben pulls his chair next to mine and captures my hand.

'How are you feeling?'

'Sad, confused, tired, angry…'

'That's hardly surprising. You should get away from here for a while. Would the trust fund approve some proper respite? A week, perhaps?'

I shift uncomfortably in my seat. He's asking questions and I don't want to trouble my aching brain to dredge up answers.

'Even a weekend would do. Take you away from here until Mark Johnson's safely in custody.'

Gethin places a mug on the table in front of me.

'You should listen to him, Gwen.' He pulls his chair up to my other side and looks at me earnestly. 'You don't want to end up back—'

I cut him short with a glare. 'No. I don't. Give me some space, Geth. I feel trapped.'

'Okay. Sorry.'

I clasp my hands on the table in front of me. I'm trying to work through the fog in my brain and I don't want these distractions. Whatever it is I've been trying to catch, slips elusively from me and a sigh escapes.

Ben gives my clutching hands a squeeze.

'I'd be much happier if I had you safe and away from here for the time being.'

'I can't.' I'm pleased that my voice sounds practical now; less defeated. 'Even if I had the money, Cranston Care would need time to set up a team to work round the clock.' I manage a smile. 'The meeting to decide what happens to Mark's children is this morning. There'll be no point in him putting pressure on me after that. The decision will have been made.'

The Stylophone's faltering strains of Rod Stewart's *Sailing* reach me. An image materialises of Granny lying by the pond. I've no doubt now that Mark was behind it. I need to keep her protected. 'Anyway, I wouldn't be happy leaving Granny here.'

~~~

The harsh bright sky of yesterday is gone, replaced by heavy grey clouds that hang low over the fields. I fetch a cardigan and am about to go through to the patio, when I change my mind. I simply can't face it. I hear movement and turn my head to see Ben standing in the sitting room doorway, watching me. He comes to stand behind me and puts his hands on my shoulders.

'I've cancelled everything for the next few days. Why don't we get away from here for a few hours?'
~~~

I turn to face him. 'I just want to stay here for now. I can't explain it, but I *need* to be here.'

'That's all right. We can do whatever you want. But I'll stay here too.'

I put my hands against his chest. 'Please don't take this the wrong way, but right now I just want to be alone to work my way through all of this. So much has happened recently and I need to sort it out in my head.'

I simply want him to go. His worry adds to mine.

He looks as if he's going to put up a fight; insist on being with me. I'm braced for it, but he backs down. The frown line is back and the tic in his cheek.

'Sure?'

'Certain.' I can't find the words to explain, but I try. 'I need you to go back to work. Having you here adds another consequence to my life. Having you here means you're a part of the collateral damage. I just want to limit that damage. I'm suffocating.'

'But—' He stops and runs a finger gently down my cheek. 'You do know that none of this is down to you, don't you?'

'That's why I need some space. To add reason to the jumble in my mind.'

'And my being here adds to that jumble?'

'Yes. Your being here, rightly or wrongly, makes me feel guilty. I know that it's because of me and if you're not here, I can let that thought go and focus on everything else.'

'I'm here because I like being with you. We both know that the guilt isn't yours, but I'm doing my best to try to understand your twisted logic. I want to help. I want to be here for you. But if my going back to work makes things easier, I will.'

'Thank you.'

His kiss is almost my undoing. The temptation to let him take control, do my thinking for me, builds with that flare of intensity. But there's something troubling me, something just beyond my grasp, and having Ben there would be a distraction.

He pulls away.

'Okay. But I'm going to make some conditions before I go.' He waits until I'm focused on his face. 'Promise me you'll stay inside. I don't want you leaving the house on your own.' He adds, 'For any reason.'

'I promise. I've absolutely no intention of moving from these four walls.'

'Good. I'm glad we have an agreement on that.' He smiles, but that muscle is still twitching in his cheek. 'I don't want you answering the door. Get Gethin to check the door cam first.

'Check!'

'And keep the windows shut.'

'I hadn't thought of that. You're beginning to scare me.'

He takes me by the shoulders again.

'I want to scare you. Your grandmother's *accident,* the fish, and now the sadistic killing of your robin, scare *me*, and if you won't let me stay and protect you, I need to know that you're protecting yourself better than you have been doing.'

'Okay.' My head's filling with tumbling images of the wheelchair on its side, the fish, the robin, Flossie. I can feel the stirrings of panic inside. I need time to calm it all down.

'I'm going to work from home for the next couple of days. Give me a ring if you want me, for any reason, even if it's only for a few minutes. Okay?'

'Thanks. And for giving me the space I need to do this.'

He gives me the gentlest of smiles and leaves.

I steel myself to go back through to my bedroom where I sit on the bed and crush the fresh pillow to me. I need to keep control.

~~~

There's a tap on the door and Gethin comes in carrying a mug and a plate with some buttered toast on it.

'You haven't eaten anything so I've made you a snack and some ginger and lemon tea.'

He puts them on the bedside cabinet and the mattress sags as he sits beside me.

'You look drained.'

I lean against him.

'I'm so tired.'
~~~

‘Have your toast and tea and slip between the covers. I can manage Gran.’ He gives a rueful grin. ‘Though I might need to extend her bloody repertoire on that thing she picked up yesterday.’

‘Sorry.’

He pats my knee.

‘You weren’t to know the full horror of what you were unleashing.’

We sit together in silence until then he picks up the plate and thrusts it at me. ‘Go on. Get this down you and then grab some sleep.’

‘Thanks, Geth. I don’t know what I’d have done without you here to pick up the pieces.’

‘I worry about you, Gwennie.’ He looks down at his feet. ‘When you collapsed after that idiot chucked you into the sea, you were completely out of it for several days. I wasn’t sure if it was going to be *possible* to pick up the pieces. I don’t want you to end up like that again.’

‘You and me both.’ I try to smile. Then I distract myself with the tea and toast and he leaves me to it.

~~~

It’s over six hours before I resurface. My head is still cluttered and chaotic. I do my breathing exercises to push down the panicky feelings that threaten to overpower me. My brain feels broken. I start a thought and before I get to the end of it, another one has formed.

It's quiet in the house and I patter through on bare feet to the sitting room. Rain is hitting the windows and the colour has leached out of the garden under sullen black clouds. A movement on the other side of the road catches my eye. It’s gone under the canopy of trees. I think I caught a glimpse of mustard yellow. Part of me wants to rush out and see if it’s Ian; demand to know what he’s playing at. The other, rational part, tells me that going outside on my own is what Ben specifically warned me against. I stand and watch for several minutes but all is still and quiet.

I back away from the window and go through to the sitting room. Geth’s sitting at the old desk, looking at his laptop.
~~~

Granny is asleep in her chair, mouth open and drooling. The Stylophone is on her lap and one hand still clutches it in her sleep. I feel a surge of affection for her and go across and gently kiss her on her forehead.

When I look up again, Gethin's staring at me. He gives himself a little shake and comes across to me.

'Don't wake the old bat,' he whispers. 'She's only just dropped off. Come on through to the kitchen. I could do with a cup of tea to fend off the downpour blues.'

He makes me a regular tea but he's ladled sugar into it. I pull a face.

'Don't look like that. It's supposed to be good for you after a tough time.'

'Not sure about that. This is a tough call in itself!'

'How about something to eat?'

I sip the syrupy tea.

'No. This'll do me.'

'Wrong answer. Let me rephrase the question. What am I going to cook for you?'

'It's too muggy for cooking. How about a sandwich? There should be some cheese in the fridge.'

While he's buttering the bread, I mention seeing the yellow cap. He goes completely still.

'You think Ian's still out there?'

'Yes.'

'But I thought he was on a cruise to a new life somewhere?'

'I know, but everywhere I've gone recently, I see the same mustard-yellow cap. What if he hasn't gone? What if he's behind the … behind the fish … behind the fish and the robin? And Granny?'

My voice is so quiet by the end I'm not sure if he's heard me, but he understands and sits next to me, taking my hand in a firm grip.

'Listen, if the bastard's still here, you need to stay inside and let Stafford deal with him. Promise me you won't go after him yourself.'

I just sit there, prompting a more forceful response.

'Gwen, promise me you won't go after him.'

'Okay, okay. I know it makes sense. It's just unsettling, that's all.'

~~~

We sit in companionable silence for a while and when Claire arrives in the early evening to help Granny, Gethin says he's going for a run. He's been jittery for the last couple of days, we all have, and I assure him that I'll be fine and he can take his time. The rain's still coming down in torrents but he isn't bothered and I watch from the window as he turns right out of the drive and heads up towards Stinky Ditch.

He's been gone for barely five minutes when there's a gentle knock at the door. I stand and back away before remembering the door cam. I look on my phone and I can see that it's Becky. There seems to be somebody behind her.

Leave it, my brain tells me. But I look at her familiar face, rain trickling down it, and I break my promise to Ben and open the door.

She doesn't come in.

'Hello, Gwen. I know you might never want to see me again but I wanted to explain.'

Shut the door! says my brain.

'Come in.'

I stand back and then see the person hiding behind her. It's a young woman I recognise as Mark's wife. She hesitates on the step and I beckon her through, too.

We stay in the hall.

'Gwen, this is my sister. My *other* sister. Georgia.'

I'm still wary but I take in the bruised face and the plaster cast on her arm.

'Come on through to the kitchen.'

Becky starts. 'You have to believe me, Gwen. I've done nothing wrong. I've been trying to get Georgia to leave Mark for years now. Three days ago, she was given a place at the refuge and she's been told that Justin and Kaylee can move in with her.'

When I look at Georgia, I can see the truth for myself. She's been under Mark Johnson's thumb and I wonder was it the last beating, or maybe her missing children, that has given her the impetus to leave the monster.
~~~

'I'm sorry, Gwen. I should have told you at the start, but when you assumed it was to do with Lisa, it was easier just to go along with the deception.'

Her sincerity is obvious and Becky has otherwise been a good friend to me. Something inside tells me I can trust her again.

Georgia speaks next. She mumbles and her body language is still cringing. 'I'm sorry about Mark, Miss Meredith. I let him bully me and Becky's made me see how stupid it was to stay with him. I love my children and now I can have them with me again.' A bitterness crosses her face. 'When I found out he was seeing Lisa, that was the last straw.'

'Lisa?' I'm not making much sense of anything today.

Becky intervenes. 'Mark's got a nasty track record of flings and so it wasn't a surprise to find he'd latched onto Lisa – Lisa who worked here until recently.'

The cogs turn slowly.

'So that's how he could access the place. Lisa had the keysafe number.' I reach out to Becky. 'I'm so sorry to have doubted you. You've been there for me so many times recently.'

She clears her throat.

'No. Wait. I do have a confession to make.' She rushes on. 'Georgia was in such a state about the children being in care, I tried to sound you out about whether they were better there or at home. Fortunately, the decision's been taken out of my hands.'

'The hearing! What happened?'

'There's now a restraining order on Mark preventing him coming anywhere near Georgia or the children. Once things have calmed down, he can apply to have supervised access to the children.'

Georgia adds darkly, 'He's really mad at you, Miss Meredith. Says you've taken everything from him. I'd keep out of his way if I was you.' She waves her plaster cast in the air and I get the message. I rub my fingers across my forehead, trying to ease the tension that's building there.

Becky touches my arm. 'Gwen? Are you all right?'

'I'm okay. Just feeling a bit jetlagged after all the excitement recently.'

'How's your grandmother?'

'She's fine.' A thought occurs to me. 'Does this mean you can come back?'

'Yes. That DS Stafford followed everything up and then gave us both some really good, practical advice and has given Cranston Care the all clear. I'm back on the rota and restart next week.'

'That's brilliant news.' I spoil the delight with a yawn I can't keep in.

'We'll go now, Gwen. Thanks for being so good about all of this. Lie low for a while. I've seen Mark when he's been crossed and it's not nice.'

Once they've gone, I lock the door and fix the chain in place. I take the kitchen towel and mop up their wet footprints.

If only I weren't so tired and confused. I sit quietly in the kitchen, breathing slowly in and out. I'm so focused on bringing my anxiety down that at first I'm unaware of the knocking on the door. I scramble to my feet and look at the door cam image on my phone.

It's Gethin.

When he sees that I've put the safety chain on, he applauds my caution and I can't bring myself to tell him that I've let Becky and Georgia in the house while he was gone. It'd only upset him unnecessarily.

He's so wet, puddles have already formed around his feet and his hair is plastered to his skull.

'The water's been on all afternoon. Why don't you get out of those sopping clothes and have a bath?'

'Sounds like a plan!'

He ruffles my hair as he passes, leaving it so damp I know it's going to frizz uncontrollably later.

Chapter 31

When I wake, rain is still lashing the window and night has descended. The house is silent apart from Granny's snores. I check Gethin's room and he stirs when I open the door and then his rhythm of sleep is restored.

I'm feeling a little better and raid the fridge for something to eat. It's so muggy and humid, I settle on a bowl of cereal with chilled milk and have just started eating it when I notice Bramble's food bowl on the floor. It's untouched. I go around the house looking for her but she's nowhere to be seen. The forecast said it might thunder tonight and Bramble is terrified of storms. I open the patio door and call gently for her, rattling the tin opener on an empty can. Nothing.

I go to the front door. Same thing.

I do my best to forget about her. She's a cat. She'll be fine outside for one night. But I know I won't be able to settle knowing that she's out there somewhere. What if she's trapped? What if she's been shut in the shed? She likes to lie in the patch of sun motes that dance in the light from the dusty window.

Sighing, I put on my coat and break another promise. I'll only be a minute and the shed's only a few steps away.

The driving rain drowns out all other sounds and I'm twitching with paranoia as I cross the patio. This is stupid. That rational part of me knows I should go straight back inside to safety, but the knowledge that I won't be able to relax if I do, spurs me on.

The beam from my torch dances crazily as I fumble with the padlock, the rain transformed into bright needles. I hold it in my mouth to free up my other hand. The lock clicks and springs open and as I transfer the torch back to my hand, the hair lifts on the nape of my neck.

I spin round.

Mark Johnson.

He's swaying on his feet. I register his dripping clothes and the fury in his eyes.

My gaze drops to his hands. One of them is clutching a hammer.

An unpleasant grin twists his features. 'You wouldn't listen. You had to meddle.'

The words are slurred and I wonder if I can outrun him in his drunken state. I'm only a few steps away from the safety of the house.

'I warned you.' He raises the hammer to waist height and I know he wants to frighten me as much as he can; feed off my fear. My eyes return to his face. I don't want to give him the satisfaction of knowing how scared I am.

My thumb creeps over the off switch on the torch. He raises the hammer to head height.

'I said you'd pay.'

As my torch goes out, I throw it at his face and catch him by surprise. He stumbles. I scream for help and race for the patio doors. As I reach for the handle, my fingertips making contact with the metal, he catches my flapping coat and drags me back. I lose my footing and fall backwards onto the slabs, the air knocked out of my lungs. He bends over me and through the rain I see his distorted face as he swings the hammer up in the air.

I can't take my eyes off the weapon.

He gives a sudden scream of pain and spins round.

Atticus! Atticus has him by the arm and is pulling him off his feet. There's other sounds, too. Running feet. Two men grab Mark, disarming him and handcuffing his hands behind his back. Then Ben's there, sweeping me up and crushing me to him. I turn my face into his shoulder and cry.

~~

Later, in the brightly-lit sitting room, I feel strangely calm. It's over. Two policemen had been sitting in an unmarked car watching the house. They'd missed Mark, as he slipped unnoticed across the road and up our garden path, but had noticed the torchlight and come to investigate. Atticus had overtaken them.

Ben isn't calm. Stafford's barely gone before he starts on me.

'How could you? How could you put yourself at risk like that? You promised me you wouldn't go out!'

'I'm all right. It's over now.' I try a smile to soothe his ruffled feathers. 'No harm done.'

He's furious and I flinch when he shouts, 'No harm done! How *dare* you say that! If it hadn't been for Atticus getting agitated and insisting on coming out, who knows what would have happened.'

He hasn't finished, his anger boiling over messily like milk on a hob. 'I heard you scream. Have you any idea how that felt? How it felt to find you on the ground with Johnson standing over you with a hammer in his hand?'

I put out a hand to try and calm him but he shrugs it off.

'You said–no, you *promised*– you'd stay in. I thought you were safe.' That muscle in his cheek is working overtime. 'You lied to me.'

'I didn't.'

His fists are balled at his side and he's rigid with rage.

I try again.

'Well, okay, I did. I meant to keep my promise but Bramble's missing and I thought maybe...'

He's so livid, he struts across to the patio doors and stands with his back to me.

That's when I consider things from his viewpoint and how I'd feel if the situation was reversed. I walk up to him and rest my head against his arm.

'I'm sorry. I didn't think.'

'No. You didn't.'

'I was stupid. I know that now. I was worried about Bramble and thought it would take a minute at the most to check the shed and come back inside.' He's unyielding. 'I didn't think Mark would be out there at this time of night. It was so wet, and it must have looked like we were all asleep.' I swallow, the sound loud in the silence between us. 'I've never been so glad to see Atticus.' I whisper, 'I'm sorry, Ben.'

He sighs. It releases some of the tension and he curls an arm around me and rests his chin on the top of my head. When he speaks again, the anger's dissipated a little.

'For a moment there, I thought… he'd killed you.'

'Oh, Ben. I was very, very stupid and you were right to be angry.' I pull him in even closer.

'Cwtch,' he says with a ragged breath.

Gethin gives a cough from across the room. I'll check in on good old Gran and then go to bed.' He grins and adds, 'And to think I used to consider the big city exciting.'

~~~

After a morning at the police station giving statements, Ben and I return to the house.

I'd expected to feel relief that it was all over, but Stafford has raised significant doubts in my mind.

'He confessed pretty much straight away to most of the incidents you reported.' He pauses before saying, 'I should have taken the incident with the mask more seriously. It was an unforgivable oversight on my part.'

I'm surprised by his admission and feel the need to acknowledge his apology, but he pushes on.

'Sober, and in the clearer light of day, he's frightened himself with his intentions. He admitted that he wanted revenge and that he meant to kill you.'

I rub my hands on my arms where goosebumps have risen at the realisation of how close I came to dying last night.

'However, he denies the burglary, the attacks on your grandmother and Gethin, and the killing of the fish and the bird.' The statement is like a physical blow. 'In view of his admission of intention to murder, I have to consider very seriously that he might well be telling the truth.'

My first attempt to reply fails. My mouth's too dry and I can't get the words out. I swallow and try again.

'So you think whoever did those things is still out there?'

'It's a possibility. Yes.'

I remember the yellow cap.

'It's Ian Weston! He's been hanging around. I've seen him several times on the road outside and I think he was at the 70s Extravaganza at the castle.'

'I thought he was on a cruise.'

'That's what we all thought. But I've seen him.'
~~~

'When you say "seen him", has he come onto your property? Made any threats?'

'No.' I falter. 'I haven't actually seen his face. But he wears a distinctive cap in a mustard yellow and I've seen it several times recently.'

'Ah. So you've seen a yellow hat, not the person wearing it?'

'Yes.' Stafford doesn't seem convinced. I plough on, desperate for him to understand. 'It must be him. It's the only explanation.'

I look at Ben for support. He appears as doubtful as Stafford. In fact, they both look at me as if I'm a silly child. I don't know what's wrong with me, but I have an urge to lash out; wipe their concerned expressions off their faces. The sudden bubble of rage frightens me and I look at my feet.

'All right, Miss Meredith, we'll get in touch with the cruise ship and check that he's actually on it. In the meantime, can I stress that you need to be especially careful at the moment. My advice is to stay indoors and lie low until we get to the bottom of this.'

I look up at Ben. That muscle's twitching in his cheek again.

~~~

Gethin's edgy. He tries to hide it, but the news from Stafford has thrown him. He's prepared a simple lunch of pasta for us but eats very little of his own. When he sits at his laptop, he spends most of the time staring at the screen, his hands resting inactive on the keyboard.

Ben is distant, too. We haven't discussed Stafford's advice and I don't want to risk a repeat of last night's anger about my stupidity. The mood in the house mimics the weather outside; dark, brooding and threatening a storm.

I want to put things right between us but don't know how. That fatigue has swept over me again and my brain is clogged and muddled.

Ben's said something but he has to repeat it. 'Come back. You've disappeared somewhere.'

His tone's light but I can see his disquiet.
~~~

'Sorry. I was just trying to put things in some kind of order, but I can't.'

Gethin suggests I go to bed and catch up on some sleep. Ben agrees with him.

'Yeah. Go to bed. I'm popping back to the house for a while but you have me on speed dial if you need me.' He hesitates. 'You won't leave the house on your own or do anything stupid, will you?'

'No. I've learned my lesson.'

He drops a kiss on my head and leaves.

'Come on, you.' Gethin hauls me to my feet. 'Bed!'

'How's Granny?'

'She's still tired after her day out at the castle. Joyce phoned earlier. I filled her in on last night's events and she said she'll come round and help with Gran. She said she'll be here as soon as she's collected her prescription from the pharmacy.'

There's something else.

'What about Bramble? She never stays away like this.'

'Bramble's a cat. Cats prowl. Cats do their own thing. Stop fretting about her. I'll rattle a can every so often and she'll come back when she's ready.' He gives me a shove. 'So, go! Get out of my hair and give a man some peace.'

When I turn to thank him, I'm disturbed by the worry I see in his face. I've brought all of this down on top of him at a time when he's up to his eyes in other problems.

'Sorry, Geth. You could do without all of this at the moment.'

'Says the person who nearly died last night.'

He points at the bedroom door and I do his bidding. Despite my anxiety, I'm asleep in moments.

~~~

The sun is warm on my back and I'm giggling as Gethin throws the ball again. It's much too high and although I strain to reach it, all I can do is follow its course far over the sparkling water. It bounces twice back up to the surface before bobbing tantalisingly beyond our reach. My distorted voice fills my ears.

'Mummy! Daddy! Get it back! Quick!'
~~~

I hear my mother, happy and reassuring. 'It'll come back in a minute. Build a sandcastle while you're waiting.'

'No! It's going away!'

'Don't be silly, pumpkin. If it doesn't come back, I'll buy you a new one.'

'It's my Kermit ball. ***Please****, Mummy,* ***please****!'*

'I promise you can choose any ball you want if this one doesn't come back.'

'No! I want this ball. I don't want any of the others.' I hear my childish voice plead and whine.

'Okay. No need to cry. I'll get it for you.' She rises gracefully from the towel beside my father, brushing grains of sand off her slender body.

But I know what's to come and the scream builds in the pit of my stomach as Mummy splashes into the deeper water and starts her slow, powerful crawl towards the ball; Kermit's bobbing face mocking her approach.

Something's wrong. She's drifting to the left and despite swimming back towards the beach she's moving further away from us. Her left arm rises in the air and she calls out. 'Peter! Peter, help!'

I watch as she disappears under the waves before Daddy gets to her. Then Daddy's calling out for help and a young man runs into the waves with a big board.

The young man has Daddy lying over the front of his board but they're not getting any closer. His hand comes up and he's shouting something at us but I can't hear what he's saying.

We sit together on the beach. There's no more shouting. There's only the waves carrying the bobbing ball further away from us.

Gethin's crying.

'This is your fault!' he shouts in my face.

'Gethin?'

'You made her go after the ball.'

I don't understand.

The beach fills with people and someone wraps our towels round us.

Gethin says he's sorry. He didn't mean it. He tells everyone that it wasn't my fault.

'It's not her fault.'

I sit up. Sweat's pouring off me and I'm shaking so badly, I can't pick up the glass of juice by the bed.

It's never-ending. I'll never be able to delete these memories. They're a fixed part of my life now and I'm damaged by them. I had counselling when I was in hospital, but I walked away from it. It was just too painful endlessly reliving the agony, each telling as acute as the first.

I revert to my breathing exercises and the panic slowly subsides.

It's 5.45 am and I'm the only one up. I get dressed in the bathroom and then go through to the kitchen on bare feet and put some water in the kettle. It's going to be another one of those brooding summer days and I can almost feel the weight of the air pressing down on me. Granny's call drags me out of my reverie and I go through to her room. She's switched on the bedside lamp and is stretching for her water glass.

'Here. Let me help.'

'I don't need any help! Why do people leave it so far away?'

She lets me hold it for her while she gulps the liquid down.

The simple act saps her strength and she sags back against the pillows.

'Can I get you anything else?'

'No.' Her lips purse in displeasure. 'What time is it?'

'5.50.'

'In the morning?'

I nod.

'You've had that dream again, haven't you?'

I'm looking at her and it's only then that it hits me. It's not satisfaction I'm seeing in her face, it's sympathy. Granny hasn't changed; I have.

I give her hand a gentle squeeze.

'Yes.' It's a whisper but she hears it all the same.

'Silly girl. It doesn't help, you know. You're too sensitive for your own good.' The words seem brutal but the tone and the expression in her eyes aren't.'

I give her a brief kiss on her dry cheek.

'Shall I turn off your light?'

'Yes. It's far too early to be up. I can't think why on earth you'd think to wake me at this ungodly hour.'

She rolls onto her side and I return her room to darkness and close the door quietly behind me.

Chapter 32

Gethin and I have just finished breakfast when there's a knock on the door. I get up to answer it but am pushed firmly back on my chair and a finger is wagged in my face.

'We don't want to make Ben angry again!' he says with a wicked grin. He looks at the door cam and hands me the screen. It's Cat and Joyce.

He lets them in and they come through to the kitchen like conspirators, looking around them and speaking in whispers.

Gethin's puzzled. 'What on earth's going on?'

Cat points to Joyce who fills us in. 'Well, I was talking with Gwen about something the other day and I've dug out a couple of things that I hope will cheer her up.' She puts a hand on my arm. 'It was such a shock to hear about the attack on you, my dear. I'm just glad they've got him and you can put it all behind you now.'

I daren't flash a warning at Gethin in case it's noticed but he does nothing to disabuse them of the notion that it's all done and dusted.

I point to the big cloth bag that Cat's holding. 'So, what's in the bag?'

Joyce looks around again. 'I don't want Edith to see. Not yet, anyway.' She takes the bag off Cat and puts it on the table. 'I had Catrin's phone number, told her what I'd got, and asked if she could drop me off here.'

'Joyce, I love you to bits but you're going to have to stop talking in riddles!'

Her eyes twinkle as she pulls out a large book.

'It's a photograph album!'

'It is.' Her face crinkles in delight

'I've brought two of them for you to see. There's one of some really old photos and then there's another of later ones from when you came here. I'm pretty sure there's some of Catrin as well.'

I have an urge to take it and dance around the room in my excitement. But when I reach for it, she delivers a playful slap to my hand. 'Not yet, you little minx! I thought you and Cat could have a chat and catch-up first – while I spend time with your grandmother. When Edith has a nap, I've some things here that I think will surprise and entertain you!'

I'm a mix of delight and curiosity. When I look at Gethin, he's regarding me with a solemn expression. I follow him into the sitting room. 'Why the long face?'

He fidgets a bit, not looking at me.

'Geth?'

'I just don't want you to get hurt.'

'Why would I get hurt?'

'You know why. There are some memories best left buried.'

'You think I don't know that? You think Joyce doesn't?'

'But who will save you from yourself?'

'What do you mean by that?' I'm annoyed. 'Tell me!'

'Forget it.'

'No. You can't say something like that and not explain it.'

He sighs.

'It's just that you're very…sensitive…about the past and I don't want her to trigger bad memories for you.'

'Joyce would never hurt me.' I rein in my unreasoning temper. 'Gethin, I'm beginning to see the past for what it was. Ben's been helping me put things in context and I know that I've got things twisted. When all of this fuss has calmed down a bit, I'm going to find a counsellor who can help me. As he says, it's the only way to move forward.'

'You really like him, don't you?'

'I do. He's kind and funny and I trust him. I'd trust him with my life.'

Gethin says nothing for several seconds. He simply stares at me then he shakes his head. 'Okay. I just don't want you hurt again, that's all.'

'I know. You've been the best brother a girl could have, but you can't be expected to drop everything and come running whenever something goes wrong. I need to face my problems head-on and deal with them like an adult.'

He gives a faint smile.

'As long as you remember I'm always happy to ride shotgun.'

'I know. And I *am* grateful, pardner.'

He groans. 'For someone with a gift for languages, that was dreadful.' He heads back towards the kitchen. 'Come on, then,' he says. 'Let's mosey along and torment that Cat gal.'

~~~

Joyce is true to her word and, when Granny's asleep, we sit around the table in the kitchen. There are two huge albums stacked on top of each other and I can feel the excitement coursing through my veins. Joyce has one hand on the top album, ready to open it, when there's a knock on the door. Gethin checks the door cam before going through and letting Ben in.

'Well, young man, have you come to join us in a trip down memory lane?'

'I'd love to.'

Joyce is sitting at the middle of the table with Gethin and I on either side of her. Cat's sitting as close as humanly possible to Gethin without actually sitting on his lap, in order to get as good a view as possible. Ben pulls one of the stools across and sits next to me, resting his arm along the back of my chair.

'Right girls and boys! Let's start at the beginning.'

She opens the album and the first page contains neatly arranged black and white photographs, some of them faded and scratched. They're smaller than the ones I'm used to and some of the images aren't perfectly focused but the likenesses are clear enough to make some comparisons with the faces we know now.

Joyce points to a stiffly-posed couple in front of a painted forest backdrop. She's not very old, in her twenties, perhaps, and wearing a white pin-tucked blouse and a long skirt with an impossibly small waist.

'What do you think?' asks Joyce. 'See any resemblance?'

It's Gethin who twigs first. 'It's Gran's grandparents, isn't it?'

'Well spotted. This is Cecil and Emily Meredith. He was a banker who did very well for himself and went on to own a large house in Carmarthen. Here's a picture of them in front of the house with their staff.'

'Beautiful building,' says Ben, awestruck.
~~~

'Impressive. Must have cost a bomb,' adds Gethin.

I can't help laughing. 'Say the architect and the investment banker!'

Cat points to the family group and the ranks of servants, all stood to attention, 'They don't exactly look full of the joys of life, do they?'

Joyce is amused by the comment.

'I daresay the servants weren't. But these weren't – what do you call them? – selfies? This one would have been taken by one of those early cameras that required a long exposure. Easier to hold a sober expression than a grinning one.'

In a later picture, Emily's holding a child on her knee. It's hard to make out the features under all the lace but Gethin has a guess.

'Is that Great Grandma Hannah?'

'Right again. Here's another picture of her taken with her brothers when she was about ten.'

This one's less formal and Hannah is smiling at the camera and has one hand resting on the head of a large spaniel.

'Now, this one is of Hannah on her wedding day just before the end of the Second World War.'

She's wearing a long, sleek white dress and is standing next to Great Grandad.

Cat coos over the photograph.

'Aw, look at him in his uniform. Though I can't believe he actually *chose* to wear a moustache like that!'

'That, my dear, is called a handlebar moustache and I believe Edward was quite proud of it. Hannah's dress was made from parachute silk. Rationing was in force during the war and many women married in regular clothes. Somehow, Edward got his hands on a damaged parachute; I daresay one of the perks of being in the air force. Emily had it made into this rather charming outfit.'

Joyce turns over a few more pages of posed pictures of Edward and Hannah but stops at one where Edward's standing with his arm around Hannah, who's making sure that her baby is facing the camera.

We can all see that it's Granny. Even though the features aren't fully formed yet, the imprint of my grandmother is already visible.

The pictures become less formal as the decades pass. When we reach the 50s, our excitement and hilarity build.

'Who on earth is *that*?' squawks Cat. 'And what on earth is she wearing?'

A teenager with hair piled high is sporting a just below knee-length skirt that sticks out as if it's swallowed an upturned bowl.

'Oh dear,' says Joyce. 'Look more closely.'

We all lean forward but it's Ben who makes the connection.

'I believe that stylish young woman is sitting in our midst right now.'

It takes a second or two for the penny to drop and then we're all peering at Joyce who dips her head and says, 'Guilty as charged. Over the page, there's one of the two of us taken by a boy who fancied himself in love with Edith.' She points to the snapshot and there they are, posing with big grins on their faces.

Cat squawks, 'What *have* you done to your hair?'

'Those were the days of the beehive. Basically, you used a comb to tease the hair down towards the roots and it gave you a raised nest of hair that you sprayed with lacquer until it had all the softness and flexibility of concrete.' She points at the full skirts. 'You were judged by the number of layers of petticoats you wore. Some used starch but a lot of the underskirts then were made of nylon and starch didn't work on them. I knew several who soaked them in a strong sugar solution. It did work, but remind me sometime to tell you about the time our friend Cynthia missed the bus and walked to the party in driving rain.'

We move into the 60s and it's a mix of mainly black and white photos, but now there's also a few in colour.

The skirt lengths seems to creep relentlessly upward until Cat gasps at one that shows the pair wearing miniskirts and knee-length white plasticky boots.

'Joyce! That skirt's practically indecent. It barely covers your…derriere!'

'You sound just like my father. "You're not going out in that get-up, young lady. That's not a skirt, it's a belt!" Though, looking at this now, I see he may have had a point.' She looks at the picture with a fond expression. 'Mind you, we thought we looked fab and groovy but the photographic evidence tells a rather different story. I must admit that the look we're sporting there was probably better suited to someone of daintier proportions.'

She sneaks a peek at the next page and begins to laugh.

'I'm not sure if I can bring myself to inflict the next ones on you.'

Of course, we're intrigued and she slowly does the reveal.

Cat collapses against Gethin, who looks as if he's trying not to laugh, but I give way to the giggles.

'What,' asks Cat between guffaws, 'were you thinking?'

Joyce grins happily.

'That would have been around 1967, I think. It was the days of hippies and flower power and, more tragically, these huge bellbottomed trousers called loon pants.'

'Oh dear!' I gasp, 'they're not exactly subtle, are they?'

'No, my dear. And I think maybe dayglo orange, lime green and fluorescent pink aren't the best colour combinations, and perhaps your grandmother might have been better choosing something with a less…er…*busy* pattern.'

There's some more pictures taken of the two of them in their psychedelic garb and Joyce is turning the page when I stop her and peer closely at one of the shots.

'What's that? There? In Granny's hand?'

Five heads come together. Then Gethin groans.

'It's a bloody Stylophone!'

I pull the album closer. 'Let me see.' Granny's sitting cross legged on the grass and I can almost hear the strange vibrato sound from here.

I'm ridiculously pleased to see her with the one she'd had all those years ago. 'This is amazing!'

'Well, my dear, amazing is perhaps too kind a word for it. We couldn't get Edith to shut up.'

She turns to the next page and Granny is standing, arms folded and wearing an impressive pout.

Joyce sighs.

Your grandfather, Paul, eventually took the wretched thing off her and threatened to throw it in the river. As you can see, she didn't take it well. I love Edith but she's always been quick to take offence. The times she's stormed off because things weren't going her way! She was an only child and I blame her parents who rather indulged her, I fear.'

As we move through the years, my grandfather begins to appear more frequently and goes from posing as one of a group of friends to his place next to Granny. He doesn't escape Cat's critical fashion eye, either. 'Orange daisies on a brown shirt was not a good look.'

The next one is of him wearing a satin shirt with ruffles down the front. Cat is even more horrified.

'My dear,' responds Joyce, 'that's *fashion*. In another decade, people will marvel at those dresses you wore that looked like skimpy underslips, and the notion of distressed jeans and shabby chic will no doubt confound those born today.'

She turns over a few more pages and then we come to the wedding photos. In the middle of the page, I find an identical one to the one that was stolen along with its silver frame.

'Oh, Joyce! You've a copy of the missing one. We can get a replacement! You've no idea how happy that makes me.'

She turns and places her hand over mine and clasps it.

'I wanted to reassure you as soon as possible, Gwen.' She gives me a beaming smile. 'When I went looking for these, I found a couple of tea chests in the loft labelled 'For the Children'. I haven't opened them and will pass them on to you and Gethin when someone brings them down for me. From what I remember, there's more photos, first shoes, books, clothes and some video tapes.' She sighs. 'To be honest, I'd completely forgotten about them.'

She looks reflective for a moment before giving herself a little shake and returns to the album. The next photo is a large one of a wedding group.

'You know the central characters, of course. There's your grandparents, with Hannah and Edward on your grandmother's side and Pru and Cyril next to your grandfather. I'm the bridesmaid in that horrific puce dress with all the frills.'

Cat and I are enthralled with the wedding pictures; Gethin and Ben, less so.

We all coo over the images of Granny proudly showing off baby Peter to the camera, just as her mother had done with her.

They're photos of their time, including the obligatory posed studio photographs of them wearing smart clothes and smiles that have frozen into an unbecoming stiffness as they've waited for the flash.

The resemblance to Gethin is uncanny and I lean across the table to look at him on the other side of Joyce.

'You're the spitting image of him, Geth, from those dark eyes to the mischief in his face.'

'Nah,' he says, 'I don't see it.'

'I'm with Gwen,' chirps Cat. 'Put your father in something less stuffy than that shirt and tie and you could *be* him.'

Our resident fashion critic is distracted by the next pictures of eighties power dressing.

'Your grandmother's shoulder pads are twice the width of her skirt in that one, and you could land a plane on your grandfather's tie!'

We're all laughing, Ben has an arm around my waist, and I'm cocooned in love and happiness. It would be great to live in this moment forever.

When the first album's finished, Joyce suggests that I go and check on Granny before she risks opening the second one.

I don't need to go into the bedroom, I can hear Granny snoring halfway down the hall. As I head back to the kitchen, I hear Joyce saying in a hushed voice, 'I've filtered these recent ones. I don't want any references made to the tragedy.

Gethin's annoyed. 'We're not stupid, Joyce.'

'What I'm saying, Gethin, is that you constantly telling Gwen things aren't her fault only reinforces the opposite notion in her head.'

'I'm just trying to stop all her ridiculous atonement.'

'And that's understandable, but unnecessary. Just let her experience what's in this album without reference to that dreadful night.'

As I cross the threshold into the kitchen, the conversation becomes animated and there's much banter about what to expect from this next book. I move quietly into my place, feeling taut and anxious at what awaits me. Ben replaces his arm around my waist and gives me a reassuring squeeze; some of the apprehension eases, but I'm on edge.

~~~

The second album is mainly of Gethin and me as children. Some are of our early years but most of them are from since we came here to live with Granny. I thought I'd be sad but distance lends a safe enchantment and it's like watching scenes from an old film – familiar and predictable but with nuances not noticed the first time around.

The first shots are of Gethin as a baby being held by anonymous arms. He's grinning at the camera, chubby hands outstretched towards it. Then he's taking his first unsteady steps, Granny behind him, ready to scoop him up. There's a couple of him sitting in a highchair covered in something gloopy that had once been in the empty bowl now resting on his head.

Cat nudges his shoulder. 'Gross! To think I thought of you as my knight in shining armour!'

'Ah! I'm wounded.' He puts his hand over his heart. 'But surely you wouldn't trust a knight whose armour was shiny and untested.'

'Depends if he was wearing his dinner on his head, Sir Gethin.'

Our mother's parents died prematurely and neither of us knew them, but there are lots of snaps of Gethin with Granny and Grandad. There are ones of him at Christmas, the camera flash turning his eyes scarlet, as he clambers into a cardboard box.

'Young man,' reproves Joyce, 'your grandparents spent a fortune on a Thomas the Tank Engine train set but all you wanted to do was sit in the box that held it.' She chuckles. 'I think the next shot shows why your grandfather and his friends were so grateful that you did.'

Four middle-aged men are are kneeling on the ground assembling the train set with determined expressions on their faces.
~~~

There are gaps on the pages, marked by small paper triangles that once held photographs in place. I assume that these were of our parents and removed by Joyce. I want to ask about them. I have so many questions, but I hold them in. Joyce told them she doesn't want any fuss and perhaps it's better to speak with her when we're on our own–when I can reassure her that I won't go to pieces.

'And here, my dears, is one of the first appearances of Gwen.'

I'm in Granny's arms, swaddled in a lacy shawl, and Gethin has his back towards us as he clutches her knees.

Cat gives him another nudge to the shoulder. 'Don't you know you're supposed to *face* the camera?'

Gethin shakes his head. 'It's as well I'm not. Apparently, I didn't want a baby sister and I told them to take her back.'

The picture underneath it is of Granny sitting in an armchair with me on her knee while my brother appears to be attempting to burrow between us, his head hidden and his bottom sticking up in the air. I laugh.

He grins back. 'I really didn't want you. You were a girl, you smelled funny and you weren't any good at games.'

Joyce turns the page and this time he's sitting in the corner of the sofa with me on his knee and he's planting a kiss on my head. There's a chorus of, 'Ahs.'

'Of course,' he says, straight-faced at me, 'I must have been told to do that, or someone bribed me!'

There's a picture of us at Easter, Gethin wearing fluffy ears and me with a large bonnet covered in chicks. At Halloween, Gethin's an orange ball on legs and I'm wearing a Casper the Friendly Ghost outfit. He's holding a toffee apple for me and, from the expression on my face, it's the best thing ever. There are other scenes where he's pushing me on my tricycle or holding down a branch for me to reach the blossom. In one of the snaps, we're standing side by side at the fair and I'm holding a giant fluffy green thing.

'I remember that frog!' I exclaim. 'You won it throwing hoops over numbered blocks and gave it to me.'

'Oh yeah! It split a few days later and loads of tiny polystyrene balls spilled out.'

'Yes! I was in so much trouble for the mess but you helped me pick them up.'

'Wish I hadn't. It took us hours. They were full of static electricity and stuck to everything, do you remember?'

Joyce turns the-page and Cat squeals, 'It's me!'

She's standing next to Gethin, their heads touching as they peer at his cupped hands. She delivers yet another nudge to his shoulder. 'You told me it was something precious!'

'It was.'

'I was expecting something pretty and sparkly. It was a horrible big black beetle.'

He grins at her. 'Like I said – precious.'

The next picture shows the two of them sitting on top of the garden wall, legs dangling at least two feet from the gravelly ground.

And then Joyce taps a finger on one of Granny lifting me up to place me on the wall beside them. Her expression makes me catch my breath. It's gentle and tender. The words slip out, 'She did love me.'

I feel Ben's grip on my waist tighten as he says, the words quiet but firm, 'Told you so.'

I look at Joyce and she nods in acknowledgement. She wanted me to see this and this *is* something precious.

Cat leans across Gethin to get a closer look. 'Well I never! Your grandmother's wearing daisies.'

She is. Both of us are sporting long, gangly daisy chains around our necks and circlets on our heads.

'It was a lovely day, Cat.' Joyce has a faraway look in her eyes. 'Edith sat on the grass for ages with Gwen and taught her how to link the daisies whilst you and Gethin squabbled together.'

I'm amazed. 'I don't remember it.'

'Ah. I don't suppose you remember this either then.'

Joyce's camera has caught me, a blur, as I fall from my stone perch.

She shakes her head. 'One minute you were sitting there quite happily; the next you slipped off and fell to the ground. You cut your knee on the stones and then, to top it all—'

Cat turns to Gethin again. 'Oh yes! You tried to catch hold of her and fell too.'

‘Sadly,’ Joyce shakes her head at him, ‘you hurt your ankle and you both had to be carried back to the house. It was a sad end to such a happy day.’

Over the page there’s a small square of paper inserted into the photo holders. It has “For Granny” written in neat but uneven letters on the front. Joyce carefully removes it and hands it to me. It opens into a handmade card with a pressed daisy in the middle of it. In that same hand, it says “Lots of love Gwen” followed by three kisses.

‘I’d forgotten all about this.’ I feel overwhelmed with a happiness that’s akin to pain. ‘She kept it.’

‘Oh yes. As far as I know, she’s kept all the little keepsakes you made her. She isn’t one to demonstrate her feelings, I think maybe she sees it as a form of weakness, but that doesn’t mean she didn’t cherish these things.’

I look up and Gethin’s watching me. He mouths ‘Okay?’ and I simply nod and beam at him. I feel very much okay. I know that one day, soon I hope, I’m going to ask to see the photos Joyce hid from me.

She quickly closes the album and puts it back with the other one in the cloth bag when a voice issues from the sitting room. ‘Where is everybody? Why haven’t I had my breakfast yet?’

Chapter 33

Bramble's screeching. I need to bring her into the house.

Something stabs the sole of my foot and I'm startled awake.

It's quiet. I must have dreamed Bramble's cries. The room's in darkness and it takes several confused seconds for my eyes to make sense of my surroundings. Everything's obscured by the night apart from a thin vertical sliver of grey. It looks like a gap in my curtains–but it can't be because it's too long. As I struggle to orient myself, an outline forms to the left of me. It's an armchair.

Gradually, the rest of the sitting room takes shape in monochrome. I'm standing at the patio doors in my nightdress.

I've been sleepwalking.

I stumble to the chair and collapse into it, tucking my feet under me. It's been two years since my last involuntary roam in the night. I thought it was over; a random part of my life that had settled into permanent obscurity. The knowledge that it's resurfaced is a blow. It's a physical indication of my inner turmoil. It's a warning that I'm losing control.

In the early rise of the sun, the room develops like one of yesterday's old photographs. I've no idea how long I've been sitting like this but the sound of a door opening penetrates the fog in my brain. Before I can organise myself to move, Gethin appears. He walks past me to the patio doors and pulls open the curtains. The bright light hurts and I must have made a noise because he spins round.

'Good God, Gwen! You scared me half to death!' He comes closer. 'Are you all right?'

'I'm fine.'

His right-hand ruffles through his hair, leaving it in untidy tufts. It reminds me of the young boy in the photo album. Since the night of the beating, the puffiness has gone from his face but the bruising has come out in a dull purple that's fading into yellow.

'How are *you*? Does that bruise still hurt?'

'No, I'm fine, too.'

'Honestly?'

'Cross my heart and hope to…' His words tail off and the air's heavy with the unspoken word hanging between us. He gives himself a brisk shake. 'I'm fine, Gwen. All I had were some scrapes and a few bruises; they're already healing.'

'Let me have a look at you.'

I stand and give a small yelp of pain. I lift my foot from the floor and he takes my arm to steady me.

'What is it?'

'Something's stuck in the sole of my foot.'

He helps me back into the chair.

'Which foot?'

'The left one.'

He kneels down and I'm relieved to see that he can do so without wincing.

'I see the problem. You've got a large thorn in it. Hang on and I'll remove it.'

I hold in another yelp of pain as he locates it and tugs it out, and then he gets up to grab a piece of kitchen roll which he holds firmly in place.

'It's nothing major but it's bleeding a bit and so this is more to protect the nice furniture than you.'

'Thanks!'

He grins, stretching his scabbed lips. 'Hold this for me for a sec while I get a plaster to stick over it.'

While he fixes it in place, I look at the path of sunlight streaming onto the kitchen surface. Something seems out of place but I can't put my finger on it. Then the image of the stolen copper pig comes to me. If Mark Johnson didn't take it, then who did?

'There we are. Good as new!' He stands again but I catch the momentary flinch of discomfort it causes him. Before I can comment, he heads for the counter and fills the kettle. I watch him as he moves around making us mugs of tea. It's a comforting scene and I feel the anxiety ebb, leaving me lethargic. We've survived, Gethin and I. It's my over-sensitive responses to the recent situations that has exaggerated the drama - to no one's benefit, particularly not mine. Stafford might not completely believe my version of events but I can live with that. It's time to move on. The image of the slowly turning spokes on the upturned wheelchair flits through my head but I chase the thought away. Enough.

I stand, testing my foot on the floor. There's a residual tenderness but that's all. I go and join Gethin. I'm hungry. I can't remember when I last ate. 'Do you fancy some breakfast?' I look at the clock. 'Is it really only 5.35?'

He gives me one of his grins.

'If that's what the clock says.'

'What are you doing up so early?'

'I could ask you the same thing.'

'I was just…I wanted…I came through to get the book that I was reading.' Now that I've started, the words rush out of me, adding justification to the lie. 'Cat recommended it. She says it's a real page turner with a wicked twist at the end.' Before I can gabble any more, he holds an admonishing finger up.

'Hush, Gwen. This is me, Gethin. I know you better than you know yourself.' His next words drop quietly into the gap between us. 'You've been sleepwalking again, haven't you?'

'No.' I look down at my toes peeping out under the hem of my nightdress. I'm determined to hang on to my positive spin. Even if it means lying, I'm not going to give Gethin more reasons to worry about me. 'It's was so hot last night and I couldn't sleep.' I clamp my lips together. I know I'm overegging things.

'Gwennie, there's no shame in sleepwalking.'

'I know! Please, Geth, just drop the subject. I think it's going to be a beautiful day. Don't spoil it.'

I can tell from his fixed expression that he's chasing thoughts in his head. Then he gives a smile, hands me my mug of tea and says, 'Shall we sit in the garden and enjoy the birdsong?'

'Great idea.'

~~~

Bramble still hasn't put in an appearance and I can't settle. I go to the doors, calling her name but there's no response. I feel sluggish, everything is such an effort. When I try to pin
~~~

down a thought, others tumble into it creating a mental chaos in which nothing's resolved

Yesterday felt good but today's different. Despite the sunshine, today feels brooding and unhealthy.

I go to the window and stare at the front garden. The rain's restored the lawn to a lush green and I can see new grass is coming up in the newly-dug flowerbed. When did Ben and I do that? I can't work it out. It seems like such a long time ago now. Curiously, it also seems like no time at all.

It's while I'm standing there, listless and useless, that a movement catches my eye. On the other side of the road, partly hidden by the overhanging trees, is a mustard-coloured cap. It's Ian Weston.

I go to the door, ready to confront him, when I remember my promise to Ben.

I grab my phone and click on his name.

'Gwen? Is everything all right?'

'It's Ian. He's outside.'

'Where?'

I peer through the window but he's disappeared. 'He was here. He was under the tree across the road by you. I can't see him now but he was there just a couple of seconds ago.'

'Stay there.'

He hangs up.

Gethin comes through. I tell him and he's out of the door before I realise what's going on. Then I worry that Ian will hurt them? I want to go out and warn them to be careful but I keep hearing my promise to Ben. So I stand, ineffectual, watching from the window.

I see both of them check around the tree, and run off in opposite directions before meeting up again in front of the house. Then they're coming up the path together and the immense relief I feel that they're both unharmed is overshadowed by my wondering where Weston disappeared to.

Ben shakes his head. 'No sign of him, I'm afraid.'

Gethin's hovering. I recognise the signs. He wants to say something but isn't sure how. I turn to him. 'Just say it, Geth. Whatever it is, just say it.' My voice sounds edgy and an expression of remorse flits across his face.

'It's nothing.'

'*Tell* me.'

'It's just,' he wipes his feet on the doormat, 'What did you *actually* see?'

'Ian Weston. He was there. Over the road. He was wearing that yellow cap.'

'Are you sure?'

'Of course I am!'

'I had to ask, Gwen. You've been under a lot of strain and sometimes that can — …twist… things a bit.'

He looks wretched. Ben is watching him. I can almost see the cogs in his brain making sense of the words that condemn me as unreliable; unstable, even.

Gethin asks again, 'What did you actually see?'

'I'm telling you, I saw him. Ian Weston in that ridiculous cap.'

'Was he wearing the sunglasses?'

'I don't know.' There's an oppressive silence as I try to force my brain to work properly. Once I've replayed the memory, the truth is damning. 'I didn't see his face.'

'So you don't know if it *was* Ian?'

I'm floundering when Ben speaks, his voice calm and soft.

'But you did see the mustard yellow cap.'

'Yes. You have to believe me!'

'I do. And the disturbing thing about it is that neither of us saw anyone wearing a cap like that. The only people around were a teenage couple in a clinch in the driveway of a house. So,' he continues, 'why is the person in the yellow hat hiding from us?'

He draws me close and I bury my aching head against him. I hear him say, 'I don't like this, Gethin. I'd be much happier if she came to stay with me for a few days until we know for certain that Weston is actually on the cruise ship.'

Gethin sounds irritated.

'Are you suggesting that I can't keep her safe here?'

'Of course not. But I can spend all my time watching over her and he won't expect her to be in my house. You have enough on your plate. You're still not fully recovered from the attack.'

I push against him. 'No. I have to stay here with Granny.'

Gethin sighs. 'Perhaps you're right, Ben. She might be safer with you.'

I'm so angry, I stumble and they both grab at me to stop me falling. '*She* is here!' I yell. '*She* can make the decision for herself.'

Gethin is instantly contrite. 'I'm sorry, Gwen. I just want to keep you safe. I'm worried about you and I can see how all of this has upset you. You need a break before…' He stops. I know what he was going to say and this time I don't push him to say the words I dread. I pull myself free from their supportive hands.

'I'm sorry too,' I say with a calmness that's at odds with the spinning in my head and the roiling in my stomach. 'We're all overreacting here. I have both of you on my side, I'm…I'm untouchable in the house and now we have a…a…' I can't remember the word. 'A thing that shows who's at the door.'

I start to limp away from them.

'What have you done to your foot?' Ben catches my arm and turns me to face him.

Before I can respond, Gethin says, 'She was sleepwalking and got a thorn in it.'

'Sleepwalking?'

I push myself in front of him.

'I wasn't. I wasn't! I was up early to read my book.' Even I can hear the desperation in the lie. Gethin sighs again.

'All right, Gwen. It's all right. I must have got it wrong.'

~~~

The day passes, blurred and cumbersome. I can't shake off the feeling that a storm's coming and that I'm in the eye of it. I try to join in with the forcibly light conversations around me but it's such an effort. An added weight is knowing that Gethin's watching me. He tries to hide it, but I catch him studying me and for the first time since all of this…this…I can't think of the word. This…unpleasantness started, I want him to go back to London. I can't stand his overbearing concern.

Joyce has come across again and takes much of the responsibility for looking after Granny off my shoulders.
~~~

She's concerned about me, too. She doesn't fuss or flap but she's also watching me. In all the chaotic half-formed thoughts, a phrase percolates to the surface "I am cabin'd, crib'd, confined". It's from Macbeth, I think. He's described my situation in a nutshell. I hate to be trapped inside. I hate this situation that's closing in on me. I'd like to run free and keep on running. A part of me acknowledges that thinking in this way is as dangerous as the rest of it. But wouldn't it be wonderful to leave all of this? To escape from my past and start over without the horror and guilt. Ah, but I know that's not possible. I'll carry the guilt with me always. There's no outrunning it. There is no hiding from it.

A ring on the doorbell snaps me out of my desperate thoughts and Ben and I stand and watch as Gethin checks the … the *thing* on his screen.

'It's Stafford,' he says as he crosses the room to open the door.

Even Stafford seems to pick up on the mood in the room. My mood. 'Everything all right?'

Ben gets straight to the point. 'Have you verified that Ian Weston's on a cruise ship?'

'That's why I'm here. We heard back this morning and we've been told there's no doubt that Weston's cruising the Atlantic Ocean as we speak.'

'No!' I can't hold it in. 'How do they know it's him?'

'They have him and his passport and the two match.' He's saying something else about raising concerns but I'm tuned out and looking out of the window.

I see him. He's there, walking under the trees.

I stumble to the door and race outside. They're calling after me, closing in on me, but I reach Ian and I grab hold of his arm. They'll have to believe me now!

He lurches round.

It's not Ian.

It's a teenage boy.

'So sorry, mate. Case of mistaken identity.' I hear Gethin say as he tugs at me.

But I have to know. 'Where did you get that cap? Did someone give it to you?'

He takes it from his head and holds it towards me. 'I got it from Youz in Carmarthen.' His gaze takes in the others. 'I didn't nick it, if that's what you're thinking. I bought it with some of my birthday money. I've got the receipt somewhere.' His rising panic causes mine to ebb.

'I'm sorry. I'm so sorry. I've made a mistake.' I'm still apologising as I'm led back to the house.

~~~

Ben stays for a while. He sits with me, holding my hand and chatting about nothing in particular. I'm so tired, I'm struggling to focus on his words and it's an effort to keep my head upright.

I hear him say, 'You're dead beat, Gwen. You need to sleep.' He stands and holds out his hand. I take it and try to pull myself up but I don't seem to be able to get my legs to work properly. Nothing seems to be working properly.

Then he scoops me up in his arms and carries me through to the bedroom. I'm aware of being lowered gently onto my bed and being covered by the throw from the chair.

'Sleep tight,' he says, dropping a kiss on my brow.

As I drift off, I hear him say in the doorway, 'I'm worried, Gethin. She's not well. Shouldn't you get a doctor to see her?'

'It's all right, Ben,' Gethin replies quietly, 'we've been through this before. I'll keep an eye on her.'

I want to shout at him to stop. I hate him for telling Ben this. But my head isn't working and I can't get my mouth to work, either. I drift off.

~~~

Gethin comes in later to check up on me. He's brought me a cold drink and asks me how I feel.

'I can't stop thinking about that poor boy.' I rub the heels of my hands against my forehead.

'Headache?'

'A bad one.'

'I'll be back in a sec.'

'Here.' He gives me two tablets and I swallow them down with the juice.

'Sleep, Gwen. All's quiet here.' I close my eyes again and he adds, 'Everything's going to be fine. Trust me.'

Chapter 34

When I next look at my clock it says 6.35 and I can't work out whether it's morning or evening. I can't clear the muddle in my head. When I stand, I almost lose my balance and knock into the bedside table, rattling the empty glass against the clock. Pulling back the curtain, the shadows and the tint of the light tell me that it's early evening. My mouth's dry and I need to drink something.

I can hear Granny and Joyce chatting in the sitting room and bypass them on my way to the kitchen. Gethin's sitting there with a piece of paper in his hand. He gives a start when he sees me and tries to hide it under the table.

'What's that?'

'Nothing.'

'Tell me.'

'It's nothing. Would you like something to eat?'

'Show me.'

'Show you what?'

'Don't do this, Geth. Let me see what you're hiding from me.'

He sighs and brings the sheet of paper back into view. He's screwed it up.

I hold my hand out and he wavers for a second before passing it to me.

He's saying, 'It'll only upset you, Gwen,' as I start to open it out.

It's one of the photocopied newspapers that accompanied the mocked-up ball. I sit down at the table and smooth the paper flat in front of me. 'It's okay,' I say. 'I can cope.'

I'm surprised that I can read it so dispassionately, but it's as if I'm reading someone else's story.

''It's old news,' he comments casually. Too casually and tries to take it back from me. 'I'll put it in the bin.'

I move it closer to me, beyond his reach.

'No. What don't you want me to see?'

'Don't be daft. I just don't want you upset by it all again.'

His eyes keep darting to the print and I work my way down the page.

The account has clearly been sensationalised for maximum effect but I recognise the basic truth of it. Then I see what he had wanted to hide from me.

'Pascoe!' It comes out more as a breath than a word, but Gethin's picked up on it. He stiffens.

'It's just coincidence, Gwen. Don't go reading things into it.'

I read aloud, 'Jason Pascoe ran to get help, but tragically his twin brother John drowned trying to rescue Pembrokeshire couple Peter and Chrissie Meredith. The brothers' heart-broken parents are flying out to support Jason and to arrange for John's body to be flown home.'

Pascoe! It has to be a coincidence. 'Of course, it's a coincidence,' I say. 'It's not that unusual a name.'

'That's what I hoped you'd say. I feel silly hiding it from you, now.'

'Why *did* you hide it?'

He looks uncomfortable.

'I just didn't want you jumping to conclusions; putting things together and making them more than they are.'

'Like what?'

He stands. 'I'll put the kettle on and rustle you up something to eat.'

Again, I have that feeling that I'm missing something. My head's still not connecting the dots.

'What did you think I'd get wrong?' I ask.

He busies himself filling the kettle and I know that he's hiding something.

'Gethin?'

'It's not important, Gwen.'

'It is to me.'

He says nothing while he pours boiling water into a mug, adds some honey and stirs it.

'Here,' he says. 'Some delightful camomile.'

I'm not letting go.

'Tell me!'

'If I tell you, you'll only start to make connections that aren't there.'

'For Pete's sake, Geth! Just tell me!'

'Keep your voice down.' He looks over his shoulder towards the sitting room. He lowers his voice almost to a whisper. 'Okay. I'm working through this myself to put things in perspective. If you remember, Stafford implied that when Ben arrived, all the unpleasantness started. Then there's Stafford's questioning Ben about the night of the attack on me.'

'Are you suggesting Ben was the one who attacked you?'

'Of course not. I think it's very likely that he saved me from serious injury.'

That scene with Stafford replays in my head. I remember the way he looked at our hands and the insinuation behind his raised eyebrow. I picture the upturned chair with the slowly spinning wheel. Stafford queried Ben about being at the house as I came back from the shunt on the road.

I feel the blood draining from my face.

'Oh God, is Ben only trying to get to know me so he can punish me?'

'Bloody hell, Gwen! Are you mad? The man's crazy about you. This is why I didn't–don't–want to say anything.'

It's as he says. All these seeds of information are taking root and I'm already viewing things differently.

The camomile tea is still disgusting despite the sweet honey, but I gulp it down. I need to push back the rising panic.

Then Gethin says something that causes that panic to sear to the surface.

'How well do you know him, Gwen?'

My heart tells me that I know he loves me and that's all that matters. My head, my poor, battered brain, tells me that I've known him for days rather than weeks and his laptop screen displays a picture of his father and his dead uncle. *They shared a birthdate.* Would he have been the right age to be John, the drowned surfer?

When I compare him with me and the relative ages of my parents, I know that it's quite possible.

Has Ben been setting me up? Is he faking an interest in me to settle old scores? Is this why he wants me to move in with him? If Mark Johnson didn't kill the fish and the robin, who's left? Who else knows the layout of the house? The code for the keysafe?

'Gwen, I like the man and I can't believe he'd do anything to hurt you. But…' he stops.

I look at him and wait.

'You're my priority and I had to view things as objectively as possible to keep you safe. Just be careful, that's all.'

I must look as bewildered as I feel because he comes across and pulls a chair round so he can face me.

'Gwen, you have to believe me, I don't think Ben's responsible for any of this. I just wish I knew who is.'

A montage of events swirls, disjointed but increasingly incriminating. Has Ben been winding me in all this time? Did he deliberately leave that screen saver for me to see and hope it would lead to an opportunity to get me to confess?

I'm vaguely aware of the doorbell going and Gethin returning with someone. When I look up, it's straight into Ben's face. I push back from the table and scramble to my feet.

'Gwen?'

He puts out a hand to catch me but I stumble backwards.

'Keep away from me!'

I register his shock as I back further away from him.

'Gwen, what's going on?'

'Have you known all along?'

'Known what?'

'About the accident? Is your uncle the man who drowned?'

His forehead's creased, his eyes troubled.

'I don't know what you're talking about.'

He turns to Gethin.

'What's going on, Gethin?'

Gethin looks uncomfortable, his eyes darting from Ben to me and back again.

'This is all my fault, Ben. I was looking at the report of the drowning when I noticed that the surname of the surfer who died was Pascoe. I didn't want Gwen to see the article in case she jumped to conclusions and my very act of withholding it made her suspicious.' He mumbles, 'I tried to warn her about coincidences and making connections that aren't there, but she's a bit jumpy at the moment. It's not her fault.'

I've heard it so often. It's not her fault. It's not her fault.

Different emotions play over Ben's features. Then he looks tired. He looks defeated and beaten and I have an urge to run to him and take the look away.

I remember his kiss on the Ferris wheel – and it comes to me that he couldn't have burgled the house. He was with me.

I open my mouth to speak. I want to apologise. Of course it's nothing to do with him! My brain's finally connecting some of those dots and I know that Ben wouldn't do anything to harm me.

But he speaks first.

'I thought you knew me better than that.'

I struggle to find the words.

'Ben, I'm sorry.' I'm still trying to explain as he walks to the front door. 'I don't mean it. I'm just confused.'

He simply leaves and is gone.

The realisation of what I've done hits me full force. I've made another mistake. There's no return from this one either.

I feel anger build against Gethin. If he hadn't tried to hide the article, I'd be none the wiser and that moment of callous idiocy and paranoia would never have happened.

Joyce comes through to the kitchen.

'Edith fancies another cup of tea and I must say I'd quite like another one myself.' She looks at me and stops in her tracks.

'Gwen? What on earth's happened? You're white as a sheet.'

'I've messed up, Joyce. I've just accused Ben of something horrible and now I've lost him.'

'Then go get him back.'

'I can't. I can't take back what I said.'

'Nonsense, girl. If he's worth having, he's worth fighting for.'

A wave of dizziness hits me so strongly I have to put my hands against the wall. Joyce helps me through to the bedroom.

I can hear Granny calling and Joyce dispatches Gethin to deal with her.

‘Now then, my love, what’s going on?’

‘I don’t know, Joyce. It’s all been too much for me lately and now I’ve ruined things with Ben.’

‘Gwen, you’ve been through a terrible time. It’s no surprise you’re still reeling from things. If Ben loves you, he’ll understand.’

She pats my hand and sits quietly for a while. She adds, ‘Don’t worry about Ben. We can fix that.’

‘Do you really think so?’

‘Tell me what happened.’

I try to tell her but some of the words get stuck and I have difficulty retrieving the right ones. I’ve never felt like this before and it’s terrifying.

All she says at the end is, ‘You can sort this, Gwen. When you’re feeling better you can explain and I know enough about this Ben of yours to know that he’ll listen.’

‘But I’ve been…I’ve been…’ the word’s eluding me, ‘unforgivable.’

‘No one’s ever unforgivable, my dear. And, yes, it might take time to mend the damage, but you can do it.’

I’m drifting off and she bends forward and kisses my cheek and says, ‘Sleep, Gwen. You need to sleep.’

My cheek feels damp where she kissed me – as if she’d been crying.

~~~

I can hear Bramble. She’s begging to come in but something’s wrong.

I’m standing at the patio doors in my nightdress.

A sallow dawn is seeping through the crack between the curtains and I can smell the scent of rain-drenched soil before I look outside and see the glistening patio tiles. I must have slept through the afternoon and the night. Perhaps that’s all I needed, my head feels clearer now.

I’ve lost track of the time that Bramble’s been missing but it must have been at least two days. I can’t go outside to search because of my promise to Ben.

Then I remember. There is no Ben. He’s no longer part of my life, so the promise no longer counts. Everything seems so
~~~

grey and miserable. How has it come to this? Now that my thoughts are less jumbled, I can see that things have come to this because of me.

I let things happen. I've tried to leave behind the child that put herself first and to make amends by giving way to others. By doing that, I've still hurt them but in a different way. I see Ben's face as he left yesterday. I still don't know how it happened. Perhaps there was a part of me that didn't believe that he could be interested in someone as flawed as I am. But I'm convinced that I have a chance of happiness with Ben and I'm prepared to fight for it. Joyce said that there's always a possibility of forgiveness and that chink of light gives me hope.

I'll apologise and pray that he'll give me a chance to explain, despite the dreadful accusations I made.

Right now, I need to do something about Bramble.

The patio door's partly open. Perhaps Gethin forgot to lock it last night. I pull the door wide and take in lungfuls of cool air. The sky is a soft smoky pearl.

Where are you, Bramble? I can't remember if I actually checked the shed after my run-in with Mark Johnson. I'm sure I'd have heard her if she were in there, but I have to eliminate the possibility otherwise it will nag at me until I do.

Five minutes later I'm dressed and approaching the shed. The sun is almost visible as a pale shimmer on the horizon. It's going to be one of those heavy days. Although I know that Mark Johnson is in custody, I still keep looking over my shoulder in case he appears, weaving unsteadily towards me with hate in his eyes.

The shed door is rough to the touch and has a triangular web in the corner with a wolf spider lying brazenly in the middle of it. I stand to one side as I raise the latch, in the hope that if the spider drops it won't make contact with me, and then I slip through the gap into the interior.

There's no sign of Bramble. I use my torch to sweep into the corners, past the black bag containing the broken statue, just in case. Nothing. I leave, gently closing the door without disturbing the web.

I'm reluctant to return to the house. I cross the garden to the pond and sit on the bench, forearms resting along my thighs as

I lean forward gazing at the still water. There aren't any fish to disturb the surface. Another image of fish floating on their sides comes to me. Another pond. Then there's movement on the patio slabs.

It's my robin! He flutters to the soaked earth and roots in the soil, coming up with a worm.

'Hello,' I say, softly.

He flies off in alarm. It's not my robin. Perhaps it's his mate, or maybe it's another bird that's moved in on its rival's territory.

I don't know how long I sit there, but the pale sun is fully visible now and muted colour is returning to the garden. The side gate isn't shut and I'm brought out of my reverie by a scampering noise. Atticus bounds into view but when he reaches me, he slows down, sits at my feet and rests his head on my knee. The awful feeling of loss hits me again and as I fuss him, my vision blurs and he's reduced to a wet, hazy smudge.

I know, without looking up, that Ben's arrived and I dash my tears away with my sleeve. I have to say something in case he leaves again.

I raise my head and meet his eyes. He looks drawn and unhappy and dissolves before my gaze into another distorted blob.

'Ben, I'm so very sorry. I can't tell you how…' The words stop as I fight to regain control of my voice. I swallow audibly and start again. 'I know what I said was appalling and I don't expect you to understand. You must hate me, but I know I was wrong. I couldn't have been more wrong and I want you to know that…to know that…' That lump of emotion is in my throat again.

'Gwen, it's all right.' He sounds flat and resigned.

'No, Ben. It's not all right. I made an unforgivable mistake.' I remember Joyce. 'I'm hoping that you might be able to see past it and we can at least be friends again.' I add, 'In time.'

He sighs. I hold my breath, praying he doesn't walk away again. He doesn't and all I can do is wait for what he says next.

'Gwen, I couldn't sleep last night going over what's happened. We've been under huge pressure and that's bound to affect how we see and react to things.'

He's telling me that our relationship's been a mistake.

'You've been through a truly traumatic time and I should have taken that into account.'

My head comes up at that. I don't know where he's going with this.

'When we first met, I made several false assumptions about you; assumptions that I bitterly regret. I know how easy it is to jump to conclusions.' He's looking at the ground. 'Last night, it was your fear and exhaustion talking. I can see that now.'

He's speaking without emotion and I'm dreading the caveat to come. It comes.

'Everything's happened so fast and we've not had an opportunity to get to know each other properly.'

Am I grabbing at straws thinking there's still hope? He's not slamming the door shut on our relationship?

Atticus still has his head on my knee. I look into his mournful eyes and wait for whatever happens next.

Ben comes round to the bench and sits next to me. 'Gwen, I don't want your friendship.' My heart sinks. He takes my hand and clasps it lightly in both of his. 'We've come too far for that. We're good together and I don't want to lose you.'

'I don't understand.' I shake my head. 'Are you saying you want to see me again?'

'Yes. That's what I'm trying to say. We've both said and done foolish things but I think we can overcome them.' His face comes closer. 'Can we start over? Clean slate? Put the past where it belongs and move forward?'

'Ben, I'm so confused. I don't know if I'm hearing what I want to hear rather than what you're actually saying.'

He smiles. 'I saw how shattered you were yesterday. I even had to carry you to your room.' His eyes crinkle at the sides in that way I love. 'Your hearing's fine at the moment.'

'You still want to see me?'

'I think that's what I've been trying, in my own clumsy way, to say.'

I smile with relief and burst into tears.

He pulls me in and I cry. I can't stop. The barriers I'd built up to deal with his rejection disintegrate and I sob against his shirt whilst he holds me close and murmurs, 'It's all right, Gwen,' over and over.

Eventually, I'm reduced to hiccupping sniffles and Atticus nudges his nose under my hand for a share of the fuss. I pull away from Ben and point to the dark patch on his shirt.

'I'm sorry, Ben. I'll give it a wash for you.'

He smooths the hair back from my face.

'No need, Gwen. I have a perfectly decent washing machine of my own and, what's more, am not afraid to use it.'

I laugh and lean back into him.

Then I push away again. A fresh start needs to be an honest one.

'There's something I need to say. I lied to you.'

'You don't need to tell me—'

'I do. Clean sheet and all that.'

'All right then.' He sounds wary.

'I *have* been sleepwalking again.'

'Why on earth did you feel the need to lie about something like that? Lots of people sleepwalk.'

'I don't know.' I'm chewing on my lip now, like my brother. 'I suppose it's because I worry that if I can walk in my sleep, maybe I do other things, too.'

'One of my brother's friends used to stay over with us sometimes and he walked in his sleep. It's all he did apart from talking a lot of rubbish. We'd guide him back to bed and never gave it another thought.'

There's a noise from the direction of the house and Gethin appears. He gives a whistle.

'Well, well. I see we've kissed and made up. Thank heavens! I thought I was going to have to come up with some kind of Shakespearean ruse to get the two of you back together again.'

It's strange how quickly life can turn from comedy to tragedy and back again.

Chapter 35

Ben says it's time for some old-fashioned courting. The two of us together, getting to know each other better without all the drama skewing things. It sounds perfect. He has some work to do on-site but later he's to take me for lunch in one of the village pubs. Gethin and Joyce couldn't be more delighted for me. I worry about offloading responsibility for Granny onto a woman who's the same age as she is, but she assures me that it's nice for her to spend more time with Edith instead of twiddling her thumbs in her empty house.

Gethin's brilliant. He makes me eat and teases me about Ben. He's had some phone calls from work and, judging from the heated tones issuing from the garden as he paces, I think they want him back.

I'm bringing him a cup of tea and hear him say, 'No. I've told you. These things take time. My sister needs—' He breaks off, saying he has to go, and hangs up. I challenge him about it. I don't want him getting into trouble because of me but he tells me he's a big boy now and can look after himself.

He adds, 'I'm good at what I do and they know that. I lay the golden eggs and that gives me immunity.'

It's reassurance of sorts, but I tell him, he's going back there by the weekend.

There have been no more 'incidents' and I push Stafford's warning about Mark Johnson to the back of my mind. Mark Johnson was irrational and possibly delusional as well.

I'm confident that with him locked, up and Ian Weston sailing the high seas, everything should be fine.

I start sorting out clothes for the washing machine but a dreadful lethargy takes hold again and I'm having to fight to stay awake.

Gethin stops when he sees me hunched over the laundry basket.

'You all right?'

'I'm suddenly very tired.'

'I suppose that all the past excitement and worry has taken it out of you. Why don't you go to bed for a couple hours?'

'I'm going out in a bit.'

'You look knackered.'

'Thanks.'

'Go and get some beauty sleep. Ben isn't going to want you tipping forward into the soup like Alice's dormouse.'

I take him up on the offer, lie down on top of the bed and drift off almost instantly.

~~~

I can hear Bramble crying. The sound drags me out of a deep sleep. Was it a dream? But I'm sitting up in bed and I can still hear her.

She's screaming.

I blunder through to the patio where Joyce and Granny are sitting together under a parasol.

'Where is she?'

Joyce looks up.

'Who, dear?'

'Bramble. I heard her just a few seconds ago.'

'We've not heard anything.'

Gethin's out there too and Ben's with him. I turn to them.

'It's Bramble.'

Gethin says, 'Great. I told you she'd come back'

'No. I heard her. Just now. She was—' I break off.

When I'm out of Granny's earshot I take Gethin's arm and drag him towards the wall.

'She was screaming, Gethin. She's hurt. I know it! She was outside my window.'

He moves towards the window and looks around.

'There's no sign of anything unusual here. Perhaps you dreamed it.'

'No! I thought it was a dream, at first, but I heard her again when I was sitting up, awake.'

'Did Joyce hear anything?'

I sway. This is beginning to feel like one of those frustrating situations with Stafford.
~~~

Ben holds me steady. He doesn't say anything; his expression hard to read. I try to explain.

'Joyce says they didn't hear her. Perhaps they were too lost in … in … conversation to notice.'

'Well, I can't see or hear anything.'

Gethin's humouring of me takes me from anxiety to frustrated anger.

'I heard her. I did! She's in trouble.'

He starts to rationalise the situation.

'Gwen, you're exhausted. I think you've probably dreamed you heard Bramble and in that same dream you sat up in bed and heard her again. I can't think of any other explanation. No one else heard her and if she was in pain, I'm sure we'd all have been aware of it. Stop worrying about her. She's only been gone a couple of days and she'll come back through the cat flap as soon as she's ready. Okay?'

I'm filtering his words through the fog in my head. It does sound plausible. I've made this sort of mistake before, haven't I?

'It was so real.'

'I know, Gwen. The mind can play tricks.'

There's the sound of Joyce's rubber-tipped stick thumping on the ground as she approaches us. 'What's going on? No more trouble, I hope.'

Gethin answers her with a calm I'm far from feeling. 'It's all right Joyce. Gwen thought she heard Bramble but she thinks now that it was just a dream.'

She studies me. Her grey eyes are steady and thoughtful. 'How are you feeling, my dear?'

'I'm fine, Joyce. Just not thinking clearly yet.'

'Don't rush things. You're still looking a bit peaky but a good rest and some fine company will work miracles.' She smiles warmly at Ben.

He responds with a smile of his own, adding, 'Edith's been very lucky to have had you as a friend all this time. Nothing much phases you, does it?'

There's a shake of her head. 'I used to get upset at all sorts of things. One Christmas, as a newly-wed, I had a complete meltdown because I'd forgotten the cranberries. Another time I wept for ages because I'd lost the chiffon scarf I wanted to wear with my new outfit.' Those grey eyes become more wistful. 'Once you've seen the patterns repeating themselves with the next generation, and the one after that, you begin to gain a bit of perspective. When you've sat with someone in pain or with a terminal illness, that chiffon scarf becomes a mere nothing.' She taps her stick on the ground. 'And it's hard to work up a head of steam over some missing cranberries when you know that there are people in the world who are literally starving.'

She looks at me as if she has something more to say, but she simply gives a nod of acknowledgement and hobbles back to Granny.

I look through the glass towards my bed. The dream was so vivid.

Ben whispers in my ear, 'You do know I'm only with you so that I can spend more time with your grandmother and her friend?'

It's a gentle tease and I lean into him.

He holds my hand and links his fingers with mine. 'I know I suggested we go out for lunch, but perhaps sitting quietly in the shade in my garden with something chilled to drink and a light bite to eat might be nicer. I've put up one of those swing seats with a canopy and we could sit together and gently rock the afternoon away. What do you think?'

I'm still struggling to find the words but my grin is my answer and he tucks my hand into the crook of his arm.

Gethin seems relieved. 'That sounds just like what the doctor would order. You two go and rock and I'll wrestle with some figures. Of course, if you can't bear to be without me, I could bring my laptop and sit with you.'

Ben laughs. 'I'm afraid the swing only holds two. See you later, Gethin.'

We walk back across the patio and down the drive to Ben's garden and it's as if I've left all the panic and anxiety behind.

~~~

There's something very peaceful about Ben's informal garden and I sit back in the canopy's shade, watching blackbirds hopping along the lawn and flowers bobbing gently in the
~~~

breeze. It's a muggy day and everything feels lazy and unhurried–until a frantic scurrying alerts me to the arrival of Atticus. He jumps straight up onto the seat next to me and pushes his head under my hand.

'What a good, brave dog you are,' I croon gently. 'I don't think I thanked you properly for saving my life.'

His tail thumps on the cushioned bench and I stroke his silky fur. It's soothing and I feel my eyes close. I'm half asleep when Atticus snuggles in closer and I feel the seat move as Ben sits down next to him and draws my head against his shoulder.

This would be perfect were it not for my faltering brain. There's also something I'm still missing that I can't quite grasp. Some of the dots are almost lined up, but every time I try to focus on them, they blur out of reach again.

I give in to the gentle rocking motion and drift back into sleep.

~~~

I'm in the dark and I can hear Bramble squealing, but I can't reach her. I'm running towards the sound of her cries only for the direction they're coming from to change. It's Atticus who pulls me out of the nightmare. He's giving little yaps and whines that shatter the darkness and restore me to the almost painful white light of the sun as it emerges from the low cloud.

'It sounded like you were having a nightmare.' Ben is leaning over, encroaching on Atticus who lays his head in my lap and looks up with those liquid brown eyes of his.

'You were making little whimpers in your sleep. Was it your parents again?'

I shake my head. 'No. It was Bramble. She was crying but I couldn't find her.'

'It's probably as Gethin says, she'll be back when she's ready. Maybe she's found a male companion somewhere and is enjoying his attentions.'

We sit in silence, the gentle rocking calming my heartbeat. Then he speaks again. 'Do you have any photos of Bramble?'
~~~

'Yes. I took one a few weeks ago of her sitting in the garden. She was rubbing the side of her chin against the little statue…' I falter as I picture the stone fragments.'

'Good. So why don't I run up some posters of her that we can put up locally. We can ask that people check their sheds and outhouses.' There's a pause, and then he continues, the tone light, 'I'd rather we used *my* phone number on it.'

'Why?'

'Well, because you've only just changed yours and it would make me happier. It's just a precaution, Gwen. It wouldn't hurt to keep your contact details private for a bit longer – until I'm breathing more easily again.'

I recognise how much this has affected him too.

'Okay. Thanks. It'll be a relief to be actually doing *something* about Bramble.'

'Good. I'll get the photo and details from you when I take you home.'

I stretch and then look at my watch.

'Have I slept for nearly three hours?'

'You have. Do you still want to go to the cinema later?'

I hesitate and he picks up the thread seamlessly. 'Only, I was thinking I might prefer a quiet night in. Can you play Rummy?'

'The card game?'

He nods.

'Love it! Used to play it at college.'

'So, how about we have some dinner and then we can have an evening together and perhaps rope Gethin in for a game of cards, too?'

The pressure in my head eases and I'm beginning to feel more like myself again. A couple more days like this and I'll be fine.

A replay of Gethin's voice surfaces asking how well I know Ben and the implications behind the question. I push it back.

Ben would never hurt me. I'm certain of it.

~~~

'Rummy!' I slam my cards down on the table with a flourish and Ben and Gethin groan.
~~~

Ben mutters something about wishing he'd never suggested it and Gethin pushes his chair back and says he needs a coffee.

'You can't have a coffee at this time of night,' I squeak. 'You'll never get to sleep.'

'But how else am I going to compete with my card playing ninja of a sister.'

I giggle happily and he goes to the kettle.

'What do you fancy?' he asks Ben.

'Do you have any decaf?'

'We do. We have decaf tea and coffee.'

'I'll have the coffee please, Geth.'

Ben suggests we go to the patio door and look at the moon but I can hear the torrential rain from here.

'What moon? It's bucketing down out there!'

Ben sighs and Gethin says over his shoulder, 'Have you no romance in your soul? The man's trying to get you on your own.'

Ben pulls a rueful face.

'Oh,' I say giggling and pulling him up. 'Perhaps we'll see some shooting stars, too.'

We go through and stand by the door. The world ends there. There's nothing but darkness beyond the glass and when we kiss, even that disappears.

Gethin dramatically singing *All by Myself* brings us out of our clinch.

Ben whispers, 'I've never felt like this before.'

'You feel it, too?' The happiness bubbles up and surfaces in a grin that must extend right across my face. Then I tug on his hand and head back to the table. 'Quick! Before he sings the chorus again!'

We sit back down in our places and Gethin brings across our mugs and places them next to us. 'I didn't make the coffee too strong, I hope?'

Ben takes a sip. 'Just the way I like it.' He looks over at mine. 'What on earth have you got there?'

'It's camomile. Gethin thinks it helps me sleep.'

'It doesn't look terribly appetising from where I'm sitting. What's it like?'

'Pretty dreadful. Here.' I pass him the mug and he takes a cautious sip.

'Do people actually choose to drink this stuff?'

I laugh at that. 'This has been sweetened with honey. You should try the unadulterated stuff. On the plus side, it does have a reputation for calming the soul and curing insomnia.'

'I'll stick with my decaf coffee, thanks.'

We play on to the accompaniment of the falling rain. We're fairly evenly matched but, perhaps it's the camomile, I'm beginning to feel tired again. I lose four games in a row. I'm struggling with the next game as I work out that Gethin has the card I need to complete my sets. When he slaps it down, I snatch it up and yell, 'Rummy!' before he can change his mind. Then I take his cards from him and check them.

'You deliberately lost to me!' I'm touched and indignant.

'No, I didn't.' He looks sheepish.

'Gethin, you had a winning hand when you put down the card I needed.'

'Did I? I didn't notice.'

'You're a poor liar. Anyway, it has to stop. I'll win on my own account, thank you.'

He reaches across and tousles my hair. There's a rage rising from somewhere that I try to push down. I scowl and we resume play.

Before long, I'm in trouble again and, worse, I'm confusing the cards and putting down incorrect sets. I decide that I've had enough.

'Sorry, gentlemen, but all this fun's tired me out. I'm off to my bed.'

Ben stands and enfolds me in a hug. Then he holds me away from him and says, 'I'll come round first thing and perhaps we can go for a walk?'

'That'd be…' I yawn, 'great.'

Gethin points to my mug. 'Want to take the remains of your tea with you?'

Ben picks up the mug and holds it out to me.

'No, thanks. I'm not going to have any trouble sleeping tonight.'

He swallows the dregs and grimaces. 'I wish I hadn't done that.'

Gethin's delighted and teases him. 'Aww, Ben. Admit it. You wanted to put your lips where Gwen's had been, you old softie.'

Is Ben blushing?

Tiredness swamps me, but I'm feeling happy and loved.

''Night, gentlemen.'

Chapter 36

Someone's talking to me but I can't make out what it is they're saying. The tone becomes more insistent and my shoulder's being rocked. Slowly, I rise to the surface like the dead fish in the pond.

The curtains are still closed, but in the shadows Gethin's face swims into view.

'Come on, sleepyhead,' he says, still gripping my shoulder. 'Time for you to get your glad rags on if you're going to have that nice stroll. Ben's waiting in the kitchen.'

I'm thirsty and my tongue feels too big for my mouth. That muzzy feeling has descended again.

'Time?'

All I can manage is the one word and I watch as his eyes narrow. He places the back of his hand against my forehead. The jovial note has gone from his voice as he says, 'I think you might be running a bit of a temperature. There's a bug going round. Perhaps you've caught it.'

It takes me a while to process the information. That would explain the muddled feeling. I want to tell him that it's a relief to know that it's not because I'm going crazy and I find another word. 'Good.'

'Good?' His face comes closer and he's peering at me. 'I think the walk might be off for today. You need to sleep. I'll tell the boyfriend and he can take you for a stroll when you're up to it.'

'No. Want to see Ben. Give me a minute.'

He leaves me and I struggle into some clothes and wend my way through to the sitting room.

Ben has his hands up and is backing away from Edith and Joyce. He looks up at my entrance. 'Gethin's just said that you're not feeling too good. I'm feeling a bit rough today, too.' He turns back and says, 'I hope I haven't passed a bug onto either of you two. I'd better keep my distance, just in case.'

Gethin's opening and shutting cupboards and drawers in the kitchen. I go through with Ben.

'What are you looking for?'

'Oil.' He runs his hand backwards through his hair. 'My bedroom door squeaks and I thought I'd give it a drop to quieten it down, but I can't find it. It used to be in here.' He points to our 'bits' drawer that contains pieces of string, rubber bands, tubes of glue and other oddments.

I shake my head.

'It's in the shed now.'

'Ah. Right. I'll go and get it. Where will I find it?'

It's hard to find the words to describe where it is.

''S'okay. Easier if I go.'

Ben says, 'I'll come with you.' But before he can join me, he's summoned by Joyce who says they need his advice on something.

He heads in their direction as I open the patio door and walk, carefully, to the shed on legs that feel more unsteady than they should. The rain has stopped but the ground glistens and there's a strong smell of soil and mould.

It's when I pass the lavender that I see her.

Bramble.

I know already that I'm too late. She's lying on her side. Fat flies buzz away as I reach to touch her, and when I pick her up, there's blood left on the tiles. In life, she was soft and warm now she's stiff and cold. I remember Flossie like this, years ago. Flossie with her tail cut off. Without looking, I know that the same thing has happened to Bramble.

Somehow, I'm back inside the sitting room, still cradling my bloodied burden. It's Granny who looks up first and sees me. Her mouth falls open and her eyes are huge in her face. And then she's screaming.

I just stand there.

Then the screaming stops and she's yelling at me. 'Get out! Get away from here! Go. Go now!'

I hear Joyce. 'Hush, Edith. Hush.' She looks at me and I can see tears pooling in her eyes.

I don't know what to do.

Granny shrieks at me again.

'Get out of here! What are you waiting for? Go!'

Then Gethin's there taking Bramble gently from my arms.

'It's all right, Gwen.' He turns to the others and says, 'It's not her fault.'

It's not her fault. It's not her fault. How many times have I heard that?

'It *isn't* my fault,' I say. 'It isn't!'

Ben stands beside me and anchors me with his arm around my shoulders. I look up into his face and can see horror, confusion and pity there. But I don't want his pity. I need him to know.

'I didn't do it, Ben. I couldn't have. I've only just woken up.'

Joyce is steering Granny towards her bedroom, the shouts for me to leave, trailing after her.

Ben applies some pressure to my back. 'Come on, Gwen. Let's get you cleaned up.'

I look down at my hands. They're streaked with dirt and blood. This can't be happening. Not again.

'I didn't do it, Ben. You have to believe me.'

'I do.' It's a simple affirmation that holds back the threatening hysteria.

'You do?'

'Of course I do. I know you don't have it in you to hurt a living creature.'

Gethin comes back. He no longer has Bramble. His hands are wet. He's washed them.

I'm guided to the bathroom where Ben cleans me up and then I'm back in my own room, sitting on my bed.

I hear Ben's voice but it's not me he's talking to. 'We need to call the police.'

'No, Ben. Leave this to me.' Gethin's firm.

'Are you crazy? Someone's killed and mutilated your cat and you're not going to get in touch with Stafford?'

'No. You don't understand. You have to let this one rest.'

'What don't I understand?'

'I'll fill you in later. It's complicated. First, let's get Gwen back to bed.'

That muddle in my brain is hindering my responses but I realise that my brother is telling Ben that I did this. That I killed Bramble.

‘I didn’t kill her! I didn’t! Tell me you believe me, Ben.’

‘I believe you. It’s all right.’

Gethin’s looking at my chest of drawers. One of the drawers is open and there’s some material hanging out of it. It looks dirty. He gives it a tug and the rest of a nightdress appears. The bottom edge is filthy and the dark patches further up might be blood. I reach up and snatch it out of his hands. The hem is still damp.

A piece of paper flutters to the floor. Gethin picks up the paper and holds it for Ben to see.

It’s the original eye picture that I’d stuffed in there all that long time ago. Someone’s gone over it with a black marker and put a cross over the eye.

‘I think you’ve been sleepwalking again, Gwen.’

I hear the keening sound that escapes me as darkness sweeps in.

~~~

When I come to, I’m lying on top of the duvet and Ben is sitting on the bed, holding my hand. Gethin is standing at the window. I can’t see his face.

I push myself upright.

‘I didn’t hurt Bramble, Ben.’

‘It’s okay, Gwen. No one’s accusing you.’

I slump back. ‘I don’t understand any of this, Ben. My head hurts. I’ve not been able to think properly for days now.’

Gethin moves across and hunkers down next to me.

‘It’s all right, Gwen. You don’t need to worry about any of this. You just need to get some more sleep. This is all a mistake and I’ll deal with it. Okay?’

‘Sure?’

‘Scout’s honour.’

Ben removes my sandals and drapes the throw over me.

I close my eyes. Everything’s such a struggle. Before I drift off again, I hear him say, ‘What are you going to do?’

‘I’ll get in touch with her doctor in Manchester. This isn’t the first time this has happened. I’m afraid all this stress has triggered a relapse.’
~~~

I want to protest. I want them to know that there hasn't been another time. Then I see Flossie and I know that's not true.

Joyce must be outside my door.

'How is she?'

Gethin answers her.

'She's in a bad way, Joyce. I should have realised that all of this recent upset has been too much. But she's sleeping now and we'll keep an eye on her. How's Gran?'

'Understandably upset. I'll stay with her until she's calmer, if that's all right.'

'Of course. I'd be very grateful if you did.'

'Thank you, my boy. It's all been a bit of a shock.' There's a disturbing tremor to her voice. 'Ben, could I trouble you for a lift back later, do you think?'

'You don't have to ask, Joyce. Let me know when you're ready.

I'm confused and angry but the need to sleep is overwhelming.

~~~

When I next manage to open my eyes, Ben's still sitting on the bed holding my hand. The wretched expression on his face worries me. Perhaps it's the connection between us, or I've simply moved my hand, but he looks at me and gives a faint smile. It goes nowhere near his eyes.

'How are you feeling now?'

I can't answer. I don't really know.

He bends nearer to me and says, 'Don't worry, Gwen. I'm still here. I'll make sure you get the help you need.'

I turn away from him and his sympathy. *He should know me better.*

That image of Flossie resurfaces. The details elude me. They always have. Someone told me it wasn't my fault. The guilt that I'd felt over my part in the drowning of three people and the death of my grandfather had sought an outlet through an uncontrollable anger. It wasn't my fault.

I never believed I'd hurt Flossie but Granny screaming at me just now to leave has shaken me. I thought we were getting on. I'd come to believe she loved me and didn't hold me
~~~

responsible for all the bad things. I've totally lost my bearings. I no longer know who I am or how I fit into my family.

Thoughts circle, wrapping me tighter in constricting knots. Who am I? What do I really know about myself? Am I capable of hurting Bramble? When I'm sleepwalking, does a side of me come out that is normally hidden, even from me? What makes me so sure that I'm innocent?

'Gwen, whatever's going on, we can sort it.'

I keep my face turned to the wall. I don't want to be sorted. I don't want any of this. There's an anger simmering close to the surface now. I'm angry with Ben for believing Gethin. But I'm *raging* inside at Gethin for the way he's depicting me and for his apologies on my behalf. Is this anger who I really am?

I turn back to Ben.

'You can go now. I'll be all right.'

'I'm happy to stay.'

'Go.'

'Gwen—'

'Go.' Then the rage ebbs and exhaustion takes its place. Under the turmoil I recognise my need to face the past head-on. I need to know everything. Once I have the bare facts, I can decide what to do with myself.

But first, I need my head to clear so that I can think. I *know* there's something tantalisingly out of my reach. Something that's niggling at me.

The mattress under me moves as Ben stands. He drops a kiss on my forehead and leaves, closing the door soundlessly behind him. I need to sleep.

~~~

Someone's come into the room. I open my eyes. Ben's standing by my bed and that muscle's ticking in his cheek.

'Hi,' he says softly.

'Hi, yourself.'

He's so still and quiet. I wait for whatever it is he has to say.

'Gwen, I'm sorry if I've handled things badly.' He swallows. 'I'll admit to being out of my depth here.'

He's telling me he wants out.
~~~

'That's okay. I understand. This must all be a bit of a shock for you. You didn't sign up for this and I don't blame you for backing off.'

'Backing off?' He looks puzzled. 'I've no intention of backing off.'

'You don't?'

'No. We've talked about this. We've got something special between us, you and I. That hasn't changed.'

'But you think *I've* changed.'

'Things here don't add up. I don't have to have known you for long to *know* you. There's an innate goodness in you. I can't explain your grandmother's hysteria against you. I think it's obvious Bramble was hurt by the same person who killed your robin and fish.'

I clutch at this crumb of hope for a few seconds before shaking my head.

'No. There's Flossie. I have to tell you about Flossie.'

He sits on the bed by my feet and waits for me to carry on.

'Granny had a dog called Flossie.

'I remember. That's what she called Atticus at the Bishop's Palace.'

'She was a lovely, gentle dog. A…what's the name? … a spaniel.' There's a pause while I regain control. 'I was playing with her one afternoon and that night she went missing. The next day she was found where we'd been playing.' I'm struggling now but I push on. 'Her tail had been cut off.' The words die away and I wait.

He exhales slowly and audibly. I watch him, still waiting. When he looks at me again, the expression in his eyes is bleak.

'I'm as lost as you are, Gwen. I think we need to talk with Joyce and try to get to the bottom of this once and for all. Even if we don't like what we find out. Then we'll know what we're dealing with and have a foundation to work from.'

He's still using 'we'. Such a comforting word but, in this case, a temporary one. Once we know the whole, ugly truth, it'll remain lodged in us no matter how hard we try to justify or ignore it. He'll be watching me, alert for signs that I'm relapsing. I couldn't bear it. What we had was tentative but filled with glorious potential. Confirmation of my callous brutality will destroy any hope of a happy-ever-after. He knows it too. I can tell. He looks down at my feet and absently massages the soles. I flinch and there's an abrupt end to the movement of his thumbs.

He sits upright, alert.

'What is it, Ben?'

'There's still a puncture wound here.' He traces his thumb lightly over the place.'

'It's where I got a thorn in it.' There's a pause before I add in a hushed voice, 'When I was sleepwalking.'

'And obviously you weren't wearing shoes?'

'No.' I can't meet his intense gaze. 'Apparently, I get out of bed wander around and then return again.'

He's about to say something but there's a tap on the door and Joyce appears.

'How are you doing, my dear?'

I shake my head, too upset to answer her. She stumbles and falters as she comes across to me. Her skin has a greyish tinge.

'Gwen, I know this must seem impossible to bear at the moment, but there is always light at the end of the tunnel. You just have to keep going to reach it. You might not be able to stop all those thoughts jumbling around in your head but don't listen to them.'

She cups my face with her hand and gives me a tremulous smile before turning to Ben.

'Could you give me that lift back now, do you think?

He hesitates for a fraction of a second.

'Yes, of course.' He stands and then leans over to kiss my forehead. 'I'll be back tomorrow, Gwen, and we'll get started on what we agreed. Keep resting. We *will* get through this.'

I give the briefest of nods and he says, 'I mean it, Gwen. We *will* get through this.'

Chapter 37

I'm tired but the relentless slideshow in my head prevents me from sleeping. I'm lying there in the dark when the door opens and Gethin comes in.

'How's things?' he whispers.

'Jumbled.'

He takes Ben's place by my feet.

'You've had a nightmare of a time recently and I've done so little to help. I feel so guilty, Gwen'

'It's okay.' I'm whispering back. 'I'm your sister, not your burden of responsibility.'

'But we're family and I should be pulling my weight. All of that's going to change, Gwen. You'll see.' He peers at me. 'Can't you sleep?'

'I've got a blinding headache and, well…' I reach across for the glass of water by my bed and drink it down.

'Come on, poppet.' He takes my hand and pulls me upright. 'Let's get you something for that headache of yours. And some food – you've not eaten for hours.'

He leads me through to the sitting room and sits me in Granny's comfy chair, drawing it round on its castors so that it faces away from the television.

'What would you like to eat.'

'I'm not hungry.'

'What about a mug of soup?'

Before I can reply he says, 'Good' and walks through to the kitchen.

I look down at my top. Dried blood and earth stain the pale green. There's no escaping it.

Gethin's back in a few minutes with two mugs and hands one of them to me.

'Drink that up. It's tomato and basil and will help settle your stomach; your head will thank me for it.'

I'm not hungry but he's insistent. I know it's not going to take the edge off my anxiety.

He drains his down and waits for me to finish mine.

'Good girl. What about some camomile?'

I shake my head.

'All right. How about some regular tea?'

'No. This was enough.' I point to my empty soup mug. He removes it and returns moments later with another mug containing sweet tea.

'No objections. You're dehydrated. Drink it now, while it's hot.'

His pestering is irritating but I give in. It slips down easily.

'How's the headache feel now?'

'A bit better, I think. Thanks.'

'I'll get you some painkillers and they should see it off.'

It's a relief to realise that the headache is improving. I desperately need to be able to think clearly. When he reappears with a small glass of water, I take it and the couple of tablets he hands me. Gethin nods in approval and recovers the glass. He sits opposite me on the other armchair, leaning forward with his hands clasped together.

'We went through hell that day at the beach but we've both survived it. I've focused on my work but you're still caught up in it. How long have I been telling you that there's nothing to make amends for?'

He sighs, the sound unusually loud in the quiet of the house. It's gone nine-thirty and Granny will be asleep now.

His eyes narrow.

'You're not listening to me, are you? You never do. You simply carry on in your own sweet way and let people walk all over you.'

'I *am* listening. I do hear what you're saying.'

'You *hear*, maybe, but you don't *understand* the words.' He pushes back in his seat, irritation visible in the snappy movement. 'You accept this life because you think it's the one you deserve. But life is what you make it and you've made nothing with yours.'

I'm stung by his criticism.

'I *had* made my own life. I was happy in ... in … Manchester … and had a good job that paid well.'

'So why aren't you still there?'

'Because Granny needed me.'

'You didn't have to come running back.'

'I did. There was no one else.'

'There was no need to martyr yourself on her behalf.'

'Geth, we could have been separated and … and … fostered … or adopted, but Granny took us in. She looked after us when we needed it. I couldn't turn my back on her, now she needs help, it wouldn't have been right.'

'That's your guilty conscience talking.'

'No. It's …' Why can't I remember the word? 'It's … natural. It's what families do. They step in and support each other when it's … when it's necessary.'

The temperature's rising in the room.

'Something wrong?'

'No. It's just getting warm in here.'

'Shall I open a window?'

'No. I'll be fine. I'm just feeling drained after …after everything.'

'I'm sorry, Gwen. You keep drawing the short straw.' He shakes his head and gives me a sad look. 'I wanted to punch Ben on the nose but I thought it would upset Joyce.'

I've no idea what he's talking about.

'Why would you want to hurt Ben?'

'Because of the way he treated you tonight.'

I frown at him. He carries on.

'Telling us that he hadn't realised just how unstable you are, and then leaving. I hate to tell you this, but he's packing up tonight– doing a runner.'

'No.' He's not making sense. 'No. He wouldn't.'

'Yes. I'm sorry, Gwen.' He glances down before looking back at me. 'I have to ask, did he deny being the nephew of John Pascoe, the surfer who drowned?'

'I'm sure he did.'

I try to replay the talk we had. There's nothing in my poor brain where he actually said he wasn't related to him.

Gethin's watching me. 'He didn't, did he?'

My flustering is enough.

'I knew it. The bastard's been after you from the start. He's led you along and played games with you until he's pushed you over the edge, and now that he's succeeded, he's left.' Gethin's furious.

This isn't right.

'No. He wouldn't.'

'Oh, Gwen. I'm so sorry. He's not worth breaking your heart over.'

'No.' I'm firm. 'Ben's not like that.'

'I wish I could deny it, but all the evidence points to him doing these malicious acts. He was here when Gran was tipped into the pool, wasn't he?'

'No. Not the way you mean.'

'Stafford's onto him. Stafford told me to keep an eye on you while he does some digging into Ben's past. I think that's one of the reasons Ben's running away.'

I'm feeling nauseous and a bit light-headed but I know Ben and he *couldn't* be that brutal to me. 'No. I don't believe you.'

'You're deluded, Gwen. You can't see what's in front of you, can you?'

My mouth's gone dry and I can feel my energy draining away.

Something bad's coming.

My hand creeps along to the pocket in my jeans where I keep my phone. I have Ben on…on…what is it? On speed dial.

My fingertips are just slipping into the opening when Gethin brandishes something in front of me.

'Looking for this, Gwen? It must have fallen out. He gets up and crosses to the bookcase in the corner. 'I'll just pop it on here for safekeeping.'

This is weird. What's he playing at?

'Gwen? You don't look too good. Are you feeling all right?'

My tongue feels too big for my mouth again.

'Dizzy. I'm a bit dizzy.'

'Can I get you anything? Another drink?'

I stare at him.

'You've gone very pale. You look like a ghost.'

Then it happens. The dots begin to line up. The photo of us at Halloween swims into view, me as Caspar and Gethin in his pumpkin costume.

'Pumpkin,' I say.

'What?'

'Mummy always called you pumpkin.'

'She loved you, too. You were her little pixie.'

I connect the dots.

Don't be silly, pumpkin

'It was you.'

There's a strange stillness about him now.

'You made her go for the ball.' I focus hard, trying to remember the exact words. 'She said "*Don't be silly, pumpkin. If it doesn't come back, I'll buy you a new one.*" but you made her go in. *You* made her get the ball.' I'm breathless. 'It wasn't me. It wasn't my voice – it was yours I kept hearing in my head.'

He winces as if I've slapped him and rubs a hand across his face. Then he sits back in his chair. A faint smile lifts his mouth.

And I know it's true.

'You've finally remembered.'

Chapter 38

'All these years you've held the truth in your little hands but couldn't see through my spin on the situation. You were so trusting and malleable then. You still are.'

The smile's replaced by a frown.

'I was so scared,' he says. 'I thought I was going to get into trouble and so I told everyone that you were the one who made her go in the sea. I didn't want to, but I had to. You do see that don't you?' He leans forward, earnest. 'I was so young and I did tell everyone that it wasn't your fault.'

Tears glimmer in his eyes.

'I love you, Gwen. You're my little sister. I tried to make it up to you. I tried. I fought your corner and stood up for you. You've no idea what it was like. I was desperate to make amends for my cowardice.' He blinks back the tears.

'And then I realised that Gran didn't hold you responsible anyway. It was an accident. That was all. You were blameless.

'Have you any idea how much it hurt to hear that? All of that penance and I could simply have told the truth. I loved you, but I hated you so much, too. Gran would settle you down on her knee to read to you and I just wanted to drag you away and hurt you.'

My face must show my horror at these revelations. More dots are connecting and the picture that's forming is deeply disturbing. He continues matter-of-factly.

'I did love you. I *do* love you. You were a gentle little thing but while you were good and innocent, *I* felt evil. There were times when that feeling took over, like the day Granny took you into Carmarthen to buy you some new clothes. She left me behind and when you came back, she told Joyce what a lovely day you'd had together and how you'd sat in the park eating ice cream and making up stories about the people you saw there. So, I went to the pond and took the fish out one by one. When they were all dead, I put them back. I tried to implicate you but no one understood.' He chews his lip then he looks at me and his amused expression alarms me.

‘Then there was Flossie.’

I flinch.

‘Gran watched you from the window one afternoon as you were fussing her. “Gwen’s such a sweet child” she said. “There’s not a bad bone in her body”. Did that mean that I had bad bones? If I couldn’t make her see the good in me, I’d make her see the evil in you. So, I killed Flossie and put the blame on you.

It worked better than I could have imagined. After that, I had all the attention and you were the one left on the sidelines.

His face looms into mine as he comes across and picks up my hand. He drops it. It’s heavy and I let it fall. His face splits into a vicious smile that sends a shiver through me.

It’s as if there’s a weight pressing down on my body. It’s a struggle to keep my eyes open and part of me wants to give way to sleep, but what he’s saying holds me fixed in the unfolding horror.

His voice carries on in that same matter-of-fact tone.

‘I did wonder sometimes if Gran worked out what I was doing. I’d catch her watching us and then looking swiftly away. When she showed you affection, sometimes I’d have to punish you for it and I think she may have made the connection. I don’t know. I *do* know that she saw our father in me and there were plenty of times she gave me the benefit of the doubt or made excuses for me.

‘That day you spent ages with Granny making daisy chains, when she placed you next to me on the wall, I simply nudged you off.

‘Then they started fussing over you so I had to throw myself off, too.

‘There were other fairly trivial occasions, but when we were older and I’d ‘accidentally’ bumped into you on the pavement and you lurched into the road. I grabbed you back and was genuinely sorry. I knew I’d gone too far and promised myself I’d stop hurting you. That same month, Gran pulled some strings and got me a place at Forsters Browning. She bought the flat for me and set me up with a fund that would take care of my expenses. It suited me down to the ground but – I’ve always had a nagging doubt that perhaps she was just getting me out of the way. Then you were accepted at the university in Manchester and our lives took off in different directions.'

The nightmare rumbles on.

'I do love you, Gwen. It's been us against the world for most of our lives, and when I heard you'd had a breakdown I came straight up to be with you and help you back on your feet.'

He'd been so supportive. His patience and gentleness had reached me and brought me out of my personal lockdown. I'm trying to reconcile that with what he's just told me.

'Your Skype call about the harassment you were under was really upsetting. All I wanted to do was to sort it for you. You have to believe me.'

He pouts, and the mood changes.

'Thing is, when you Skyped to tell me, I saw a way out of a predicament. You see, I've been going to the casino. I made a small fortune at first. I knew what I was doing and the money rolled in. Then my luck changed. Somehow, I lost it all over a few weeks. Zoe begged me to stop but I knew that if I stuck with it, the odds would turn in my favour again and so I took money out of the company and used that. But it wasn't enough to turn my luck around. Then I had to repay all that I'd borrowed before the auditor spotted what I'd done.'

He groans and runs a trembling hand over his face.

'When a couple of heavies called at the house, Zoe found out about the loan. She'd had enough and upped and left. I just needed one big win and it would all be sorted. One win! I think the bastards had rigged it so that I'd lose. Then the loan sharks started circling and I had to sell the car, TV, everything.'

I remember the patch on the wall and his story that Zoe had thrown a paperweight at the TV.

'When you Skyped me, I realised if I came to Dernant I could help myself to some of Gran's jewellery and other valuables. I knew they'd cover the debts and she wouldn't miss them. It was the perfect let out.

'Remember when she woke up screaming about someone in her room? The light from my torch woke her. I ran into the bathroom, ripped off my top, wrapped a towel around my shorts and stuck my head under the tap for a few seconds.

'After that, whenever I got the chance, I searched the place. Grandad's coin collection, the liberty clocks, some of those small Chinese pots would have been all I needed–but then you told me that most of the valuable things had been stashed away.'

I don't want to hear any more, but I'm hooked on his words, simultaneously fascinated and repelled by the horror of them. He looks away and when his eyes return to settle on my face, they're hard as flints.

'It should have been easy, Gwen. I'd pay the loan back and everything would have been put right.'

Even through my malfunctioning brain, I know that he's delusional.

He presses a hand to his ribs.

'I ran out of time with the loan company. They wanted their money back. The boss sent some of his men here and they made it clear he was expecting payment. I panicked. I wrangled on the phone for some more time and promised to double their interest. I was going to get rid of Gran, you see. I tried to tip her into the pond but you and Ben came back before I could finish it.

'Then it came to me. There was another way out. All I needed was enough for a night at the casino. So, I waited until you went off with Ben to Folly Farm, nipped back to the house and took anything I could find of value. Once I had some chips, I could get into a game and win back what I'd lost.'

His lips twist into a rueful expression.

'That copper pig? I lugged it all the way to London and turns out it wasn't worth the trouble. The other stuff was well worth it, though.'

He slams his hand down on the arm of the chair.

'They cheated me! I lost *every single* game!'

He chews his lip and I wait. It's all coming together despite the darkness descending in my head.

'They were waiting for me when I left. Said my time had run out. That's when I had no option but to do what I'm doing now. You do see that, don't you?'

He doesn't seem able to look me in the eyes.

'I told them I was coming into an inheritance. I'd be able to repay them handsomely.' Then he does lock eyes with me.

'So, it was your life or mine. I chose mine.' He grimaces. 'I was in so deep, I needed everything, not a half share.'

'You made it so easy at first. I was going to pin your demise on one of your loony persecutors but when Weston left and Johnson was arrested, I had to think up something else.'

The sad expression is replaced with one of triumph.

'I've done my best to make you look as unhinged as possible. I can't believe how easy it was. I've been putting Gran's sleeping tablets in your tea and playing you the sound of Bramble crying – though I needn't have bothered because you slept through it most of the time.'

He sighs. 'It'll soon be over, Gwen. There's no one left to help you. Ben's had enough and walked out on you. He couldn't get away fast enough. I dare say he'll feel he's had a lucky escape when he learns of your suicide. I've given you enough sleeping tablets and muscle relaxants to send you to a permanent rest. I'll tell everyone how upset you'd been and how tragic it all was.' Tears are welling in his eyes again. 'It'll be a gentle end. You might panic a bit at first but I'll make sure you're okay.'

The light from the corridor flickers for a moment. Am I passing out? He draws me back into his mad narrative. The tears have gone.

'Of course, I've decided on a nice dramatic touch. I'll show you soon. And in a couple of days, I'll have to dispose of Gran but that should be a piece of cake.'

'Nooooh.' The word is drawn out of me–a bovine groan.

'Don't worry. Everything's going to be all right. I'll take care of both of you.' The crooning tone forms a startling juxtaposition with the menace behind his words.

He stands, picks me up in his arms and carries me through to the corridor and on to the bathroom. I try to struggle but it's such hard work. I realise what he intends to do just before he places me in the bath.

'No. Please. Noooh.' I'm pleading with him to stop. He turns away, puts in the plug and turns on the taps.

'I didn't think to turn the immersion heater on but this makes it more like the sea, doesn't it?'

My eyes go from him to the tumbling water. I'm fighting as hard as I can, my movements slow and clumsy.

'Don't, Gwen. Better to just accept it gracefully.'

The water's gushing out of the tap and my hand flails out against the top of the tub, trying to gain purchase.

'When it's nice and deep, I'll hold you under and it'll soon be over. You're doped to the eyeballs and you'll barely be aware of it. Trust me.'

He kneels down next to the bath so that his face is close to mine and, for a while, all he does is stare at me.

'Geh, noh.'

The level's rising. It's covering my legs now and as it creeps upwards, he continues.

'It's not been easy, you know. Take Bramble, for instance. If that second door cam had arrived, I'd considered putting on one of your ridiculous nightdresses and tottering across to the shed, but I knew that wouldn't work. Anyone could have seen it wasn't you. We don't look anything like each other. We're not alike at all, really, are we?'

The chill water is lapping at my hip bones. I can't believe he'll go through with this. He's my brother. I stop thrashing and try to focus on his face.

He's gazing at me, curious about something. He explains.

'I've never killed a person before. I've been working up to it, you could say. Insects hardly count, but the fish were more substantial and surprisingly satisfying. Then came Flossie. Flossie was hardest and yet, in some ways, the best. She was so trusting. I looked into her eyes while she struggled to stay alive, and I could really see the difference in them when she died.'

He gives a little shake. I can't tell whether it's one of horror or pleasure, but I'm trapped in his narrative, unable to ignore the poisonous words dropping so casually from his mouth. Gethin's sick.

'Bramble's demise worked a treat. Gran went completely over the top. I loved it. Such drama and all focused on bad, crazy Gwen.'

He brings his head close to mine and touches a finger to my cheek.

'Crying, Gwen? Don't. It'll all be over soon.'

He pulls up one of my eyelids and is so close our heads touch.

'Now I have *you*. I've pictured your death in my head and soon I'll be able to see if it's like I imagined it to be.'

'S'op, Geh.' I'm begging him to stop. It's a real struggle to stay conscious. The cold water is above my waist. I don't look down at it but I can feel the cold creeping upwards, pulling the weight of my clothes against my clammy skin.

'There's something mystical about the experience, you know. One minute you have a living creature and then it's as if the spirit's flown and you're left with nothing but a shell. You can tell the precise moment – the moment when something's no longer there.'

I can't tear my gaze away from the pleasure in his face as he describes the moment of death.

'It's not that they stop moving. That's what people think, isn't it? No, it's an actual moment when that internal spark goes and a dullness takes its place.'

I'm lying against the back of the bath and the water's up to my chest.

I attempt to pull myself forward but I don't have the strength.

'Gwen. There's no need to panic. They say it's quite peaceful–drowning, that is.'

I'm terrified. He attempts to sooth me.

'I know it didn't look that way when we were in Fuerteventura. I think, maybe, that it was the panic that made it hard for them. If they'd simply accepted they were going to drown, it would have been fine. They say it's just like falling asleep.'

'Nooooh!'

'That's always been your problem. You're afraid of water. There's no need.'

He dips a cupped hand into the water and pours the contents over my head. The shock of it makes me gasp. He does it again, and I'm aware of it running down the back of my head. The next scoopful is tipped over my face and flows over my nose and into my mouth.

My terror makes him smile.

'It's just water, Gwen. There's nothing to be afraid of.'

I've inhaled some of it and splutter and choke.

The level is creeping up to my neck and it must be my deep-seated panic that's keeping me awake. That and the cold.

'Geh'n.' I need to reason with him but it's not possible without words and all of mine are buried, locked away, inaccessible.

The churning water has reached my chin and I cough and spit as some of it fills my mouth. Once more, I try to grab the top of the bath with my right hand to pull myself up. My strength has gone but I'm still fighting inside.

'The water's coming in faster than the overflow can cope,' he says with satisfaction.

The light from the corridor flickers again and he smiles at me.

'Time to ease you to your rest, Gwen. It's for the best. Trust me.' He puts a hand on my shoulder and effortlessly pushes me back and down – but not before I see Granny in the doorway; Granny swinging the cricket bat at his head. I hear the thud through the rush of the water and then Granny's bending over, trying to lift me out of the bath.

'Get up, Gwen! Get up!'

I'm buoyed up by the depth of the cold water. Between us, we manage to roll me over the edge and we tumble to the floor. I cough up water, barely able to raise my head.

She's lying on her back looking dazed. As I watch, the dazed expression morphs into one of fright and I turn to see Gethin pulling himself to his knees. He has the bat in his hand.

'You miserable old woman!' he snarls. 'You just had to stick your nose in and now I'm going to have to deal with you tonight, too.' He shakes his head. 'I was going to give you a peaceful end. Perhaps a soft pillow or a bit of an overdose. Now it's going to be messy.'

He rises unsteadily to his feet and moves towards her. I dredge up my remaining strength, pull myself over her and tuck her head under my shoulder as he brings the bat down. I feel it strike but it doesn't really register. The sedatives are dragging me under and soon I'll be unconscious. He raises the bat again. I want to just give in to sleep but the need to protect Granny gives the energy for one more lunge. I throw myself sideways at his legs, knocking him to the floor. The bat skitters across the surface away from him. It's all I have left. I roll over and let my weight pin him down.

Gethin pushes me off him and crawls to the bat.

'Don't, Geth!' I'm begging in my head.

He stands over me. He's holding the bat in both hands and sweeps it up in an arc.

There's shouting. At least I think I can hear shouting. I can't see properly but there are others in the room. Someone's holding me. I can't see them. I think it's Ben. I think I hear him say, 'It's all right. I've got you.'

But it could just be wishful thinking. It's a comforting thought at my end.

I can't hold back the dark any more.

Chapter 39

Strange faces loom into view and out again. I hear words but their meaning is beyond my comprehension. My eyes are opened and lights are flashed into them. Perhaps I've had another breakdown. Perhaps this has all been a product of my unstable imagination.

I swirl around in a disturbing maelstrom of images, until there comes a time when things still and I manage to open my eyes. It's dark. I can't feel anything. I let myself drift back to oblivion.

When my eyes open again, it's daylight. I try to move my left hand. It's cumbersome and I see that I'm wearing a sling and I'm hooked up to an intravenous drip. There are laminated signs on the walls. I must be in a side ward. I pan round the room, past the monitor screen of blips and changing numbers, past the TV mounted near the ceiling and on to the right-hand side.

He's there. Ben. He's leaning back in a chair, asleep. A stubble has grown on his face and there are dark shadows under his eyes. Then I notice the cut on his temple, held together with surgical strips. I feel my stomach flip and bring my right hand down to still the feeling there. It must have been the movement because his eyes open and then he registers that I'm looking at him.

'Gwen? Thank God!' He takes my hand. 'You're in hospital. You're going to be fine.' He pushes a button on the handset and a buzzer sounds.

'Everything's okay now, Gwen. You don't need to worry about anything.'

'Granny?' It comes out as a hoarse whisper.

'She's going to be fine, too, my love.' His Adam's apple bobs before he adds, 'You protected her.'

I smile and he kisses me before being ushered out by a nurse who needs to make some checks.

I've had my stomach pumped and my fractured shoulder blade should heal without surgery. I'll need physiotherapy when it's settled down again. I can expect to feel very tired and weepy for a few days.

I try to speak but my mouth's parched. The nurse holds a plastic cup of water for me to drink from. He's calm and reassuring.

'Granny?'

I need to know the truth.

'Your grandmother is making a good recovery. She doesn't remember the details. We can't say if she might have flashbacks, but at the moment she has her friend with her and is coping well. You can see her tomorrow, perhaps.'

'She's not hurt?'

'No. You shielded her from the blow, which is why you're in a sling. She's bruised from the fall and her dementia's a bit worse for the time being but that's only to be expected.'

Another buzzer sounds. He puts the disposable cup down, makes his apologies and leaves.

Ben is back almost instantly. He stands looking down at me.

'Hi.'

That's all he says but the smile that accompanies it is enough to reassure me.

'How are you feeling?' He pulls the chair closer, sits on it and takes my hand.

'Groggy.'

'Hardly surprising.' His smile dies. I should never have left you alone with him. If it hadn't been for your grandmother, I'd be attending your funeral now.'

'How is Granny? The nurse said she's recuperating well.'

'She's pretty shaken up. We all are. But she already seems to have forgotten what happened.'

'She saved my life.'

'I'll always, *always*, be grateful to her. Joyce had warned her to be on her guard but neither of us knew whether that registered or if she'd even remember it beyond our leaving.' He raises my hand in his and kisses it. 'I think I was already working it out when I left. Your feet were clean and you couldn't have been out in that rain. I mentioned it to Joyce and she told me that your grandmother thought Gethin was jealous of you. When she was screaming at you to leave, it was to protect you.'

He clears his throat, his voice husky now.

'Anyway, she not only remembered the advice, she pushed her panic alarm whilst I was with Joyce and it recorded and relayed all that was being said.'

He rests his head on our clasped hands for a second. When he looks up again, I'm startled by his bleak expression.

'You can have no idea how dreadful it was hearing Gethin threatening you like that and knowing that I wasn't there. I got Joyce to phone for the police and came back driving like a madman.'

'I thought I heard Stafford.'

'He arrived after the squad car as I was using the key from the keysafe. I took Gethin by surprise but he struck me with the edge of the bat, knocking me out of the way before turning back to finish you off. If one of the other policemen hadn't used his taser from the doorway …'

He can't go on. It's my turn to return that powerful grip.

'What about Gethin?'

'He's been remanded in custody.'

I start to cry.

'I'm so sorry, Gwen.'

The tears continue to fall. I'm not sobbing, just swamped in a quiet sorrow.

I don't seem able to stop and Ben leans over and pushes my buzzer.

He stays at my side, alternately encouraging me to let the grief out of my system, and begging me not to cry. Eventually the nurse is back and I'm given something that lets me sink back to sleep.

When I resurface, Ben is still there.

I don't know what I think now. My past and present are almost unrecognisable. Ben's presence is a balm that helps to calm my chaotic emotions.

'Gwen, I'm struggling with all of this so I don't know how you must be feeling. Try to let it go for now.'

I'm tired again. I can't understand how it's possible to still be tired after all that sleep. Ben's tuned into it.

'Why don't you close your eyes and have a nap? I'll stay, if that's all right, and count my blessings.'

~~~

My sleep ebbs and flows. Whenever I surface in panic, Ben's there. There's a lot to process. I've gained a sort of closure regarding the past but I've lost Gethin, somehow, along the way. I've never really understood him or been aware of his dark side. The childish nightmares I've suffered so frequently have been supplanted by a different, edgier terror. Ben's right; I have to let it go and I know I'm going to need help to do that.

I'm given the all clear to return home and am waiting by my bed when Ben arrives pushing a regulation hospital wheelchair.

'What have you done with Atticus?'

'He's fine. He's ingratiated himself with Vera and Rachel who've been taking him for long rambles and feeding him treats from their capacious pockets. There's a possibility he might never return to me.'

He looks at my overnight case on the floor.

'Ready?'

'They tell me I can visit Granny. They're keeping her in for another couple of days as a precaution and then she should be able to come home again.'

'No problem. The desk tell me that rules dictate you have to exit here in this wheelchair but we can roll along to her room on our way.'

As we arrive at Granny's side ward, my anxiety returns. What will she say? Will seeing me remind her of the horror we experienced?

'I'm sure it'll be fine.' He's tuned into my thoughts again.

'Ready?' He tips his head in the direction of the doorway.

'Yes.'

Joyce is helping Granny to a drink of water. Their heads swivel towards the door at the same time. Joyce flashes a
~~~

smile in my direction, but Granny simply stares blankly at me. There's no recognition there.

'Look, Edith. Gwen's come to see you.'

'Gwen?'

'Yes. Gwen. Your granddaughter.'

She continues to gaze at me. A stillness has fallen over the room.

It feels like I've lost her. Ben's hand reaches over the back of the chair and clasps mine.

'Gwen?' she says. Then she stiffens, 'Gwen? What are you doing here? You should be in school.'

'I've come to see you.'

'What have you done to your arm?'

'I…er…I fell.'

'Does it hurt?'

'Not really.'

'Stupid girl,' she grunts. 'How are you going to help me if you can't look after yourself?'

I smile and Ben pushes the chair close enough for me to stretch forward and kiss her cheek.

'No need for that!' But she's smiling at me. Her expression changes.

'Where am I? This isn't my room? Where have you brought me?'

Joyce intervenes.

'You're in hospital, Edith. You had a fall but you're going to be all right.'

'A fall? I thought Gwen had a fall.'

'She did. You've both had a fall.'

I brace myself for what might be coming.

'That nasty carer pushed me. I don't like it here. There's no TV.'

'I point to the wall mounted screen with my good hand.

'There's one up there for you.'

'Well why didn't you tell me?'

Joyce grins and Ben reaches across for the remote control and switches it on. By some miracle, the second channel he comes across is showing Downton Abbey. I hear Joyce's sigh of relief combined with Granny's humph of satisfaction. They're both, sadly, short-lived as the episode ends and the credits start to roll. Full grumpiness surfaces and, despite Ben patiently going through the channels, she's gone full Chicken Licken on us; the sky's falling down, all is lost and no one cares.

This short interlude has sapped my energy and I'm at a loss what to do.

'Go on,' says Joyce. 'Go home. You need your rest. I have a trump card up my sleeve and I think now's the time to play it. We'll be fine.'

'Sure?'

'Certain.'

'I owe you, Joyce.'

She smiles.

'Time to put all that debt talk where it belongs, Gwen, and start over.' She directs her next words at Ben.

'Cherish her. She's going to need someone at her side. It'll be particularly nasty when all of this goes to court.'

'Don't worry. I'm going to make sure she's safe and knows how much she's loved.'

My vision shimmers at his words.

It's going to take time to find my balance again. I've wasted so much of my life on a stupid fiction but I've been given this opportunity to start over and I intend to make the most of it. I love this man and I have my chance of happiness.

We're at the door when Granny calls out, 'I need Liquorice Allsorts. And some of those choc chippy thingies.'

I'm feeling stupidly tearful as the door shuts behind us. Ben bobs down in front of me.

'It'll be all right. It'll take time but that's something we have – time and each other.'

He gently holds my face in his hands and kisses me. Despite the pain and the exhaustion, that familiar sensation builds and when he draws back again, I'm smiling.

'Right, m'lady. Time to take you home.'

Ben's barely pushed me a couple of feet when he stops.

For a second, I don't know why, but then I hear it.

Joyce has played her trump card.

We move along the corridor to the tinny vibrato of *Yellow Submarine*.

Acknowledgements

My book would not have been possible as it is without the support of others. These people behind the scenes mean so much to me and I'm very grateful for all the many things they've done to help.

First, there's my family who've not only put up with me but have actively played a huge part in the finished result. Kevin, Beth, Ellie and Jen: take a bow!

Marcia Meara, a wonderful friend, generously shared her blog with me so that my betas and hers had access to my work as it progressed. It took countless days of her valuable time but she remained determinedly upbeat and encouraging throughout.

Then there's the beta readers (or critique groups) themselves, who've stuck with me during this journey and have given invaluable feedback. David Western was first in line and I've shamelessly taken on many of his suggestions and appreciated his insight. Each chapter was then pored over by the following and *every one of them* made a positive and significant difference. In alphabetical order:

Dian Colwell, Dawn Dehtiar, Lois Grantham, Gail Grimes, Sharon Helton, Denise Murfitt and Tina Power. You have my love and thanks.

I also need to thank Emma Owen from Folly Farm. Unable to leave the house during the pandemic, I've pestered her with queries that she has patiently answered in order for me to write accurately about the place. I trust I've done it credit!

Lastly, but perhaps even more importantly, I need to thank you, the reader. Without you, like that tree falling in the empty forest, this novel doesn't exist.

Printed in Great Britain
by Amazon

39388287R00195